PRAISE FOR EBOLA ISLAND

kevin

5.0 out of 5 stars **A great read.........**

Reviewed in the United States on December 4, 2019

Verified Purchase

I started to read this book yesterday and kept it reading until I finished it last evening.............. I am going to be on the outlook for the next book written by this author and will purchase it as soon as it is on Amazon. I have emailed some of my friends already to alert them that they should get a copy of this great read now.

Floatdust

5.0 out of 5 stars **Extremely Relevant to Today!**

Reviewed in the United States on August 13, 2021

Verified Purchase

I was drawn to this book for its relevance to the current pandemic. Mr. Pratt did not disappoint and it was as though he had seen the coming of a plague that has become so well known to us all. *Ebola Island* takes the reader behind the scenes into the world of power, greed, sinister intent, and satisfies with enlightenment and integrity. I hope there will be a sequel, and one after that as well.

J. Mark T.

5.0 out of 5 stars **Ebola is not Covid but this book is too close**

Reviewed in the United States on July 22, 2020

Verified Purchase

Fascinating book which will surely make the hair on the back of your neck stand up! How prescient is Pratt to envision this outbreak before the Covid outbreak worldwide. And the conspiracy theorists will surely appreciate his cynical perspective of government and profiteers!

Kitty from Florida

5.0 out of 5 stars **Fiction th**

Reviewed in the United States on May 26, 2020

Verified Purchase

Great story and grew to love the characters. Interesting I found the book during this time in our history, almost afraid this could truly happen. I recommend the book to anyone who enjoys suspense and/or a good love story. Good job, Gregor! Looking forward to more adventures.

Jim G.

5.0 out of 5 stars **If you like to watch "Jack Ryan" or "Scandal", you will love this book!!**

Reviewed in the United States on December 4, 2019

WOW what a great thriller novel! I was going to read this book leisurely at the beach but I started on it the night before I left and couldn't put it down until I finished it (that has never happened to me before). So much for relaxation. It drained me emotionally – I was in disbelief, angry, had tears from sadness, disbelief again, angry again, a bit queasy, had tears from happiness, depressed, cheered, worried, had hope, had satisfaction, was afraid to find out what was next – couldn't wait to find out what was next.................I can't wait for his next novel.

PRAISE FOR DRAGON'S EYE

"Maddy and Jack Gamble seemed to have the perfect life...until it wasn't. When Maddy is kidnapped, it seems like an eternity. Captive on an ocean vessel bound for China, there's tension at every turn. The story twists and turns, and you can't trust anyone. Filled with crackling energy, a fabulous storyline, and a glimpse into the exciting future of technology, Dragon's Eye is a must read!"

> \- Don Bruns, Editor/Contributor Hotel California,
> USA Today Best-Selling Author

"Gregor Pratt's DRAGON'S EYE is a high seas, high stakes, high-tension thriller. Not only is this a riveting, well-researched adventure story, but it also has fascinating main characters the reader will root for all the way to the final page. Don't miss it!"

> \- David Bell, USA Today Best-Selling Author of
> SHE'S GONE and THE FINALISTS

DRAGON'S EYE

Who's Watching You?

This is a work of fiction. The characters and events described herein are imaginary and are not intended to refer to specific places or to real persons alive or dead. Some of the places referred to in this novel are real, however all events depicted there are purely fictional. All rights reserved. No part of this publication may be reproduced, distributed, or transmitted in any form or by any means, including photocopying, recording, or other electronic or mechanical methods without the prior written permission of the publisher except for brief quotations embodied in critical reviews.

Copyright © 2022 by Gregor Pratt

All rights reserved.

No part of this publication may be reproduced, distributed or transmitted in any form or by any means, including photocopying, recording or other electronic or mechanical methods without the prior written permission of the publisher.

Published by St. Armands Press, Sarasota, Florida
www.gregorpratt.com

Cover Design: Mary Beth Wilker
Cover Illustrator: Evelyn Pence

ISBN (hardcover): 979-8-9869193-0-0
ISBN (paperback): 979-8-9869193-1-7

THE JACK AND MADDY GAMBLE SERIES

Dragon's Eye is the second thriller in the Jack and Maddy Gamble series.

Ebola Island the first in the series is a pandemic novel published just before the world learned of COVID. A stunning thriller about a greedy lawyer, a beautiful woman and a corrupt government.

Dragon's Eye takes place later in Jack and Maddy's lives and begins in Nelson, New Zealand where they have settled down and begun a family. Those idyllic dreams are shattered when Maddy disappears. The clues unravel slowly, but the plot moves quickly through twists and turns as Jack sets out to rescue her.

The author plans at least one more book in this series. All are available at Amazon.com

Thank you for purchasing *Dragon's Eye,* my second published novel. This story continues the adventures of Jack and Maddy Gamble who many of you met in my first novel, *Ebola Island.* Some quotes from the reviews of *Ebola Island* can be found on the preceding pages. *Ebola Island* is available for purchase on Amazon or through Barnes and Noble.

Self-published authors like me thrive on strong reviews and word of mouth so after you have finished reading this novel please go back to the site where you purchased it and leave an honest review and if you enjoyed it, please tell others about it. Word of mouth is the best recommendation of any book, in my opinion.

And feel free to reach out to me via my website www.gregorpratt.com or by email prattgregor@gmail.com.

Gregor

This book is dedicated to my wife Patty.
Thanks for believing in me.

DRAGON'S EYE

Who's Watching You?

GREGOR PRATT

ST. ARMANDS PRESS

CHAPTER

1

The Palazzo Motor Lodge
Rutherford Street
Nelson, New Zealand
March 8, 2033
8:25 p.m.

Julia Adamson sat back in the outdoor balcony corner on her room's second floor at the Palazzo Motor Lodge. She was finishing her wine and trying to decide what to do. The man she slept with discreetly had just left to go home to his wife, and she should probably be leaving to go home to her husband, but she wasn't sure she wanted to. Ever. This affair she had allowed herself into had incredibly complicated her life. She knew it was wrong, well, at least it wasn't the way she had been raised to behave, but things at home were not good. They didn't fight; not anymore, her husband just ignored her. Not entirely, they sometimes had breakfast together before they both went off to work, and they still attended family get-togethers as a couple and pretended, and once in a while, he would demand wifely services. If she tried to say "No," he made her miserable until she gave in and then would go back to ignoring her.

It was a beautiful night, clear, warm, with a slight breeze, so she sat back in the corner of the balcony with all the lights off and sipped on her wine, a Sauvignon Blanc from the other side of the island and one of her favorites.

From her chair, she could see across the pool area and out to the drive. Not much was going on, everyone was in their rooms or still out, and she knew the pool was closed for repairs. Earlier, about sunset, she had seen a woman, a beautiful woman, let herself in through the back gate of one of the other units. She smiled and thought, *Well, I am not the only one.* The woman had on a pair of *Manolo Blahnik* pumps, magnificent shoes. She wished she could afford shoes like that.

She had seen this woman enter the rear of this same unit one other time, last week. She remained quiet and hidden in the shadows, sipping her wine, lost in her dilemma. As she looked out, a van turned into the driveway. It had its headlights off. The sun had just gone down, so maybe they hadn't realized that yet. In the city, other lights could make one forget. She was surprised the lights weren't automatic. Nothing was exciting about the van; but she watched it as there was nothing else to look at. It was so quiet she knew it must be electrically powered. Most vehicles were, that, or hydrogen fuel cell. There were still internal combustion vehicles around, but they seemed fewer and fewer except for the collector vehicles. The van was white with a yellow roof that came about a foot down the sides. She thought that was probably to make it more visible to other drivers or something. The van went quietly past toward the parking area in the rear of the property.

Julia took another sip of her wine and was just getting up to leave when she thought she saw someone moving in the shadows along the drive and near the pool area gate. As she watched, six people dressed head to toe in black came silently through the pool area gate and moved along to the patio where she had seen the woman enter earlier. One of the men was scanning the balconies and pool area. She sat back in her chair as far as she could. She didn't dare take a drink of wine. She held her breath. What was going on?

Then all of the people in black went in through the patio door she had noticed earlier. No one had seen her. She let out her breath, finished her wine in one gulp, and put her glass on the table beside her. She leaned forward to listen.

She heard a slight scuffle and muffled voices and then nothing. There was no sound at all. She looked over, and the van had returned; she had not heard it. It parked right beside the pool gate. It looked like the side door to the vehicle was partly opened. No lights were visible inside, and the headlights were still off. The van must have been in park because the brake lights were not on either. Mesmerized, Julia sat back into the darkness on the balcony to see what would happen next. After a couple of minutes, one of the people in black, clearly a man, came out of the patio door carrying two suitcases, a backpack, and another smaller case. He set them on the patio, and noiselessly went back inside. Three more black figures came out carrying a large black bag. It seemed heavy. *Could there be a body in there? The way it drooped, there was something bulky and oddly shaped in the bag. Be quiet, be quiet, be quiet,* she said to herself as her breath became ragged. Then two more of the black-clad men, she was sure now they were all men, came out, one on each side of the woman she had seen earlier. The men each had a hand on her arm. Suddenly the woman ran toward the pool. Julia could see that she was barefoot. The woman screamed, "Help me!" And then the two men were on her. The woman hit one of the men in the face and then the other man put his hand over her mouth and she went limp and quiet almost immediately. What did they drug her with? Julia looked around; no one else in the motel seemed to have noticed. Julia was afraid and watched in shocked silence as the men bound her hands, put something over her head and picked her up like a rag-doll. Julia covered her mouth with her hand.

The three men with the heavy bag had reached the van, and as they did, the side door opened completely. They climbed in, taking the bag with them. The two men with the beautiful woman lifted her into the van and climbed in after. And where were those fabulous shoes? And her hair didn't look the same. *Was there a hood over her head? Oh, my God!* Julia sat forward. Then the last of the men came along with the suitcases, backpack, and case and put those in through the van's side door. Before he got in, he stopped and looked around the pool area and across all the balconies. His gaze seemed to stop at her balcony. *Could he see her? Did he know she was there?* She looked about frantically. *Had she left a door open or a light on? Was light reflecting off of her wine glass? Damnit.*

But no, the last of the men climbed into the van and closed the door. On the door it said in green lettering "Global Logistics," and there was phone number and a website. She didn't get the phone number because the van quickly pulled away, turning its lights on as it turned out of the hotel driveway onto Rutherford Street.

CHAPTER

2

The Gamble House
Victoria Road
Nelson, New Zealand
March 8, 2033
9:00 p.m.

"Daddy, when will Mommy be home? I'm hungry."

JJ is always hungry. And his mother is quite late. I've kept her meal warm or tried to for over an hour. I made Maddy's favorite, blackened tarakihi. Now it was probably ruined. Some things don't keep well, like fish. I texted her again. After five minutes and still no response, I said, "Come on, kids, let's eat." JJ came running into the kitchen, followed by his sister, Allison.

"Where's Mom?" Allison asked.

"She must be delayed at work," I said with more confidence than I felt. Tonight was the fourth time in the last two weeks she had been late.

As we ate, I glanced down at my watch; there was still no reply from Maddy.

"Daddy, this rice tastes good," said five-year-old Allison. I smiled and looked over at their plates; they had pushed the fish to the back of their plates, their rice was disappearing, and their salads were gone. I moved my fish to the rear of my plate, too. It was somehow dried out and greasy at the same time.

I'm so lucky to have two great kids. After resolving the Ebola Island matter and after our marriage in Malagasy, Maddy and I had come straight to New Zealand. And after traveling around and looking for houses, we settled on Nelson. By the time we did, Maddy was pregnant with JJ. Jack Albert Gamble. While he's not technically a junior, everyone calls him JJ, short for Jack Junior. He's my six-year-old wild man, sweet and kind and sensitive and wild. A little under a year later, JJ's sister came along. Allison was Maddy's grandmother's name, so we named her Allison Delin Gamble. She is beautiful. She saw me looking at her and smiled up at me.

I am happy here with Maddy and the children; the happiest I have ever been in my life. My trial lawyer swagger is gone, as are my skirt-chasing days. When I found Maddy, I found myself, the good parts of me, and I overcame my distrust of women. Maddy came to Ebola Island to help with my rescue and had helped me wind up what was probably the most significant lawsuit ever. And I mean ever for anybody. Time was when I would have known the answer to that and would be looking for an even bigger case. Not now, not anymore. Now I looked for Maddy to come home for dinner. Where is she? Being late is so unlike her, at least until the last couple of weeks.

The early years here were so busy; I don't know how we had time to have and raise children.

Both Maddy and I received Presidential Medals of Freedom and Congressional Gold Medals for our part in resolving the Ebola crisis. Then Congress appropriated twenty-five million dollars as a "reward" for our service and as further "payment" for what our government did to me. We received high honors and honorariums from many other governments as well, generally tax-free. Then we authored a book about the whole thing, which was done by a ghostwriter, and that had sold well, and then it got picked up as a movie, which made us more money. And then just like that, after about two years, after the film had run its course, the world forgot all about us and left us alone to raise our two young children.

Maddy is a great mother. Since we don't have to work, we spend all of our time with the children, usually all together but sometimes one parent with one child and one parent with the other. I must be the luckiest man in the world; Jack Gamble, husband, father, lover, friend, adviser, problem solver, nighttime story reader, punching bag, wrestling partner, horse, carrier, supplier. Yes, sir, I have it all. The people in Nelson are great to us. They know who we are pretty much everywhere we go in Nelson, but after the first year, they don't fuss over us or try to give us things. They treat us with extraordinary, trusting human kindness that New Zealanders deliver so freely. And the kids are treated well but not like they are special. Things are the way we want them. I hope I speak for Maddy, too.

Both children attend Auckland Point School and are in the same class. Since Allison had turned five just before JJ was six, we could enroll them at the same time. At least they would know someone, we thought. Auckland Point School is our zoned school from our address, so we had no trouble getting the kids into school to begin what the New Zealanders call 'Kura.' Their school even has a Maori name, 'Te Kura o Matangi Awhio' which means school of the whirring wind. I always mispronounce it, calling it 'Te Kura o Matangi Ohio' just to get a reaction from the kids. They are still young enough that it works every time. Maddy just shakes her head at me.

As we finished up our meal, I brought out a plate of cookies Maddy had made earlier before leaving for work. Shortly after the kids had started school, she got a job teaching English to non-English speakers. Most of her students were Chinese. She loved it and told me all about her classes and students, and we laughed together at the things they said wrong. A session was just finishing up, and some students needed extra help. That's what Maddy had told me. She especially mentioned a Chinese student named Li Wei. I glanced at my watch again.

"Bath time," I called out. Allison ran ahead to get to the tub first. JJ slumped in his chair, "Do I have to?"

"Yes, JJ, you played hard after school today; you have to. But you can go second."

I went down the hall to find the tub already filling, and Allison had her pajamas all laid out in the bathroom. She smiled at me again. "Will you wash my hair, Daddy?"

"Sure, sweetheart, sure." She could probably tell I was distracted, so I tried to refocus. *Get in the moment, Jack*, I told myself. JJ was next, and he didn't want any help, but he didn't get his own pajamas.

Before long, they were both in bed and drifting off to sleep. It was just after ten p.m.. Still no Maddy. I tried calling her. The call went straight to message; maybe her phone was off. I tried the location app we both had on our phones, but it said location not available, which was the message if her phone was turned off or if the battery had died. I looked at my watch again.

I sat down in the kitchen. Then I got up and looked out the window at the driveway. I checked my watch. I sat down again. I turned on the news. I checked my watch. I got up to pace and sent Maddy another text. I tried to call her. I checked location services. I looked out the window. I sat back down. I walked down the hall and checked on the children; both were sound asleep. I walked back to the kitchen, looking out the window again along the way. I pulled my hair back along the sides of my head with my hands. I went out on the deck off of our bedroom. The night was calm and clear, much like last night.

Last night after getting the children bathed and to bed, I had come out here with a glass of wine, two actually, one for Maddy. Maddy said she wanted to take a quick shower. The bedroom lights were off, so I sat in the semi-darkness and listened to the night and enjoyed my wine.

Maddy came to join me dressed in her robe, with her hair still wet and uncombed. She picked up her wine and went to the railing, and looked over. When I wasn't looking, she undid the belt to her robe, so I could see her naked body barely hidden by the robe when she turned back around. She smiled. Impish. Like she was doing something taboo. I motioned for her to sit on my lap, and she did, facing me. She kissed me hard and long and then soft and then softer. My hands slipped inside the robe. I couldn't believe this slender sexy body had given birth to two children. Maddy worked hard at her fitness. She began to unbutton my shirt, and her hand found my chest. It was hard for me to sit still. I slowly pulled her robe down from her shoulders until it fell behind her and then to the deck floor. She kissed me more urgently and pulled me up, and undid my jeans. Soon they and my underwear had joined her robe. I still had on my unbuttoned shirt when Maddy pushed me gently back down into the chair, and as she sat back down, she put me inside her. And she kissed me. I began to rock my hips forward ever so slowly, and she pressed back, slowly, slowly. I kissed her, and my hands caressed her breasts. She let out a soft moan and moved her hips just slightly faster. Her moaning and breathing quickened my pace. I stood up and lifted her with me. She wrapped her legs around me, and her hips moved faster, slower, more quickly, and then faster still. I did what I could to keep up, and suddenly Maddy's head and shoulders fell back against my grip, and she moaned my name, "Jaaaack." And then, "I love you, Jack."

Tonight, I am alone, kept company only by the breeze and the sounds of rustling leaves and insects and an occasional car. Now and then, I could hear the ocean. *Oh, Maddy, where are you? Are you alright? Don't you know how much I love you?*

At eleven-thirty p.m. I called the police. After two rings, "Nelson Central Police Station, Sergeant Taylor speaking."

I stammered, "My name is Jack Gamble, and I'm calling about my wife."

There was a pause. Then, "Yes, Mr. Gamble, how can I help you?"

From his tone, it seemed the sergeant knew me or at least recognized my name. And there was something else, curiosity, bemusement; I wasn't sure.

"Well, she hasn't come home, and I can't reach her cell phone," I said.

"How long has she been missing?" the sergeant asked.

I had been expecting this question. "Not that long really, but she's never late, and if she will be even a little late, she calls or texts to let me and the children know." I hoped the children were a nice touch, and I decided to keep to myself Maddy's lateness three other times recently.

"Okay, Mr. Gamble, let me get some information from you. Since she's only been missing a few hours, that's about all I can do at the moment." *It's been more like four hours*, I thought, *and you don't know Maddy*. But I said, "Okay, what do you need?"

"Her full name."

"Madison Delin Gamble, but she goes by Maddy." Her middle name was the same as Allison's.

"Description?"

"About five feet five inches, light brown hair, shoulder-length, slender, very attractive." I didn't add that she had a million-dollar smile and gorgeous eyes, but I could have.

"Last known whereabouts?" The sergeant sounded a little bored, so I decided to try to make Maddy more human.

"Maddy teaches at the Nelson English Centre to give back to this great country that has given so much to us. Her class tonight was over at seven-thirty, so the two children and I were expecting her by seven forty-five or eight at the very latest."

"Wait a minute. Gamble? Do your kids go to Auckland Point School?"

"Yes, they both do. Why?"

"Well, it's a small world. I have a son, Nikau, who goes there, too. He just started, and he has mentioned your son to me. I guess they're friends."

I sighed to myself. Thank God for unexpected connections. "I'll have to ask JJ about your son in the morning."

"Yeah, please do. Now back to business. What kind of car does she drive?"

I could tell he had much more enthusiasm, compassion even. Maybe he was thinking about his son and his son's mother. "She was driving a 2031 Tesla coupe, bright red with a black hood and a white convertible top, License number TYB702."

"Anything else you can think of, Mr. Gamble, that might help?"

"Call me, Jack, please. If our sons are friends, we should be friends, too." I could almost hear him smile over the phone. *Treat people like you want to be treated*, I could hear my father say. "The only other thing I can think of is she was providing some special tutoring to a Chinese student named Li Wei. I don't know much about her class or her students, but I'm sure the school could help you with that."

There was a pause, so I added, "The class was winding up, tonight was the last one, and I guess he needed more help."

"Okay, Mr. Gamble, Jack, I'll have the guys look for her or her car tonight. I'm not supposed to do anything until someone has been missing for twenty-four hours, but I can keep this unofficial. And tomorrow, I'll make sure the detectives know about this first thing. I will stay over until they get in to be sure."

"Thank you, Sergeant Taylor."

"Charlie and you're welcome."

I willed myself to be patient. This is so unlike Maddy. She is never late without calling or texting. Never. Something is definitely wrong. I can feel it. *Did one of her students harm her? What should I do? Besides call the police. Is there anything else I can do?* The children are asleep in their beds and there is no one I can easily call to come stay with them, especially this late and with no notice. I leaned forward and raised both of my hands to my head, pulling my hair away from my face and forehead as I did so. I sat like that for many minutes. *Maddy! Maddy! Where are you?*

CHAPTER

3

Dockside
Port of Nelson
Nelson, New Zealand
March 9, 2033
2:30 p.m.

Li Wei turned and stirred. He tried to lift his head, but it fell back down to the mattress he lay sprawled across.

"Li Wei? Li Wei? Can you hear me? Li Wei?" Maddy got up and went over to where Li Wei lay. They were in some sort of a cargo box or shipping container. They had been here all night. Whatever they had injected into Li Wei must have been potent because he had been out for fifteen hours or more. She had been alone in the dark. "Li Wei?" She shook him gently. His eyes opened only to close again without focusing. He groaned and then rolled away from Maddy. "Li Wei, you have to wake up."

Maddy's mind turned toward Li Wei. What did she really know about him. *She remembered meeting him outside the Supreme Court when the law firm she was then working for had won the case against China preventing extradition from New Zealand due to human rights issues. Then he and six other Chinese students had shown up in her English class Coincidence? And immediately she had been attracted to Li Wei. She was secretly pleased when he requested private tutoring. She had met him discreetly in his hotel for the fourth time last night. Maddy, what the hell is wrong with you?*

And what about Epoch Times where he was supposed to be going for a job?

Maddy could see Li Wei's face in the small amount of light that crept in from the doors.

He groaned again, opened his eyes, rubbed them, closed them briefly, and then forced them open. He rubbed the back of his head. "Maddy?" He looked around. "Where are we?"

"I'm not exactly sure. Are you okay?"

He started to speak in Chinese, then shook his head and said, "I think so. My head hurts. How did we get here?"

"What's the last thing you remember?"

He sat up, groaned, and lay back down. He rubbed his eyes again. "I remember men coming into my room from the patio door. I should never have had you leave it open. I knew better."

"Yes, and what else?"

I remember sharing with you my work on why the Chinese communists are threatened by Falun Gong's logic on perspective and its embrace of compassion and tolerance."

"Okay, what else?"

"I remember kissing you and you kissing me back."

Maddy blushed and wondered what might have happened if those men had not burst in. "What else?" she said.

He rose slowly. He sat silently for a moment and then said, "That's all. No, wait, someone stabbed me or struck me or something, then I remember nothing."

"Okay, that's pretty much what I thought. You had gotten up to confront six men, all dressed in black wearing face masks. One of them injected you with something, and you've been out since."

He looked around. "What time was that? What time is it now?"

"Last night; it was eight-fifteen or eight-thirty or so when they injected you. Then they put us both in a van and drove us here. It's not far from the hotel, and I think they drove around in circles to confuse me. I was conscious part of the time but had a dark hood pulled over my head."

"I'm so sorry, Maddy, for getting you into this. It's me they want. Not you."

"Who are they? They won't tell me anything."

"They may be Chinese State Security. If not, they are doing this work for State Security. I have been in fear of them my whole life. Because of my work and beliefs, they want to get me inside China where they can neutralize me."

"You mean..."

"It can mean many things. Detention, torture, forced confessions, and yes, even death. I should have left with the others."

"Did you know they were after you?"

"They are always after me. I have not been entirely honest with you. I change my name and move about, trying to stay ahead of the Chinese Communists. I have been hiding from them all of my life, pretending to be someone else, living in different countries and with different friends, always staying ahead of China. They killed my parents for simply trying to protect the rights of Chinese citizens as promised under Chinese law. I am only alive because a neighbor woman took me in and when I was eight years old smuggled me into Vietnam where she left me with her nephew and his family. Only then did she tell me my parents had died in detention, arrested because they were Falun Gong and dead now like so many others. I grew up in Vietnam thinking of my parents often and studying Falun Gong. At first, I thought I would be a lawyer, too, but then I realized I would have no more power and no more effect than they had had. I determined Falun Gong was the only group of free Chinese strong enough to have any chance to unseat the Communists. So, I joined them and worked my way up through that organization, all the while collecting evidence of Communist abuse and then either hiding that evidence away or sending it out to others in the world at large. This job for *The Epoch Times* was to be my stepping-stone to real influence. All of the other Chinese who were with me are also Falun Gong. My parents were Falun Gong. My friends and I have seen people follow and watch us many times. While we were all together, we felt fairly safe, at least safer."

"Why do they not like Falun Gong?"

"The simplest answer is because our philosophy of a cosmic perspective and compassion and tolerance for all threatens the Communists effort to have the only perspective that exists and that things be judged only good or bad only as they are for the communists."

"Why did they take me?"

"I'm not sure. Maybe just because you were there?"

"Where are they taking us?"

Li Wei swallowed. "Either to China or somewhere to be killed. I am so sorry." He reached out for her hand. Maddy did not respond. She was looking at the door.

"I think we're on the docks in or near Nelson. Can you smell the salt air? And several times, I've heard horn blasts like the horns on large ships."

Just as she said this, a loud blast from a ship's horn was very close, and they started to move. They could feel both forward motion and the rocking motion that only the sea can give.

They sat in silence. Li Wei finally asked, "Have you seen anyone since they brought us here? Has anyone spoken to you?"

Maddy thought for a minute about what to tell him and decided on the complete truth. "Last night, when we arrived, two men brought me in and removed the hood from my head and cut the zip ties on my wrists. Then they brought you in, unzipped the bag you were in and dumped you on the bed. One of them said to me, 'How do you like your new love shack, missy?' and 'If your boyfriend there can't make you happy, just let me try.' Both of the men laughed when another man, a leader, I guess, came in and spoke harshly to them in Chinese, and they both left without saying any more. This man looked at me and said just to keep quiet, and they would probably release me. He said it wasn't up to him. He left two water bottles and pointed out the toilet." She motioned toward a bucket in the corner of the room.

"This morning at about eight a.m., by the sun, they opened both doors, and two different men brought in breakfast for both of us. When they saw you were still out, they took yours away. I could see we were on the deck of a ship, and this is some sort of shipping container surrounded by more shipping containers. I haven't seen anyone since."

"And no one has hurt you?"

"No, I'm fine. No one has touched me. I'm just frightened."

"Me, too," he said. "We have every reason to be." He put his arms around Maddy. She returned his hug for a long time.

The ship was still moving forward, gaining speed ever so slowly. A slight breeze slipped in through the crack between the doors, not much but something. And then both doors burst open, and five men, five Chinese men, stood in the doorway. In the front of the men was the leader who had told Maddy she would probably be released soon. And now they were putting out to sea. In his hand was a wand of sorts, black metal with some kind of leather handle. He held it up. "Well, look at my two little love birds. Do you know what this is?"

Li Wei shook his head no.

"I like to think of it as a wake-up stick, something to help you clear your head." With that, he touched Li Wei's thigh with the stick and pressed something in the handle. Li Wei jerked and screamed as the shock wracked his body. Two of the other men held Maddy back.

"Are you fully awake now? Good. We have important matters to discuss." Then he turned to Maddy and said, "You are a guest of China. No harm will come to you. We hope you will learn to see the true, gentle and kind nature of China." He bowed slightly.

And the men took Li Wei out of the storage container, closing and locking the doors and leaving Maddy trapped alone. She heard the stick arc again, and Li Wei cried out. And then she heard only the wind through the door. Maddy paced the tiny room. *Who was Li Wei? Was he telling her the truth? Who were these men? What did they want from her? Would they torture her? How would she survive that? Would they kill her? Would she ever see her children again? Or Jack?* She tried the door; it gave slightly but was obviously locked from the outside. *And where would she go if she got out?* She could still feel the motion as the ship put further out to sea. *Damn! What have I done?*

CHAPTER

4

The Gamble House
Victoria Road
Nelson, New Zealand
March 9, 2033
4:30 p.m.

I picked the children up from school. Before she even had the door closed Allison asked, "Is Mommy at home?"

I looked at the driver's side window to hide my face. "No, not right now. Should be home soon." Composed, I looked back at Allison. Jack told me all about his day, really all about recess and his exploits on the soccer field. I was half listening and hoped they didn't notice.

When we arrived home, there was a strange car in the driveway. I wonder if it has anything to do with Maddy. For the first time, I thought of kidnappers, and then immediately, I'll pay anything. I drove slowly up the driveway toward the grey sedan parked in our driveway. The brake lights came on and then the backup lights, and then they went off, and the driver's door to the car opened as I came to a stop behind it. A woman got out of the sedan as I was getting out of my car.

"Mr. Jack Gamble?" she asked, looking squarely at me.

"Who wants to know?" Then I noticed the badge on her belt. "Yes, yes, I'm Jack Gamble."

"Detective Wirihana." She stuck out her right hand, and I shook it. Firm grip, and she looked me in the eyes the whole time. I searched her face for clues. She had large dark eyes she kept right on mine and her full lips were pursed in a semi-smile.

I sent the children into the house. They looked wide eyed at this detective.

"Yes, Detective Wirihana."

She said, "You can call me Detective Wilson if you prefer." She handed me a business card with her name Detective Amelia Wirihana (Wilson).

I noticed that her extension matched her badge number as she said, "Sergeant Taylor asked me to look into this first thing, so I came as soon as I could. I hope I didn't startle the children"

She was looking at me strangely. *Does she think I had something to do with Maddy's disappearance? Surely not. Sergeant Taylor's kid is a friend of JJ's. Maybe he is apprehensive.*

"Thank you, Detective Wirihana." I've lived in Nelson for more than six years and was getting used to the Maori names. "Would you like to come in?" I motioned toward the house. The front door was unlocked, and the main entrance was standing open. Another of Detective Wirihana's cards was stuck to the screen door. I took it off as we entered and turned to look at her.

Before I said anything, she said, "I found the door open like that, Mr. Gamble. I did not enter your house if that's what you're wondering."

I looked down, collected my thoughts. "I'm distraught, Detective. I don't usually leave my front door standing open." I remembered her job. "I mean, I know Nelson is safe and all that."

She put up her right hand to stop me. "It's all right, Mr. Gamble. I can see that you're very upset. Is there somewhere we can talk privately?"

We went out onto the side porch and closed the door behind us. She said, "Why don't you tell me about Maddy?" She smiled for the first time.

We sat in the kitchen. "Maddy is my wife, the love of my life. She is the mother of our two wonderful children, Allison and JJ, who I just picked up at Auckland Point School. That's where I'm coming from." I looked back towards the front door. "I haven't been gone very long." She nodded. I continued, "Maddy teaches at Nelson English Centre, she knows Mandarin Chinese, and she had a class last night, the last one of this session, I think, and she didn't come home afterward, didn't call, didn't answer her phone. My wife isn't like that, Detective; if she was going to be late or something was wrong, she would let me know. Let us know." I looked at her face again. "Do you know anything? Do you know where she is, what happened?"

"No, Mr. Gamble. It's still really too early for a missing person case. But I owe Charlie, Sergeant Taylor, a favor, and he asked me to come over here first thing, that's all. Try to remain calm."

I realized I had my hair pushed back with my right hand which was resting on my scalp. I dropped it to my side.

"New Zealand is not that big. We'll find her. We'll find Maddy." She patted my hand, which I realized was shaking. "Why don't you give me a picture of your wife, tell me what she was wearing last time you saw her, type of vehicle she has. That type of thing?"

I was reasonably sure I had given all of this information to Sergeant Taylor last night. Maybe she did suspect me. But I gave her the story without hesitation. "I'll get you a picture. Maddy is stunning. She is about five feet five inches tall, slender with long light brown hair, her natural color. She left here about four o'clock yesterday afternoon to go to the Nelson English Centre to teach a class. After class, she was going to tutor one of her students, a young Chinese man named Li Wei. She drove her car, a bright red Tesla convertible with a white roof and a black carbon fiber hood and mirrors She was wearing a light blue blouse, black slacks, and her favorite shoes, a bright blue pair of fancy pumps, kind of sparkly. Expensive, I forget what brand, but Maddy loves her shoes." Detective Wirihana had checked her notebook but hadn't written anything down until I mentioned the shoes.

She said, "That should be enough to go on, for now. How about that picture?"

"Sure, sure." I got up, knocking the chair over in the process. I picked it up and retrieved my phone. While I did, Detective Wirihana excused herself and called someone on her phone. All I heard was, "Get someone over to the Nelson English Centre right away, find out what time her class was, who saw her, when she left, anything else you can find out, and put out the information on the red Tesla. We should be able to find that pretty quickly." She came back into the kitchen.

I didn't pretend I hadn't been listening. "Thank you, Detective, for getting this moving. Here are several photos, including a recent one in her blue shoes. Do you want me to send those to your email address?"

"No," she said, "send them to my phone." She gave me the number, and I sent the photos. She checked to make sure she had them and said, "That number is the best way to reach me, day or night. Feel free to call anytime. It's not on my business card, but I don't mind giving it to you."

I nodded.

"Are those Manolo Blahniks?" she asked, looking at the pictures I had sent her.

"Yes, that sounds right. Maddy bought them in Auckland last year."

"Nice shoes."

She looked at my face carefully again. "Can you think of anyone who might want to hurt Maddy or you, Mr. Gamble?"

"Please, Detective, call me Jack. And no, I can't think of anyone who would want to hurt Maddy."

"What about someone from your past? I vaguely recall a story about you two and Madagascar when you first moved here."

I looked back at her. "I've almost forgotten about that part of our lives, Detective. We were instrumental in bringing down a plot to leave millions of people to die who were said to have Ebola. They were all dropped on Madagascar, and meanwhile, the governments of the world looked the other way, and two masterminds of the whole matter made hundreds of millions of dollars on the death and misery they inflicted. Yes, we could still have enemies from those days, but it would be hard to say who they are. Most of the governments involved have repented and are trying to fix things. Madagascar is a free nation again called Malagasy. Good friends govern there, and the criminal masterminds are both dead, so I don't know who might be after us for that." I added, "But it is possible."

"How about anything else you or Maddy have done since moving here to Nelson?"

"I don't think so. We've been pretty low-key, having and raising kids, walking them to school, and Maddy works at the Nelson English Centre, and I do a little writing, but no one knows anything about that. Wait a minute!" It occurred to me that Maddy's prior job may have made her some enemies. "Before Maddy started teaching she worked for a New Zealand law firm that successfully argued in the Supreme Court here that based on China's record of torture, secretive imprisonment, mass discrimination, political influence over its judicial process and harassment of Chinese defense lawyers, that New Zealand would not extradite or transfer persons to China. Basically, the court found China did not honor basic human rights. That might have caused some hard feelings."

"Hmm. I remember that case, it got a lot of media attention and undoubtedly infuriated the Chinese. I don't see any obvious connection but we will see. Meanwhile, if you receive a ransom demand you will let me know right away?"

My hand went to my head. "Ransom? Do you think Maddy has been kidnapped?"

"Maybe. I checked, you and Maddy have lots of money and it is no secret; it's all over the internet."

I hadn't thought of that, I grabbed the detective's arm. "I will pay anything they ask. I just want Maddy back."

Detective Wirihana put up her hand. "Let's not rush off here, Mr. Gamble. It's only a possibility. Only one possibility."

Detective Wirihana was closing up her notebook. "Any other jobs either of you has had here in New Zealand? Is your wife a lawyer?"

"No other jobs. Both of us are attorneys in the United States, but neither of us has become licensed in New Zealand. Maddy worked as a paralegal for the firm here, but she is very capable and was told she was a huge help in winning that case. She dug out mountains of evidence of Chinese abuse of its citizens and even foreigners in Chinese custody."

I realized I still had hold of the Detective's arm. "I'm sorry." And I let go.

She patted my shoulder. "It's okay. I can see how upset you are. Normally, you would be the prime suspect here, but I would be wasting our time investigating you. But you will have to forgive some of the other officers if they ask you probing questions; they're just doing their job."

I nodded. How could anyone think I had something to do with Maddy's disappearance? I would never hurt her, and what about our children? - waste of precious time. But I remained silent.

"Mr. Gamble, many times in missing person cases, we find someone ran away. Was everything all right between you and your wife? Was she acting differently?"

"Everything was fine between us. No issues."

"Well, why would she wear Manolo Blahniks to teach an English class?"

CHAPTER

5

The Gamble House
Victoria Road
Nelson, New Zealand
March 9, 2033
6:30 p.m.

My cell phone rang. I rushed to grab it. Caller ID told me it was Detective Wirihana on her private number. As soon as she left here yesterday, I put it in my phone.

"Yes, yes. Hello?"

"Mr. Gamble, Jack?"

"Yes, speaking," I said as I was walking out the back door to the rear porch so the children wouldn't hear me. They had both come home from school, bounding in, looking for their mother. I had lied to them again, but I couldn't keep that up for long. I didn't want to worry them needlessly. I could still remember when my parents had been killed in a car accident when I was young. The realization that they would never be coming home, not ever, was with me always. I didn't want that to be true for my kids, not if I could help it.

"Detective Wirihana here. I have some news."

"Yes, Detective. Do you know where Maddy is?"

"Not yet, but we're getting closer. We found your wife's Tesla parked on Nile Street. It was legally parked, and one of the neighbors said he thought it had been there all night. A red Tesla kind of stands out."

"Nile Street? Where exactly is that?"

"Nile Street West is a fairly quiet side street, mostly residential, that intersects Rutherford Street, a busier commercial street. The Tesla was parked about a block and a half from Rutherford Street. Two blocks down Rutherford Street is a place called the Palazzo Motor Lodge; it sits in an area with lots of hotels. Are you familiar with it?"

"No, should I be?"

"Not necessarily, but we think your wife was."

"What do you mean?"

"This morning, the cleaning crew was making its rounds. They were surprised to find that one of their guests had left early. A man named Li Wei had taken all of his things and left even though he was paid up through the fifteenth when he was supposed to leave."

"Li Wei, you mean like the student Li Wei my wife was tutoring?"

"We feel certain they are the same, Mr. Gamble. This Li Wei was Chinese, according to the desk clerk, and had arrived with a group of other Chinese men, all of whom have checked out in the last couple of days. We have tracked these men from their hotel check out dates to flights out of New Zealand, some to Malagasy, some to Cincinnati, Ohio, others to other countries. Even though the desk clerk said they were Chinese or at least spoke Chinese, none of them went to China. Li Wei had a Vietnamese passport that he used for identification at check-in. I have a copy if you would like to see it. What do you think that all means?"

"No, the passport wouldn't mean anything to me. I never met Li Wei. And I don't know what it all means. Why do you ask me like that?" I used both hands to pull my hair back.

"Well, sir, for starters Malagasy was the scene of your last great international adventure and Cincinnati, Ohio is where you used to live. Are you sure you don't have anything to tell me?"

"I see. Is there something more Detective, something to do with Maddy?"

Detective Wirihana paused, apparently digesting my answer. "Yes, I hate to be the one to tell you this, but the cleaning crew found a pair of sparkly blue Manolo Blahnik pumps under the bed in Li Wei's room. And when we showed the desk clerk Maddy's picture, he remembered seeing her here last week with Li Wei; they were in the lobby to get a soft drink and laughing. He said they were touching each other, fighting to be the first to buy a drink. The clerk thought they seemed to be in love."

What? Maddy in love? With someone else? A student. "The clerk must be mistaken, Detective. Maddy wasn't in love with anyone but me."

"I am sorry. The people at the Nelson English Centre said they often saw Maddy and Li Wei together and alone."

I sat on the floor of the porch. *Maddy?*

"As I said, I am so very sorry. There doesn't seem to be much else for us to do here. Would you like to come get the car? We're done with that and have no good place to keep a car like that. We would like to keep the shoes just in case."

"Yeah, yeah," I said. "I'll get the car tomorrow sometime. Where is it?"

"Police headquarters."

"How did you get it there?"

"One of our officers drove it. To tell you the truth three officers fought over who got to drive it."

"How, I mean you don't have a key?"

The detective laughed softly. "Ever since car makers allowed cell phones to start cars we have always been able, in this country at least, to call the manufacture with a Vin number and explain ourselves and they give us a code that will start and operate the car for seventy two hours."

"That's kind of scary," I said.

"Jack?" she said softly.

"Yes?"

"If it's any consolation, I think they're still in New Zealand somewhere. I have checked airports and ships leaving here, and no Li Wei has been on any of the passenger manifests or Maddy Gamble either, and Li Wei still has a plane ticket for the fifteenth, leaving from Auckland and ending up in New York."

I wasn't sure how to respond, so I didn't. I knew more small talk about the car was not working. I leaned back against the house. *Maddy. Come home. Why oh why?*

"Maybe she'll come home," she said, and then she hung up.

My thoughts rushed back over my life. Had I been wrong to trust Maddy? After my parents had died, I had lived with a whole cast of different relatives when I was young. All nice enough if you were a stranger, but none of them loved me. And from them, I had learned that love was not real, just a pretense put on to get what you wanted. That had been reinforced by Barbara, my college girlfriend. When we were inseparable after years together, she had dropped me because I wasn't rich enough to keep her usual style. After that, I had grown good at pretending and was vengeful about making money. As a high-profile lawyer in Cincinnati, I had made bundles and, along the way, had bedded many a beautiful woman. At first, that's all Maddy was to me, but then I came to believe in her, to believe that she loved me. That she loved me like my mother had, only better. She had come to Madagascar to rescue me from the men who were trying to kill me to cover up their heinous crimes. And we were in love; I know we were. We had come here together, halfway around the world from Ohio to New Zealand, and we had settled down and started a family. And I thought she was happy. I was. Maybe I should have seen something coming. Was I just naive? Had the law job and the teaching only been a way to get out and meet others? Other men? Oh, my God, Maddy?

Not you. And this detective, could I trust her? She had gone from accusing to sympathetic in about thirty seconds. It had to be manufactured emotion, just doing her job, trying to get me to slip up, still suspicious of me. And I couldn't blame her. Malagasy and Cincinnati made it look bad and even though Maddy had confided in me about some of these placements for her students I couldn't calm my own lawyerly suspicions.

CHAPTER

6

Somewhere off the coast of New Zealand
March 9, 2033
Midnight

Maddy paced around the container box she was locked in again. It was eight feet by forty feet. She used the golfer's technique Jack had taught her. For her, a slightly exaggerated stride was three feet, give or take. Her prison was almost but not quite three paces across and just over thirteen paces long. And it was slightly higher than it was wide, only over eight feet. She could jump and touch the top but could not touch it standing on her flat bare feet. She had been over every inch of the container.

The seas seemed choppy; the ship surged and fell, surged and fell. *What was Jack doing? And the children? They would all be so upset. Why, oh why had she tutored this Li Wei? Did she have feelings for him; was that it?* I wore my fancy shoes *just* for him. If only I had come home to dinner after class. And what would become of me now? Did anyone know where I am or who had taken me?
Why was I even teaching? Boredom? Adventure? Was I really look-ing for something else? Something more than the life I have with

Jack and the children? No, I love my life, love Jack, he had become a great husband and father. And I love my children? What was it then? She took a deep breath and tried to calm herself. *Think, Maddy, think.* What did Jack do to survive Ebola Island? *Be like Jack, Maddy, be like Jack,* she kept telling herself. But she wouldn't listen; couldn't calm herself.

Were they going to kill me? Torture me? Rape me? Imprison me forever and ever? Make me confess something to be played on television? How can I be strong? I can do this. I will live through this, no matter what, to get back to Jack and my children. I have to. I will. Surely the United States and New Zealand, and maybe others would press China for my release. Surely. They had all been so warm and complimentary when Jack and I had exposed Ebola Island for the crime against humanity that it was. China was committing yet another crime against humanity. I will expose this one, too!

And what about Li Wei? What are they doing to him with that electric stick? The burn on his leg looked terrible. And now they are at it again. And why? Calm down, Maddy, calm down. No one has hurt you yet; just calm down. You will have to take charge. Li Wei is not able.

Maddy looked closely at the door. It was two doors, one hinged on each side, and they closed together in the middle. The door to her right closed first, and then the one from the left closed over it and had *a* long locking *pole* that slid down into a metal loop that was part of the container to keep the doors shut. When the doors were open, she had seen metal loops that matched up when the doors were closed, and she had heard her captors put a lock through those loops after they shut them. Near the top of the entries in the middle where they met was a small gap. She could see outside. It was dark. She looked closely and saw an identical opening at the bottom of the doors; she hadn't noticed it before because it didn't let in as much light. She heard voices in Chinese, and she quickly went back and sat down on her mattress.

My mattress, she thought. The other one was Li Wei's. The doors were unlocked and opened. Their captors dropped Li Wei into the front of the container. He was unable to walk. Two of the men kicked at him, and he crawled to his mattress and fell onto it. Maddy could see red and black burn marks on both of his thighs. The wounds were oozing blood, and Li Wei smelled of burnt flesh. The apparent leader emerged, carrying the electric shock stick. He was dressed in dark blue pants and a matching shirt. His hair was dirty and he smelled of alcohol. He caught Maddy looking at him and smirked. "We are returning your boyfriend." His English was passable. Then he pressed the switch, and the bar arced loudly, and Li Wei flinched. All of the men laughed. The leader only sneered and looked again at Maddy with dark beady eyes and said, "See, we don't even have to punish this dog anymore; he suffers when we let him see the stick."

Maddy got up and went to Li Wei. She stroked his head. "Are you alright? Oh, my God, what have they done to you?" He moaned but did not move.

"Were you lonely here in your love nest without your lover, Miss Maddy Gamble?" the leader said. Maddy looked up at the use of her name. How did this monster know who she was?

"Did you think we wouldn't figure out who you were, that you were one of the human rights lawyers that viciously attacked China. And at first, you volunteered; you were not even paid. You did it because you hate China. You Americans are all afraid the world will see that the Chinese way is better. Do you think we don't know who hangs out with the enemies of China? Enemies like Li Wei. Now you will have a chance to reflect on your improper opinions. We know much about you, Maddy Gamble. We know you noticed the cameras following you. We watched you trying to hide from them. Who did you think was watching you?"

The way he said her name made her skin crawl. And how were the Chinese monitoring cameras in New Zealand? She wanted to throw up but squinted her eyes and tried to look tough. "What do you want with me? Let me go. And leave Li Wei alone."

The leader laughed. "Let you go? Where? Overboard? The big boss says he has plans for you. But you are lucky; he says not to harm you; he wants you to be fresh when we get home to China. For now, all you need to do is think about the errors of your past and be prepared to confess and apologize for them when we reach China."

Plans for her? Confess and apologize? To whom? For what? What the hell did that mean? Maddy remembered Li Wei's speech in his motel room. This man could stand no dissent. The Communist way was the only way.

He lit up the stick again, and Li Wei started. Maddy stroked his hair to calm him. The leader looked at her with that same leering grin. "But we don't want you to miss all the fun. The next time we have a chat with Li Wei or as we call him Wee Wei." All of the men laughed. "We are going to let you watch. Let you see what you are missing. Maybe it will help you correct your false thinking about the Chinese justice system. You two stay with them while they eat dinner; the rest of you come with me." Maddy looked through this man. She would show this man no fear. None. The Chinese vassals may follow and fear him, she would never. No matter what they did to her.

He turned and left, and all but two of the men went with him. The two that remained handed Maddy two plates of food, one for Li Wei. Her plate had some dried meat, rice, and a salad of some sort. Li Wei's dish had only two small steamed buns. Maddy began to divide the food into two equal parts. One of the men stopped her and said, "No. That plate is for you. You cannot share it with him. If you try, I will take both plates, and we will leave. He may only have what is on the smaller plate." He spoke in Chinese, but Maddy understood every word. She stopped trying to divide the food.

Li Wei looked up at her from the bed and motioned with his eyes for her to not argue. She tried to help him up, and he cried out in pain and put out his arm. Maddy pulled back, and slowly, he worked himself up to a sitting position. She handed him his two small rolls, and he ate both down. Maddy worked on her meal, and twice when the guards weren't looking, she hid some of her food under her leg for Li Wei.

As soon as she finished, which wasn't long since she was famished, the two men took the plates and left. She heard the doors close and lock, and the two men walk away.

She gave Li Wei the food she had hidden for him. He devoured it. In the darkness, she asked, "What else can I do to help you?"

"Nothing, let me sleep; they will be back soon enough." His head dropped to the mattress. "I am sorry. What about you? Can I do anything for you?"

Maddy shook her head. "No, you get some rest." She looked around at the small dark crate with just a sliver of light from somewhere creeping in from the joint between the doors. The trace of light accented the lock. Maddy turned away. Something wasn't quite adding up here. Why all of this effort to capture Li Wei, a private citizen with an ax to grind against China? The scale was all wrong.

CHAPTER

7

The Gamble House
Victoria Road
Nelson, New Zealand
March 10, 2033
6:00 p.m.

I finally told the children that their mother was missing. As soon as they came home from school, I sat them both down. "Your mother has disappeared," I said.

JJ said, "What? No!" and Allison just stared at me.

"She went to tutor a man after her class was over two nights ago, and now both of them are missing."

"Are they together, Mommy and this man?" asked Allison.

"I don't know, honey." I had convinced myself that no one knew for sure. All of us were crying. "The police are still looking for them and I'm sure they will find them, and your mother will be back with us soon." What else was I supposed to say?

JJ asked, "Can I go to my room now?" He was my little stoic warrior; he always processed things on his own for a while and then came up with questions and his understanding of things. I nodded, and as he left for his room, he put his hand on my shoulder, "We'll be okay, Dad."

Allison didn't seem so sure. She curled in close to me and was silent. Now and again, I could feel her sigh. I didn't dare look at her for fear my tearful face would only make her worse. She grew quiet, and I hoped she had fallen asleep.

I watched as two cars turned into our driveway, Detective Wirihana's grey sedan, followed by Maddy's red Tesla. Shit! I had forgotten all about picking up Maddy's car. I dried my eyes the best I could.

"Who is that, Daddy? Is that Mommy's car?" Allison asked. So much for her being asleep. I could feel the excitement in Allison's voice. I felt terrible squashing her hope when I said, "That's the police bringing back Mommy's car. She's not with them, sweetheart. Why don't you see how your brother is doing? I'll take care of this. It shouldn't take long."

Allison went to join her brother, looking back over her shoulder at the Tesla and me the whole time.

As I went out onto the front porch, I saw she had stopped and watched as Detective Wirihana got out of her sedan with two pizza boxes. A uniformed officer got out of Maddy's car, followed by a small boy on the passenger side. "Jack, this is Sergeant Taylor and his son, Nikau," said Detective Wirihana.

"Call me Charlie," said the officer, sporting a friendly grin. "Nikau and I thought we'd come over and hang with your kids for a bit, if that's okay? And Amy here sprang for a couple of pizzas."

I didn't say anything. I remembered Sergeant Taylor and his son from the telephone. I just wasn't sure why they were all here and with pizza.

Amy said, "There's been an important development in your wife's case. I need you to come with me for a little while if you will. Entirely up to you, but I think you'll want to hear this for yourself. And Charlie here and his boy volunteered to bring your wife's car back and stay with your children while we take care of a little business."

She was slightly smiling, so I didn't think they had found Maddy's body. And she seemed tense like she wanted to spring. "Let me tell the kids."

JJ was already running down the steps, and Allison was on the porch watching. JJ said, "Nikau?"

"Hey, JJ. I heard about your mom is missing. Very sorry. Detective Amy may have some new information that would help and needs your dad to go with her, so my dad and I came to hang out and eat pizza. Okay?"

Leave it to kids to sort things out quickly. JJ said, "Sure, pizza sounds great. And after we eat, I can show you my room." And then, "Is that your dad?"

Charlie smiled and said, "Just call me Nikau's dad, that's how most people know me. What's your name?" he said to Allison, "I hope you like pizza."

She nodded, and as they all went inside, I shouted, "I'll be back as soon as I can, kids."

After I got into Detective Wirihana's car, I asked, "What's this all about, Detective?"

"Well, Jack, and please call me Amy; I'm not exactly positive, but a witness showed up at the Palazzo Motor Lodge who thinks she saw several men in black abduct your wife into a van."

"What? When?" I brushed back my hair.

"Two nights ago, the night Maddy went missing. The witness is there now, at the motor lodge with a patrol officer waiting for us to take her statement; really, for me to take her statement. I know you were a lawyer and all, but leave this one up to me, please. But I want you there to hear what is said and see if it gives you any ideas. If it does, you can just relay those to me."

"Okay," I said, "I'll try. Where the hell has this witness been? We could have used her information two days ago!"

"I know, I know I have been thinking that as well. Let's see what she says about that."

Amy pulled up and stopped right in front of the door to the motor lodge. As we went in the front door, the desk clerk motioned to his left and said, "They're in there." We went left into the manager's office. There was a patrol officer seated near the door. Further into the office was a woman, about my age, not bad looking, not good looking, either. She had her hands clasped together. She started to stand up, but Amy told her we would be right back and please sit down. Amy motioned for the officer to come out into the hall, and she shut the office door as he did.

"So, what can you tell me, officer?" Amy said as she strained to look at his badge.

"McAdams, Officer McAdams," he said.

"What can you tell me?"

"She just showed up here, all upset, according to the manager. She said she saw a kidnapping here a couple of nights ago and then gave me this fantastic story about six men all in black taking a woman out the back. I have it all down here." He held up his notebook.

"Why don't you let me have that? Her story may or may not be fantastic; that's what I'm here to figure out. Nice job, McAdams. I can take it from here."

McAdams nodded, handed Amy his notebook, and left. Amy opened the door to the manager's office. "Mind if we sit down?" she asked. The woman nodded.

"I'm Detective Wirihana of the Nelson Police." She handed the woman a card. "We're here to hear what you told the officer. Would you mind telling me again from the beginning?"

The woman was obviously nervous but nodded.

"Why don't you start with your name?"

"My name is Julia Adamson."

"I have your address here. What is your date of birth, Julia?"

"June 21, 2001."

"Okay, when you were last here at the motor lodge?"

"Two nights ago."

"And what were you doing here?"

Julia looked down. "Meeting my boyfriend."

"And are you married, Julia? No judgment, just a question."

"Yes, that's why I didn't say anything at first."

"And now?"

"Well, I've finally had it. The bastard hit me this morning. I told him all about my boyfriend. I was no longer afraid he'd find out. Wanted him to know, wanted him to feel bad." She started to cry. Amy looked over at me with raised eyebrows and immediately said, "There, there, Julia. I completely understand. The bastard hit you, and you hit him back with what you had done. No one is blaming you."

The woman, Julia, composed herself and looked up. "So, that's why I'm here now. I know I should have come forward earlier but I was worried my affair would then be discovered. I'm sorry."

"Why don't you tell us what you saw on Tuesday?" Amy had still not introduced me.

Julia took a deep breath. "I was sitting on the patio of room 217. We had finished, you know, and my boyfriend had left, so I had gotten dressed and was sitting out back sipping wine thinking about going home." Amy nodded, and Julia continued, "I saw this woman, a beautiful woman, come up the driveway and let herself in through the pool gate. I thought she was another secret lover like me. Only she was classier. She had on a light blue blouse, dark pants, and these bright blue high heels. I think they were Manolo Blahniks." She said this to Amy, thinking I wouldn't know anything about shoes. I leaned forward, and Amy motioned me back with her eyes. I could tell she was very interested in this story. She made a note and said, "Go on."

"Anyway, this woman goes onto the patio of room 103 and lets herself in."

"Have you ever seen this woman before?"

"Yeah, I think so, I mean, last week also on Tuesday, I saw her in the lobby as I was leaving. She was with one of the Chinese guys that were staying here. She and this one guy were laughing and having a good time. And all of the Chinese guys stayed in those rooms on the first floor near the lobby."

Amy nodded again. "Do you come here every Tuesday?"

"Yeah, well, I did anyway. I don't know now. It may not be necessary. I mean, now that my marriage is over."

"What about your boyfriend, is he married?"

"Yeah, my boyfriend is married."

"Julia, you know I have your boyfriend's name here from the officer who first talked to you. You can use his name."

"Yeah, it's okay. I know you have it, and if you have to talk to him, you do. He was gone before any of this happened."

"We'll try to be discreet if we decide we need to talk with him."

"Thanks."

"Go on, please."

"I was getting ready to go when I saw this van pull into the driveway of the motor lodge with its lights off. It was real quiet, like it was an electric vehicle or something. I remember thinking they must have forgotten to turn their lights on when the sun went down."

"What time was it?"

"Somewhere around eight-thirty, maybe a half-hour after sunset."

"Okay, then what happened?"

"The van went by, on back to the parking lot, I guess, and didn't come back, and I was about to get up again when I saw motion along the pool fence. I had to squint to see, but there were six people all dressed in black moving along the fence and through the pool gate."

"You're sure there were six?"

"Yes, ma'am."

"Were they men or women?"

"Hard to be sure, but men, I think. I saw one in the light of the patio, and he had a black mask on, too, like a ninja or something."

"What happened next?"

"These men went in through the same patio door the woman had entered. First, I heard muffled voices and then a scuffling sound, and then everything was quiet."

"What did you do?"

"I sat back into the dark corner of the patio I was on and watched. Pretty soon, one of the guys in black comes out with a couple of suitcases and a backpack and something else and puts them all down on the patio. He goes back inside. That's when I noticed the van was back. I didn't hear it, but it had pulled up right outside the pool gate, its lights were off, including its brake lights, and the sliding door on the side of the van was partly open."

"How well could you see all this from where you were?"

"It was dark where I was and lighter where the van and the people were so that I could see pretty well."

"Okay, after this, we'll go see where you were and where they were, if it's okay?"

"Sure."

"What happened next?"

I was trying not to lean forward in my chair. Amy was taking notes as she talked and still managed to keep things conversational.

"Then I saw three of these people, men in black, come out the patio door carrying a huge dark bag. They were struggling a bit like it was pretty heavy."

"When you say large, how big? Big enough for a body, maybe?"

Julia's hand flew to her mouth. "You don't think... Yeah, it might have been big enough for a body. Maybe. The thought crossed my mind that night, but I convinced myself I was just excitable."

Without prompting, Julia continued, "Then two more of these men came out, one on each side of the woman I saw."

"Are you absolutely sure it was the same woman?"

"Pretty sure. She had on the same light blue blouse and dark pants, only this time she was barefoot."

"How do you know she was barefoot?"

"She tried to get away, she ran toward the pool and I could see her feet clearly."

I leaned forward and asked, "What happened next?" I couldn't help myself and I tried not to look in Amy's direction.

"The men caught up with her and she hit one of them, hard and right in the face, but then the other man grabbed her from behind and he held something over her mouth and she went limp almost immediately. Then they tied her hands behind her back and put a bag over her head and carried her to the van."

"A bag over her head?" I asked, unconsciously pulling back my hair.

"Yes, I watched them pull it down and then I couldn't see her hair anymore."

Amy looked at me with raised eyebrows and I sat back.

Amy continued, "What did you do then?"

"I squeezed back as far as I could into the corner. One of the men was looking at all of the balconies. I don't know if he heard something or was just checking. Anyway, he gets in the van, closes the door, and the van starts moving without a sound. It gets to the end of the drive-way and turns left and then turns its lights on."

"Wow," said Amy. "That's quite a story. Can you describe the van? Did you get its license plate?"

"I didn't get the license number, but I can describe it. It was white with a yellow top. I was looking down at the top from the second floor. The yellow came a foot or so down the sides of the van, and then it was white the rest of the way down. On the door in green letters, it said Global Logistics and then globallogisitics.co.nz. There was also a telephone number, I think, but I wasn't able to get that."

"Did you see anything else, Julia?"

"No, that's it."

"Did you make notes about what you saw? Your memory is excellent."

"Yeah, I went in and made notes right away. I felt bad for that poor woman, but I was afraid, afraid my husband would find out where I was." Then she kind of snorted and laughed at the same time.

Amy stood up. "Let's go take a look at the two patios," she said. Amy tilted her head toward me. "You stay here. I'll be back in a few minutes."

"No way, if this can help find Maddy I'm coming with you. I might see something you miss." I stood and followed the two women out of the office.

Oh, my God, Maddy, who took you? What do they want with you? Where have they taken you? Part of me wished she had run off with Li Wei, at least she would be safe. And part of me wondered what Maddy had been doing here. Perhaps Li Wei had a hand in this.

The patio where Julia had watched Maddy's abduction provided an excellent view of the pool area, the gate and the patio of room 103. She could have seen what she said she saw and she never hesitated once when describing where she had been sitting or other details.

Before long Amy released Julia. "Ready?" was all she said and we went down and looked at room 103 and its patio. Not much to see as the room had been cleaned and made up one or more times. Amy showed me where Maddy's shoes had been found and I was so overwhelmed with the question of what Maddy had been doing here in the first place to notice much else. Amy didn't seem to notice much either.

Once we were back in her car, I said, "Wow. I believe her. Who do you think kidnapped Maddy?" I pulled back on my hair.

Amy looked over at me. "I'm not sure. Maddy was here at least twice voluntarily, so that theory still has legs. Sorry."

"But you heard what this woman said."

"I did, and I believe her, too. We have to stay open-minded. We do want to help you find your wife. Look, it's late; I'll take you back to your kids and pick up Charlie and Nikau. Tomorrow first thing I will investigate Global Logistics and start checking footage from area security cameras. There are many in this area."

CHAPTER

8

The Gamble House
Victoria Road
Nelson, New Zealand
March 11, 2033
11:30 a.m.

After I walked JJ and Allison to school, I gathered my thoughts. At breakfast, they had asked me about what I did last night with the detective. JJ said, "She's pretty."

I must have blushed because both of the children were pointing at me and laughing. I said, "A witness came forward and she had seen some things that might help us find Mommy."

"Like what kind of things?" Allison asked.

"Came forward from where?" JJ asked.

"Just some people near where she was at a meeting, and these people weren't acting right. So, the police are going to try to find those people and ask them some questions."

Allison asked, "Does this mean she didn't run away with a man?"

Before I could answer Allison, JJ said, "I hope they find her soon."

"Me, too," I said. I hated not telling the children everything that was going on. I tried to be sure that what I told them was accurate, if not complete. I remembered my lawyer days. When a witness was sworn to tell the truth, the whole truth and nothing but the truth, it was usually the whole truth where the problems came in. Most people tried to tell the truth, just not all of it. Now that person was me. And I was relieved that so far, it was working. Only a parent understands how hard it can be to stay ahead of a five-year-old and a six-year-old.

I was walking back home when I noticed one of the cameras mounted near an intersection. My conversation with Maddy came back to me. Could that camera have anything to do with her kidnapping? It had behaved strangely in regard to Maddy. But wasn't it a City of Nelson camera? Why would they have any interest in Maddy? Some lecher at the controls? Although I didn't think anyone really controlled or monitored these cameras. I was at the intersection of Britannia Heights and Victoria Heights, not much here really. There were a few houses across the street and then a point of untended land that was part of the yard of the nearest house or maybe municipal property. And there near the tip of the point was a light pole with a camera mounted on it about twelve feet up. I walked across the street and the camera swung rhythmically. I walked back across the street and still the camera droned on, back and forth, not at all like what I had witnessed when Maddy walked past this same camera. Whenever one of the cameras spotted Maddy it followed her as she went, rather than swinging back and forth, and kept pace with her if she sped up or slowed down. I'd promised Maddy I would look into that for her, but hadn't. I needed to do that today like I had promised Maddy I would do days ago. Maybe if I had... I stopped myself mid-thought. *Jack Gamble, you get your sorry ass together right now. Maddy's situation isn't your fault, but it is your responsibility. Someone has taken the mother of my children, and I need to step up and get her back.*

When I got back to the house, I grabbed a cup of coffee and got onto the computer right away. First, I searched for Global Logistics,

Nelson, New Zealand. Nothing relevant came up. I found all sorts of references for global logistics as a topic or a service but no company by that name and no connection to Nelson, or even New Zealand. I tried Globallogisitics.com in addition to Globallogistics.co.nz. I couldn't think of any other ways to search. I gave up. I knew the police would also be checking that lead, so I moved on to surveillance cameras.

"Chinese surveillance Cameras" brought up a large number of articles, ads from camera companies, product ratings, and some references to spyware contained in the cameras. I started there. In 2025, the United States banned specific Chinese cameras or software or components made by certain Chinese companies because the cameras provided data back to the company in China and the Chinese Communist Party. The Chinese surveillance camera had been widely used against the Uighurs in China, a subculture that had been all but wiped out after first being monitored virtually everywhere, then retrained in internment "schools" and then murdered in large numbers by the Chinese state forces. I was breathing deeply and sighing while reading the extent of the Uighurs' plight at the hands of the Communists. The cameras were widely used in Hong Kong when the Chinese Communists went back on their word and obliterated the democracy there. The stories were all so sad. I found several other brands of cameras made in China that were either suspected or proven to have spyware. Some of them could even be controlled or reprogramed from China. What I also found most interesting was the strides the Chinese had made in facial recognition. Their cameras were very good at it.

Starting with the Uighurs, they could program the computer controlling the cameras to focus on or look for individual faces. Then the cameras, if they found that face or those faces, would follow them as far as possible and alert other nearby cameras to try to pick up that face that could be heading their way. With that methodology, the Chinese could pinpoint within a couple of blocks the location of anyone they chose. As bad as that was, they had made it even worse. The

Chinese had developed an algorithm that told the cameras also to record and follow the faces of any other individuals it saw more than once at the same time or within a specific time frame of spotting a person of interest. So, if you happened to be crossing a street on your way to work at the same time as a person of interest did two or more times, your every move could be subject to constant scrutiny by the Communist Party. *Unless you were smart like Maddy and noticed the actions taken by the cameras in your presence. Maddy, and who knows how many other persons of interest.*

I wrote down the suspect camera manufacturers' names and went out to my car to go and recheck the cameras in Nelson to see if I could tell who had manufactured them. I put a small ladder and a couple of tools in the trunk and took my phone to take pictures. I didn't have to go far; there was a camera right around the corner. I pulled over, got out, got my ladder, and walked behind the pole where the camera was mounted. Standing on the top step of the ladder and holding onto the pole for balance, my eyes were even with the camera's housing as it made its rhythmic back and forth sweep. There was nothing on the housing anywhere. I looked underneath the camera. There was something there, but I couldn't read it. I got down and moved the ladder. There on the housing, it said: "Manufactured for the City of Nelson, NZ." I held my phone under the street camera, took a picture of the signage, and checked it to make sure it was a good image. I climbed down and went and checked four more cameras. They were all the same. Whoever had made those cameras wasn't broadcasting it. I took pictures of all of them.

I drove home and decided to check in with Amy before she went out for lunch. I called as I was walking up to the house. "Jack, hang on a minute."

Then she was back. "Sorry, I was just finishing something up. What's on your mind?"

"Mainly, I'm wondering if you've had any luck following up on the information we learned last night, from Julia Adamson."

"It's slow. So far, nothing on Global Logistics; it seems to be a dead end."

"Yeah, I did a quick check myself and found the same. I was hoping you guys had better resources and would come up with something."

"Oh, we have better resources but a dead end is still a dead end sometimes. We have also been reviewing security camera footage for March 8. We pick up the van at the corner of Nile and Rutherford near where Maddy parked that night. We think that is just coincidence before you go off on that. Okay?"

"Okay." She had called that one right.

"After that, we're having trouble following the van. It's hard to predict where it traveled or where it ended up. And to top it off, the stupid software that came with the cameras isn't working as it should. We ask it to find all pictures of this van on March 8, and it kind of sits there and spins. Very frustrating."

"Let me ask you something. Do you know who manufactured the cameras used by the City of Nelson?"

"No. But I can probably find out. Why?"

"Maddy believed the cameras were tracking her and showed me one day. When I walked past a camera, it kept swinging back and forth, but when Maddy did, the camera followed her movements."

"Huh, what do you make of that?"

"Not quite sure, but I was doing some research online this morning, and the United States has barred certain Chinese cameras or components or software from many uses in the US. And there are some horrifying articles about how China uses surveillance cameras against the Uighurs and others. All in all, there are about six companies called into question. And the cameras here have no manufacturer's markings. I have pictures of the bottom of four of them I can send if you want to see them. Tell you what. I will email you the companies' names, and you can check and see if one of them manufactured the City's cameras and let me know. Okay?"

"Okay. And no need to send the photos. I believe you. And I've got one for you. The more I get into this, the more I believe your wife was abducted by professionals and maybe even professionals working for a nation-state. I spoke to a friend of mine with counter-terrorism experience as a kind of unofficial consultant, and she thinks the same thing."

"Who?" A counter-terrorism consultant? I listened intently.

"Her name is Sara. Let me tell you about her credentials. I think you'll be impressed. She was a member of the elite Army Special Forces, New Zealand Special Operations Force or just SAS; then the even more elite New Zealand Security Intelligence Service, NZSIS or SIS, recruited her. She became a top-level spy, in other words. In that capacity, she thwarted an assassination attempt on the Governor-General by enemy agents. She was wounded and given a discharge and pension, and she lives right here in Nelson, not far from you. She now goes by Sara Singh, and she's a good friend of mine."

"Okay. Do you think it's a good idea to involve her? I guess it couldn't hurt."

"My thoughts exactly."

"What did she have to say?"

"She agrees this looks like a state-sponsored kidnapping. She reminded me that there's been no ransom note. She listened to what Julia Adamson told us and immediately said it sounded like the Chinese. She said the hood over the head was almost a trademark for them; Sara asked if there were any Chinese victims before I had told her about Li Wei. When I said yes, she said to focus on Li Wei, and she promised to get back to me soon. And now the cameras seem to tie into China, too."

"I've been wondering about that, too. Maybe Maddy wasn't the target. But what happened to Li Wei? Could he be involved?"

"Maybe, or maybe he was in that large bag Julia saw being carried out."

"Maybe," I allowed, "Let me know what you find out about the cameras and what else this Sara has to say."

"Will do."
I had to sit down with my head in my hands.

CHAPTER

9

Somewhere off the coast of New Zealand
March 11, 2033
3:00 p.m.

The sound of the waves lapping against the boat was soothing, something expected in her otherwise bizarre circumstances. Maddy was still thinking about Jack and the children. She couldn't help feeling like she had let them down. What would they do without her? What would happen to her?

The rhythm of the ship moving through the sea was smooth, Maddy tried to focus on that. The waters must be reasonably calm. The rhythm failed to help her sleep. She tossed and turned and slept a few minutes here, a few minutes there. She was afraid. The unknown plans for her made everything worse. She knew that she might never see her family again. She could endure whatever they did to her if she knew she would see her family once more. But she didn't know that. As far as she could tell, Li Wei never stirred. She was alone. The small container smelled of perspiration and waste and burnt flesh. Her feet hurt; her head hurt. She thought that was from not having much water. Her lips were dry and chapped. A couple of times, Maddy heard the sound of Li Wei's breathing. Occasionally a noise from outside the container would drift in bringing a welcome distraction. Some of the noises she thought she could identify; others remained a mystery. She knew when the sun came up by the small opening at the top of the doors, a crack really, but it allowed her to maintain a sense of time. Still Li Wei slept. Her world went no further. And maybe it never would again. Trapped in a small box on a big ship in the middle of the ocean. What could change to give her a chance? Any chance?

The doors to the storage container opened loudly to the bright sun of the afternoon. Maddy caught a glimpse of the sun in the sky to their left. They must be heading north.

Two men stood in the door with two plates. "Lunch," they exclaimed. There had been no breakfast, no contact from anyone since last night. Li Wei had to be awakened, which was accomplished by a sharp slap to his face. He startled and opened his eyes. Li Wei's hand went to his face, he groaned, and looked down at his legs and then around at their surroundings. Maddy hoped he had a peaceful sleep.

Maddy said, "Can I use the bathroom, please?" And then she repeated her request in Chinese. And she held herself between her legs to be sure they would understand, one of the men pointed to the bucket in the corner.

"I can't."

From outside the storage container, she heard, "Take her to the restroom. Deputy Minister Chen said we were not to harm her. And be more careful what you say in front of her, she can speak at least some Chinese."

Chen, she thought. Deputy Minister Chen and he said I was not to be harmed. And she lamented letting her captors know she could understand Chinese. That had been stupid. She would have to become more mindful, more cunning.

The man in the doorway replied, "Yes, sir. Shall I handcuff her?"

"Why bother? Where can she run? We will let them eat lunch when she gets back." Even though they now spoke mainly in Chinese it was understood they she knew what they meant. *Stupid, stupid, stupid.*

Maddy followed the man through stacks of storage containers, four containers high and seven rows deep, all across the front deck. She looked up to see the bridge. She could vaguely see two men there, dressed differently than the men she and Li Wei had seen. So there must be crewmen, and the kidnapping group, at the very least. As they started down alongside the bridge, Maddy could see that the rear deck also had containers stacked in rows. How would anyone find them even if they came on board? She realized the Chinese held them in a box at the bottom of the stack for ease of access. Would anyone else think of that? Would anyone else ever get that chance? What could she do if she got free? Was there anywhere she could hide? How long would she have to hide without food or water or a bathroom?

Maddy took in everything she could. Midway along the ship's quarters was a doorway. The man stopped, turned the wheel and opened it, and motioned for Maddy to enter. He didn't say anything, but she didn't like the way he looked at her. Then he pointed to a door to her left. Maddy took in the interior hallway and the metal stairs going both up and down directly ahead of where she had entered the quarters. She saw the infirmary straight ahead when she stepped through the doorway. She closed the bathroom door behind her. The room had a light, a stainless-steel toilet with a few bad spots, and a stainless-steel sink with handles for hot and cold water. There was no towel, and the only toilet paper was a half roll on the floor partially wet from something.

The man knocked on the door. "Come on. You hurry up."

Maddy said, "Okay." She was standing in the rundown head on a rundown ship, and she didn't want to leave. It was safer here than where she had been, where she would return. She went to the sink. Only the cold water worked. At least it was something. She splashed cold water into her face. She flipped her hands down sharply to shake off some of the water. She opened the door, bowed her head slightly, and said, "Thank you." And they retraced their steps back to the container prison cell.

Several men had moved into the container when they returned, the same men as always. As she entered, one man handed her a plate and bowed slightly. "Just for you, eat," he said. He gave Li Wei a plate, too, but with far less food. The leader got up from a chair in the container and motioned for Maddy to sit down. He held her chair for her as she sat. Again, she had a meal of soup and rice and some sort of meat; she couldn't tell what. This time Li Wei had the same food, but only about a one-half portion. They both started to eat rapidly. She was so hungry.

After only a couple of minutes, the leader took Li Wei's plate away, with more than half of his food still uneaten. "Lunchtime is over for you, Li Wei. Now we talk." He turned to Maddy, "You can keep eating. and I already know your name," he said as if it was a threat and then he bowed his head slightly. Maddy just looked at him. "And we all know you understand Chinese, so don't pretend otherwise."

Two of the men pulled Li Wei down onto the bed, held his shoulders down, and pulled his legs apart. Li Wei cried out. His wounds began to bleed again. From somewhere, the electric stick appeared, and one of the men fired it up. "Do you remember yesterday?" sneered the leader. "Today, we will let your girlfriend watch while you cry like a baby and beg for mercy."

Maddy tried to get up, but firm hands pushed her back down in the chair. Her plate fell to the floor. "My name is Wang. It is all you need to know. You can call me Mister Wang." Then he fired the stick and touched it to one of Li Wei's existing wounds. Li Wei suppressed a cry, as another guy held Maddy down.

Wang looked back at Maddy. "We will tie you to the chair if we have to. Do we have to?"

Maddy shook her head. "Why don't you leave him alone? Can't you see how badly you have hurt him?"

Wang looked at Li Wei as if contemplating what Maddy had said. "He has it within his own power to stop this at any time that he wishes. All he has to do is tell me what I want to know. Let me demonstrate."

"Li Wei, what are the names of the men you conspired with against your birth country?"

Li Wei remained silent. The stick lit up and bit into his other leg, and Li Wei cried out. Maddy squirmed in her chair to stay seated. Wang turned to her. "Perhaps you can answer for him. What were the names of the other students in your class?" Maddy looked at the floor and didn't answer. Would they torture her next? She knew the names they wanted, the names of the other students in her class and she suspected they already knew those names.

"There, you see? Li Wei will not cooperate. We know you conspired with lawyers to defame China's justice system; we have copies of your communications. Why do you deny this? Did you not meet with this woman, this Maddy Gamble, to help her win her big case in New Zealand?"

The stick fired again. Maddy called out, "Wait. I'm not a lawyer in New Zealand; I was only a helper on the case. And I didn't even know Li Wei until after the case was over." She wondered if she was the cause of all of this.

"Is this true, Li Wei, or is she lying to me?"

Li Wei said, "It is true."

The leader turned the stick off.

"Tell me the names of the lawyers you met with to discuss the Chinese criminal justice system."

Li Wei said nothing, and the stick stung him again. Li Wei groaned and then went slack. The leader nodded at the two men holding Li Wei. They jostled him, and he groaned, but he did not move.

The men slapped Li Wei in the face, then they splashed water in his face, but he did not regain consciousness.

"Too bad," Wang said. "Just when we were starting to get somewhere. "It is useless to try to resist, Li Wei. Sooner or later, you will tell me everything I want to know." He fired the stick but didn't attack Li Wei, and Li Wei didn't notice.

Maddy said, "Why do you torture him to provide information you must already have? Surely Chinese intelligence knows the names of men he traveled with." She glared at Wang who seemed pleased that she had spoken to him in Chinese.

"This man needs to demonstrate that he will cooperate and that he understands his first and only loyalty is to China"

"Oh, bull shit," Maddy said and several of the men chuckled. Not Wang. He stood and pointed the stick menacingly at Maddy. "Perhaps you would like to tell us the names of those lawyers? I can only hope I get the chance to have such a discussion with you."

So, she did have some latitude she thought and these were definitely Chinese intelligence agents.

The sun was still up but was now low enough in the sky that the stacks of containers blocked it from shining into the doorway. Still, the breeze was pleasant, warm, but cooling. Maddy stayed in her chair and took a deep breath. Wang looked at her strangely. She looked back, trying to memorize his every feature.

After a minute, Wang picked Maddy's plate off the floor and offered it to her. She shook her head. Wang and his men left, and the doors closed and locked. The chair and the plate of food remained.

Li Wei didn't move. Maddy had only her thoughts for company. *Am I the cause of all of this? Did the Chinese kidnap us because of the human rights lawsuit I worked on? No, wait. Li Wei says the Communists consider Falun Gong a severe threat; indeed, that is more important than a court case from New Zealand. And it makes more sense since he was in Nelson with other Chinese Falun Gong, and they were all staying at the Palazzo Motor Lodge. Or did the Chinese follow me there, and Li Wei got caught up in it? Was this supposed to be a lesson to lawyers and others in New Zealand and around the world? Were Li Wei and his friends something other than what they said they were? Had they committed some acts or crimes in China or were they planning to?* Maddy sat very still for a very long time, searching her mind for answers while she nibbled at the food on the plate, taking care to hide some away for Li Wei.

CHAPTER

10

The Gamble House
Victoria Road
Nelson, New Zealand
March 11, 2033
7:00 p.m.

I was in the kitchen cleaning up after dinner. Dinner had taken a long time, and no one had eaten much. I had finally explained to our children that Chinese agents had kidnapped their mother and that we were trying to find her with the police and others' help. They had lots of questions. *Who are these people?*

Why did they take Mommy?

What will happen to her?

What will happen to us if we can't find her? That one brought tears, first from JJ, then Allison, and then me. And that had brought an end to any eating. We stayed at the table and talked until all of us had stopped crying.

"You okay?" I asked them.

JJ said, "Yeah."

Allison said, "Yeah, but not really."

We shared a group hug.

And JJ added, "Yeah, not really for me, either."

I fought back more tears.

That was how I felt, too. I had control over most of myself to shoo the children off to their rooms, I could clear the table and do the dishes, but I was not okay. Not at all, not even close.

What had happened to our little life here, to our family? How had everything changed so rapidly, going from simple happy times to insurmountable worries and overwhelming anxiety and fear? I wasn't sleeping well, now none of us had eaten much, and I had no good ideas what to do. The Chinese had kidnapped my wife, and no one knew for sure where she was or if she was even still alive.

And why had they taken her?

What was she doing at the Palazzo Motor Lodge?

How would I ever find her?

Through the window, I saw Amy's grey sedan and two other vehicles pull into the driveway. I dried my hands and tried to wipe away any signs of tears and went to the front door to meet them.

"Amy." I nodded.

"Hello, Jack. Sorry to drop in on you, but it's essential. You know Charlie and Nikau."

Charlie said, "I thought maybe your kids would like to go with Nikau and me for ice cream."

Only in New Zealand, I thought, did the police help with childcare.

Amy continued, "And this is Sara Singh, who I told you about this afternoon."

I reached out and shook her hand. "Nice to meet you. Thanks for agreeing to help."

"Happy to," she said, watching me intently the whole time. Her grip was solid. Still, I had trouble imagining her as an elite warrior. She was older than me by a decade or more, had short graying hair, a slight limp, and was dressed in jeans and an oversized billowing shirt tucked into a still trim waist.

"And this is Detective Noah Montgomery from our office; he has agreed to help on this case."

I shook hands with a large, fit, clear-eyed young man. Now he looked like an elite soldier.

"Come in. Come in, all of you." I stood back to let them enter and saw JJ and Allison looking on from across the living room. They must have heard someone come to the house.

"Hey, guys. Nikau and his dad are going to take you for ice cream."

Nikau excitedly said, "You know that little place by the school where you can eat your ice cream outside."

JJ was equally enthusiastic. "I want chocolate." But Allison just shook her head. JJ saw her and stopped. I went over and knelt before them. "I know you probably don't feel like going right now and don't feel like doing anything. But we need to talk about finding your mom, and it would be better if you gave us a little time by ourselves. Okay?"

There was a long pause. No one in the room said anything. Finally, Allison said, "Okay, Dad." And then she hugged me. JJ and Nikau were discussing what flavors of ice cream were best. JJ came back and took his sister's hand, and the four of them went out the door. I silently watched until they were down the front steps.

"Let's sit at the kitchen table."

We all found a seat, Amy set up her computer, and Sara and Noah both opened notebooks. I got up, found a notepad and a pen, and sat back down.

Amy began, "Jack, your thoughts on the camera were right on point. The city bought cameras from a company now known as C3 that was previously known as the Chinese Camera Company, with three Cs in the name. Not particularly original but apparently adopted because the United States broadcast that equipment and software from the Chinese Camera Company couldn't be trusted. It seems our city fathers, in their wisdom, ignored that because of price and because they already had a hundred or so Chinese Camera Company cameras and had never had any problems. Noah, why don't you pick it up from there."

Noah looked at his notes. "As Amy said, the City of Nelson decided on C3 cameras based solely on price, and four thousand cameras were installed all over Nelson between 2025 and 2029. Generally, they work pretty well, but we noticed just like your wife did, Mr. Gamble, that when certain people walked by a camera, the camera tracked them. Mostly the cameras focused on Chinese persons but we did find one known instance where our cameras followed a New Zealand intelligence agent and an agent from your CIA. We couldn't figure out why but we're working on it after the CIA alerted us to it. We couldn't figure out who turned on the tracking of these people. The concerns expressed in other parts of the world about these cameras became louder and more troubling. Police from around the country, around the world really, were complaining that bad guys seemed to be able to hack into these cameras. Rather than replace the cameras and admit a mistake, the City found a band-aid approach. And as part of that, we had a company from Wellington install what is called a traffic filter on the camera system."

"What exactly is a traffic filter?" I asked.

"Well," Noah said, "It's not like it sounds. It has nothing to do with vehicular traffic. It records, separately from the camera system, all signals sent to or received by the camera system. And the guys who installed it said no one from the outside would ever know it was there."

"Okay?" I asked.

"Tell him what you found, Noah," Amy said. I could tell by looking at Sara; she already knew about the cameras.

Noah continued, "We checked the data logs of the camera system against the data logs of the traffic filter, and specifically, we checked for the period from eight p.m. until nine-thirty p.m. on the night the Chinese abducted your wife. And what we found were some differences, very slight, but different, just the same. Up until around eight-forty, everything is the same, identical. Then we can see the white van with the yellow roof leave the Palazzo Motor Lodge and turn left on Rutherford and pass the camera at the intersection with Nile Street.

Then things change. The Chinese sent an electronic command to the camera system that didn't register digitally but was captured by the traffic filter. We can't read it, but we think it was a command to the camera system to delete or obscure all images of the van in question. Can you show him, Amy?"

Amy had turned her computer toward me. Sara was leaning in to watch. So far, she hadn't said anything after the greeting on the porch. I got as close to the computer as I could.

"First, you'll see the van at the intersection of Rutherford and Niles. The camera won't tell you where it is but take my word for the location. Pay particular attention to the top of the van. In addition to the yellow paint, it has black stripes across it like the old SKU system. We think that acts as part of a command to the camera system. Watch."

She let the video roll, and we watched just what she described. We all looked up at her. I had seen what she described but was taking her word for what it meant.

Amy continued, "What we do when we're trying to track a vehicle or a person for that matter through the camera system is take an image of the vehicle from the system, like the image you just saw of the van, and then we ask the system to show us similar images in the same general area and time period. When we did that here, nothing came up. Usually, that would mean it went to ground before it passed another camera. But Noah here, figured it out. Noah, you explain, and I'll run the video when it's appropriate."

I could sense that something important was about to be shown. And I could see Noah's pride in his work. "Okay, so I knew we couldn't find the van, and I knew how big the image of the van would normally be. From eight forty-five until nine-thirty p.m. on March 8, the traffic filter showed slightly more data traffic than the camera. We can't view imagery from where the reader is from the traffic filter, just data. So, data was missing from the camera system. I admit my imagination went wild here. I thought what if someone removed images, specifically images of the van from the footage, how would they do it? I guessed it would be done manually. So, bear with me here. The men grab your wife, get in the van and take off and send a message to somewhere to take the van out of the system. It takes a little bit to activate the command because the van is visible at the first intersection it passed, estimate a few seconds later. Then it's nowhere to be found. And we searched everywhere around Rutherford and Nile; it didn't stop there. So, how do you identify the image to be ignored? I decided the most efficient way would be to see it on display and hit the hide command while it's in view to hide future images of this same item. And the black markings must be designed to help in this regard. I decided to test my wild assed theory by cutting the van's image in half and searching for just the front half and so on. Finally, I got the image down to just the front three to five percent of the van's images. Amy, why don't you show them."

Amy was ready. We were again looking at the picture of the van in the intersection. A click and the back half of the van disappeared. Another click and half of the half disappeared and so on until finally there was just a narrow sliver of the van visible, and no one would have known what they were looking at if they had not watched the systematic reductions. "Now watch this," Noah said. "Now we ask the system to track this sliver of the van, and this is what we get."

Dozens of images popped up on the screen displayed in a small format with all pictures on each of three screens. Sara smiled and patted Noah on the back. "Damn," I said, "that was some fine work, Detective. But what does it all mean?"

Noah sat back, obviously pleased with his work. Wild assed idea or not, he had been right.

Amy continued, "We think someone pushed a button just a little bit too slowly, but Noah was the only one I know ever to figure it out, and obviously, the city has a camera problem. We have forced the city to turn them all off. Here are the multiple images of the sliver of the van identified by their location on a city map. It's too small to display the actual images, so they're all just numbered. The van moves from lower number to higher number in order."

I leaned forward to see. Sara sat back; she must know where the pictures lead.

Amy narrated for my eyes. "You can see the van driving around in circles or aimlessly, just another layer of confusing signals or maybe they were waiting for a confirmation that the image block worked. After about ten minutes, they then take a direct route to Port Nelson. The van is last seen turning into a fenced lot at the port adjacent to several older warehouses. That was at nine twenty-two p.m.. At nine twenty-eight p.m., the camera system's data comes back in sync with the traffic filter. That was the van's final destination."

I stood up. "Let's go there before the bastards paint the van and take off again."

For the first time, Sara spoke. "We've already been there. Not us personally, but other police officers and intelligence agents. Maddy isn't there, but we're sure she was there. And the van is there. Bear with us just a little longer, please. We have a plan, and we do have hope."

I would try to be patient. "Intelligence agents? Spies?" I asked.

"Yes, Jack. Spies. And that means we believe agents of a foreign government, specifically agents of Communist China, took your wife. It's why I'm here. Can I explain?"

"Yes, please do."

"When Amy called me this afternoon and relayed the problems with the cameras and the witness account of your wife being taken by force with a hood over her head, I immediately suspected the Chinese. They often use hoods to terrify and disorient their victims."

Maddy terrified? Poor Maddy, what she must be going through. But the Chinese? Really?

"And the camera problem didn't surprise me. When I worked on the Premier's protection detail, we knew that their makers could remotely control certain cameras manufactured by the Chinese and find certain people or lose certain people. Just like what Noah uncovered here. We called them Dragon's Eye, an unblinking ability to see everything. Here it is more an ability to make things disappear, but it is the same problem. Those damn cameras.

"The advantage to the Chinese in clandestine matters on foreign soil is immense. And we warned all levels of government in New Zealand, but pricing remains a big issue for government and they thought these things would never happen in their community. So, the Chinese fingerprints were all over this from the beginning. But why? Amy told me of your wife's involvement in the human rights case here in New Zealand."

I looked over at Amy. I didn't remember telling her about that, but maybe I did.

Sara went on, "In my mind, that isn't enough for the Chinese to abduct a foreign national on another nation's soil. If she were in China, maybe, and I'm sure China would love to see misfortune befall her, but I don't think they would take the risk of international fall out. Especially, since you and Maddy are international heroes for your roles in exposing the Ebola debacle on Madagascar. No, I don't see it. But Amy also told me about Li Wei, so I spent part of the afternoon researching him. Both of his parents were human rights lawyers in China, in Wuhan specifically. In the aftermath of the coronavirus crisis, they accused the Chinese Communists of suppressing the truth, first about the existence of the virus and then about the number of deaths and the need for no further restrictions. According to Li Wei's parents, China had let many thousands of Chinese die and put millions more at dire risk in an attempt to make the Party look good. A huge second wave of the disease in China and beyond followed because the Communists pretended to have everything under control. Some lies cannot be contained.

"But the Communists tried. They arrested and incarcerated Li Wei's parents and other lawyers making the same arguments. None of them were ever heard from again. A neighbor took in Li Wei and then later smuggled him out of Wuhan and China to Vietnam. This woman claimed Li Wei had died of the virus, during its second run through Wuhan and his body incinerated. It was a clever lie. Many were incinerated without any record, while the Chinese Communists were suspicious, this woman stuck to her story, and the Communists couldn't prove anything. That didn't stop them from imprisoning her for six months."

"How do you know all of this?" I asked.

"Amy may have told you I was in intelligence. I still have many friendly contacts. And I must say, mentioning that you and your wife were involved gained me better cooperation from the CIA than I am accustomed to."

That surprised me, but this was no time to consider it. "So, what's our plan here?" My patience worn; I wanted to act, to rescue Maddy.

Sara said, "Be assured others are working on implementing the plan even now while we fill you in." I nodded, and she continued, "In about 2029 when Li Wei was still a teenager in Vietnam, he began a campaign of sending messages about the Wuhan tragedy and his parents and others 'over the Wall' into China. He sent pictures of his parents and pictures of piles of bodies waiting to be incinerated. So, from that point on, the Communists knew who Li Wei was or at least who he claimed to be. He became an unofficial lawyer, researching human rights and government abuse cases in China. But he wasn't satisfied. He is still very young. He joined Falun Gong and told some members that it was the only group with enough members to bring down the Communists. One of those other members was later revealed to be an agent of the Chinese Communists. Then Li Wei disappeared for about four years. That concerns me very much. Where was he? What was he doing? Did the Communists have him? Then he resurfaced and gathered a group, determined to take his message to the rest of the world, coming first here to New Zealand to study English and then spreading out to the corners of the globe to tell their story. And it's always possible that Li Wei was actually a spy for China and turned in his group members before he himself was extricated. I can understand why the Chinese would want to stop that group but not why they would act recklessly. To them, Li Wei was and always would be Chinese. And they believe they can treat Chinese however they want wherever they want. So, to me, Li Wei is the key, and it becomes a near certainty that the Chinese took him and your wife."

I must have had a question on my face. Sara said, "He was in the bag. The heavy dark bag carried by three men out of the hotel to the van. I have seen those bags before."

"Even so, could he not have still been a willing participant?"

Sara shrugged but I could tell from the way she looked at Amy and Noah that she wasn't particularly concerned about that.

I was struggling to keep up. "Now what?" I willed myself not to brush back my hair.

Amy took over. "Once we determined, with Sara's great help, the Chinese had taken Li Wei and Maddy, we tried to think as they would. Noah's tracking of the van to the Port got us started. They want to get out of the country, we thought. It turns out that was right. We have every reason to believe Maddy is on a cargo ship, *Eternity*, registered in Belize. The Chinese Ocean Shipping Company formerly owned it. Who owns it now is unclear."

"Where is it now?"

"Somewhere between Nelson and Tauranga, closer to Tauranga. It's due there at about two a.m. tomorrow," Amy said.

"Tauranga?" I asked.

"Yes, Tauranga is a port in New Zealand, very busy. That's not the final destination for *Eternity*. She's due to ship back out tomorrow afternoon at about four p.m. and hasn't yet filed her itinerary from there. I'm told that's not uncommon."

"So?"

"So, we go to Tauranga. I have already alerted the authorities there, and they will standby, and Noah and I will leave here by private plane and fly there first thing in the morning."

Sara added, "And some friends from SIS, the intelligence service will also be there."

"I want to be there," I said.

Sara and Noah, and Amy all looked at each other. Amy said, "I don't know. Who would watch your children?"

"I will," Sara said. "I've always wanted to be a grandmother. Don't worry, Jack; I will take excellent care of them."

Noah said, "Maybe Charlie can help, too."

Amy looked daggers at both of them. I knew Amy hadn't been happy with my participation in the questioning of Julia Adamson and I could imagine she didn't want me tagging along here. I said, "I won't be any trouble, Amy."

Amy threw up her arms. "We'll pick you up at five-thirty a.m., Jack."

CHAPTER

11

Onboard Eternity
Near Tauranga Harbor
Tauranga, New Zealand
March 12, 2033
3:00 a.m.

Captain Zhao of *Eternity* was at the bridge on a calm and peaceful night outside Tauranga's harbor. He would be glad to get to the port. He loved his country, and he loved being the captain of a big ship. The sea was a free and magical place; it didn't care about politics or religion or language or nationality. It gave no expectations and accepted none. It just did what it did, sometimes the same, sometimes different, sometimes predictable, often not. The sea was not mean or evil, although it could be. The sea was not kind or loving; it merely was. That's what he loved. You had to accept whatever the sea offered each day and make the best of it. And *Eternity* was a good ship. Not the newest or the fastest or the prettiest of ships, but it was seaworthy, and it was his ship. That was what was most important to him. He didn't own it; he sailed it for others. "Others" now meant the Chinese Ministry of State Security hidden under some company name. But his orders for this trip had undoubtedly come directly from Deputy Minister Chen. Zhao had known Chen since they were boys. That is how he had gotten his position and he had never forgotten it. He also knew Chen, had watched him change from a boyhood friend into an aspiring Communist, first locally, then regionally and now nationally. His old friend had devoted himself to party politics and avoiding personal political disaster since they were about twenty. He never saw Chen anymore, but saw some of Chen's poorer relatives who were oh, so proud of Chen. Chen wasn't really a bad man but he was also one you could not count on, regardless of how long you had known him. He would do what was best for Chen and for his perception of the leading faction in the Communist party. Zhao was not impressed with political survival skills. Still, he did like his job.

Sometimes, like this trip, he was ordered to transport people, usually prisoners, back to China. And like this voyage, that meant that there would also be State Security agents or other thugs on board. His crew was small and close-knit, like family. Most of them had been together for eight years now. They knew their jobs and to keep their mouths shut, but sometimes these State Security thugs would drink and cause trouble or pick fights. They had weapons they would never surrender; his crew did not carry weapons, although they kept a few guns locked on the bridge. The State agents sometimes tortured the people they had brought on board. He heard them scream many times. Yes, he was glad to be close to Tauranga. When they had berthed, he would disembark for a two-week vacation while a replacement Captain took over his ship. In two weeks, the ship would return, he would get on, and a different replacement captain would get off. Ship's captains had become a way to get Chinese in and out of ports. But when the ship returned, it would not hold any prisoners and would not house any State Security agents.

"Tauranga Port, this is *Eternity* coming in for scheduled berth," he called on the radio.

"Roger, *Eternity*, hold on, please."

After a couple of moments of static, the port radio operator came back on, "*Eternity*, this is Port Tauranga; we need you to slow down your approach; no berths are currently available. I repeat, no berths are currently available. Do you copy?"

"*Eternity* here. Yes, I copy. What's the problem?"

Captain Zhao cut the engines by two thirds.

"Port here. We had a collision in the harbor this morning; three ships that should have been gone collided and are damaged. Two of them need to stay at berth, or they might sink. So, things are a little f'd up in here right now. Give me a little time, and I can give you a better estimate of when we can get you in."

"Roger that, Port."

"Port here. Do you have cargo to unload or to pick up *Eternity*?"

"Only me, Port. Tauranga is my vacation port. I'm coming in to change with another Captain."

"Roger that, Captain. Vacations are good. Let me see what I can do for you."

"Thanks, Port. *Eternity* out."

Captain Zhao hit his fist softly on the ship's wheel. From behind him, Wang said, "Something wrong, Captain? I noticed the engines have slowed."

Captain Zhao turned. He didn't like Wang, didn't trust him, and had to take orders from him when he was on board his ship.

"No big problem. We may have to wait a little bit for a berth. There was a harbor collision today, and three boats laid up that weren't supposed to be here."

"I see. How long will it take?"

"I don't know yet. The Port will get back to me."

"Captain Zhao, it is not important that we pick up a replacement Captain here, only that we drop a certain one off on the return trip."

The radio crackled, "Port here, *Eternity*. Are you there?"

"*Eternity* here, Port, I copy. What have you got for me?"

"We won't have a berth here for you for five or six hours at the soonest. Best I can do. Sorry, Captain. And for what it's worth, it's not a bad night to hang out, out there."

"Roger, Port. I understand. Let me get back to you."

Beside him, Wang was shaking his head. As soon as the radio crackled off, he said, "That will not do, Captain. I have a schedule to keep. There is nothing to be done here that is more important than the security of China. Tell them we have plenty of fuel and file the next leg of the itinerary we discussed. Is it ready to go?"

"Almost. But Honorable Wang, I was supposed to be on vacation and get off here, and a replacement Captain gets on."

Wang was enraged. "Fool. Do you think your vacation is more important than the security of your country? Maybe you and I should have one of my little chats together. I told you this replacement Captain is unimportant; getting the return replacement Captain into New Zealand was the real goal. The Minister will find another way. File the new itinerary; explain to the Port and make it good. We are going to China as quickly as possible. Do you understand me, Captain?"

Two of Wang's men had joined them on the bridge, both with weapons on their hips. One of them said, "Is there a problem, Wang?"

"Not yet," he said, glowering at Captain Zhao. The Captain thought it is always the same 'the security of China,' like this is the one task that is essential. He hated these men, acting like monsters and masquerading like patriots and in control of his ship and him.

The radio crackled, "Port here *Eternity*; today is your lucky day. Your replacement captain, Captain Hu is here now. I can send him out in a tug, you can meet us with your tender, and your ship can be on its way if you have enough fuel."

Wang was shaking his head no, furiously.

Captain Zhao looked at Wang, looked at his two men with holstered weapons, and said into the radio, "We have plenty of fuel. Send Hu now, Port. I will be underway in the tender in a few minutes."

"Roger that, *Eternity*. Two more things. You need to file your onwards schedule, and I think I can see your lights from here. Why don't you flash them right now to be sure, so I send the tug in the right direction?"

Captain Zhao turned the ship's light off, then on, then off, and the radio shot back, "Got it, just where I thought you were. Captain Hu is on his way."

Captain Zhao turned to face Wang and his men. Wang had a pistol in his hand. "What the hell do you think you are doing, Zhao?"

"I'm going on vacation. I haven't had one in two years. You wish to command my ship; it is all yours." Zhao bowed slightly.

Wang raised the gun.

Zhao's gaze was steady. "If you shoot me, who will file the updated itinerary? Do you know how? And now the port is sending my replacement. If something happens to me outside this harbor, the New Zealand authorities will impound the ship here, and there will be a full inquiry, including a search of the ship. Is that what you want, Wang? And if you have killed me, don't count on my crew to lie to the authorities for you."

Two of *Eternity*'s crew members had entered the bridge and stood staring at their Captain and Wang and his two thugs and the pistol in Wang's hand.

No one spoke or moved.

Captain Zhao finally said, "If we have an understanding, Wang, I will now file the revised itinerary for Port Vila." He turned to his two crew members. "Go and lower the tender. You two are taking me to the exchange with Captain Hu, who will be guiding the ship the rest of this journey." His men were glad to get away from the guns and left the bridge immediately.

Wang lowered the gun and waited for Zhao to update the itinerary. After sending it, Captain Zhao stood with his back toward Wang and waited for the confirmation.

Zhao was shaking inside. He had had enough of these barbarians masquerading as Chinese patriots. Deep inside; he was proud of himself for finally taking a stand. He said to Wang, "If there is nothing else, I'll be going."

"Just one more thing, Zhao. There is nothing in this itinerary to prevent me from simply setting a direct course to China, is there?"

Zhao smiled inwardly. He was going to be allowed to leave. He replied, "No, sir, there is nothing to prevent that. Technically, you should revise your itinerary, but sometimes ships change course and don't do that. However, at some point, you will need to let the port where you will be landing know."

Wang nodded; his face was red, the gun still in his hand but now at his side. He had lost face and in the presence of two of his men.

Slowly he stepped out of Zhao's way, watching his every move. Wang said, "Yes, you may go now, Zhao, and when I get back to China, I will tell your family you said hello. Do they still live in Shanghai?"

You rotten bastard, you had better leave my family alone. Then Zhao smiled pleasantly and said,"Yes, very close to where Deputy Minister Chen grew up."

That should slow him down.

CHAPTER

12

En route to Tauranga, New Zealand
From Nelson, New Zealand
March 12, 2033
5:30 a.m.

Detective Montgomery came to pick me up. I was waiting at the bottom of the driveway at five-fifteen a.m., pacing back and forth. He pulled up at five-thirty.

"Well, you're up early," he said, motioning to the front passenger seat for me to get in.

"Where's Amy?" I asked as he was pulling away. "She'll meet us at the airport. There's always paperwork with a flight and our boss Commander Li was asking her all sorts of questions. She's been at the airport since four-thirty or five. We got to sleep in."

He smiled to make sure I knew he was kidding. He seemed remarkably calm to me. I was a mess and couldn't stop worrying about everything. *Was Maddy okay?* I was wearing an old Cincinnati Reds ball cap to try to keep my hands out of my hair.

Would we find her?

Would there be violence?

Would we get there in time?

How were the kids?

How would they be if their mother never got back?

What if neither of us did?

All kind of in that order.

Maybe Montgomery sensed that and was putting on his calm act for my benefit.

"How long will it take us to get to Tauranga?" I asked.

Noah said, "Flight is about an hour and a half, and then maybe fifteen minutes by car, call it thirty minutes, time we unload and get picked up. Amy has arranged for a Tauranga Police Lieutenant she has worked with before to meet us at the airport at seven forty-five, and then he has a team standing by supposed to be ready by eight-thirty. Figure nine o'clock with normal delays."

I recognized all the hard work Amy and Noah and who knows who else had put into this operation overnight.

"Thank you, Detective, for helping pull all of this together."

"No problem, man." Then he looked over at me. "She's going to be all right Jack. We have this all well covered. They're still in New Zealand."

"She's got to be all right," I said, "Got to be. Can I ask you a question?"

"Sure."

"Why not just close the port?"

"Good question and we thought of that. If we closed it in advance, *Eternity* would remain at sea with all the risks attendant to an open sea boarding and rescue. And if we closed it after they made port, they would be alerted and perhaps eliminate their captives, maybe try to drop them overboard. No one is certain but we decided this was the least risky approach."

"I hope you're right."

"Me, too."

We drove in silence for ten more minutes before turning down Trent Drive. Ahead of us was a modern-looking airport terminal, not brand new but maybe ten years old. I had flown out of it numerous times. Before we got to the terminal, Noah turned through a gate labeled 'General Aviation,' and there ahead of us was a small plane waiting on the tarmac. Amy and a man in a light jacket and ball cap were standing beside it. Amy waved us over, and Noah drove up near the plane.

"Good morning, Jack. Noah. Everybody ready to go?" She looked significantly at me as she said this.

"Yep," said Noah, "Ready to roll."

"Yep," I echoed.

"Guys, this is our pilot, Joe Huang. Joe, Detective Noah Montgomery, and Mr. Jack Gamble."

We all said hello. Joe turned to me, "Mr. Gamble, I remember reading about you and your wife and the Ebola crisis." He bowed his head. "The world owes you a great debt, and I'm very honored to try to help you today."

I was humbled that this man remembered that especially at this time. "Thank you. Thank you," was all I managed.

We climbed into the plane, which had a Beechcraft Bonanza sticker on the tail fin. Amy climbed in upfront after the pilot. Noah and I climbed into the third row so we could be facing forward. I was happy to see the second row of seats, even if it was facing backward. I was looking forward to coming home with Maddy right in front of me, where I could see her.

We pulled on the headsets, and Joe went through his pre-flight checklist. Then he said through the headphones, "Everyone ready?" We each pushed our talk button and said "Ready" all at the same time. Joe gave a thumbs up and started taxiing toward the runway. I watched him, looking left and right and ahead and talking into the radio. In a minute, we were second in a queue behind a New Zealand Air commercial liner. We were off, climbing over Nelson, while l looked down at the coastline and the city. And then we were above the clouds. I must have dozed off. I had hardly slept. Something about the noise or the motion of the plane woke me as we were breaking through the clouds. There below me was another city and coastline. Joe came over the headsets. "Tauranga dead ahead. Should be on the ground in about ten minutes."

No one else said anything. We all squirmed a little in our seats, adjusted our clothing and seat belts, and contented ourselves with looking out the window at another beautiful view. Ahead of us, I could see the harbor. Everything looked small from up here, but I thought I saw several large ships, including some stacked with colored boxes. Cargo container ships, I thought. And Maddy is on one of them. *I'm coming, Maddy, I'm coming.*

As we were taxiing toward a small terminal building away from the main terminal and the big planes, I saw a police SUV coming out to meet us. Joe killed the engine, and we clambered out to meet Tauranga police Lieutenant Palmer who passed handshakes all around and had a hug for Amy. Noah and Joe were busy unloading a couple of bags from the rear of the plane and putting them into the back of the SUV. Joe called out to us as we got into the police vehicle. "I'll be waiting right here until you get back. Good luck."

As we drove, the lieutenant filled us in. "It is now five minutes after eight. We should arrive at the dock at about eight thirty-five. When we do Detective Wirihana, I will see the harbormaster and find out where *Eternity* is berthed. Then we'll take a few minutes to make a precise plan based upon the exact berth. The docks can be closed off, and we will quietly put men in position to board *Eternity*. We have a helicopter ready and two small, fast boats to watch the water beside the ship. Once everyone is in place, we all go at once. Mr. Gamble, I will have one of my officers wait with you at the harbormaster's office until the ship is secure and then bring you on board. And try not to worry. This is not the first time we have searched a ship for people the Chinese were smuggling out of the country."

I took a deep and loud breath. I wanted to protest. I wanted to be there to save Maddy. I took another deep breath and said, "Okay, except I'm going onboard with you. She is my wife."

Amy threw up her arms and everyone turned away from me, but no one said no.

We drove through a quiet city, waking up to a busy seaport area. Cranes were running, lifting cargo boxes on and off ships. Vehicles were going here and there, and even on the water, small boats hustled back and forth. There was a security gate to access the parking area for the port. Tauranga police already manned it. They waved their lieutenant through. Once inside the parking area, I saw several unmarked SUVs with police officers in SWAT gear hanging around them. They spread out so as not to create a stir, I guessed. Taken all together, I thought there were about forty officers.

I overheard Lieutenant Palmer telling Amy and Noah, "The harbormaster and the COO both cleared this operation, technically they have their own security force, but they are ill-prepared for an operation like this. The harbormaster wanted to be here and promised he would be in by eight. *Eternity* is scheduled in port until four this afternoon. It will take a while to search the ship if the Chinese do not cooperate. The helicopter and the boats will be watching to prevent any last-minute violence or things from being thrown or jumping overboard. We will move quickly throughout the ship to cover everything, but it will take a while. These officers are well trained and well equipped, and we have three advisers from SIS, who will be going on board with us."

I knew because of Sara, that meant national intelligence officers. I knew this was a moment of great danger for Maddy. Her abductors could try to kill her at the last minute or maybe kill Li Wei or both. I heard the lieutenant mention throwing them overboard and could see them trying to hide the evidence. It seemed like the police and national intelligence had everything covered. I prayed silently, *Dear Lord, let Maddy be safe, let her be home with the children and me tonight. Please, Lord, I will do anything you ask.*

And I pretended not to be listening to the police conversation.

Amy came up to me. "Okay, Jack, we're ready to go to the harbormaster's; everyone is in place. Are you okay?"

"Yeah, I'm good," I said. I took my cap off and brushed back my hair.

I hated it when she looked at me like she was now. She could see the scared little boy inside me.

She said, "We decided Noah will stay and wait with you in the harbormaster's office. You know him, and I can reach him by radio as soon as it is safe for you to come on board. And I will, I promise."

"Okay," I said. Amy gave me an unexpected hug. I was trying not to cry. "Let's go," I said, and I took another deep breath.

CHAPTER

13

Harbormaster's Office
Tauranga Port
Tauranga, New Zealand
March 12, 2033
8:47 a.m.

Noah held the door for me. I could see the harbormaster at his desk firing up his computer. He still had on his jacket, and his briefcase was on the floor beside his desk chair.

"Good morning, lieutenant, good morning, all," he shot back over his shoulder. His computer screen came to life. I could see that he had to log in. Then he had to look at the screen to be recognized. Finally, the port logo showed on the screen, and the harbormaster began to click away. We stood in silence. Finally, he said, "Ah, yes, here we are. *Eternity.*" He stopped talking, clicked again at the screen, and then again.

"Oh no," he said and then, "Oh my God, no."

"What, what's wrong?" said the lieutenant stepping closer to the harbormaster's desk and looking at the computer screen.

"*Eternity* never berthed last night. She's not here. I'm so sorry. I didn't know."

Amy came forward now. "What do you mean it's not here? It was supposed to get in around two or three this morning and be here until four this afternoon." For effect, she looked down at *Eternity*'s printed itinerary folded in her hand.

"I know, I know," he said, "but look," pointing to the screen. "*Eternity* radioed in at three o seven ready to come into port. Port responded that we didn't have a berth ready yet. You see," he said, turning away from the screen, "we had a wreck out here yesterday morning, and as a result, three ships that should have been gone were back at berth. There was no room at the inn, so to speak." He turned back to the screen. "The deputy harbormaster on duty last night reported that *Eternity* had plenty of fuel, had no cargo to load or unload, and was putting in here only to exchange captains before the next leg of its journey."

"Where's that?" Amy asked.

The harbormaster clicked over to another screen, "Port Vila, Vanuatu. The exiting captain filed the new itinerary at three forty-two this morning."

The lieutenant was exasperated. "Why weren't we notified? You knew we had this operation planned. Do you know how much it costs to put something like this together?" He stepped forward toward the harbormaster.

"I didn't know until just now, lieutenant, I swear. The Chief Operating Officer and I were the only ones who knew about this operation until this morning. Saturday mornings are not busy here so there was no need to alert our workforce. We told no one, just like you asked. My deputy didn't know there was anything special about *Eternity*. And I didn't find out the timing until the COO called me on my way to work this morning. I swear."

Amy asked, "Is it unusual for a ship to not stop where their itinerary says they will?"

"Unusual, yes, officer, but not unheard of, especially with the Chinese. They always seem to be in a hurry. And now their next stop is only three days away, and they said they had plenty of fuel."

"Is that something you check, sir?" asked Amy.

"No, we rely on the ships for that. They should always know how much fuel they have and, besides, they are stuck at sea if there is a mistake. So no, we never check that."

"But is there a way to check it?" Amy asked.

Where was this going, I wondered?

The harbormaster thought and said, "Maybe you could check at Nelson, the port they embarked from, and see what fuel records they have for *Eternity*."

"And where is *Eternity* now?" asked the lieutenant. He had cooled off a bit.

"Well, without tracking it via satellite, it has been traveling for roughly five hours from here toward Vanuatu, at twenty knots per hour, pretty standard anymore for these cargo container ships, that puts her about one hundred nautical miles out to sea. A satellite could give us a precise location."

"Damn," the lieutenant said, irritation creeping back into his voice, "Well beyond our territorial waters."

"I am so very sorry," the harbormaster said.

I thought, you have no idea what sorry is. Noah put his hand on my shoulder. "Do you have a wife, sir?" I said to the harbormaster, pulling off my cap. He didn't answer.

"I'm so sorry, Jack," said Amy. She sounded defeated.

The harbormaster looked at his desk and shook his head slowly back and forth.

The lieutenant was on his radio. "The operation has been aborted. All personnel stand down."

The five of us looked at each other.

"Is there anything else?" the lieutenant asked, as the harbormaster handed him a copy of *Eternity*'s onwards schedule.

The harbormaster turned back to his screen, made a couple more clicks. "Wait, here's a little more. It seems like *Eternity* was able to exchange captains without ever putting into port."

We all became alert.

He continued, "My deputy noted that a Captain Hu had checked in expecting *Eternity*. He said the captain currently onboard sounded so miserable at missing his vacation, and he felt bad that we didn't have the scheduled berth available. Hence, he sent Captain Hu out in a pilot tug, and they were met partway by a tender from *Eternity* carrying Captain Zhao. The captains each transferred to the other vessel, and Hu went to *Eternity*, and Zhao came ashore."

"Any information about this, Captain Hu?" Amy asked.

"Nothing here, but it will be available from the Maritime New Zealand registry. All ships are there, including owners, tonnage, and the like. Find the ship first, then the owner, then search captains under the owners. He should be there, including what he is qualified to captain," the harbormaster rattled off, pleased to be of some assistance finally.

"And how about this Captain Zhao? Did he come ashore here?" Amy asked.

"Yes, he came in to thank my deputy for getting him ashore for his vacation. He said he hadn't had one for years. My guy thought he looked exhausted."

"Any idea where he may have gone after leaving here?" Amy asked.

"No, we don't track captains when they're on shore, but he did ask my deputy to call an Uber for him. And there may be some footage of him or the Uber on the Tauranga security cameras that are now city-wide."

Amy and Noah and I just looked at each other.

CHAPTER

14

Trinity Wharf Hotel
Tauranga, New Zealand
March 12, 2033
11:30 a.m.

It hadn't been hard to find him. There aren't many Uber fares at four a.m. in Tauranga, then add that the fare was Chinese and probably in some sort of uniform or at least cap. He had registered under his own name, Wang Wei Zhao, and listed Shanghai, China, and nothing more as his permanent address. He had left a credit card on deposit, and Lieutenant Palmer's office was now running a check on that.

The problem was the guy wouldn't talk to us. Palmer had called in an interpreter, and we all gathered in Zhao's hotel room; Amy, Noah, Palmer, the interpreter, and another Tauranga officer who was never introduced and me.

It seemed clear that Zhao knew something, but all he would tell us was his name and his employer. But when Amy asked about Li Wei and Maddy, he seemed to start, notably when I showed him their pictures. Noah and the interpreter stayed in the room, while Amy, the lieutenant, his confederate, and I stepped into the hallway.

"He knows something; I can smell it," the lieutenant said.

"Agreed," said Amy, "but how do we get him to talk?"

The lieutenant said, "He was the skipper of a ship that we have reasonable cause to believe held two kidnap victims. We can hold him for a while with that. Even if he didn't participate in the kidnapping, he must have known they were on his ship and did nothing to let anyone know. Hell, he may be the ringleader for all we know."

"Maybe," Amy said, "but I don't think so. Let me make a call. I have an idea. Jack, come with me."

Amy and I went back downstairs, and at Amy's request, we took a small office. She sat down, dialed a number, put her phone on speaker, and set it on the desk.

"Amy?"

"Yeah, hi, Sara. Jack is right here with me. You're on speaker."

"How'd it go in Tauranga?"

"Not so good. *Eternity* never put in here, some sort of a crash filled all the berths, and they kept sailing. Now they're out of our territorial waters."

"Shit! So, you didn't even see the ship?"

"Right. But the captain who sailed the ship from Nelson to Tauranga got off here via a tugboat, and a new captain took over. We ran down the captain who got off, a guy named Zhao. We have him with us now, but he won't talk. Tauranga Police want to arrest him and sweat him in custody. And we might have to do that, but it could take days. And we don't have days. *Eternity* will be at Port Vila in a couple of days now, maybe three, and after that, I predict it will head straight to China, meaning we would have to take it down on the open sea."

"Not a good idea. Even if you could get the New Zealand Navy to intercept it, *Eternity* will see the navy coming and eliminate Li Wei and Maddy and try to dump them overboard. And that would be hard to stop. And it would take days or weeks for the navy to decide to act, and we don't have that much time."

"Right, exactly what I was thinking. I wonder if you'd be willing to talk to Zhao?"

"What, me? It would take me hours to get there, and I would have to have Charlie or someone watch JJ and Allison."

"Sara, Jack here. How are the kids doing?"

"Just fine, they're great kids and have been very sweet to me. This morning we made chocolate balls together. I'm cleaning up now, and they're outside playing with Nikau under Charlie's watchful eye."

Amy said, "Getting back to this guy, I was thinking of having you speak to him over my phone, a video chat if you will. You speak Chinese, don't you?"

"You know I do. I was stationed in Beijing for eighteen months and spent four months after that in a Chinese prison until I was part of a prisoner exchange."

"Yeah, I know. I hate to open old wounds, but we really need your help."

The pause was so long I thought the call had been cut off.

"Okay, I'll do it. But give me one hour to gather some intelligence on this guy Zhao. Send me by text everything you know about him. And are the SIS guys I had standing by this morning still around somewhere?"

"Don't know, I can ask Lieutenant Palmer and see if he can find them."

"Okay, see if he can round them up and get them to where you are. Where are you anyway?"

"The Trinity Wharf Tauranga, right on the bay. You'd think a ship's captain would have had enough of the ocean, but that's where he is staying."

"Okay, give me an hour and send me the information."

We said our goodbyes and went back upstairs. Amy called the lieutenant out into the hall.

She said, "So, here's my plan. We may have to sweat this guy in custody. But let's hold that for Plan B. It might take too long to do us any good, but if it is all we have, it is all we have. First, I want to have someone else question him, a woman I know, former SAS, former SIS, and former NPD, served in China, whole kit and caboodle. Let's let her have a go at him. If she can get him to talk, we are days ahead. And if not, we are only a few hours behind."

The lieutenant said, "Worth a try. And I think I know who you mean. I've read about her."

Amy said, "Shh, she's trying to remain anonymous, live a simple life. But she is willing to do this for Jack and his family."

I was starting to realize how fortunate I was to have a national hero working on our behalf.

The lieutenant said, "Mr. Gamble is no slouch himself." He bowed his head, and I bowed back.

"One more thing," Amy said, "See if you can track down those intelligence agents who were on standby this morning and get them here within the hour."

"On it," he said and went down the hall dialing his phone.

Does this guy have a wife or kids, I thought. The Chinese can't be that much different in that regard. But what if he is hardened, ex-military or something? I sat on the edge of the bed and looked around the small hotel room; pleasant, but still confining. I wondered where and how Maddy was being held. I balled my fists up when I thought of someone hurting her. I pushed my hair back. I forgot where my cap was. I stood and walked out of the room to have some time to myself.

CHAPTER

15

Trinity Wharf Hotel
Tauranga, New Zealand
March 12, 2033
2:15 p.m.

Sara sent a text message at one thirty that she needed a little more time. The intelligence agents had gathered and were in the room next to Zhao's. The Tauranga police had now commandeered the rooms on either side of Zhao and had the hotel empty this wing of the third floor, where Zhao's room was. I was with Amy when Sara called back, "Okay, I'm ready. Sorry for the delay."

Amy said, "Okay, I'm going to put you on face to face so Zhao can see you on my phone. Then I will go in and chase everyone else out except Zhao and me."

Sara said, "And take Jack in with you. Jack, if you can hear me, are you alright with that? You will mostly have to be quiet."

"I hear you, Sara, and I can do that. Whatever it takes."

It took a few minutes to clear everyone else out of the room. Zhao sat in one of the comfortable chairs in the room. Amy motioned me into the other chair. She sat on the bed across from Zhao, placed her phone face up on the small table between the two chairs.

Sara took over from there. She spoke first to Mr. Zhao in Chinese. He answered her, she responded, and then she immediately switched to English. "I have determined that Captain Zhao speaks excellent English, and he and I agree to continue in English so that you two will know what's going on without my having to explain things."

"Now, Captain Zhao, let me make sure you know who is in the room with you. The woman seated on the bed is Detective Wirihana of the Nelson Police, and she is investigating the disappearance of two individuals from Nelson. She believes Chinese state security abducted them." No visible reaction from Zhao.

"The man in the room is the husband of the woman who was abducted. His name is Jack Gamble. Look at him, Captain."

Captain Zhao did as instructed. Emotion played across his face and across mine, too.

"Mr. Gamble and his wife, Maddy, are Americans: American heroes. They were instrumental in bringing an end to Ebola Island eight years ago."

Zhao looked at me again. It was clear he had at least heard stories about the Ebola crisis, undoubtedly spun by China to blame all on the evil United States.

"The other person taken by Chinese state security was a young man known as Li Wei Yang, raised in Vietnam, but born in Wuhan like you were."

Captain Zhao started at this and looked at the face on the phone. Sara acknowledged his look with a slight head bow.

Sara went on, "In fact, I think you may have known his parents, or your parents knew them. They were both human rights lawyers. Do you remember the Yangs? They disappeared shortly after the coronavirus crisis, and Li Wei never heard from them again."

Zhao wiped his brow and stared at the phone, but never said a word and never looked at Amy or me. We exchanged a glance.

"And my name used to be Mina Kaur. I now go by Sara. I worked in Beijing as a spy for my country, New Zealand. Let me tell you what happened to me, Captain Zhao. Everyone in Beijing involved in security knew I was a spy. It was an open secret. In intelligence work, most of us know each other, regardless of our allegiances. When you work in and out of the New Zealand embassy, your likeness and identity are not secret. There is a sort of unwritten code about what is and is not acceptable behavior. A large portion of intelligence is gathered from public sources and also from individuals. Computer hackers or data thieves gather some from computers, but I wasn't involved in that. In any event, I had been in Beijing for eighteen months, far too long, and I was about to be transferred back to New Zealand to be with my family. Do you have a family, Captain Zhao?"

Zhao nodded, yes.

"I know you do, Captain, forgive me. You have a wife and two daughters living in Shanghai. I had two daughters. Mr. Gamble here has a daughter and a son."

Zhao again looked at me. I only nodded the truth of what she had said, then closed my eyes briefly. Zhao turned back to the camera.

"Just before I was to be sent home, a Chinese agent was captured in New Zealand after he attempted to infiltrate New Zealand's SIS, its spy service, the same organization that employed me. So, when I arrived at the airport in Beijing for my flight home, I was arrested. The man who arrested me is now Deputy Minister of China's State Security. Do you know who he is?"

Zhao's face was transparent. He knew the name. He said, "I know of that man; he grew up with one of my distant cousins. I have never met him."

Sara smiled. "I wish I had never met him. For four months, the Chinese kept me in a secret prison. For the first month, I was allowed very little sleep. I was interrogated daily by Chen. My food rations were tiny; I was starving. But I never talked; I never told Chen the identities of other agents. Finally, an exchange was agreed to, me for the Chinese agent captured in New Zealand.

"It turns out that while I never disclosed anything, this Chinese agent had, he had identified dozens of undercover Chinese spies working in New Zealand and Australia and a few in Europe where he had previously worked. These agents began to be rounded up one by one, and a few months after the prisoner exchange, our sources say Chen tortured his own agent. The one who was previously captured, and he admitted what he had revealed. Chen was furious. We know he told others New Zealand had deceived him, made him look like a fool, and he vowed revenge. Do you know what his revenge was, Captain Zhao?"

Zhao shook his head. He was sweating and rubbing his hands together. Amy had not told me any of this, and I was engrossed in Sara's story. Amy , as calm as a big cat, was watching Zhao .

"Chen slaughtered my entire family while I was in Wellington on official business. Oh, he didn't do it himself; he sent a group led by a man named Wang. And not only did he murder my family, but he also audiotaped it while he did it and sent me the tape. Chen felt New Zealand, and I, had made a fool of him, and his revenge was to destroy my family and to try to destroy me. I know what and whom we are dealing with here, Captain Zhao. I hope you do." Tears were streaming down Sara's face, but she kept looking straight into the phone.

Zhao was visibly upset. He was shaking his head.

Sara waited and then asked in a soft voice, "Have they threatened your family, Captain Zhao?"

Zhao remained silent. So did Sara. Amy and I exchanged a look.

I spoke up, out of turn again. "Captain, I realize you're in a difficult spot. Try to imagine my position."

Zhao was looking at me, expressionless.

"This is my wife, the mother of my two small children, the woman I love more than anything, my partner, my friend, my lover, and I would do anything to save her. I would gladly trade places with her." I showed him a picture of my family on my cellphone. "She is out there somewhere." I pulled back the drapes to the view out to

Tauranga Bay. "She is on *Eternity*, your ship, sir." I combed my hair back with my right hand.

Sara added, "Maybe we can help protect your family, Captain Zhao. Maybe. But first, you have to help us. We know you're just a ship's captain. We know you didn't kidnap anyone, but we think you know who was on your ship. Were there Chinese security agents on *Eternity* as you sailed from Nelson to Tauranga?"

"Yes," Zhao spit out, "yes, and I hate them, Chen, Wang, all of them." His shoulders fell and his eyes closed. "I hate them," he repeated.

"Was it one of them who threatened your family?"

"Yes, a man who goes only by Wang. And from what my cousin has told me I know Chen will not save them."

That answer made Sara pause, which seemed to throw her off track. "Yes, Captain Zhao, I know the men you mean; the same men who led the slaughter of my family. I would not want them to do the same to your family or to Jack's wife."

I wondered if Sara had ever met Wang face to face. Would he really harm Maddy? It sounded like he was vicious, but wasn't Maddy a private citizen whereas Sara had been an enemy combatant? In my heart, I knew it wouldn't matter much. I stayed silent now. Sara was doing a masterful job.

Amy was taking a few notes. I knew she was recording the call.

"Tell me, Captain. Did you see the two individuals we showed you pictures of on *Eternity*?"

Zhao looked at me and said, "Yes, I saw the woman for sure. She came out and entered the quarters of the crew. I think she used the restroom."

I knew I shouldn't, but I couldn't hold back. "Are you sure it was her? Was she okay? How did she look?" I was immediately afraid I had broken the magic spell. I could see from their eyes, both Sara and Amy were fearful of the same thing.

Captain Zhao looked over at me and said, "I am very sure it was your wife, Mr. Gamble. She looked just like the picture, only more tired, dirtier, and she was barefoot. But it was she. I did not observe any injuries to her, but I only saw her very briefly. I am sorry I do not know more. If it was my wife..." His voice trailed off.

"What about the man, Captain Zhao?" Sara asked, "Was he the man in the pictures the detective showed you?"

"I am not sure. The man looked Chinese. Wang tortured him. The one time I saw him, two of the security agents were dragging him. He could not walk, and I could see wounds on his legs. I did not get a good look at his face. At times we heard his screams. We hate the State Security, my crew, and me. We only want to sail the seas and deliver cargo, but the Communist Party makes us take spies, prisoners, security agents, and stolen property. If we complain, we will disappear, and our families will disappear. Enough! And yes, Miss Sara, I remember Li Wei's parents. They were very nice people and helped my grandfather with some small matters before they disappeared."

"Where on the ship are Mr. Gamble's wife and Li Wei being held?"

Zhao gave some thought before answering, "There are rows of stacks of containers on the ship. Many are stacked right beside other containers. On the front deck, there is a small passageway right below the bridge. On the ship's port side, you go down that passageway about halfway, and one of the bottom containers on your left is used to hold the two prisoners. The container is red and yellow and old, and the doors' seals are missing to allow some light and air into the container."

I was fighting my anger. The Chinese are holding my wife in a storage box? On your ship, and you did nothing about it? Amy must have sensed something. She put one finger to her lips.

"Can you think of anything else, Captain, that we may need to know?"

"The captain, Captain Hu, who replaced me is a spy. He is slipping out of New Zealand on my ship, but he knows nothing about commanding a vessel."

Sara said, "Captain Zhao, there may be some more questions for you later. You have been very helpful. Will you promise to be as helpful with others who may have more questions?"

Captain Zhao bowed again to the phone. "Yes, I have had enough."

"One more thing, Captain. Is the information on file in New Zealand as far as your address and next of kin accurate?"

"Yes."

"No promises, Captain, but let me see if I can do anything to help your family."

Amy and I left Zhao's room and brought Sara still on the phone with us. Noah and the lieutenant took our place with Zhao.

I said, "Thank you, Sara. You were outstanding. I had no idea what you had been through."

Sara gave me a sad smile and then a salute and said, "Well, you can believe it, Mr. Gamble, and you can count on me to protect your family. No matter how long you need to be gone." She tried to smile. "Now take me to those SIS agents. Are they still there?"

Sara made Amy turn off record on her phone, leave it with the intelligence guys, and leave the room. Amy and I waited in the hall. The lieutenant joined us, and Amy filled him in.

When he had heard it all, he said, "Okay, we'll take Zhao into custody. It's for his own protection. We'll have to wait and see what Wellington says about any charges against him."

Amy just frowned. She moved on with, "We now have an eyewitness to the transporting of abducted individuals from New Zealand by Chinese agents. The kidnapping occurred in New Zealand, and the ship set sail from here. That's more than enough to stop that ship if we can figure out how to do it without endangering Maddy."

CHAPTER

16

Onboard Eternity
The South Pacific Ocean
March 12, 2033
10:00 p.m.

Captain Hu had abandoned the bridge two hours ago. The crew was relieved; the man knew nothing about ships. Why had he pretended? The sailors knew he was a security agent or a spy pretending to be a captain so he could quietly leave New Zealand.

The first mate had the controls. Everything was computerized, and the ship sailed itself if you first set it up right. That is unless you happened to be in a storm like the one they were in right now. Manually he tried to keep the ship on course, for every time he would pull the wheel to the right, the sea would force it to the left. And if he let it drift too far to the left, a wave would come crashing over the deck. They had lost one container off the front deck so far. He wasn't sure about the back.

Two of his fellow crew members were with him on the bridge. They were all experienced hands, which meant they knew what to do, and they also understood to be afraid, at least a little. One of the crew said, "We could sure use Captain Zhao tonight."

The first mate said, "Yeah, he knows how to sail in any weather. Good man, not like that Hu."

The crew laughed. The other one said, "Why do these spies even pretend? We are lucky he didn't sink us before he went down to drink with Wang, and they know each other from somewhere."

The first crew member said, "All of the state security have holed up in the lounge, drinking except for the ones who are seasick."

The first mate laughed. "Yeah, some heroes of the state. The weather turns bad, so they can't continue their important state security work of torturing a boy who can no longer walk or make lewd comments about the American woman they keep locked up in a can. I wonder what kind of night they are having out there?" As he spoke, he watched a wave slide across the front deck. He had to believe water was coming into the prisoners' container, and there was probably nothing to hang on to in there so they would tumble with each rise and fall of the ship. He went back to his wheel. The remaining crew was resting or trying to. In this storm, shifts were six hours, three men each shift. There were only cold rations, and no work on the ship was occurring. From the radar, it looked like this would be a long storm. He slowed to sixteen knots to better match the rhythm of the storm. Still, the storm was pushing them, driving against their stern, propelling them forward.

***

Maddy fell against the side of the container again. The ship tilted and turned and rose and fell, and she slid across the wet floor, sometimes on her wet feet, sometimes on her rear end, and sometimes lying flat. Li Wei had been bouncing across the container, unable to exert any control in his injured state. Maddy had torn strips from his mattress with great effort and tied them together until she had a length long enough to lash Li Wei to the door. The lash went around his waist and wedged into the opening at the middle of the doors. After several failures, Maddy had gotten the lash over the lock and back through the doors to secure Liu Wei to the front of the container. He hung there like a rag doll, swinging from side to side and groaning occasionally but no longer was he crashing helplessly from side to side.

Maddy tried to hang on to the crack in the door near Li Wei. She could try to help protect him with her body and keep herself upright as well. The ship lurched, and the doors slammed on her fingers. If not for Li Wei's lash through the opening that kept the door from completely slamming shut, her hand would get crushed. As it was, it was only bruised. Maddy adjusted her grip and rode the swells for a while. Then the doors slammed shut again, this time with a rush of water under the doors. She adjusted her grip once more, trying to position her hands to keep the doors from slamming shut. That worked until the skin rubbed off her knuckles, and the pressure on her hands from the doors became unbearable.

She let go of the doors and made a new plan. Maddy tried to ride her mattress. It absorbed some of the crashes into the side walls and protected her from falling to the floor. The waste bucket skittered across the floor with every wave. The floor was now very wet and the container smelled even worse than before. Sometimes the ship rolled so hard that Maddy and the mattress slid into and partway up the side wall or the rear wall, and Maddy would fall off and have to climb on again when she could. She used the putrid mattress to protect her head and body the best she could. Many times she grunted or gasped when she was thrown violently into one of the walls. She caught her breath whenever she had the chance. There was no one to call out to but God. So she did. Sometimes the mattress would carry Maddy forward into Li Wei, and there was no telling who might hurt whom. Through it all, the lash on Li Wei held. She took pride in that it wasn't perfect, but it was as safe as she could keep him in his helpless state. Now she just had to fend for herself. She held tight to the sides of the mattress, which meant her hands got banged up. A strong wind whistled into the container through the crack created by Li Wei's improvised body sling. It was cool, cold even against her wet clothes. She didn't have time to give that much thought.

For hours there had been no sign of their wardens. No food, no restroom, and no torture; just a terrifying, unpredictable, unending ride inside a tin can, thrown violently about in total darkness with water coming in and out along the bottom of the doors. And a chilly breeze slipping in through the crack in the doors. And Maddy thought, *this is better, at least for Li Wei there is no torture and maybe he can heal a little, maybe he can sleep a little.* However, she didn't see how anyone could sleep through this storm.

Early this morning, Wang had brought a man to see them, a man he said was the new captain. Captain Hu, he said. They were both drunk. Wang had his arm around Hu's shoulders and looked like he would have fallen if he hadn't. The seas were rising even then. Some of the men gave Li Wei and her breakfast, which was the last they had seen of anyone.

Maddy tried to think of Jack and JJ, and Allison. She wondered how they were doing, and then she crashed into one of the walls. Maddy thought about how much she loved them, and she bounced off the floor. She prayed that she would see them again, and her head banged into the front wall.

Jack, I am so sorry, she thought, and the wind whistled through the door openings with the force of its invasion into the container. Maddy was shivering despite all the energy she was spending. *I have to get out of here. But how? And what do I do if I get free? I am on a ship somewhere in the middle of the ocean. And I can't leave Li Wei. Not like this. But I can't carry him, and we don't have any food or water or anything. Help me, dear Lord, please help me.*

The wind howled, the ocean rose and fell, the night wore on, Maddy and her thoughts sloshed about, and Li Wei swung back and forth from his waist across the door. The sun rose; the sun set, and only then did the storm start to subside.

CHAPTER

17

Tauranga, New Zealand
March 13, 2033
5:30 p.m.

The wind howled, and the rain fell all day. I imagined what it must be like out at sea. The harbor waves rolled and crashed onto the shore, ships at berth, over the tops of docks, over the tops of seawalls. The rain was non-stop. Still, I went for a walk at a point where I thought there was a let-up in the storm. I had to do something.

I walked out of the Trinity Wharf Hotel into the open courtyard in front of the hotel. The opening was triangular and I hugged the right side of the building and turned right after I passed it with the wind at my back. One of the Tauranga police officers loaned me a rain slicker, conspicuously marked with "Police." He hesitated to give it to me until his lieutenant nodded that it was alright. I pulled the collar up and started. There was no one else to be seen, but the rain was light even if a strong wind drove it.

I remembered so many things, so many things about my life and Maddy. I had been a shallow greedy man when I arranged for Maddy to come work for me. She was a brilliant young lawyer, eager to help make the world a better place. Shallow. As it turned out, Maddy knew better than I did who I was, at least who I was capable of being. When I ended up on Ebola Island by trickery and faced nearly certain death, Maddy could have given up on me and gone her own way. We had only dated a short while and had only lived together a few weeks at that point. I laughed at myself. I was trying to make up for a past romantic disappointment by accumulating as much as possible and always thinking about getting more. I shook my head in disgust at myself.

Then came the island, a death-defying journey of weeks overland across a strange terrain with cannibals and mercenaries trying to kill me at every stage. And through this valley of death, I was led by two fearless Malagasy brothers, Albert and Roderick. At any stage, I knew they could have abandoned me and been better off, safer. They never did; never have I met nobler, more honorable men than those two skinny ragged-looking Africans. From them, I had learned humility and compassion and how to be a man, and how to love. I remembered when I realized I loved Maddy in Madagascar's rain forests, then known as Ebola Island and now known as Malagasy.

And with their help, I had battled across the island only to be severely wounded near the end and then rescued by Maddy and nursed back to health. Then I had the chance to prove to Maddy and myself that I was a new man, a man deserving of respect, a man to marry.

Within a few weeks of my return, I settled the largest class action in the history of courts anywhere, and then I waived my fee, which would have been immense. I turned my back and walked away from the profession so I could marry Maddy and settle down somewhere quiet and raise children together. No matter what I told myself, I would rescue her, as she had saved me, and I wanted to think 'or die trying', but I couldn't because of the children. My simple life had two significant complications in it, JJ and Allison. And I loved them very much and knew Maddy did, too. We all needed to be together.

The wind began to gust, and when it did, it pushed me along a little faster. Because of the rain, I had my head down unless I was crossing a street. When I looked up to be sure I could cross the street safely, I saw a rotating camera mounted on a post across the street from me. It looked identical to the cameras in Nelson. *Were those damn things everywhere? Were they watching me now? Could the Chinese be monitoring me and know what our rescue plans were?* I didn't think so but the thought concerned me. I put my head back down and knew the rain would help also. I was in sort of an industrial area. There were fenced lots with storage containers stacked on them. Storage containers probably like the one Maddy was locked inside. Large windowless casket like containers.

So far, I had seen two vehicles and no people. I lost track of how long I had been gone, but I was still on Mirresees Road, off of Dive Crescent where I had started at the hotel. I was walking along the harbor, trying to stay close to where Maddy was, at sea. I had counted eight cameras so far and didn't know if I had missed any. Those damn Chinese. Did they have eyes everywhere?

I thought, there might be a little more shelter from the wind inland a bit. I turned and looked back the way I had come. The rain hit me in the face like little pebbles. It was starting to rain harder. I decided I better go back the way I had come. The wind driven rain pummeled my face. At the first side street, I turned left and went one block back away from the harbor. I hoped this was a straight parallel road. When I got there, I turned right immediately and hugged the buildings again; only this time, there were buildings between me and the wind. Much, much better. I noticed fewer cameras here on a back street.

I moved along back to the hotel, and my thoughts returned. *Why, oh why Maddy, did you go to tutor Li Wei?* Was there more to it? I hoped not, but I knew how it looked. Amy had made that apparent. And now I might never get her back, never see her again. Was Maddy being punished for straying? If that was it and I didn't know, the punishment was too severe, and what had the kids or I done to deserve this? My anger and frustration and my love and worry all fought with each other.

I looked up to check for traffic at a cross street and caught a blast of rain squarely in the face. I had to wipe my eyes to see. I should have taken the rain hat the officer had offered me to go with the jacket.

Back in the shelter of a building, the ridiculousness of Maddy's situation struck me. I was barely able to walk along here on 'dry' land, and she was somewhere in the middle of the ocean, a captive on a container ship. There was no doubt in my mind that the weather at sea was much worse. I hoped she was as dry and comfortable as possible. But how comfortable would men who had put a hood over her head make her? I hated those barbarians who had taken her. Who knew what they might have done to her. She could be, no, would be forever changed. My Maddy. In the hands of barbarians. That's what they were, barbarians. And it ignited me further that they were now vying for power with America and the rest of the civilized world. *Barbarians! I will stop them!*

And then there was another camera.

I was at the last cross street before the Trinity Wharf Hotel. I could see the open courtyard area to the front of the hotel ahead of me. I turned left, and for a moment, I didn't move forward. The wind was so strong it took great effort to make any progress, and the driving rain was blinding. I worked my way across the side street and along the side of the hotel. I had my right hand across my forehead, trying to shield my eyes. Finally, I was at the corner and turned toward the hotel entrance. Even the large awning over the hotel entrance didn't provide much relief; the rain still drove into me. As I approached the door, a bellman held it open for me and said, "Come in, officer, come in out of that weather."

I laughed to myself but didn't bother to correct him. Maybe those cameras thought I was a police officer, too. *What the hell was I going to do?*

When I squished my way back upstairs, Amy and the others were waiting for me. My shoes and socks and pants were soaked, water was still dripping from my hair.

Amy put her hand over her mouth to try not to laugh. The others couldn't help themselves.

"Did you have a nice swim?"

"Should have taken your hat."

"Nice day for a walk."

"Who says Americans are crazy?"

"Did you learn anything?"

I really couldn't tell who made which one of the cute comments. I just smiled and bowed and took off and returned the rain jacket. I said, "Thanks, not sure what I would have done without that." Then to everyone I said, "I'll be right back." I shook the water off my hands and pushed my wet hair back out of my face as I went to my room to change. When I had put on dry clothes, I came back out. Everyone was now in the room we had designated as the command center, and the door had been left slightly ajar for me.

Amy was at the computer. She turned to look at me and said, "Drier is better, Jack. Have a seat. I'll fill you in."

I sat on the edge of one of the beds beside Noah, who moved over just a bit to make more room for me.

Amy said, "This storm certainly complicates things. We can't get out of Tauranga, and we can't tell where *Eternity* is. In a storm like this, a ship can be blown way off course. If that gives us more time, it could be a good thing. But they could also reroute, and that might be good or bad depending. When the storm lifts, we should be able to pick up the signal from *Eternity* with our satellites."

"Depending on what?" I asked.

"On where they reroute to. Vanuatu is fairly friendly with New Zealand; not every country around here is. Some are very pro-Chinese, which could make everything more difficult. And Papua New Guinea may be even better than Vanuatu, so it just depends."

"I see," I said, "and we don't know where *Eternity* is?"

Amy said, "Right. The satellite cameras are no help in this kind of cloud cover, and *Eternity* has turned off its tracking beacon or..." She let that sentence drop, but I knew she meant that *Eternity* could have sunk. *Shit! Wasn't it already bad enough?*

"So, what do we do?" I asked.

"We wait. As hard as it is, we just wait. When the storm finally clears, we can then confirm a plan. Right now, we tentatively plan a rescue in Vanuatu, but it may or may not happen. We will just have to see."

CHAPTER

18

Trinity Wharf Hotel
Tauranga, New Zealand
March 14, 2033
4:00 p.m.

Amy was the central figure in our new operation. We had taken over several rooms at the hotel, the same wing of the same floor we had emptied to interrogate Captain Zhao. He was no longer here; the Tauranga police had taken him into custody. They had searched his meager belongings and found nothing of real value. Amy did find a picture of his family, which she scanned and sent to Sara.

Sara called again for the third time today, this time for a video chat. We organized as a task force with Amy as the official leader. No one would deny that Sara was invaluable. She opened with, "I went to the fuel depot at Port Nelson. It looks like *Eternity* put out of here with a full tank of fuel, over one point eight million gallons. She could sail for a month on that fuel, easily enough to reach China without stopping at Vanuatu. Easily."

"Damn, I bet that's exactly what they plan or what they will plan if the storm has moved them toward China," said Amy.

"I'm afraid you're right," said Sara. "If this damn storm ever lifts, we can see where *Eternity* is. Mind you, she may be off course because of this storm, it's a beauty, but shortly after things calm down, we will likely be able to determine her course."

"What do we do if it looks like they're headed straight for China?" I asked.

No one answered.

I took a deep breath, "What about Zhao saying that Hu was a spy and didn't know anything about ships? Will anyone on board know how to correct course?"

Amy answered, "That's a good question. I've been assuming the first mate would know, but that's not a certainty. I've been thinking of Hu's being a spy as additional justification to stop *Eternity* on the high seas. Sara, what do you think?"

Sara said, "I think we have enough to justify the stop, and that's what I've been pushing for through some contacts in Wellington. At this point, we'd need the Navy to make the stop. Lieutenant Palmer, are you there? Hu boarded in Tauranga, so that would be your case. What do you make of it?"

Lieutenant Palmer said, "Yes, I'm here for the duration. And I agree that it is enough to stop the ship all on its own. When coupled with the eyewitness testimony of kidnapped persons held on board, persons abducted in Nelson, I think there's more than enough."

Sara said, "And take a good look at the identification photo of Hu. Doesn't it look like it might be doctored, like he has makeup or something here, under his nose near the left corner of his mouth?" She brought it up on the computer. Palmer took a look, pursed his lips, shrugged and took another look.

I was relieved; there was an answer to my 'what if they are heading straight to China' question.

Amy nodded her agreement. "Sara, where are the SIS men who were here yesterday? We haven't heard back from them."

"And you won't. They'll report back to me. One of them is in Wellington lobbying SIS and the Navy and the Premier. So far, that's going nowhere; they haven't said no, but they are studying it. One more reason we need to know the whereabouts of the ship and its probable course. They keep talking about the dangers of stopping a ship on the high seas. *Eternity* may not willingly stop, and Wellington is unlikely to sink it at sea, so they try to work through any other options first. That same agent is trying to monitor the satellite imagery of the sea between you and Vanuatu. Just clouds right now, as I said."

"And the other two?" Amy was nothing if not relentless. As good a quality in a police officer as it was in a lawyer. I was glad I didn't always have to be the one to push things.

"One of the others is in Port Vila, trying to put an operation together should *Eternity* put in there. And the last man is in Guam."

"Guam?" I asked.

"Yes, you should know the US Seventh Fleet and Pacific Fleets are still based there. If it comes to firepower at sea, that's the place to go around here. Overpowering force may be the only way to affect a rescue," Sara said.

Amy asked, "Do you think you could get the United States involved? I mean, that would be great but is it realistic?"

"Let me worry about that," Sara said. "I do have some friends there from the old days. You never know. And Maddy is a US citizen, an American heroine even, and Li Wei was on his way to a job in the United States. So, we have things to talk about."

"What else do we have?" Sara asked.

Lieutenant Palmer said, "We're tracking down Captain Hu with the help of yet another SIS agent. Thank you, Sara. Our working theory is that the real Captain Hu is dead. Three months ago, his registration was updated, and a new photo added. A current photograph is required. Even with the hat and sunglasses, our people are convinced that the new photograph is someone different. We're thinking they have been planning this spy exfiltration for some time. Amy and I have even discussed that the Nelson abductions may have been a last-minute decision by the Chinese. They had the opportunity and the mode of transportation, so why not."

Amy nodded. "More and more, we think Maddy was just un-lucky."

Sara said, "I agree, and that makes me more fearful for her safety. So far, though, the Chinese don't know we have an eyewitness who can place both Maddy and Li Wei onboard the ship. Lieutenant, if I decide to broadcast that in the media to make it harder for China to eliminate them at sea, can you keep Zhao safe?"

Eliminate them at sea? Or take them to China, where I may never hear from Maddy again? I was searching my contacts for any-one who might be able to help. I was glad I hadn't cleaned them out as Maddy kept suggesting. Stored on the cloud, they didn't take any space or affect my phone's functionality, so why bother? Let's hope my laziness would get its reward.

"One more thing going on," Amy said. "Officers in Nelson are try-ing to track down Li Wei's friends from the Nelson English Centre, especially the four who also stayed at the Palazzo Motor Lodge. On our first check they were booked on flights out of New Zealand the day they checked out of the Palazzo, but in checking further none of the four actually made their flights. For all we know they've been ab-ducted, too, and could even be onboard *Eternity*. We'd like to know if they or Li Wei knew they were being watched or suspected any of this, and we want to find out a little more about them."

"Good detective work, Amy, as always. You all work on that, the police issues. I'll do my best on policy and other planning. Call if an-ything new develops, and I'll do the same, and we'll all talk again as soon as the storm stops; sound good?"

Then she said, "'One more thing, Jack. Your kids are fine. If they aren't with me, Charlie or another police officer, a parent or two are watching over them. So, you don't need to worry about them."

"Have they asked about me?"

"Some and about Maddy, too. They know I don't have much to tell them, but yes, they ask some questions."

"Thanks, Sara, take good care of them."

"Wait a minute, Jack. Here they come now. Do you want to talk to them? I had Charlie pick them up today and they are just pulling in."

"Yes, absolutely."

"Hang on a minute."

I could hear the door open and then Sara telling the kids I was on the phone and then running feet.

I smiled to myself. When I saw them. "Dad!"

"Hi Daddy!"

Allison said "Where are you, Daddy? Did you find Mommy? When are you coming home? You said it would be soon." Then she took a breath and reached out to touch the screen.

I did too. "I am still in New Zealand and will be gone a little longer. We know where your Mommy is but still have to get her back."

Allison said, "Those bad men better not hurt..." and then she was interrupted by a wail from JJ. "Is it my fault Dad? I can be better. Did Mommy run away because of me? I promise I will do better. Tell her Dad, please. I am studying harder. I am sorry." And he started to cry. I could only see him in the corner of the screen.

I overheard Sara telling him it wasn't his fault.

"JJ, listen to me. It is absolutely not your fault that Mommy went away. She didn't go because of you or Allison or me. She didn't want to go at all but some bad men took her away. And now I am going to get her back. It's nothing that you did or even about you at all. I promise."

JJ sniffled.

"Or you either Allison, both of you can put those ideas right out of your heads. Your Mommy and I love you both very much and would never ever leave you. Okay?"

Two sheepish okays came back across the line.

"Promise?"

"We promise Daddy" they said in unison, standing side by side. It was hard not to cry looking at them.

We talked a little longer about school and some new favorite flavor of ice cream and about Nickau. I was having trouble staying in the conversation thinking about how hard this was for them. When we ended the call I couldn't remember what either of them had been wearing. Now that they couldn't see me my tears were falling.

CHAPTER

19

Onboard Eternity
The South Pacific Ocean
March 14, 2033
11:00 p.m.

"Finally," Hu said, returning to the bridge. The first mate's shift was over, and he had left the bridge. Crew member Chang was at the helm. His name was stitched onto his shirt, marking him as an experienced sailor. Chang looked up but did not speak. Instead, he gave a small head bow of deference. Hu still stank of liquor. Twice he stumbled as the ship rolled a little to and fro. The storm had finally passed, but it would take a while longer for the seas to calm down. Chang had been working on ships for many years. He was used to this and prided himself on never getting seasick, no matter how rough the sea.

This past storm was intense and rough; half of the crew and all of the security men had been helplessly sick. The first mate, Chang, and a few others had managed the ship through the storm. That gave them a sense of power over the helpless security agents who all the crew hated to have on board. He didn't blame Captain Zhao for wanting to get off the ship. He admired him for standing his ground against that monster, Wang. No other word could describe him; he was cruel just to be cruel. Chang sensed that Wang's men feared him; they did not respect him. Captain Zhao, now that was a man to admire. During rough storms, he was always at the helm, for however long the harsh weather lasted. Often during the middle of the night, Zhao would come to the bridge to check on things and would stay and chat with whoever was there. On Sunday mornings, while sailing, he insisted on personally serving breakfast to all of the crew.

Wang stumbled on to the bridge. "Whew, what a night." He held his head and shook it slowly side to side. If he thought he was funny, no one else did. Hu looked at him oddly and simply said, "Lieutenant Wang." So, that was his title. He only went by Wang most of the time. Wang stopped clowning and nodded. "Captain Hu." It seemed to Chang that Hu outranked Wang. Yes, he was sure of it. He kept to himself.

Hu asked, "Do you know how far off course the storm blew us, Chang?" He was pleasant enough, at least at the moment.

Chang replied, "Not far, Captain, and the storm also drove us forward faster than we would go under only our own power. We may end up being slightly ahead of schedule and we are closer to China if you determine to change course." Remembering his position, Chang added, "Of course, the determination is up to you and the first mate, but I think we may arrive at Port Vila in the next thirty-six to forty hours or we may proceed as you order."

Wang didn't even pretend to be interested. Hu said, "That sounds about right to me, too. Depending. We'll see about our course later."

"Right, sir, depending." Chang wished they would leave the bridge. He knew Hu had no idea where they were or their course. Hu looked out over the port side of the front deck. The containers were intact, although some were moved or tilted, and the doors on one had opened, spilling what looked like milk all over the deck.

"What is that, Chang?" Hu asked, motioning to the mess on the deck.

"Looks like milk powder, sir. It's been pretty rough. I guess one of the containers came open. I will get someone to clean it up right away." Chang immediately called the quarters below for all available hands to clean the foredeck and secure the spilled load.

Hu turned to Wang. "How did our prisoners pass the night? Where did you move them?"

Wang's face answered. He hadn't moved them anywhere, and he had no idea how they were doing. He said, "I was just going to collect some men and go check on them, sir."

Hu's face displayed his displeasure. He did not speak it in front of Chang and the other crew member. "I will come with you. I wish to see for myself."

After they left, Chang turned to his crew mate and said, "No one should have to spend a night at sea in a storm locked in a storage container. I don't care who they are or what they have done. Wang deserves discipline for his cruelty."

The crew mate with Lhao written in marker on his shirt was new this trip; he just grunted and turned away. Chang would have to be more careful around him and check to see what the first mate thought of him. Chang got back to his duties. The ship was self-correcting its course to get back to its plotted destination, Port Vila. Chang was ready for a few hours ashore. If he only knew how, he would stay ashore. But he could never endanger his family in that way. That would be dishonorable.

Chang looked out over the ship and was pleased to see several crew members cleaning up the deck. The crew had secured the opened container, and any milk powder that had not split open was safely back in place. He chuckled to himself at the mess. Milk powder and seawater combined to make milk, salty and undrinkable milk, but milk nonetheless. Often *Eternity* and other ships he had worked carried milk powder and other foodstuffs back to China. It was growing harder and harder to feed China's population. He was glad to have the helm and not be among the crew mopping the deck or hosing it off the side of the ship. He turned and looked back at *Eternity*'s frothy wake and smiled. The ocean would soon absorb it, so there was no trace.

When his eyes came back forward, he saw Wang leading two men and Hu bringing up the rear. They were going to where Chang knew the prisoners were.

When Wang got to the container holding Li Wei and the woman, he stopped short. Chang could see a ragged piece of cloth was secured somehow, going from inside the box around the locking loops and then back into the container.

Wang held it in his hand and turned to one of his men and issued a command.

One of the men stepped forward, pulled a knife from his belt, and cut the cloth.

***

Maddy heard Li Wei's body fall to the floor. He grunted as he hit. Through the door she heard a shout, "Unlock it, you moron."

As the doors were opened a man stepped forward to see inside. Maddy didn't recall ever seeing him before. He was a handsome man with perfectly combed hair, tall by Chinese standards. At first she thought he was smiling, but then she determined he had some sort of scar or defect at the left side of his mouth so that he always looked to be smiling or sneering. Both doors were pulled fully open. There in the doorway lay Li Wei in a heap. He didn't move. Seawater still sloshed around the bottom of the container; some of it ran out and past their shoes. One empty soaked mattress was in the back corner of the box. It was tattered and torn; pieces were missing that seemed to match the lash around the door locks. Li Wei had more of the lashing around his waist. Still, he didn't move. The other mattress was against the side wall. Maddy slowly pulled herself up and blinked to look at the men, this new man especially. Her face was bruised and swollen; her hands bled. She was dirty, disheveled, and disoriented. She tried to rise, but failed; tried to speak, but didn't.

The new man released his anger. "Wang, what were your orders as to this woman? That she was not to be harmed? That is my understanding." Maddy listened closely. So, this man was over Wang. He continued, "And Li Wei, tell me Wang, has he told you any useful information? Look at him, look at them. The Deputy Minister will not be happy when I tell him; no, show him what you have done." He began taking pictures with his phone. Maddy had been thinking the same thing. Wang tortured Li Wei for no useful purpose other than to satisfy his own sadistic temperament. She slumped to the floor, playing up her condition for the pictures.

Wang put up a hand to try to stop the picture taking. The new man slapped Wang across his face. "Never put your hands up to me, Wang. Never! Have you forgotten who I am? When the Deputy Minister sees this, he will be furious, especially when he hears you were drinking all night instead of following your orders. Now, where are the other prisoners?"

Maddy made out other prisoners from their conversation. *What other prisoners? There must be a thousand containers they could be in. And who is this new man who can order Wang around at will?*

The new leader turned to the two men. "Take these two to sickbay. Let's see what we can do with them." As they left, Maddy watched him disarm Wang and lock him in their container. As he left, he said through the locked doors, "Reflect on your failings."

Through the locked doors, Wang said, "Sir, please." They all walked off. Maddy looked up to see someone watching from the bridge and smiling.

CHAPTER

20

Trinity Wharf Hotel
Tauranga, New Zealand
March 15, 2033
7:00 a.m.

During the night, the storm had abated, and the clouds were thinning. Amy and I were alone in the control room, looking at satellite imagery of the South Pacific. We had found *Eternity*. It was about ninety miles east of its plotted course and also farther along than we expected. It had taken a few minutes to find her given that she was not where we expected. And, of course, I feared that she sank. In that, I was relieved.

"Well, good news, I think. I'm positive that's *Eternity*, the profile image matches, and there aren't, or at least aren't supposed to be, any other ships out there. Normally, the sea-lanes would be more crowded this time of year, but some ships stayed put at berths rather than tackle that storm. I've heard that Papua New Guinea really got hammered; there was lots of property damage, flooding, and twenty-seven dead. *Eternity* should be happy to be afloat still." She looked at me, horrified. "I didn't mean it like that, Jack. That wasn't how I wanted it to come out. I just meant that given the power of the storm and with Captain Zhao replaced by a counterfeit captain, *Eternity* must have a good crew."

I put my hand up. "No offense taken. Can you tell me anything about its course?"

"Yes, I think so. The next hour will make things clearer, but it looks to me like they're correcting course from where the storm left them to get back on track to get to Port Vila. And if I'm reading this chart correctly, they could be there early tomorrow morning."

"That would be great if they aren't heading straight to China. It gives us a better chance, at least. So, what do we do?"

"We arrange to meet them. Joe and his plane are still here standing by. Sara says her guy in Port Vila has some help lined up, so we find out more about that and mobilize. Rescue Maddy Gamble, take two."

"Thanks, you're great. I want you to know I really appreciate you." *Rescue Maddy Gamble take two. We have to succeed this time. Have to—please, Lord.*

"No problem. Just doing my job. Now let's watch that ship until we're sure."

We called down to the front desk for coffee and some breakfast rolls, and slowly other team members began wandering in. Noah was next. We filled him in. "Okay, I'm in," was all he said. Then came Lieutenant Palmer with one of his men. We filled them in as well.

He said, "I'm sorry, Amy. Sorry, Jack. I've been discussing this scenario with my Commander, and he called in our legal counsel, and they're refusing to allow any Tauranga officers to participate. They say Vanuatu is foreign soil, which could lead to an international incident with China, one of New Zealand's largest trading partners. I tried everything; I really did. I asked what difference did it make if Nelson police or Tauranga police created an incident. They said the difference was their asses weren't on the line if it was the Nelson police. That's what they said. And then they dared to ask me to wish you good luck. I am so sorry. I really am. Amy, I have to ask, what did you say to your Commander to get his permission to go?"

"Simple, I didn't ask."

Noah looked up at Amy after her comment, shook his head, nodded, smiled, and went back to his attack on a breakfast roll.

I asked, "What about Sara's guy? Will he be in?"

"Yeah, I think so. He's a spook; the rules are different," Amy replied.

"Okay," I said. "We've been watching this screen for an hour and a half. Where is *Eternity* headed?"

"It's tough to tell. The storm may have blown them off course, but *Eternity* is well west of Vanuatu, actually seems to be heading more for the Solomon Islands."

"The Solomon Islands?" I asked. "Is that good or bad?"

"Not sure. I'm not even sure that's what's going on. I really have only a couple of minutes to go on here. I know where they are, but it's harder to tell yet where they're headed."

"If you will allow me," the lieutenant said, "this is what I do all day every day." He motioned to the computer, and Amy got up and backed out of the way.

The lieutenant sat down and began working on the computer. He did something which showed where *Eternity* probably had been. It was a little tough to follow, but it looked like she had started out for Port Vila on a direct course. Then the storm had hit, and *Eternity* was probably lucky to be still floating, let alone on course.

While we were waiting, I asked Lieutenant Palmer, "Do you know who manufactured the security cameras on the streets of Tauranga? I saw them yesterday and they look identical to the ones in Nelson. And those cameras were surreptitiously complicit in my wife's kidnapping."

The lieutenant gave me a knowing look. "I would have to look up the name of the company, but they're Chinese and we don't trust those cameras. The Chinese seem to know things about Tauranga that they shouldn't have access to. I've read any number of similar reports from around the world."

I nodded and looked at Noah and Amy. Noah said, "Dragon's Eye." The lieutenant smiled like he had heard the term before.

Amy asked, "Can you turn them off when we leave for the airport and from the airport?"

"I'll see what I can do."

We all watched the screen for a few minutes. The lieutenant assured us *Eternity* was in the open sea. "We should be able to see her turn east toward Port Vila any minute. Then we'll know."

Only *Eternity* did not turn east. We watched for ten or fifteen minutes that felt like days and days. The lieutenant looked up. "I'm sorry but the ship appears to be on a course almost due northwest."

"Due northwest?" I tried to figure out where that meant they were going. As soon as it occurred to me, I blurted out, "China?"

I could tell from their faces that they all thought I was right.

"Oh, dear God."

"Let me expand the map for you," said the lieutenant, and he changed the view on the computer to show a much larger area.

I bent forward to look, my hands holding my forehead, cupped as if to help me see. I could tell that *Eternity* was due west of Vanuatu and moving toward the Solomon Islands. "How far away are they from the Solomon Islands?" I asked.

"Still hundreds of miles," said the lieutenant.

"Aren't the Solomon Islands a United States protectorate or ally or something?" I asked, "Maybe they could stop the ship in their waters."

Amy put her hand on my arm, but I shook it off. I was in no mood for condolences.

She said, "Yes, the Solomon Islands are friendly to the United States, but this is a Chinese ship. All these little island nations have to be wary of angering China. I doubt the Solomon Islands could stop this ship, and I doubt even more that they would risk it."

"What about the United States? Do they have a naval base there?" I asked. There had to be something we could do.

"The United States has no significant or permanent presence there," said the lieutenant. "The United States does have bases on Guam and Palau. It looks like *Eternity* will be sailing right between the two. Let me show you." He turned back to the computer screen, and then he added, "But I don't want to get your hopes up. I doubt even they could or would safely intercept this ship. However, a common route is to pass through the Solomon Islands here and then turn northwest to China."

We all crowded around the lieutenant. He did something with the keyboard which projected *Eternity*'s course if she maintained her current bearing. The line went right through the Solomon Islands and proceeded to pass almost equidistant between Guam and Palau.

"How far will it be from Guam and Palau at this point?" I asked, pointing at the spot on the line between these two islands.

The lieutenant thought for a minute and said, "Somewhere around four hundred miles from each."

"Can the New Zealand Navy catch them?"

Amy answered, "No. They won't get involved, and I doubt they could physically catch them at this point. But I will ask Sara."

The lieutenant stayed at the computer and was looking hard at something. He clicked and clicked and focused on a distant part of the ocean. He let out a low groan and said, "Damnit, just what we didn't need."

We all turned back to the lieutenant.

"What? What is it?" Amy asked.

He pointed to the computer screen. "See these blips here? Five ships are sailing in a tight group. That's a military formation, probably Chinese. I can't think of who else they could be. And they're on the exact reverse course *Eternity* will be on after they clear the Solomon Islands and turn; they're going out to meet her and bring her in safely."

"Are you sure?" I asked. "How far away are they?"

"I can't be positive, but that's my best theory, and the matching courses make it more likely. They are very far off, but so are we, and we don't have a ship."

CHAPTER

21

Trinity Wharf Hotel
Tauranga, New Zealand
March 15, 2033
8:45 a.m.

"Sara, we have trouble, and we need your help. Call me as soon as possible. The ship Maddy is on is heading straight for China, and the Chinese navy is sailing out to escort them in. Call as soon as you can. Please."

I hung up and sat looking down with both hands pressed into the sides of my head.

Amy was on her phone. "I'm sorry, sir, I can't come back right now." Then she said, "No, sir, but I think you would be more concerned when two people, one of them a Nelson resident, were kidnapped by foreign actors right there in Nelson."

There was a long pause. "I'll have to get back to you on that. Sir." And then she hung up.

"Your boss?" I asked.

Amy almost spat out her words. "Yes, he's trying to force me to come back to Nelson. The stupid bastard."

I must have looked concerned because she added, "Don't worry. I'm not leaving. Not in the middle of this. No way."

We sat and talked about Maddy and our options. And then we talked about them again because we had few options and plenty of time. Everyone else had left the room. Just Amy and I were there when Sara finally called back.

"Hello, Jack, sorry to be so long getting back to you. I heard your message and have been trying to work on things."

"It's okay. Do you understand what's going on?"

"Yes. Your message was unambiguous, and I've been busy verifying things for myself."

"What do you mean? Verifying?"

"I called an old friend. He checked satellite images and sent me a screenshot of what we believe is *Eternity* heading toward the Solomon Islands on a course for China. And we believe it is *Eternity* heading for China because coming toward *Eternity* from the direction of China is a Chinese Escort Task Group, five ships in all. They could be out of any one of a dozen bases. I have people searching for more precise information now. Since their course is the exact complement of *Eternity*'s eventual course, there can be little doubt that this is a coordinated effort. Very Chinese to telegraph that this is their intention in an attempt to intimidate anyone who might interfere."

"Well, that's just it, who might be able to interfere?"

"Is Amy there with you?"

"Yes."

"Anyone else?"

"No, just the two of us right now."

"Okay, put this call on speaker. Let me get right to the point. Our options and resources are very limited in this situation. I spoke with a friend in naval command of the New Zealand Navy, and he looked carefully at everything. I could hear him running calculations. He doesn't think New Zealand has any ships that could get there in time. And he says China might consider it an act of war in any event. This escort group consists of two destroyers, two frigates, and a fuel ship.

It's not a huge group, but a single vessel cannot successfully confront it. My friend agreed if we found New Zealand prisoners onboard, China would likely complain but not escalate the situation. As it is physically, New Zealand could only get helicopters there. And that's not enough to stop or intimidate an escort group. The only chance would be to get to *Eternity* while it's still alone, but that has risks of its own, as we all know."

I knew she meant that the Chinese could simply kill the prisoners, and discreetly dump them into the sea.

"Will they, Sara? Will New Zealand send helicopters?" Amy asked.

"I don't know for sure, but my friend is working on it. All we can do is wait and see on that. But he did mention the US naval base at Guam and the smaller station on Palau. It's small but fairly new, and they have a part of the Seventh Fleet in there now. My friend ran his calculations and said if they act quickly, the US Navy from either Guam or Palau could intercept *Eternity* and the Chinese naval ships."

"Wouldn't they be concerned about China's reaction, too?" I asked.

"Of course. There are some differences. The US could launch an intimidating naval force; no one else around here can; Maddy is a US citizen and a hero at that, and your President is about to run for re-election and a 'tough on China' story might help him."

"Well, can we ask them? Ask the US Navy to intervene?" I asked.

"I've already put that in motion, at least as far as I know how. My New Zealand navy friend is contacting his counterpart in the US Seventh Fleet in Guam, and I have reached out to some friends in the CIA from the old days and asked for their help. They promised to take it to their boss right away and were more eager when I explained who you and Maddy were. I'm not sure when I'll hear back from my friend in the navy. As soon as he hears."

Amy and I just looked at each other. Amy shrugged. I said, "Sara, there is no one quite like you for springing right into action." I thought for a minute and added, "I have a contact in the White House and I'll call and see what I can do."

Maddy's life was on the line, this was no time to sit back.

CHAPTER

22

The White House
Washington D. C.
March 15, 2033
5:45 p.m.

"Hello, Jack Gamble here."

"Well, Jack Gamble. Surprised you're calling me. How the hell are you?" said Mitchell Drummond.

"Not so good, Mitch. I need your help. Can you talk for a few minutes?"

Mitch paused, then responded, "Yeah, I have a few minutes for you. At six o'clock I have a meeting over dinner with the President. What's going on?"

"First, congratulations on your appointment as Chief of Staff. I always knew you would go far." Mitch laughed, and his laugh brought back memories of when we were in law school together. Mitch had never really practiced law, not as I had anyway. He had his eye on politics and was elected to the United States House of Representatives at age thirty and then was appointed a US Senator from Ohio at age thirty-three.

"You know, and I don't tell many people this, but I wasn't sure I wanted this position, and now that I have it, I wonder sometimes if I should have stayed in the Senate. But let's not waste time talking about me. A national hero has called me after many years, and I want to know what he needs before I run out of time."

"Okay. Thanks. Here's the short version. You probably know Maddy and I moved to New Zealand after we got married. Frankly, I had some trust issues with the US government."

"Understood, and rightfully so. The way it treated you was horrendous, sending you to die on Ebola Island."

"Yes, well, and it's not lost on me that now here I am asking, begging if you want me to, that same government for help. Mitch, we believe agents acting for Chinese state security kidnapped Maddy."

"Whoa, can you prove that?"

"Yes. We have an eyewitness to her kidnapping and an eyewitness to her being a prisoner on a Chinese shipping vessel., There is security camera footage from Nelson, New Zealand, intentionally manipulated to obfuscate her abduction, and the Chinese navy is sailing out to escort the cargo ship to China."

Mitch whistled. "Hang on, I need something to write with. I need details."

I looked over at Amy. She mouthed, "The White House? As in The President of the United States?" I nodded and her eyes went wide.

Mitch was back. "Okay, give me some details."

"How much time do we have left?"

"Don't worry about that. The President will understand, and I had a short note sent into the Oval Office. Go on. Where exactly is Maddy?"

I filled Mitch in. He quizzed me about how we knew Maddy was onboard *Eternity* so I told him about the eyewitness.

"Where is this witness now?"

"He's being held by the Tauranga police."

"Perfect, go on, please."

"*Eternity* left the Tauranga area on March 12 with an itinerary for Port Vila, Vanuatu, and encountered a huge storm. We couldn't track her until earlier this morning when the storm abated. Now *Eternity* is essentially past Vanuatu and is steaming toward the Solomon Islands. And a Chinese navy contingent is steaming toward *Eternity* on the complement to what we think will be *Eternity*'s eventual course."

"Whew. So, you said March 15? Today?"

"Yes."

"So, you must be in or around New Zealand? It's only the fourteenth here."

"Sorry. I knew that. Honestly, I can't quite get my mind around talking to each other in real-time, and somehow it's a different day there. I know it is, but..."

Mitch chuckled. "Maybe someday we can figure that out. Where exactly is the Chinese navy?"

"They're still well west of the strait between Guam and Palau."

"And you want the US navy to head them off, and I suppose rescue Maddy from *Eternity* at the same time?"

Mitch was quick; he had gauged the entire situation and correctly surmised why I was calling. I felt a little foolish. I knew I was asking for a lot, a whole lot.

"I don't have anywhere else to turn. I don't mean to put you on the spot."

"You definitely have. And honestly, I don't know if there's anything we can do or not. Deploying the US Navy isn't done lightly. On the other hand, you and Maddy are both national heroes, and, in my opinion, you have every right to ask for help from the government that tried to kill you. A righting of wrongs sort of thing." He paused, and I held my breath. Amy noted the silence and looked across the room at me.

Mitch said, "This is above my pay grade, but I'll tell you what I'm willing to do. I am meeting with the President in just a few minutes and I will definitely fill the President in and see if he's willing to order the navy to help you."

"Thank you, Mitch. That's all I can ask. Thank you."

"You earned it, hero, no problem, and you're still a good fact man, just like you were in law school. I'm not sure anyone else could have laid out the facts any better or any faster. Now I have to get going. Is this the best number for you?"

"Yes, and let me give you another number just in case." I gave him Amy's cell number and explained who she was.

"Okay, got it. We'll see. How much time do we have to decide?"

"Almost none unless you can come up with a different plan."

"Okay, we have great resources here. If the President is interested in acting here, we can determine the locations and speeds of vessels and decide what courses of action might work. I'll be in touch when I know anything or if I need more information. You take care, Jack, and know that I'm pulling for you and Maddy."

"Thanks, Mitch. You're the best."

When I hung up, I looked over at Amy, who was slowly shaking her head. "The White House? You know the Chief of Staff personally? Mitchell Drummond? I looked him up while you were talking. You know him?"

I shrugged. My lips smiled, but I know my eyes didn't. *Oh, Maddy, my dear sweet Maddy. I'm trying, darling; I'm trying.*

"I guess now we wait," I said.

CHAPTER

23

Onboard Eternity
March 16, 2033
4:00 a.m.

Maddy and Li Wei were now confined in sickbay. It was a tiny little room but so much better than the storage container. There were lights and cots and a real toilet. Li Wei had been left alone so far. He was mostly sleeping. Maddy was still working on a plan. She now knew there were other prisoners onboard. She needed to find out where they were being held. Maybe she could free them and together they could overtake the crew. She wasn't sure but she thought the other prisoners were somehow tied to Li Wei. If only he would wake up. She knew the ship was north of New Zealand generally toward China, but she wanted to know if there would be any intermediate stops. She would only get one shot at escaping and good timing was essential. *Where could she get more information? And how could she get more information without raising suspicions?* Wang being out of the way helped but the new man was no fool. She would have to be very cautious. And she would have to figure out who this new man was. She wasn't sure about Li Wei. He had been horribly tortured so he wasn't in league with Chinese state security. At least not now she thought. His physical condition was an impediment. *Did she even need him? Could she even trust him?* More and more she was having doubts, something about his story just didn't make sense. Yet she needed information from him as well as from the Chinese. *Wake up Li Wei, wake up.*

Still, he slept. Maddy ate a little more of the food that had been left for her. Li Wei's food had all been eaten before he slept. And Maddy examined every inch of the sickbay, every cabinet and drawer, under both cots.

Finally, she nudged Li Wei. He groaned and then stirred. She was ready with a glass of water from the small sink. "Here, you need to drink this." Li Wei blinked. "Come on, sit up and drink this. We have to keep you hydrated."

He sat up and took the cup from her and brought it to his lips. After he had several drinks, she took it from him. She pressed her finger into his chest and said in her best lawyer's voice, "We have to straighten a few things out."

Li Wei sat up. "Like what?"

"Like who the other prisoners are onboard this ship."

He protested, "What other prisoners?"

"Don't give me that crap. You heard as well as I did. He mentioned other prisoners. Who are they and where are they? If you expect my help in any way, you're going to have to tell me the truth."

Again, Li Wei protested. "I don't know."

Before he could finish, Maddy threw the rest of the water in his face. She didn't say anything else. She just continued to stare at him.

Finally, he said, "I'm not absolutely certain, but I believe the other prisoners are some of my friends, some of the same students who were in your class."

"Why? Why do you think that?"

"When they were interrogating me, they kept referring to things these men were saying or had said about me. Things that implied I was a dangerous enemy of China, things that I could be put to death for. And they tried to get me to implicate certain men, certain friends of mine and to implicate you, too, Maddy, in exactly what I am not sure. Anything I guess."

"When were you going to tell me this? Don't you think I had the right to know if they were looking for evidence to use against me, even if it was trumped up?" Maddy could look fierce when she wanted to. She had never looked more so.

"I never said anything that would implicate you in any way, Maddy. I swear."

Maddy believed him but didn't let up until he had told her what the agents had asked him about and the names of the other men the Chinese had been asking about and suggesting implications from. She knew all of the names he gave her, all were former students.

"Where do you think they're holding these men?" Maddy asked.

"I am not sure. If they are in a container, it will be on the deck level or maybe one row up. Otherwise, it is too hard to go in and out. From comments I heard Wang make I think they may be somewhere below decks."

"Comments? Like what"

"Once when I think he thought I was unconscious and unable to answer or hear, he directed two of his men to 'go down' and check what I had said against the other prisoners. 'Go down' is not much to go on but it is the best I have."

Maddy thought about his answer and then helped him to his feet. "Come over here by the door and take a look at this ship's map. Let's see if we can identify anywhere these other men might be held."

"Okay, but why does it matter?"

"Because you're too beat up to be much help and if I'm going to get out of this, I'm going to need some help."

"Maddy, I am so sorry to have gotten you involved in all of this. It is not your fight; it is our fight. Please do not do anything to get yourself killed."

Maddy snorted. "Who is 'our', whose fight is this?"

Li Wei shook his head but did not answer. There were still things he was not telling her.

Li Wei struggled to his feet and Maddy helped him toward the door. Just inside the door was a map of all decks of the ship. Together they looked over each deck. They ruled out the deck where the crew's bunks were. Interrogation done the Chinese way was too loud and they both felt the crew wasn't a full partner in the events occurring onboard. There were two small rooms near the engine that could be possibilities and there were several rooms near the galley that looked big enough and remote enough, at least when the crew wasn't in the galley.

Li Wei stumbled back to his cot and sat back down. Maddy got him a fresh glass of water.

"One more thing, Li Wei. Who is the new man? The man who moved us here and locked Wang away?"

"He is called Captain Hu, the captain of this ship, but that may not be his real name. He clearly has dominion over the state security agents so I suspect Hu is just a cover. I overheard some of the men call him smart mouth behind his back."

"Smart mouth?"

Li Wei nodded.

"Because of that scar or defect that makes him always look like he is smiling."

Li Wei shrugged. "I do not know."

Maddy gave that all some thought. Captain Hu, it is then. She returned to the map and committed to memory the location of the armory and the lifeboats. She studied how to get access to the bridge and how to block it. Then she looked over the entire map again looking for a place where she could hide. She knew that could only work for a short time, in port somewhere or if help was on the way. She still didn't have a plan but she had a few things to work with.

"One more thing, Li Wei."

He looked at her but did not speak.

"You and I must speak to each other only in English. Many of these men only speak Chinese, but let's not remind them that I can understand Chinese. Maybe I can learn something if they forget."

CHAPTER

24

Naval Force Maria NAS Naval Base
Guam
March 16, 2033
6:00 a.m.

Ten naval vessels stationed at Guam steamed into the Philippine Sea. Together they were what used to be called a Surface Action Group. In no time, the three frigates led the way out of Apra Harbor south into the Philippine Sea. Next came the destroyers, then the submarine hunter and the fuel ship, then the South Carolina II, a cruiser, and finally the battleship Ohio deuce as she was known. Sending the smaller ships first allowed the navy to project out to sea more rapidly. Their orders were clear, full steam ahead to their rendezvous point with a smaller naval contingent from Palau's US base, that was putting out to sea simultaneously.

Ohio deuce and its Captain were in control of the operation. Palau was a much smaller facility than Guam. The port there was excellent, but the population and the islands themselves were much smaller. Palau had invited a US military presence in 2020, and after the typical years of Congressional wrangling, a small base was approved in 2025.

It had been completed in 2029 and allowed the US to project its presence another four hundred miles along the coast of China, the world's other superpower.

It was a perfect day for a battle and the odds favored the United States. Ten ships from Guam plus five more out of Palau against five Chinese ships, the biggest of which was a destroyer. Better yet, no Chinese submarines had been detected in the area, and better even than that was the ongoing war between Russia and China. While Russia was busying itself in Europe with threats from USEU, the successor to NATO, China had mounted a massive invasion of Siberia and captured it and its vast energy reserves in only weeks. Now Russia was struggling to take back its lands, but with little success, as China had quickly shut off the oil and gas pipelines, and mother Russia was starving, for fuel and energy, for money, even for food. Still, the Russian Pacific Fleet kept the Chinese navy busy and engaged, and no one would be coming to rescue this little escort group. No one.

The orders for the mission were posted in the bridge for anyone to see:

Your mission is to intercept the Chinese escort group and prevent them from making contact with Eternity. You are not to fire on the Chinese naval ships unless fired upon. Your superior force should be sufficient to accomplish that. Officially, you are on maneuvers, nothing more.

Find a reason to stop, board, and search Eternity, looking for two prisoners, a young Chinese man and an American woman. The woman is a national hero, Maddy Gamble. Treat her and the Chinese man with all respect and photographically document their recovery. You may fire warning shots to stop Eternity but do not fire directly on that ship unless your forces are fired upon.

Acknowledge and proceed.

God speed.

Chief of Naval Operations Roy A. Bingham

Chief of Naval Operations. That meant these orders came from the highest level. Probably even the White House was aware of what was going on or had authorized the action.

***

Onboard the Wuhan II, Captain Bi was enjoying the glorious morning at sea. He had fresh air venting onto the bridge, and even though it was warm outside, the strong breeze made the bridge cool. He looked ahead at the never-ending sea and the blue sky. This mission was easy, sail out to sea and escort a Chinese cargo ship back to the mainland. These spy captains made him laugh. They all thought they were so important, smuggling themselves into and out of countries and occasionally bringing back a captive or two. He thought it was an incredible waste of resources to send five ships out on escort duty, but he had his orders and would follow them. He knew what would happen if he did not. He knew of many mighty and powerful Chinese who simply disappeared when they did not do as told. Bo Xilai was but one example. He had died in prison after having once stood near the pinnacles of power. His death had not been reported for over two years. Such was the control the Communists had. Even Xi Jinping himself had disappeared. Perhaps if he had had a son, he could have passed on the Chairmanship, but instead, the young lions, the ying pao, around him had waited, and when the time was right, they had pounced. Many said Xi's acceptance of a third term and his attempts to control everything had been the beginning of his downfall

Now the leadership of the party was said to be more progressive. Bi knew they were more warlike, and this concerned him deeply. They were younger, which he liked, but they were even more ruthless and intent on stamping out anyone displaying any sign of disobedience. Yes, sir, he would follow his orders even when he knew it was a waste of resources. He just hoped he wouldn't be sent into an entirely hopeless position someday, as had happened to some of his friends in the War with Russia. They were sacrificed simply to buy time. He worried that the country's leaders now placed their own glory and China's destiny above reason and that they would lead the country into an untenable posture.

Captain Bi liked his ship, the Wuhan II, and felt lucky to have her. She was one of the newer destroyers in the navy, commissioned in 2029 when the original Wuhan was decommissioned. She was a Luyang class II destroyer, fast and well equipped electronically. Her weapons were adequate for a destroyer, and she had given up a little armor plating to shed weight and improve speed and maneuverability. She was a good ship, and he knew he was a good match for her. He smiled to himself. The mission might be wasteful, but he was at sea.

The Captain's radar man called out to him. "Captain, I think you should see this." His ship had very sophisticated radar equipment and a room just for tracking the surrounding sea and sky and a display station here on the bridge so that he stayed informed without going below decks.

His radar man pointed to several blips traveling in formation and coming from the area of the US naval base in Guam. "See those ships, Captain? They are the US Navy, and there are many of them. I count ten. Their course will intersect ours. And also here, five more US Navy vessels converging on us from the other direction."

Captain Bi looked intently at the screen with real interest. "We are still hundreds of miles apart. Just keep your eye on them and keep me informed. It is probably nothing to concern us. Where is *Eternity*?"

"Here, Captain, just about to clear the Solomon Islands. Then she will turn directly toward us, and we will cover the distance between us more quickly. Still, it is a day and a half or so."

The Captain nodded, took one more look at the blips, and went back to gazing across the sea.

***

Amy answered my phone when Sara called. She immediately put it on the speaker.

"I must say, Jack, you certainly have connections."

I explained, "Mitch and I just happened to go to law school together."

Amy interrupted, "And Mitch happens to be the Whitehouse Chief of Staff. Can you imagine?"

We all laughed despite the situation.

"We haven't heard anything back, Sara. Have you?"

"Yes. Quite a lot. My friend from the New Zealand navy called me early this morning. He reports that a large number of US warships set out from Guam first thing this morning, heading straight at Palau, and at the same moment, a smaller but still potent number of warships left Palau heading for Guam. That will put those two US battle groups directly between *Eternity* and the Chinese naval escort. Congratulations, Jack. I don't know how you did it, but you did. And I hope you don't mind, but I took a little credit myself with my friend. Never hurts to have a little mystique."

We all laughed again. "That's great news. What do you think it means?"

"I can't say for sure, but my friend and I were discussing it. We can't believe the United States intends to fire on the Chinese Navy and start a war even though we both personally think this is the ideal time with China engaged against Russia. Maybe get rid of two birds with one stone, if you know what I mean. Rather, we think the intention is to get the Chinese Navy to back off and then maybe stop and board *Eternity*. The Chinese will howl at that, but provided we find the hostages, the Chinese will move on to other issues soon enough."

I asked, "Do you think we can do that safely? I mean, board *Eternity* and rescue Maddy?"

"Honestly, I remain worried about it. If the Chinese Navy turns back and if the US Navy turns toward *Eternity*, Maddy could be in real danger. If there are no prisoners onboard Eternity and it's stopped and searched, the Chinese will claim to have a legitimate gripe, and who knows what they will do in retaliation. I know they would prefer that scenario, but it may not be that big of an issue. They pretty much do what they want and don't seem to limit themselves to the truth."

"Anything we can do?" I asked. The thought of Maddy being killed and thrown overboard or, even worse, simply thrown overboard to drown made me sick to my stomach.

Sara said, "I'm still working on the gang in Wellington to see if they'll send helicopters to watch *Eternity*. Besides politics, there are some practical problems. For instance, how long can a chopper stay in the air before needing to refuel, and where would it refuel? What could happen to Maddy when it went to refuel, or could we manage more than one helicopter, so one was always there? Would the presence of the helicopters only seal Maddy's fate in a bad way? Sorry, Jack. You can see there are any number of complications. But the biggest one is the lawyer's question.

"The lawyer's question, like you taught me as far as dealing with your children. When they ask to do something, ask 'and then what?' and keep asking it until they run out of answers, and in that way, you may know if it's a good idea. So here, suppose we carefully watch Eternity by helicopter, then what do we do? No one has a perfect answer to that, so maybe the helicopters are a flawed idea. But I'm still pushing the option, and I think perhaps the United States has reached out to New Zealand as well. So, we have to wait and see."

"I do understand. And I had forgotten telling you that. Good to know you were paying attention."

"Always. Always. If there's nothing else, we will stay tuned and Kia ora for now."

Amy said, "Goodbye, Sara," so I said, "Goodbye, and thanks." I thought about saying Kia ora instead, but decided it seemed phony coming from me.

***

Back in his quarters, Captain Bi radioed his home naval base in Ningbo.

"This is the Wuhan II. Please get me Admiral Fong at once."

"The Admiral, sir. He's in a critical meeting right now."

"Tell him it is an emergency."

"Captain Bi, he is directing a battle against the Russians."

"Tell him he may also be directing a battle against the Americans unless we talk."

"Yes, sir. I'll get a message to him. We'll radio you back."

Bi paced his small quarters. He wanted to come up with a plan and not just ask for help or advice. He wanted to appear decisive and courageous. He paced some more. Fifteen minutes passed, and his escort group chugged ever closer to danger.

The radio crackled. "Captain Bi, I have Admiral Fong."

"Thank you, Admiral. So sorry to interrupt you. I know how..."

"Yes, yes, Captain, get on with it. When I found out you were calling, I looked at your group on radar, and I see the two US navy groups approaching. What do you make of it?"

"Sir, I can't be entirely positive, but I think they mean to intercept us and prevent our escorting Eternity home."

"Umm, hum. And how much time do you have?"

"At current speeds, we will all be at the same point about midnight tonight."

"What are your options, Captain?"

Captain Bi had been preparing for this. "I see three." Then he said them in order of bravery required to try to make an impression. "First, we continue our course and fight our way through if necessary and complete our mission."

The Admiral said, "You want your little escort group to do battle against fifteen US warships, including a battleship and two cruisers? I appreciate your bravado, but we have no ships or sailors we want to sacrifice right now, and we have no current desire to start a war with the United States. I am a career Navy man, not a ying pao. What are your other options?"

Bi was well pleased with Admiral Fong. Like Fong, he had gone into the military as a career and as a way to provide for his family. Both were smart and hard-working and party members but were not party higher-ups. Both hoped to help navigate China through this period where the hawks of China, the ying pao, made all of the decisions. He said, "With all due respect, sir, we could abandon the mission and let Eternity fend for herself or continue on and try to confirm if the US Navy is focused on us or this is some sort of maneuver that happened to come at the wrong time for us."

"There are no such coincidences, Captain; but how would you attempt to confirm it?"

"Sir, by altering course and or speed and seeing what the reaction of the Americans is."

There was a pause. "Very well, Captain, try altering course and speed and have Eternity do likewise. I see no harm in that. I will speak with Beijing and do my best to reason with them and be back in touch. Perhaps the Americans don't realize it, but shi is on their side if they even know what shi is. If your mission erupts into battle, China could find herself encircled by warring enemies. You are not to engage the Americans, do you understand? And let's hope they do not realize that now is their time to strike."

"Yes, sir, but what if they fire on us?"

The Admiral had disconnected.

He radioed Eternity.

"Captain Hu, I am Captain Bi of the Wuhan II, the lead ship in your escort group. We have a little situation here, and I want you to reduce speed by one half and keep it there until you hear back from me. You may have to reverse direction."

There was a long silence. "Yes, Captain Bi, we will reduce speed. May I ask what the little situation is?"

"You may. We have fifteen US warships converging on our position. I am not yet certain of their intentions, but I want you nowhere near the US ships. There are too many of them for us to protect you."

"Yes, sir. Hu over and out."

The Chinese naval escorts increased speed and the US naval ships did likewise. The Chinese reduced speed and the Americans again matched their speed.

CHAPTER

25

Onboard Eternity
The South Pacific Ocean
March 16, 2033
4:00 p.m.

Maddy heard the lock to sickbay turn. Chang entered the sickbay for the third time today, bringing tea and some small rice cakes. Maddy had still not finished her lunch, but Li Wei had devoured his. He was still eating like he had never eaten before, and he knew this could all be taken away again. Li Wei encouraged Maddy to build her strength as well. Afterward, he complained his belly hurt, so he drank his water and part of Maddy's to settle his stomach. There was a small toilet area in sickbay, and with Maddy's help, Li Wei had gotten up twice to use it. She had heard him be sick, but she hadn't said anything.

Chang brought medical supplies. He looked in the bathroom and at their two plates. He bowed. "My mistake, honorable sir; I gave you too much food. I thought you must be hungry. Now I know you must go slowly. I will go back to smaller meals like the last two days. Sorry."

Li Wei looked up. "Now we both know." He bowed slightly.

"Now we all know," Maddy said, breaking her own rule about only speaking English, and they all shared a laugh.

Chang said, "I have bandages and medical supplies already here, and I brought some clean clothes." He turned to Maddy and bowed his head again. "I hope these will be suitable." He put a small stack of clothes on her cot. On top of the clothing was a pair of boots. The clothes looked to be crew uniforms, clean and sharply folded. Maddy put her hand on Chang's shoulder. "Thank you." She took up the used clothing.

The sickbay itself was small. It had two stainless steel cots with thin mattresses on top and medical supplies stored on a shelf under the beds. The cots were secured to the floor and had straps that would keep someone in the cot. There was a small desk at the back of the sickbay with shelves and cabinets lining the rear wall. The tiny restroom with a sink and a toilet, closed off by a curtain, was near the door. There was no shower, but there was a small mirror. Maddy had already cleaned herself up a bit, washing her face, combing her hair with her hands, washing her feet. She had been barefoot since her abduction. She had many small cuts and bruises.

She was bruised across the right side of her face and along the inside of her right arm. Her ribs hurt on her right side. She had already searched the sickbay for a weapon while she and Li Wei were alone. She had hidden a small scalpel under her mattress. It wasn't the best hiding spot, but her choices were few. Maddy eased over to her cot while Chang was attending to Li Wei. Slowly she lifted the corner of her mattress. *Should I pull the scalpel and use it to kill this Chang and then try to escape? No, he's the only one on this ship who has been kind. And besides, where would we go? We would be recaptured and put back in the container in no time. I need a better plan.* She eased the mattress back down. Chang turned and looked at her; he glanced at the bed. He said, "I have soap," and pointed to a bar of soap on top of the medical supplies.

"You use it first, for Li Wei," Maddy said, sitting on her cot and sipping her tea and nibbling on her rice cake. He was so kind, so careful. Chang cut away Li Wei's pants' remnants, leaving him in his underwear and tattered shirt. Li Wei looked at Maddy and covered his eyes. Maddy looked away but turned quickly back when Li Wei cried out. Whenever she looked at Li Wei, Maddy felt like she was just fine comparatively speaking. He needed attention first. She needed him to be as fit as possible and she knew she would need his help to get the other prisoners to help her.

Li Wei's wounds were awful, open sores and burned flesh in several spots on each leg. The bowl with water that Chang was using was already dark red, a mixture of blood, burnt skin, and dirt.

"Can we divide the soap, Chang? I will go ahead and clean up and put-on fresh clothes." She motioned toward the restroom. "And when you need fresh water, pass the water bowl around the curtain. I will empty and refill it."

Chang cut the soap in two with a knife. Both halves had some blood on them. He took a cloth from the pile of medical supplies, wiped one half off, and handed it to Maddy. He smiled; his whole face smiled. Maddy returned the smile.

She took the soap and the clean clothes and boots and stepped into the toilet area; she took the water bowl from Chang, emptied it, and then filled it with fresh water. She handed it back and closed the curtain.

She pulled off her ragged slacks and tattered shirt and placed them on the floor. The filthy dirty pants were frayed along the bottom and had a small tear near the right hip. The blouse had fared worse. Because it was light blue and not black like the slacks, it showed every dirty streak, every grease mark, and because it was more delicate than the pants, it had a rip in one sleeve from the wrist to the elbow, a tear in the back. She neatly folded both before putting them on the floor. Her underwear and bra were dirty too, not as bad, and they would have to do. She would rinse them, then wring them out and put them back on damp. Using the small mirror, Maddy looked over as much of her body as she could. Her black and blue ribs hurt, she had three short cuts on her right arm, her feet had multiple cuts, her left thigh had the largest slice, and the area around it was bruising. She couldn't recall where she had gotten that.

She undressed completely and began dipping the soap under the water and cleaning a small part of her body, and then repeating the process on another part. Every few minutes, the bowl would appear around the edge of the curtain along with a "Fresh water, please," and she would interrupt her bathing to freshen the water for Li Wei and Chang. She knew that each time that happened the two men could catch a glimpse of her. She kept her back toward them the best she could.

In this fashion, over the next hour, Maddy got herself cleaned up and dressed. The crew uniform was worn but clean and fit her reasonably well. The shirt had marks from removed stitching where someone's name had once been. Maddy tried to read the name from the stitch holes but could not. She sat on the toilet to pull on the boots. Her feet were tender. She would need socks. She took the boots back off and stepped around the curtain in her bare feet.

Chang had nearly finished cleaning Li Wei's wounds. He had wrapped most of them in clean gauze. Li Wei was no longer crying out; he was lying back groggy. Li Wei lifted his head briefly to look at Maddy, and then it fell back without his making any comment. Chang handed a pill vial up to Maddy and pointed to Li Wei. He held up two fingers, and Maddy understood Li Wei had taken two pain pills. She nodded and patted Chang's shoulder.

When Chang finished with Li Wei, he turned to Maddy and said, "And now you?" She lifted her feet. "They hurt. Do you have any socks?"

Chang looked carefully over her feet and then went to a cabinet in the back and retrieved an ointment. From a drawer, he pulled a pair of blue socks. After applying the lotion and gently massaging it into her wounded feet, he tenderly slipped the blue socks on Maddy. The socks had grip strips on the bottom so she would not need to wear the boots. Li Wei was snoring softly. Chang asked if Maddy needed anything else. "Aspirin?" she asked. Chang nodded, found another vial in the back by the desk, and showed it to Maddy. She nodded. He pointed to Li Wei and then her and raised his eyebrows. Maddy understood. She shook her head no; she didn't want what Li Wei had. She pointed to the aspirin.

Chang was gathering his things to go. He collected Maddy's neatly folded clothing and Li Wei's as well. He turned to Maddy and said, "My name is Chang." He pointed to his name, stitched on his chest, and gave a slight bow.

Maddy bowed back. "Maddy, Maddy Gamble." She offered him her hand, and he shook it. She wondered if that was all the English he knew.

"You are American?" he asked.

Maddy thought about what she should say and just said, "Yes."

"Very pretty." This time he spoke in Chinese.

Maddy thought, *uh oh,* and her face must have conveyed her thought.

Chang seemed momentarily embarrassed. He said, "Very pretty like my wife and my daughters." He bowed again. "Do you have children, Maddy Gamble?"

Again, Maddy struggled with what she should say and decided on the truth. She spoke in Chinese.

"Yes, I have two children; a boy six and a five-year-old girl and a wonderful husband. Tell me about your daughters, Chang. How old are they?"

"Four and seven." Chang smiled as he thought of his two young daughters.

"Chang, my children and husband have no idea where I am or what has happened."

Maddy watched thoughts and emotions war across Chang. He shook his head, saddened but then he stood and said, "I am sorry, Miss Maddy Gamble. I will be back later. If you need anything or he does, ask for Chang."

"Chang, can I ask you something?"

"Yes, you can ask me anything."

"Where are we heading?"

Chang looked down. He knew what this answer would mean for Maddy and Li Wei. He said, "Miss Maddy, we are headed to China. I am so sorry."

Maddy breathed out. "I was afraid of that."

Chang added, "But the ship slowed down a couple of hours ago by quite a bit. It is almost stopped. Maybe there has been a change. I hope so. You are the only prisoner on this ship who is not Chinese, perhaps you will be treated more kindly."

Maddy wondered if Chang really had any idea what would likely happen to her. She sucked in her breath. These were her worst fears. She said, "Are your daughters expecting you back in China?"

Chang nodded.

"Then some good comes from this."

Chang put Maddy's clothing neatly into a bag and placed Li Wei's ruined clothing in a different bag. He never commented or seemed surprised that they could converse in Chinese. He bowed as he left. Maddy heard him lock the door.

CHAPTER

26

Onboard the Wuhan II
March 16, 2033
10:00 p.m.

"Yes, Admiral Fong. I am certain the Americans are at sea because of my escort group. When I slowed, they slowed, and then when I sped up, they sped up to maintain their control of the point where all three groups will meet."

"When will that be, Captain Bi?"

"In approximately three hours, sir."

"Captain Bi, I want you and your group to stop and remain where you are. Beijing wants to see what the Americans will do. If they turn toward you and attack you, they will conclude that America wants to start a war right now while our forces are divided. That is personally what I think and what I would do if I were the Americans. And if they do, we are prepared to launch missile and air attacks then but not before."

"I understand, sir, and I do not mean to be impudent but remember the American's anti-missile capabilities and their aircraft on

Guam. They can see our planes coming and still be airborne and over my ships before our planes arrive."

"I understand your concerns, Captain, and I relayed those same arguments to Beijing. These are their orders."

"And what if the Americans do not attack us?"

"If they hold their position and do not attack, then your orders are to alter course and sail south of Palau. There you will attempt to connect with *Eternity* in some other location, somewhere the Americans don't have quite so much naval power. And we will bring the fight another day after we have defeated the Russians."

"I see, sir. We will hold position and watch the Americans. What do I tell *Eternity*?"

"Hu is a pompous fool. Wang's overreaching has put us in this position. My navy is trying to cover for one spook. Tell him his orders from me are to stay put. He is not to come one inch closer to China until he hears from me directly. He has his orders from Deputy Minister Chen, but they will not force another war on us before we are ready. I hate those spies; they think they are superior to the rest of us."

Captain Bi agreed but kept his thoughts to himself. His superior's rant could come in handy someday, and he didn't want to squander the opportunity by joining in. "Yes, sir. I will tell *Eternity* just that, sir."

And they both signed off.

"Hu? Captain Bi here. Your orders from Admiral Fong are to stop where you are. I quote the Admiral, 'You are not to come one inch closer to China.' Do you understand, Hu?"

"What is going on there?" Hu asked.

"I am not authorized to discuss anything with you, Captain Hu, only to relay the orders. Do you understand your orders?"

"Yes, understood. Over and out."

Captain Bi relayed the orders to his group to stop all engines and hold their current position.

***

Captain James was on the bridge of the *Ohio II*. He was close to a battle. He could smell it. His radar crewman came to him and said, "Sir, the Chinese have stopped."

Captain James looked up bewildered. "Stopped?" he asked. "Where?"

"About seventy-five miles from the course intersection point and about one hundred six miles from us."

James slammed his fist onto the chart table to his left. "Damn. They are chickening out. Damn. Damn. Damn. Damn."

He turned to the radar man. "All stop. Hold our positions here and relay the order to the *Lake Erie*. They are to hold their positions, too." James could think of only the Chinese naval ships just a short way out of the reach of the guns of his battleship.

CHAPTER

27

The Trinity Wharf Hotel
Tauranga, New Zealand
March 17, 2033
1:00 a.m.

Some nights and days are longer than others. This day was shaping up to be the longest day of my life. Amy and I sat near a computer screen on a computer lent to us by the Tauranga Police. We watched three groups of blips and one single blip out in the ocean, in the Philippine Sea. None of the blips were moving; they continued to blink in the same spot. And that is precisely what we wanted to happen; to continue happening, nothing. I stared at the screen, brushing my hair back repeatedly.

We had been watching the blips for hours now, ever since I had received the call from Mitchell Drummond. He hadn't said too much but alerted us to watch the radar and the satellite images. One thing he said was surprising. He said something like this was my lucky day because the United States was looking for an excuse to confront China at sea. Amy and I were still talking about that.

"It certainly could be politics, but a dangerous way to get votes," I said.

Amy replied, "I don't know. I see overwhelming US power there. I think the Chinese have no choice but to back down."

"What about saving face?"

"You never know how they will portray it except it will be from the Communist Party's perspective. Maybe something like the warmongering United States tried to lure China into an armed conflict, but China outfoxed them and deftly sidestepped the confrontation."

"Really? That's absurd."

"You wait and see. I hope I'm right about the Chinese backing down."

"What about Maddy? What about *Eternity*?"

"That is another matter altogether. I expect *Eternity* to avoid the US Navy, but I don't know if it will turn around or if the US Navy heads back to port; maybe they will plow ahead to China. I hope not, but that's a real possibility."

I nodded my head. I had been thinking about the same things.

My cell phone rang. I was getting used to it ringing at all hours of day and night. It was Sara calling.

"Hello, Sara. What do you have for us?"

"That's a great greeting. I have news and good news. Which do you want first?"

"It's the middle of the night. Start with the bad news and finish with the good news."

"Okay, like you, I've been watching the naval standoff in the Philippine Sea. Our advisers think China was trying to discern the United States' intentions. And whoever had the US ships remain stationary was brilliant. No aggressive moves and not backing down either. Knowing of your call to the White House, I suspect this strategy came from the highest levels. And our advisers say there is no way the Chinese Escort Group can engage the Americans in a battle. It would be suicide, and the Chinese need their ships and sailors. Reports are that the Russians are winning the naval battle even though they are losing on the ground."

"What do your advisers expect to happen next?"

"They expect the Chinese to turn and go a different direction, although no one is sure when. The Chinese can be very patient."

"What about *Eternity*?"

"Again, this is just speculation, but the Chinese are keeping *Eternity* well back from the action. That could mean Maddy and Li Wei are still with us, and the Chinese don't want them discovered. And then again, there could be things we don't know. *Eternity* could be hauling drugs or other contraband and want to avoid contact with the US Navy for that reason. From what our advisers are saying, the US has enough evidence to stop, board, and search *Eternity* based upon the affidavit given by Captain Zhao. If they stop trying to avoid the US ships, then I fear for Maddy and Li Wei's lives."

I took a deep breath. "Okay. I understand what you're saying. It's just hard to be relieved."

"Yes, I can't blame you there. That's what I called the news, even though it's mostly speculation. I know you're watching the ships' positions like we are, so there's no need to comment on that. But like I said, I do have some good news."

"We're all ears," said Amy.

"Wellington has decided to get off its ass and help out or at least be ready. They have three Seasprite maritime helicopters and a contingent of New Zealand Special Forces en route to the Solomon Islands. They can observe *Eternity* or even the taking of that ship. They are just on standby, but it's good to have that option."

"Why the Solomon Islands?" I asked.

"It's the closet friendly airstrip. And the Solomon Islands are friendlier to the United States than they are to New Zealand. Some historical grievance from a few years ago, I guess. But Jack, you should know the United States has been instrumental in getting clearance to base out of the Solomon Islands, and although no one will admit it, I strongly suspect the United States twisted arms to get New

Zealand to act at all. And Amy, do you know who the biggest opponent to New Zealand's involvement was? Your Commander Li. You'd think since the abduction took place on his watch, he would want to help rescue the victims."

"Sometimes I don't know about that guy. There are times when I wonder about his competence. He seems to do exactly the wrong thing at times and blow any chance for a successful operation. And I've told him that to his face more than once," Amy said.

It was hard not to laugh at Amy's dramatic remonstrations. I looked to be sure Amy was finished and said, "Thanks, Sara. I'm looking at a map now, and I see that helicopters based in the Solomon Islands can get to *Eternity* faster than from anywhere else. And we all know that could make all the difference. Anything else?"

"No, that's it. Now we wait. But I want you two to get some sleep. The men with me are monitoring the ships' positions constantly. If any of them move, even the slightest bit, they will alert me, and I'll call you right away. So, don't feel like you have to watch the monitor constantly. Sleep is an asset; get some."

She hung up, and we decided she was right. There was only one king-size bed in the room, so Amy crawled under the blankets, and I lay on top of the blankets on the other side of the bed. Just in case, we left the computer on, tuned to the radar blips, and set it up so we could quickly convert it to satellite view.

CHAPTER

28

Philippine Sea
March 17, 2033
6:30 a.m.

Captain Bi was waiting by his radio. "Captain Bi. Good morning to you. We have carefully observed the Americans, and we do not think they will let you pass. We do not wish to lose your ships and your men. Your orders are to turn slowly, do not suggest fear or panic, and then make good speed toward the Diaoyudao Islands. I suggest thirty or thirty-two knots."

"Yes, Admiral. I understand my orders." Bi was relieved. He knew his force was no match for the Americans.

"Captain Bi, after you are underway, alert your men that they will be entering a growing naval battle with the Russians near these islands. The battle is very fluid and going rather badly. We have lost several ships. When you get closer, I will have more specific instructions, but your force will be attacking the Russians from a new direction."

Bi remembered that old expression 'out of the frying pan and into the fire' he had learned when studying at CalTech. "Yes, sir. My men will be ready." Before Bi signed off, he asked, "What about *Eternity*, sir?"

The Admiral spit out his answer, "If it were up to me, I'd have you tell that spy ship to go to hell. They have caused China great trouble and kept you and your men from a battle where we could use you. I am so tired of state security thinking they are the most important people and issues."

Bi waited.

More calmly, the Admiral said, "Tell *Eternity* what they do is up to them. We cannot provide an escort any longer. All of our forces are committed. I would suggest that if the Americans stay near their current positions, *Eternity* goes back where it came from, but that is up to them. I wash my hands of it."

"Yes, sir."

In the process of getting his ships turned slowly in the other direction including trying to make it look like a Chinese decision and not one forced by the US Navy, Captain Bi forgot about *Eternity*. His escort group was forty nautical miles from where they had held their position all night and moving quickly toward China when Captain Hu radioed him.

"Captain Bi, *Eternity* here. What is going on?"

"Ah, Captain Hu. We are called back to battle with the Russians and can no longer assist you."

"Were you going to let me know? We have been holding for quite a long time."

"I was getting ready to radio you. You beat me to it."

"What are we to do now?"

"I have no orders for you, Captain Hu, only some suggestions from my Admiral."

"And what are those?"

"He said to wait and see what the Americans do and decide from there. And it looks to me like the smaller US force is turning toward you even as the larger force heads back to its base."

"Yes, I see that, too. Plus, we have limited fuel after holding our position all night. I do not think we have enough fuel to reach China, especially if we encounter any heavy seas. We were counting on refueling from your fuel ship."

"That will not be possible now, Hu. I suggest you make port in the Solomon Islands."

"Aren't the Solomon Islands a US protectorate?"

"Perhaps. I don't know the official status, but the Solomons are very friendly with the United States."

"Perhaps I should jettison my prisoners? Do you think that would help our situation?"

"I cannot give you advice there, Hu. This mission of yours is a state security mission. What are your current orders?"

"Deputy Minister Chen said the woman was not to be harmed."

"A Deputy Minister? Well then, unless you get new orders from Deputy Minister Chen, I must suggest you follow your orders."

"But I don't feel safe going to the Solomon Islands."

"Can *Eternity* reach Vanuatu?"

"Yes. Good idea. That is our filed itinerary anyway."

"Then Captain Hu, I suggest you turn for there and quickly. It is a sovereign nation and pretends to be neutral as between China and the United States."

"How will I explain my delayed arrival?"

Bi was losing his patience. Must he explain everything to this child?

"Here is what I would say, Hu. Then I am going to go. If anyone asks, tell them *Eternity* was blown way off course by a big storm and that it then experienced engine problems while you were at sea, which you eventually fixed. You may want to pay for someone there to look over and perform maintenance on your engines to bolster your story, but you can figure that out. Over and out, Hu. I really must go."

Hu gave the order for *Eternity* to make a course for Port Vila, Vanuatu.

CHAPTER

29

Trinity Wharf Hotel
Tauranga, New Zealand
March 17, 2033
11:00 a.m.

Amy hugged me, and I hugged her back. Sara hoorayed over the phone, and the Tauranga lieutenant danced a little jig. Blocked by the US Navy, *Eternity* was turning away from China. Two of the three helicopters New Zealand had sent to the Solomon Islands were in the air but staying out of visual range of *Eternity*. They could be there in minutes. Still, they could kill Maddy in seconds if *Eternity* was alerted to an attack.

I knew an attack was technically too strong of a word. But what else did you call forced boarding by armed Special Forces troops?

The US Navy had effectively blocked *Eternity*'s way toward China, but they were still too far away to intervene. As long as they eliminated the 'flee to China' choice for *Eternity*, that would help. But how did we affect Maddy's rescue?

Sara led this discussion. She had contact with the New Zealand government and with someone in the CIA. One option had been to board *Eternity* at night by stealth from inflatable rafts or even frogmen. That was the best option when *Eternity* had been stationary. Now that was too risky for the special forces. The ship had to be quickly and wholly subdued and then searched for Maddy.

Sara said, "I think a helicopter assault is our best bet. We can put enough boots onboard to overwhelm the crew and security agents immediately. If we use two helicopters to make the assault, one fore, and one aft, we can have forty men on the deck in under two minutes, and the third chopper can hover nearby and provide covering fire if need be."

I asked, "Won't they know we're coming?"

"Yes. Especially in daylight. Even if no one is paying attention to their monitors, they will see three helicopters converging on their ship from two to several minutes before we arrive. If we come in low over the ocean, we might be able to minimize that."

"And we think Maddy is still in the shipping container described by Captain Zhao?"

"Yes. We have no reason to think any differently."

"What if she were now below decks?"

Sara thought and consulted with someone. I couldn't hear what they said. When Sara came back, she said, "That would increase the risk to Maddy. Jack?"

My attention was drawn back to the monitor where *Eternity* was now moving in the opposite direction.

My phone vibrated. It was a text from Mitch Drummond. I read it aloud. "We've given you some time. Not sure if there will be anything else we can do. Still trying. Hang in there, Jack, Rescue Maddy!" We all acknowledged we had had no chance without the US Navy. I texted back, *-Thanks, Mitch.*

I didn't hear any more and knew I wouldn't.

I asked the group, "How far away is the US Navy from *Eternity*?"

The Tauranga lieutenant looked at the screen and said, "It all depends on relative speed, but the US ships are at least a day away from

Eternity, and since both are sailing the same direction, it may stay that way. It could be more."

I asked, "Any idea where *Eternity* is headed?"

The lieutenant from the Tauranga police force said, "I have been watching that, and I think they're headed for Port Vila, Vanuatu."

I nodded. "Sara, do you still have a man in Port Vila looking at an operation there?"

"Yes. Under the circumstances, he hasn't done much yet, but he did outline a possible operation for me."

"I don't need to know the details right now, but would it be less risky for Maddy than an attempted rescue at sea?"

"Yes, it definitely could be if done stealthily. It could also go sideways."

"I'm sorry, everyone, to have so many questions." Each of them assured me they understood.

I said, "Let me ask this. Do you think Maddy is still alive?" Instinctively, my hand went to my head.

Silence. No one wanted to field that question. Finally, Sara did. "Yes. We think so. But the evidence is thin. Since *Eternity* is turning away from the US Navy, we're guessing they don't want to be boarded. That could be because of Maddy, or it could be for other reasons. And one of my naval contacts thinks they may be running low on fuel. And Jack, I don't want you to take this the wrong way or be offended, but in my field, we will act as if she's alive until we know for a certainty otherwise. If she is already dead, we can do nothing, but we will still attempt a rescue until we're sure. Does that make sense to you?"

My stomach turned on itself. "Yes, that makes sense."

"I follow your logic and like it. If a Port Vila rescue is less risky, we call back the helicopters and special forces and watch *Eternity*, and if she goes to Port Vila, we take our shot there. And if she changes course or otherwise surprises us, we board and search her at sea at that time."

I nodded, and Amy said, "We all agree."

Sara said, "Okay, then. I suggest you all get yourselves to Port Vila as soon as possible. Let me know your arrival, and I will have someone at the airport to meet you."

CHAPTER

30

Port Vila, Vanuatu
March 17, 2033
6:00 p.m.

After we left Tauranga, we were over the ocean immediately. It was beautiful in its vastness, nothing but water as far as I could see. Amy was upfront with Joe again, and Noah and I were in the far back row. No one had spoken over the headsets since takeoff, and Joe had shown me how to mute my set. After a half-hour, I did just that and closed my eyes. The drone of the plane was relaxing, steady like background noise. I blinked my eyes open and saw more water, and then I slept.

Noah reached over and nudged me awake. I couldn't hear him through my muted headset, so he pointed and mouthed, "Port Vila."

I looked ahead and to our right. A small speck of land broke the endless water, and at first, it looked like popcorn floating above it in my sleepy state. I rubbed my eyes. Small fluffy clouds were hovering over the landmass. I turned off the mute and said, "How much longer?" and pointed ahead.

Joe said, "Deplane in about thirty minutes."

Amy said, "Welcome back to the living. Glad to see you get a little rest."

"How about you two? Sleep any?" I said, meaning Noah and Amy.

"A little," said Noah.

"None for me," said Amy.

"Same here," said Joe, and we all laughed.

"Hey, take a look down below. That's Tanna Island, a part of Vanuatu. And there in the middle of the southern part is one big banyan tree. Can you see it?"

"Wow."

"That thing is huge."

"I see it. Is that one tree?"

"Yes, it's one banyan tree with multiple trunks and roots. Some people say it's the largest in the world. Others dispute that. Who knows? This one even has a name, Kaluas. It's hundreds of years old, and the astronauts said they could see it from space."

"Really?" I was thinking about all the things Kaluas must have witnessed over the centuries. How many storms or droughts, how many people, how many animals had lived in it? How much violence? Maybe none here. How much love? We flew over more ocean, and I could see another island ahead.

Joe said, "We will be landing at Bauerfield Airport in Port Vila. Port Vila is the capital and biggest city in Vanuatu. But biggest is a relative term. Port Vila has about forty-eight thousand residents making up about fifteen percent of the population of the entire country." I did the math in my head; the whole country had only about three hundred twenty-five thousand people. Looking down, I could see a compact town squeezed mainly between a bay and a lake or at least a body of water surrounded by land.

Joe continued, "Vanuatu consists of eighty different islands, most of them inhabited to some extent, but you could certainly know all of your neighbors on some of them. You're looking at the Coral Sea, a part of the Pacific Ocean. Vanuatu is an impoverished country; most people fish or farm. Vanuatu imports pretty much all of its energy, oil from Russia and Venezuela, and politics here can be a little unpredictable. Vanuatu used to be governed jointly by the British and the French but then got its independence. It seems like there's always a no-confidence vote against their president. Sometimes the president is voted out, and sometimes he or she survives. Some people say the Russians stir this up to keep the government off-balance. Me? I think it's just the poverty."

From here, poverty posed as a beautiful tropical island. I knew it was part of Oceania, made up of many, many islands and inhabited by diverse people. I marveled at Britain and France getting along well enough to govern here jointly. I decided that fact didn't speak well for the value of the islands.

Noah laughed and said, "Thank you, Mr. Tour Director."

Joe bowed and smiled.

Amy took over, "I've asked Joe to fly over the harbor, nothing quite like a bird's eye view. Joe, can you mute now?" Joe did as she asked. "Keep your eyes and ears open, and I'll tell you what we're observing. See that big concrete structure with the big containership just pulling away?"

"Yes," Noah and I both said.

"That's where *Eternity* will be docked beginning tomorrow morning." No one responded, so Amy continued, "And see that island just out from the dock? That's Iririki Island, and we'll be staying there at the Iririki Island Resort and Spa."

"Spa?" Noah said.

"Don't get your hopes up, big boy; you won't have much time to enjoy it," Amy said, "Adam from SIS has a penthouse booked there and a small raft."

"Penthouse?" Noah asked.

Amy nodded her head. "Yes, it has three floors; we all get our privacy, except for you and Adam. I hope he's your type. After dark tomorrow, we'll go by raft to *Eternity* and sneak aboard. The raft has an electric motor, and those things make almost no sound. We'll scout the area earlier in the day tomorrow and finalize our plans, but I wanted you to have a chance to see things from the air."

"Thanks, Amy," I said. The island was spectacularly close to the docking area. We might not have the backup we had in Tauranga, but we should have the element of surprise on our side. *I'm coming, Maddy, and I will save you. I swear I will.*

Joe reached up to his headset, then said, "Sorry to interrupt, but *we've been cleared for landing.*"

As the propeller was winding down, Adam, an SIS agent we knew from Tauranga, drove out near the plane to pick us up. We had taxied to an area in front of a small building, the terminal, I guess. There was no one visible except for two men in uniforms, lounging against the building. Noah started to unload the gear when Adam put a hand on his arm. "Let's get those later. I may have all the gear we'll need already in the bungalow, and the VPMW has been acting a little weird. Watching me like a hawk since I got to the airport, like they knew you were coming."

"VPMW?" I asked.

"Vanuatu Police Maritime Wing. The airport is not usually their bailiwick. I don't know if I did something to tip them off, but we best be low key if they decide to search the vehicle. Just bring personal belongings, and you two can each bring a sidearm since you're police officers."

"Are New Zealand and Vanuatu on friendly terms?" I asked.

Amy answered, "Yes, but they can be a little provincial at times. Yes, provincial is the right word. And I am guessing Lieutenant Palmer was not able to disable the cameras in Tauranga."

We loaded three small suitcases and ourselves and drove toward the gate to Ring Road. An officer held up his hand to stop us. Adam rolled down his window as three other officers came out of a small office and walked alongside our vehicle. When I looked back the two men near the terminal were now standing and watching us.

He said, "Can you tell me your business here, sir?"

"Yes," Adam said. "Holiday. We have a bungalow at the Iririki Island resort."

The officer looked into the vehicle; one woman and three men on holiday didn't look quite right. "Mind if we look in the back, sir?"

We all knew Adam had no choice. I was glad he was here and glad the weapons bags were not. "No problem, officer," he said and started to get out of the car. The officer put his hand against Adam's door. "You stay put; just open the trunk, please." Adam popped the trunk. The first officer stood by Adam's door, and another officer stood near the car's passenger side. We couldn't see what the two officers at the trunk were doing with the trunk lid up. After just a few minutes, they closed the trunk lid, and the officer beside Adam said, "Thank you, we hope you have a nice visit and appreciate your cooperation. We don't want any trouble here." They never searched us individually or asked for identification. I thought that was peculiar.

Even though I was seated behind Adam, I could tell he was smiling by how his ears moved up the side of his head. "No, sir, no trouble here."

As we pulled out onto Ring Road and turned left, he said, "I wonder what all of that is about; it's not usually like that here." Amy turned around and looked back at Noah. If they knew something, they weren't saying.

I decided to lighten things up. "Is this called Ring Road because it rings the city?"

Adam shook his head. "No, it rings this entire island, even at that it's something like one hundred twenty kilometers in total, takes about three hours to make the complete loop."

I did the math in my head, about seventy-two miles. Not much at all. Hard to disappear in a space that small. Not so good when we were about to assault a colossal ship, and the local police seemed suspicious. Then I noticed cameras on about every other light pole. They looked like the same cameras in Nelson and Tauranga.

"Here we go again," I said, pointing to the cameras. "Dragon's Eye." Noah and Amy both looked out, and then back at me.

It wasn't long before we pulled up at the Iririki Lodge. We unloaded our bags, and I started for the front door of the hotel.

"No, not here, this is where we catch the ferry to our resort. Come this way," Amy said. I had to wonder if she felt like she was my mother sometimes.

"Is this still Ring Road?" I always liked to have my bearings.

"No. You may have missed it, but we angled off of Ring Road back just a little bit, onto Lini Highway. This road is Kumul Highway now."

We walked around to the back of the lodge, where there was a boat dock. I looked around as the water taxi came across the narrow strip of water. Behind it, I could see an island and what I guessed was our resort. Down this shore, I could see what I took to be the town area, Port Vila, I thought. The water taxi unloaded, and we were invited to board.

"No charge for guests of Iririki Island Resort," the boat driver said as he walked up the dock to shore. Obviously, we weren't leaving anytime soon. Island time must exist everywhere there is an island.

When we were finally underway, Adam acted as our tour director, describing the town area and its bars and restaurants and then casually describing the dock area that we could see looking across Iririki Island. He was subtle; no one overhearing his words would have picked up on their importance. I heard very little of what he said. I sat with my head in my hands, looking at the deck. All I could think about was Maddy. How was she? What had they done to her? She had no idea we were coming. I had made it across a death filled island and now I had lots of help. I could do this. I could rescue Maddy. As we docked, I stared silently at the now empty dock.

Adam had already signed us all in, so we went straight to our penthouse. Adam was laughing when he said he had told the resort office that Amy and I were married, that Amy was his sister, and that Noah was their cousin.

Amy said, "So, do we have to act like family and fight?"

We all laughed. "No, no fighting, but we do need to develop our cover, eat a little, drink a little, gamble at the casino a little, lounge on the beach, you know touristy things. And Amy, you and Jack need to act like you like each other."

"That'll be easy," Amy said. "We do like each other," and we both held hands to the loud laughter of Adam and Noah. To anyone walking by or listening from a distance, we seemed just like we were on vacation.

Our penthouse was on the western shore of the island toward the mouth of the bay. Adam and Noah took the bottom unit, just in case, Adam said. Amy took the second floor, and they gave me the top level. We dropped our things, and then everyone came up to my floor because the view was best. The sun was just setting ahead of us but still illuminated the port, which you could see from one end of the balcony off of my unit. It was massive, looked to be concrete, had several levels and a couple of cranes. Stacks of storage containers were in several places.

Adam pointed down to the beach in front of our penthouse. Our balcony was right at the water's edge with a small sandy area under it. "See that tarp? Under it is a raft, black and electrically powered, just big enough for six people and gear. The gear is in my unit below. Well after dark, we load the raft and make our way to the dock area. Friends will have taken over security there, so we won't have any trouble getting to *Eternity*; it's getting on and off *Eternity* where the rescue gets ticklish."

"What about the raft?" Amy asked. "Won't our neighbors here see us uncover and load and launch it?"

"I don't think so. Sara has arranged to rent all of the other units within two places of this one. No one else will see the raft until we're well out from the island, and it should be a very dark night, a sliver of a moon and cloudy. This raft is very quiet and as you can see it's already very near the water. Like I said, getting over there without being seen should be easy."

Amy laughed. "Spooks always have it all over us regular cops. We would never be allowed to rent extra units."

"What about getting back?" I asked. We would have Maddy and Li Wei, and there was no telling what condition they would be in, and all hell could be breaking loose.

Adam said, "Perhaps much tougher, but not if we're stealthy. I've arranged to have a vehicle parked near the dock space so I can stay and cover your rear flank if need be or use the vehicle and even take someone with me if it looks like the raft will be overloaded on the way back."

We all thought about his answer. "Amy, I want you to bring everyone back here and then take the raft out about four hundred meters from shore and use your knife and sink it. The water is fairly deep there. And sink whatever equipment you don't think we need any longer, too."

Amy nodded, and I could tell she was going over the plan in her mind.

Adam continued, "Tomorrow at seven a.m., Joe will have his flight plan filed for a return trip to Tauranga. Provided the local police don't give us any trouble, you will all be out of here on that plane."

We were all digesting the plan. To me, it was complex. I was still staring at the dock building, wondering how everything would go. I wanted to see *Eternity*.

"What about once we're on *Eternity*, Adam? What happens then?" I asked.

Amy nodded, and Adam answered, "That's the most dangerous part, probably. We plan to sneak on board, go directly to the container where Captain Zhao said Maddy and Li Wei were being held, pop the lock, grab them, and leave the way we came. If we can do so quietly, I doubt the Chinese will even mention it to the local authorities. But if they confront us, there could be violence, and all bets are off. Then we do our best to survive and get the hell out of there. Okay?"

I shrugged. "Yeah, I understand. Thanks." That was a lot to digest for everyone. I was having trouble focusing on the logistics. All I could think of was Maddy. *Where was she now? Was she being fed? Was she hurt? What was she thinking? Would she be expecting us?* I brushed back my hair with my hand.

After a few minutes, Adam sang out, "Come on now, let's go out and get noticed having some fun. I have a dinner reservation at the Azure Restaurant, and then we should drop by the casino. Lose a little, make some friends, and introduce yourselves using your cover information."

Adam and Noah walked out, laughing with their arms around each other, and Amy and I held hands. I was totally unprepared when Amy turned and kissed me under one of the resort park lights.

CHAPTER

31

Port Vila Harbor
Port Vila, Vanuatu
March 18, 2033
6:00 a.m.

Eternity had come as far as she could under her own power and direction. Captain Hu, acting on the first mate's suggestion, had overseen the pilot tugs taking over, directing the big ship into the harbor and to her berth. He had made a big show of turning it over to the first mate now that everything was under control. To himself, the first mate rolled his eyes, and he held his tongue.

Maddy heard the engines of the tugs and felt the ship moving differently and slowly. There was no sound from the engine room on *Eternity*. Something was happening. *Were they coming into port? This might be their only chance to escape.*

Maddy and Li Wei were sitting on the edges of their respective cots talking. Their knees were almost touching. Maddy looked up and they fell silent when Captain Hu unlocked the sickbay door and entered. He bowed his head; they didn't. Captain Hu smiled, anyway. Maddy watched him warily.

"I trust you are more comfortable here. You both look much better than the last time I saw you."

Maddy and Li Wei had just been discussing how much better they felt and how much better these quarters here were, but now to Hu, they said nothing. Maddy stopped talking to listen to Hu. *What did he want? What could she learn from him that would help her escape? Where were the other prisoners and who were they?* Maybe she would learn more about Li Wei. In this strong light she could see that the left corner of his mouth was scarred. Running from the corner of his mouth about an inch and a half upward and into his left cheek was a thin red scar. A permanent smile she thought. He was dressed in a crisp, creased khaki uniform, and he wore polished shoes. His hair was still impeccable.

Captain Hu continued, "I thought you would be interested to know that your former quarters have a new occupant. I have personally confined Wang as a result of the way he treated you two. China today does not need to treat its prisoners violently. I apologize for what Wang made you endure during the storm and for the torture he inflicted on you, Li Wei. As I said, China no longer needs to behave in that way. Time is on our side. You will both come to recognize the superiority of China's ways given time and the opportunity to think. Wang is a throwback to the old days, the days before we became enlightened. I truly hope that he can reform. And I have taken control of this ship and all matters on her. Mrs. Gamble, I particularly regret that you were injured during the storm. No agent of China has harmed you directly, but nevertheless you were injured by Wang's neglect. Most unfortunate. My apology."

Maddy thought, so that's how he intends to defend himself to the Deputy Minister; no direct action and Wang as the neglectful one. That's why he locked Wang up, to cover his own negligence. And he is very definitely in the state security chain of command and is not a mere sea captain. He probably reported directly to the Deputy Minister, but she couldn't back that idea up with any facts so she determined to keep working on that.

"Don't you think Deputy Minister Chen will hold you accountable as the commander of the mission?" Maddy said through a grimace, holding her side so he would remember her injuries. She also thought the other prisoners would not be in a storage container; that would be difficult to explain.

Hu nodded and Maddy realized she may have made a mistake to demonstrate her situational acumen. Hu said, "As I noted I determined Wang was at fault and he is imprisoned. It seems just to me."

Li Wei and Maddy exchanged a glance. Wang imprisoned in their storage container? That was great news. An eye for an eye, well almost. Wang was such a cruel bastard. Maddy watched Li Wei and followed his lead. He kept his gaze impassive. She, too, was cautious around this new captor.

Hu said, "I thought perhaps you would be happier." His lips smiled, the scar made it look tragically sad. "No matter. I came to alert you that we are pulling into the harbor. Where is not important. It is not New Zealand, and it is not China. I expect you both to be quiet and cooperative while we are in port. Make no unnecessary noise and no attempts to escape. That is all that I require of you. Is that understood?"

Both Li Wei and Maddy nodded. Maddy was thinking that this was her chance. "Good, and to be sure, later today, after we have docked, I will be back to separate you two, just while we are at port. If one of you tries to escape, know that I will have no choice but to kill the other. I have noticed you two are quite fond of each other. I do not think you would like that to happen. And if I have to kill one or both of you the lives of the other captives onboard will also be forfeit. Do you have any questions?"

Maddy asked, "Who are these other prisoners?"

"You do not need to know that, Mrs. Gamble. Let it be sufficient that you know their lives will be taken if you behave badly. You wouldn't want that, would you? Any further questions?"

Apparently interpreting their silence as agreement, Hu said. "Good," and turned and left.

When they were sure he was gone, Li Wei said, "I am glad Hu imprisoned that monster, Wang. Held in the dark just like we were. I can only wish for a storm so he can truly understand the horrors of that container."

Maddy said, "I can't disagree there. He was horrid. Too bad he's not getting the electric stick treatment. Hu is no prize, but better than Wang."

"Yes, I would love to see if Wang's training in resisting torture is as good as mine. I am not so sure about our Captain Hu," Li Wei said. "He is smoother, more polished, but may be even more dangerous. He says all the right things but would torture or kill us just the same. And he is more than willing to kill the others. They are both snakes, different species of snakes maybe, but snakes just the same."

He was right; there was something insincere about Hu. She was wondering about Li Wei's training comment. *Trained by whom to resist torture? Surely not Falun Gong or The Epoch Times?* She decided to keep her questions to herself for now.

Maddy said, "Tell me what will happen to us if we're taken to China."

Li Wei said, "For some time anyway, China will not acknowledge that it has custody of either one of us. And we will be separated and isolated. I thank God for your presence now." He saw Maddy's face. She was not thanking God. "Perhaps it is my English again. I truly wish that you were not here, that you were at your home with your children. But for me, you're being here is strengthening, supportive. I hope you know what I mean."

Maddy said nothing, she knew what he meant, and she badly wanted to help him, stand beside him, and fortify him.

"I am very sorry, Maddy, that we have gotten you involved in this. You must believe we never intended or foresaw your being imprisoned. We knew what risks we were taking. This is so unfair to you."

He looked truly sorry so Maddy shrugged to signify it didn't matter much and nodded to acknowledge his comments. "Please continue with what to expect in China."

"Since they cannot put us in prison under our own names, they have three choices, all bad. First, they could kill us, but I think we would already be dead if that were their plan. I know they want information from me and they must have some ideas as to how you could be useful to them. The second choice is that they put us into prison under fake names so we cannot be located. That is always possible, but it seems like those secrets leak out, prisoner to prisoner, prisoner to visitor, visitor to world. So, I think what they will do with both of us is RSDL, residential surveillance at a disclosed location. I know it doesn't sound so bad, but it may be the worst of all if anything can be worse than dying. With RSDL, you are held in an undisclosed location, often deprived of food and sleep for prolonged periods, made to assume painful positions, afforded no privacy or dignity or freedom, and interrogated for many hours, day and night. The goal is to break you. You may not be subjected to physical violence, but its real threat is always present. It would be best to decide how you will resist or advise you to give them what they seem to want quickly. You must decide and better now than after we arrive in China."

"What do you mean, by how I will be able to resist?"

Li Wei steepled his hands under his nose. "There are several ways," he said, "you can refuse to answer anything. That is very tough, and the response will be callous. I would expect little food, little sleep, and physical punishment. You can try to give them some of what they ask for, some information but withhold, for example, the names of others they are sure to seek. If, for instance, you say you were only a minor player in the lawsuit in New Zealand, they will want to know who the leaders were. It would be best if you prepared your answer in advance. Spend some time deciding what they want with you and what they will ask. The other way I have suggested for you is simply to answer their questions as fully as possible. Your treatment will be the best in that scenario, and they may even release you in a year or so. Maybe. But since you know very little, I do not think you would hurt any others by being forthcoming with your answers."

Maddy was horrified that the best-case scenario was that they might release her in about a year. "What about you? What do you know that they want badly enough to torture you?"

"You are better off remaining ignorant of that. That way you can honestly answer questions about what I intend or who I am or what I may have told you. There are things I have not told you, Maddy. It is for your own protection."

At least he admitted withholding things from her. She would have to think about his explanation.

"Do you plan to tell them what they want so they will stop torturing you?"

"No, I do not. I hope I can hold out. If I tell them what I know they may then decide I have no further value and kill me."

Maddy took that in. That option was only for her.

She said, "Do you think there's any chance we can escape here? Or that somehow we will be rescued?"

Li Wei smiled gently and said, "No one will be coming for me. Who do you think might be coming to rescue you?"

Maddy was just about to answer when the door to sickbay opened again. This time it was Chang bringing breakfast and fresh towels. Maddy wondered at the fresh towels; they didn't need them. After serving breakfast with his customary bow, he reached between the towels and pulled out Maddy's own clothes, the torn and tattered rags she had removed just hours ago. First, Chang held the pants up and let them drop; the hems looked new. He lifted the outside of the hem so Maddy could see the new stitching.

Chang said, "Now they are not so long they drag on the ground." He had shortened her pants. He showed her where he had also repaired the tear at the hips. Maddy struggled to tell where the repair had been made. Chang put them on Maddy's cot and patted them, and held up her light blue shirt. It was clean! She looked back at her pants and realized they were clean also. The repair to her shirt was more visible. The tear was closed but the thread used was heavier and darker. It resembled a scar on a pirate's face in an old movie, and her shirt was now short-sleeved. Chang held it up. He had hemmed it just above where her elbow would be. The hem was excellent but for the slightly darker thread.

Chang said, "I am sorry I could not save the longer sleeves or find thread that matched exactly, but I thought a pretty woman like you would like to have her own clothes."

Tears rolled down Maddy's face first and then Li Wei's. Maddy stood and hugged Chang. "This may be the sweetest thing anyone has ever done for me. You won't get into trouble, will you?" She held her clothes tightly to her chest with both arms. She realized that Chang had hidden her clothes in the towels to bring them to her. Who knew what lengths he had gone to to repair them without getting caught at it. Maddy wondered what would happen to him if Hu found out.

Chang shook his head. "No problem. Maybe wait a few days to wear them."

"Thank you, thank you so very much."

Li Wei added, "You are a good man, Chang, a very good man. People like you are why I fight to free China."

If anything, Chang looked embarrassed by the hug, kind words, and the attention. He turned to leave and then stopped and turned around. "We are coming into Port Vila in Vanuatu. Security will guard you more closely, and I will not be able to visit so often. You must be very careful. I have heard talk, they will kill you and the other prisoners if you try to escape or if anyone makes them uncomfortable. Be very careful. And Ms. Maddy Gamble, I hope you get to see your children and husband again."

Maddy asked, "Are they going to move the other prisoners in here with us?" She looked around the small sickbay for emphasis.

Chang said, "No, Ms. Maddy the others are already secured in galley storerooms."

How are we ever going to get off of this ship? We don't have much time and I still don't even have a plan.

CHAPTER

32

Port Vila Harbor
Port, Vila, Vanuatu
March 18, 2033
8:50 a.m.

The tug skipper used his radio to communicate with *Eternity*. "*Eternity*, do you want us to swing you around and back you in?"

The first mate looked at Captain Hu, who screwed up his face and shrugged his shoulders. The first mate nodded and said, "*Eternity* here. Why?"

The tug came back, "Just thought it would make leaving port tomorrow a little quicker. My paperwork says you aren't on the schedule to be loaded or unloaded until this afternoon, so we have time now."

The first mate conferred with Captain Hu and then said, "What about other ships coming in, any problem there?"

"No, no problems there. Nobody else due in port before you depart in the morning, and the weather looks good; cloudy but clear. Your call."

The harbormaster had asked the tug captain to see if he could get *Eternity* to back in. Said don't push it but try. He wasn't told why and didn't ask. He didn't need to know. Now he figured he had tried.

"*Eternity* here. Go ahead and back us in. Thanks. How long will it take?"

"Roger that, *Eternity*. Shouldn't take much longer, maybe thirty minutes more, then most of you can go ashore."

***

I watched it all from my balcony. I had my elbows on the balcony rail and my hands were pressed together as if in prayer, joined under my nose and over the middle of my mouth. It was like watching molasses. My heart was pounding, my mind was racing and the world around me was in slow motion. I stared at *Eternity* as if I could see through her hull and determine where Maddy was being held. I tried to send Maddy thoughts telepathically. *I'm right here, Maddy. I am coming for you. Don't give up.*

Now I watched as the tugs disconnected and chugged to the other end of *Eternity*. They were going to back her in, put her port side against the dock. Way to go, harbormaster. Way to go, Adam. That should help. Maybe we could sneak onboard, go straight to the container where Maddy is, open it, and sneak back off with Maddy and Li Wei. Maybe. I was trying to eyeball where the deck of *Eternity* would line up with the dock, It had several levels, and the closer the deck was to one of the stories, the better I thought. It would only be six or eight meters into the ship, open the container, and then run like hell. It should only take a few minutes. We might go undiscovered for that long. The plan was starting to come together. Six to eight meters there and six to eight meters back. How long could it take? But what if she wasn't there? What if she had been moved or if something had happened to her? The plan was weak in that respect. We were about two dozen Marines short of taking over and searching the ship.

Amy came back out on the balcony, showered but dressed in the same clothes she had had on last night. I had overheard her on the phone in my room with her Commander. It sounded like Commander Li had alerted the Vanuatu Police Maritime Wing of a potential problem with two of his detectives and *Eternity*. That explained the police's attention. I could hear Amy exploding into the phone. "You don't have to wipe my ass for me, Commander." And "You're going to get us killed, Commander. Is that what you want?" and, "I told you I was going to see this through; you can either call off your dogs or prepare for mine and Montgomery's funeral."

Near the end of the conversation, she said, "Yes, sir, I'm willing to accept responsibility if something goes wrong." And finally, just before she disconnected the call, she said, "When you figure out what you're going to do, please let me know."

She was still hot when she came outside. "That son of a bitch Commander Li told the Vanuatu police to be on the alert for two New Zealanders. He told them to watch *Eternity* while she was in port. Can you believe that shit? Like this isn't hard enough."

"Why the hell would he do that?"

"Because I told him I wasn't returning to Nelson and was going to see this through. He found Joe's filed flight log and *Eternity*'s filed itinerary, added them up, and then alerted the Vanuatu Police. Said he was trying to keep Noah and me out of danger and to avoid an international incident. Chickenshit! Two people get kidnapped right in his town, and he's afraid of how it will look if we rescue them. At least he didn't identify us by name to the Vanuatu Police. It's like he is trying to intimidate us, to get us to just give up."

Eternity was now slowly backed into the dock. It looked like her main deck would be somewhere between the second and third levels of the port.

This might be our only chance.

"So, what do you think about our chances, Amy? Be honest."

"Not sure. Not as good as they could be without my commander's help, I know that. And now I don't know if he can reverse it even if he tries. I just don't know. The operation itself isn't that complicated if everything goes as expected. But remember, there will be armed men on that ship; spies; the Chinese version of Adam. Men like that are dangerous. I don't want you to think this is some walk in the park. You will have to be at your very best. We all will. And we could use more people. We would give up stealth but gain firepower."

She looked at me to make sure all that had sunk in. She then said, "I'm going down now to talk with Adam and Noah; maybe they can think of something to counteract my idiot commander. We have a call with Sara at ten this morning. She's always good with things like this." She was trying to encourage herself.

I stared at *Eternity. What was going on, on board that ship? Why did they have Maddy? Where was she being held? What had they done to her? I will sink that damn ship if they have hurt her!*

"You coming?" she asked.

I didn't turn around. "I'll be down in a bit. Before the call to Sara." I brushed my hair back.

"Jack, is everything all right? If this is about last night, I hope you understand I was just playing my part." Her voice trailed off.

I waved her away. *Eternity* and Maddy had my full attention, but was that really what had happened.

"And don't worry, it won't happen again."
Good.

***

Hu entered sickbay and touched the pistol in his belt. "Li Wei, step to the back of the room. Maddy, turn around and put your hands behind your back. You are coming with me."

Both Li Wei and Maddy did as Hu ordered them.

Li Wei asked, "Where are you taking her?" Worry was apparent in his voice. This was the first time Maddy had been tied or cuffed. She was thinking that was a good sign, maybe there was some possibility of escape here, some reason Hu would be worried. She would jump overboard if she got the chance. She doubted they would shoot her in that circumstance. *Could she swim with her hands tied behind her back? She was going to find out if she got the chance. But would they really kill all of the other prisoners if she escaped?*

Hu laughed. "Oh, are you worried about your girlfriend's safety? You should have thought about that a long time ago, don't you think?" He leveled a stare at Li Wei. "But don't worry, she will be safe enough as long as both of you behave while we are in port. As I told you earlier, you each will ensure the good behavior of the other. If one of you escapes, the other will die; if one of you tries to escape and fails, you will both die and the others as well. You wouldn't want that would you, Li Wei? If you both behave, then after we leave this port tomorrow morning, you will be housed here together for the remainder of our journey. You may even be moved to larger quarters with the others. I trust I have been clear." He looked hard at both Maddy and Li Wei. He tightened the slip ties over Maddy's wrists, which were behind her back.

Maddy thought, *there is some link between Li Wei and the others that I don't understand, that is very clear. And they're being kept in a storeroom down below.*

"Let's go," he said, prodding Maddy. Once the door to sickbay was closed and locked, he stopped Maddy while taping the paper over the sickbay door's glass portion. Now no one could look in from the hall or entry door to the quarters and see Li Wei.

Maddy never got near the deck or the sides of the ship. Hu marched her down two flights of steps and through the galley. They surprised Chang, who was in the galley fixing breakfast. Hu took Maddy to one of the freezers, unlocked it, and ushered her inside. Maddy shot Chang a terrified glance. Hu grabbed a stool from the galley and put it into the freezer with her.

"You can sleep on the floor for just one night. And you will be dry even if not warm." Then he laughed at the terrified look on Maddy's face and put his hands on his upper arms in a mock shiver. He cut the zip ties and let the pieces fall to the floor. He closed and locked the door. As it closed, he said, "Sweet dreams." She heard him tell Chang, "No one goes in there without me. Do you understand? And don't tell her the freezer doesn't work. She will figure it out."

Well, that was some small comfort.

"But she will suffocate in there," she heard Chang protest. Maddy knew from Hu's earlier tirades she couldn't be allowed to die due to her conditions in light of the Deputy Minister's orders. At least she hoped that was still true.

"Then you must find a way to get air in there. If she dies, you die."

Hu might be worse than Wang. He created a problem and then threatened a crewman if he didn't fix it.

Maddy heard Hu's footsteps as he left the galley. She could feel the ship slowing; they must be almost docked. Fifteen minutes later, Chang unlocked the freezer room and gave Maddy a blanket and a pillow.

"Say you found them in here," he said. Chang checked her wrists to make sure the zip ties had not injured her. He cleaned up the pieces of the zip ties from the floor. Then he removed a part of the chiller from the back of the freezer, so a little light and some air came in. He took the removed parts with him and left food and water for Maddy.

"Thank you, Chang. You are so kind, the only one. Are the other prisoners nearby?"

Chang nodded as he closed the door.

She was alone again, locked in a small dark space, her faith her only hope. *Jack, Allison and JJ, I love you and I'm coming back to you. I'm coming home. Someway, somehow, I will get out of this. Come and get me Jack. I know you are out there somewhere. Come find me, please come find me.*

How could she get out of this freezer and find the other prisoners? She knew who they were but would they help her? Even alone if she could just get *to* the side of the *ship*. She carefully examined where Chang had removed the chiller. It was not quite large enough for her to escape through but perhaps if she could figure out a way to enlarge it or bend back the surrounding metal.

CHAPTER

33

Iririki Island Resort and Spa
Port Vila, Vanuatu
March 18, 2033
10:20 a.m.

I watched *Eternity* get secured to the dock. I watched as the tug-boats disengaged and pulled away. I could see no activity on the ship; very little of the deck was visible. Stacks of containers stood everywhere. There was so sign of anyone. Here and tonight might be as close to Maddy as I would ever get again. I told myself not to think like that, to stay positive. *Persevere, Jack, you can persevere. What would the children and I do without her? What are the children doing now? What are they thinking? Feeling? Would we stay in New Zealand? Would we ...SILENCE!* My inner voice commanded. *You will go downstairs, and you will remain on task. You will save Maddy, and you will bring her home safely. Do you understand me?*

Sara's call was in full swing when I got downstairs to Noah and Adam's room.

"Sorry to be late, everyone. I was watching *Eternity* come in: she's right there, just a short hop across the bay."

The conversation had stopped. Sara said, "It's okay. We understand this is very different for you."

I knew Sara understood. Very personal, that's what this was. I hoped the others would give me the benefit of the doubt.

"Let me catch you up," Sara said. "And after we all finish, maybe you and I can talk for a few minutes about the children. No problems, I just thought it would be nice to talk."

"Sounds good," I said, rubbing my hands and trying to appear confident. "Tell me what I missed."

Sara said, "First we discussed that chicken shit boss of Noah and Amy's. Two thoughts there. I will reach out to a friend from the old days in the Vanuatu Police. I don't think he's in the maritime wing, at least he wasn't, but I know I can trust him. Maybe there's something he can do. His name is Renee Laurent, and as you might guess, he's of French ancestry. His family has been in Vanuatu for ages. Secondly, I will call some SIS people in Wellington to see if they can call this cowardly commander off, convince him to rescind the Vanuatu police's warning, and convince him it isn't his call. Which it's not. The question is, even if he calls it off, can he unring the bell. And they can tell me if they suspect his allegiance in any way. I will report back to Amy on those issues as soon as I have any news.

"Tonight, everything is a go. Despite the police's warning, Adam thinks you can get in and out of the dock area without being noticed. None of us are sure what kind of watch *Eternity* will post. Some cargo ships post none, but many do, mainly to discourage theft. There was no real likelihood of an entire container being stolen, but one could be broken into and some of its content stolen. And here we know *Eternity* holds prisoners, so we should expect some watchmen, especially near the container holding Maddy and Li Wei. And speaking of Li Wei, I am still digging into his past, something doesn't seem quite right about him.

Later today, you'll be scouting the ship. Adam has rented a speedboat, and you're going water skiing. Do you water ski, Jack?"

"Well, it's been years," I said.

"You don't have to be any good, just able to get up on the skis and look like you're having fun. Sometime in there, Noah and Amy will be taking their turn at the skis, you will be the watch, and Adam will drive the boat. Both Amy and Noah will fall in the waters near *Eternity*, and you will be distracted and not notice, giving them a little time for an up-close reconnoiter. It's the best we can do without going on board or flying over on a helicopter. We hope to be able to get whatever guards there are to show themselves. And so you know, the ski boat is also for the benefit of the local police. Let them see you all having fun and also see you in a boat they will never see leave Iririki Island again. It will be tied up in plain view tonight while you cross the bay in the raft that no one has ever seen before. We hope that keeps them off their guard a little bit. Does that about cover what we have discussed so far?"

"Yes, Sara, that covers it," Adam said. "Let me go over equipment and logistics with everyone and especially what to do if there's trouble. Everyone will be in all black, including head coverings. The forecast is still for cloudy skies. Each of us will have night vision gear, the best made. Jack, before we leave here, I will go over it with you. You'll be amazed at the difference it makes in what you can see. Everyone will wear body armor covering his or her torso just in case we get into a firefight. All of us, including you, Jack, will carry a Glock 34s, a nine-millimeter weapon. A solid gun with a solid round. It will stop anyone you hit. Hopefully, you don't have to use it. The rest of us will also carry automatic rifles. The Chinese will fight if they become aware of us. And we will all have radios and throat mics to communicate, but Jack, I want you to stay with Amy at all times. No matter what. Okay?"

I nodded my agreement. I looked over at Amy, but she was looking down.

Adam said, "Any questions so far on equipment?"

I asked, "Will the Glocks have silencers?"

"No, no suppressors. They can throw off the accuracy of the weapon slightly, and honestly, even a suppressed round will be easy to hear on this ship," Adam answered.

"Okay then, let me move on to logistics. I have people watching to see if any of the crew and especially if any Chinese intelligence agents go ashore. If so, they will be followed if possible and kept out late if at all possible. The fewer people on board, the better. At twenty-three hundred, Noah and I will uncover and drag the raft into the water; Jack and Amy will be in the shadows and will join us immediately. It will take no more than five minutes to cross the bay to just outside and below the dock. We leave the raft there and proceed through the port, which will be manned by friends at that point. If there are local police, we'll have to deal with it or abort."

I understood, but that word abort was like a thunderclap. I had never before considered that we could fail because we aborted the operation.

"Assuming we go, we work our way through the port building, getting as close as we can to the level of the deck of *Eternity*. Then we try to align our entry point to the aisle through the stacks to make us close to the red and yellow container on the deck proper, which holds Maddy and Li Wei. We want the shortest distance possible, on and off. We sneak aboard, neutralize anyone we have to as quietly as possible, cut the lock, free the prisoners, and leave the way we came. I will leave in an SUV I have parked near the dock and can take some others with me in case Maddy and Li Wei aren't in great condition."

I blew out my breath. "And what if they're not in that container?"

Sara said, "You're good, Jack. That's one weakness in the plan. We have too few people to conduct a thorough search of the ship and too few to fight for control of the ship. If they're not there we'll have to leave the way we came without them."

No chance, I thought. If I get on that ship, I'm not leaving without Maddy.

Amy said, "Assuming we find them, Jack, you should go with Adam and Maddy and Li Wei. It's safer than the raft. Noah and I will take it back toward the island but sink it along the way and swim in. And tomorrow morning we fly out with Joe, directly back to Nelson."

Sara laughed softly. "This is what I miss the most. The plan! I always loved going over the plan and then later looking back on what didn't go as we expected and what we did instead. They all sound so good beforehand. Never fails. The most important things are to be careful and to work together."

I was thinking about how outclassed I was here. The others were professionals. They had done things like this before. Well, maybe. And it sunk in that I needed to carry a gun. The danger was evident, and also, Adam didn't trust me with a fully automatic weapon. Then I remembered that I had had no chance to survive a journey across Ebola Island, no chance at all, but somehow I had made it. *I could do this!*

"If we're all good, will you three excuse yourselves so Jack and I can talk about his kids?"

"Before they go, I have one more question everyone should hear," I said. "Vanuatu has the same type of cameras Nelson had, at least they look the same. Is there any chance the Chinese are monitoring them and know where we are at all times?"

The silence told me the others had not thought of this.

Sara answered, "That's another good point. Let me see what I can find out or what I can do. I don't want to risk boarding the *Eternity* if they know we're coming."

The others got up and walked outside. As they walked out the door, they talked about the weather and waterskiing later; they were on task and in character. I now noticed they were dressed like tourists. I was going to have to change clothes.

"So, how are they doing, Sara?" I asked, brushing my hair back with both hands.

"Great, really," Sara replied. "I know I say this all the time, but they're wonderful children. And I have a surprise for you. I knew we would be talking so I kept them home this morning and I will put them in front of the camera for a little face to face with their dad."

"Oh Sara, you are the very best."

And then there they were, Allison and JJ, all dressed for school but jumping up and down to see me. They pressed their faces in close to the screen so I did the same and gave them a big kiss. And I got two great kisses back.

"How are you guys? How is school? How's Nickau?"

They told me all about everything. There were no new favorite flavors of ice cream to discuss.

"So how do you like Sara?"

"Oh, she is great," they both agreed "but we want you and Mommy back and then Sara can come visit." Allison said.

"Or maybe live with us along with Nickau and his dad," added JJ.

"Well, we'll see when we get back. It shouldn't be too much longer. I love you both very much."

"We love you Daddy and Mommy too!"

"And she loves you. Now put Sara back on."

Sara switched to a voice call.

"Thank you, Sara. I didn't realize how badly I needed that."

"You know the most important question may be how are you doing?"

"I'll be okay," I said, brushing my hair back again. I loved seeing the children. They change so fast when they're young. What else have they been doing?

If Sara caught on that I had changed the subject back to the children she let me get away with it. "There's school, of course. Allison seems to be doing fine. Her teacher says she's a little 'far off' at times, and we decided that's to be expected. But her grades and behavior are fine. The school psychologist met with her twice and is available to meet again but Allison says she doesn't need to talk to her, she just needs her mother and father back is all."

"So, you talk to their teachers and to the school psychologist? You're pretty good at this child care thing."

"Oh, please. I love children, and I've been around here forever. I know everyone."

How could I be so lucky to have someone like Sara with my children? Kind and loving, a treat baker, checked with the teachers already, attuned to their emotions, and quite capable of defending them if need be.

"And what about JJ?"

"I just talked to his teachers today. He is slacking off a bit. No one can tell if he's emotionally distracted or thinks he can now get away with slacking off. I'll talk with him tonight."

With JJ it could be either one of those.

"Have they asked many questions?"

"No, not too many. Some, of course. I did tell them things should be cleared up in a couple of days. I hope that was right."

"Me, too."

"Jack, you know you don't have to go tonight. You can stay in the room and wait for them to return with Maddy. The raft will only take four in and have room for six out, but I have someone on standby that can take over. A professional."

I was trying to decide if she wanted me out or was just giving me a choice.

She said, "I would hate to see anything happen to you. The children need you. You really should let someone else go."

I understood where she was coming from. I suspected Amy had talked to her privately. I worked this over in my mind, what was the right thing for me to do? On the one hand, I could stay safe and send another professional and maybe increase the chances of success and guarantee the children would have at least one parent. On the other hand, I could go after my wife myself and do the best I could by her and do my best to stay alive for the children. I hoped Sara would understand me. I thought she would.

"Sara, this is my wife. I have to go."

"Understood. Try not to shoot anyone; leave that to the pros."

"Yes, ma'am," I said. Then I asked, "How are those chocolate balls coming?"

I could tell she was delighted. "I made a large batch again last night. Honestly, I don't know where those kids put them. And they never gain an ounce. I'll make a batch and freeze some at home, and they last me for months. Here, they're gone in two or three days."

"Quit bragging."

"Well, mister, I suppose you won't want to know where in the back of the freezer I hid a few for you then?"

We laughed and said our goodbyes just as the others were wandering back in.

CHAPTER

34

Iririki Island Resort and Spa
Port Vila, Vanuatu
March 18, 2033
4:30 p.m.

Amy said, "our surveillance has determined that there is one watchman on each side of *Eternity*. We didn't observe any weapons but we have to assume they are armed."

Adam said, "We may be able to surprise them. We know about the attempt in Tauranga, but they don't. As far as we know, they have no reason to be hyper-vigilant in this sleepy little port."

"Your asshole Commander didn't warn the Chinese, too, did he?" I joked.

"No, but I'm wondering if the local police may have said something," Amy said. Adam interrupted our dark thoughts when he reminded us to have fun and rammed lightly into the dock while landing the boat.

As we climbed out of the boat, still laughing, I stole a look at *Eternity*. The crane was loading a cargo container onto the ship. Adam had the ship's manifest; thirty-four containers offloaded and delivered here and twelve boxes packed on board the vessel for delivery to Shanghai. So, the unloading and loading process was coming close to ending. Adam had told me that the port personnel would first remove all containers staying here, and then all containers coming aboard would be loaded. He also said the boxes should have been loaded initially to facilitate unloading and reloading here. And for the first time, the documents made concrete that the next stop was China. I had known that but tried to avoid thinking about it. Tonight, was it. It had to be. Once the ship got to China, there was no hope for Maddy's release except for negotiations by New Zealand and the United States. And that would take time, and who knew what could happen in the meantime? The stories I had heard of treatment in Chinese detention centers were frightening. Most of these stories I had heard from Maddy when she was working on that case for the New Zealand law firm. She knew much more about it than I did. She had to be terrified. I remember her crying when reading descriptions of how the Chinese treated prisoners. They accused everyone of being a spy or of subversive activity. They would do the same to Maddy. They nearly starved them, isolated them from their families who had no idea where they were, tortured them and even killed them. Maddy could not withstand torture or imprisonment. They could not treat an American woman like that. *I will not allow it! I know where you are, Maddy. The United States knows where you are. We're coming to get you, to set you free.*

I just hoped we would be in time.

And a rescue on the high seas sounded dismal, too. First, everyone made it seem like an act of piracy, and secondly, Li Wei and Maddy would be killed and disposed of if a capturing warship got close. Tonight, was it.

I was the last one to the penthouse. Everyone was in Adam and Noah's unit on the ground floor, leaning over the table. Sara's face was on the tablet when I came in. "There you are, Jack. Like I was saying. No word yet from Wellington. They agree but are hesitant to get involved in local police matters, as they put it. So, Amy's commander is still a problem. They didn't say no. Locally, my friend Renee, who is now a captain but not of the Maritime Wing, has managed to trade shifts and will be on duty tonight. His force will work the land side of the docks and town. So, we shouldn't have any trouble there, but maybe from the waterside. He also checked, and there's nothing of record that the Vanuatu police formally warned *Eternity*. However, he cautioned that an officer could have gone onboard *Eternity* and warned them to keep their guard up tonight. No way to tell. And he told me the port building was well covered with cameras as are most parts of Vanuatu."

We all looked at each other. We knew the risk from the cameras was real.

"What do we do?" I asked.

"Unless Renee can figure something out, we abort. These cameras are from the same manufacturer as the ones in Nelson. They're all over the Pacific, probably all over the world. And China can apparently command them at will. If the dragon is awake and eyeing you, you cannot board *Eternity*."

I swallowed hard. Abort? Now? We were close, but if the Chinese were watching us approach by camera we were as good as dead. There had to be a way. I changed the subject. "The crew was registered as twenty people all specifically identified." I knew this because I had seen the information on Captain Hu back in Tauranga. The real Hu had been replaced, or worse, so the paperwork would match. "Then, from the video, there were at least seven security agents. Six went in and out of the hotel, and at least one more was already in the van. So, we have twenty-seven, maybe figure thirty to be conservative on board. We see how many take shore leave and assume the rest are on board."

Sara said, "Exactly right, Jack. You'll make a good spy yet." Then she added, "And I have some women working for me in Port Vila tonight. I have offered them two hundred New Zealand dollars if they're the first to report to me the name of a man from *Eternity* in town drinking or eating. That's all, just the name, and then we can maybe get a better estimate on crew versus security who are still on board. Both should be avoided, but the security agents are much more dangerous. I want those odds to be about even, four of us against four of them, fewer if possible."

"Sara, you're a genius," I said.

"Hey, just trying to help these girls out. Sometimes they have to do a lot more than get a name for two hundred dollars. And it's not out of the question that four or more of these security creeps will want to go ashore. If so, I hope to know. I'll let you know as soon as I hear anything from Renee about the damn cameras."

CHAPTER

35

Port Vila Bay
Port Vila, Vanuatu
March 18, 2033
11:30 p.m.

"So, what I need to do is put these night vision goggles on and leave them on?" I asked to confirm.

"Right," Adam said. "Unless we happen to go inside the ship and it's well lit. That's doubtful, but if it happens, your vision will go green, and you need to flip the goggles up until we get back out into the dark. It's almost automatic, Jack. Your vision blurs, and you act to correct it. Just be sure to pull them back down when outside. Nothing to it. Now let's try that throat mic again."

I had an earpiece in my right ear. It was easy to hear communications from the others; it overrode all other noise. They had warned me that it might not seem so simple if we were in the middle of a firefight. It was the throat microphone I had a little trouble mastering.

"Whisper, that's all you have to do. Try it again," Adam said.

"Can you hear me?" I said in my best church whisper.

"Loud and clear," said Adam, "but so can the bad guy across the room. Let's try this. I will whisper something, and you can listen to how loud it is in your ear. Then take the earpiece out, and I will whisper at the same level, and you should be able to gauge just how soft it is."

"Kiwis are cool," came across my earpiece, not loud but not soft and easy to understand. I pulled out my earpiece, and Adam whispered, "Yanks are cool, too." I could barely hear him.

So, I put my gear back on and whispered very softly, "Yeah, Kiwis and Yanks are the good guys."

Adam smiled. "Perfect. Keeping quiet could save your life. In a firefight, not only can it be hard to hear, it can be hard to remember to whisper. Don't worry too much about that. The cat's already out of the bag by then. And, if we get into a gun battle, retreat the way we came as quickly as possible. We have to be clear on that."

Amy and Noah were watching me answer.

"Got it," I said.

We had been sitting in Adam's unit waiting for over two hours, playing with our equipment, talking, waiting. It was maddening. I paced again for about the tenth time. I nearly pulled my hair out pushing it back over and over. No one told me to stop but I could tell I was annoying them.

Sara called. "I just heard from Renee. His exact words were 'the dragon is sleeping in the port building and all across the island. Tell your friends to be extremely careful and that I will be nearby'."

"So, it's a go?" I asked.

"It's a go," Sara said. "Good luck."

Thumbs up all around, and we were out the door; Noah and Adam first and then Amy and me. They all had their night vision goggles down, so I pulled mine down, too. The strap on the goggles and the head covering would keep my hands out of my hair.

Amy led me toward some mangroves near the beach. The entire island was one resort, and it was heavy with vegetation, palms, mangroves, and several flowering plants I didn't know. It was lush, which suited our purpose perfectly. We were on the dark side of the island, away from the town. On the other side, the lighting displayed numerous anchored boats.

Adam and Noah were ahead of us and to our left. Quietly they pulled the tarp off of the raft and pulled the raft out from under its cover of mangroves. They hauled it into the bay, just to the point where it started to float. Then Noah came back ashore for the two equipment bags. They were bulky; he had to take them one at a time. While Adam held the raft and acted as lookout, Noah loaded the bags into the raft.

I knew the next step was for Amy and me to join them and set out for the dock; I took one small step toward them and felt Amy's hand on my arm, pulling me back. She didn't say a word but pointed out into the bay. There was the police boat slowly cruising along the bay with its running lights off. Adam and Noah had seen it, too, and crouched down into the bay behind the raft. The raft itself was black with no markings. Even with my goggles down, I could barely make it out.

The police boat kept moving past and then turned toward the town and the other side of the island. Finally, it turned on its running lights and increased its speed. Adam waded silently out into the bay so he could see around the mangroves.

He waved to Amy and me to come, and we stole out from under the mangroves and waded out to the raft. Using his throat mic, Adam said, "I think they're going in for the night. Their base is in town just around the corner. Even if it's just a rest stop or a shift change, this is the perfect time to make our way across. Stay down to keep as low a profile as possible."

I could feel the vibration in the raft from the electric motor that was propelling it. The engine gave off only a slight hum. From three feet away, I could barely hear it. No one spoke. We watched. Under the cloudy sky, the bay to our right and rear was dark. There were a few lights on the far shore, but nothing seemed to be moving on the water. To our left and behind was the mooring bay for pleasure boats with a few lights and the town with a soft glow. There was an occa-sional sound, but not much; Port Vila was quieting down for the night. Ahead of us was the looming dock structure. It was lit but not brightly. Below it was a small landing area where we would beach and conceal the raft. Four hundred meters down near the far end of the dock structure was the stern of *Eternity*. It displayed no lights. The main deck seemed to be slightly illuminated. From here, I couldn't tell if *Eternity* had some lights on or if lights from the port were shin-ing on the deck.

We motored noiselessly along the side of the concrete port build-ing. Even its lowest level was well above us. Adam steered the raft into a small cove overgrown by mangroves. He stopped and allowed us all to climb out. The water was about waist-high. To our left and up, there were many flashing lights. We all saw them. The lights were so much higher than we were; we couldn't see what was going on. Adam came wading out from under the mangroves carrying one of the bags; Noah had the other. We worked our way ashore, still lower than the dock's lowest level and still hidden by the native plants.

Adam whispered into his mic. "You all stay here. I'll see if I can figure out what's going on back there, with all the flashing lights. If I'm not back in ten minutes or you hear shots, get in the raft and go back to the resort quickly, sinking what you can along the way."

Thumbs up. The three of us crouched down, and Adam crept up the bank. I was surprised he kept his goggles, pistol, and communi-cation gear, making it difficult to explain himself if he encountered anyone. Then again, he had done this sort of thing before.

Amy mic whispered, "You doing okay, Jack?"

I nodded yes; I figured that was even quieter than a whisper.

What was taking Adam so long? I realized how nervous I was. Did it show? I knew these three probably preferred I wasn't here. Thinking I could screw things up. And I knew they were right. I fo-cused. Never since Madagascar had I been in such a dangerous spot. And now I had children. And if something terrible happened to me, that probably meant something wrong for their mother, too. That would be horrible, the worst possible. And what did Maddy want to happen? Why was she with Li Wei? I had made my choice on that. I was committed to saving Maddy, even if I was only protecting my children's mother. What was taking so long? I looked at my watch; three minutes had passed.

Amy looked down at her phone. It had made no noise but was ever so slightly illuminated in the dark. She read something on it and then throat mic'ed, "Sara just sent me a text. There are at least three state security agents from *Eternity* in town drinking. Maybe more, she says but three confirmed. Better odds."

Noah gave her a thumbs up.

Amy and Noah were silently keeping watch. Noah looked up the bank toward where we had seen the flashing lights. Amy was looking up toward the dock building, the way Adam had gone. I turned to keep watch out across the bay.

A few minutes later, I jumped when Adam's voice came across my earpiece.

"All clear. Come on up the same way I did. I'll be waiting for you at the top. Jack, you bring the other bag."

I went first as quietly as I could manage with a heavy bag. Noah came second, and Amy watched the rear and the bank as she came. Adam crouched down beside several cargo containers. We gathered to him.

He was smiling. "Turns out those flashers are from the main division of the Vanuatu Police. A Captain Laurent has closed Wharf Road on either side of the port here for the next two hours."

"Sara!" said Amy.

"And that's not all. I was told nineteen in town, sixteen crew, so we're down to about ten to deal with, maybe six agents."

Amy said, "Yeah, I just got a text from Sara, same info, three security agents in town."

"How do you know all of this?" I asked Adam.

Adam pointed to the dock building. There was a doorway at the lowest level, just slightly opened. "My guys," he said. "They'll have the dock duty until one-thirty a.m.. One of them was outside here, taking a smoke break, waiting for us. He told me. He also told us how to get to *Eternity* without being seen, even by them. He has disabled the cameras in the port building so no one will see us and even better he thinks this Captain Laurent can shut down the cameras all across the island, same as Sara told us. It makes things easier. But we should be clear from the land side."

In single file, we moved toward the door in the lowest level of the port.

CHAPTER

36

Port Vila Port Building
Port Vila, Vanuatu
March 19, 2033
12:02 a.m.

We had an hour and a half to sneak through the port, board *Eternity*, rescue Maddy and Li Wei, and get back to the resort. An hour and a half!

Adam opened the door that had been left ajar for us. As he passed, he reached down and moved the empty pop can that had held the door open. He put it down just outside the doorway. We all had on gloves so there would be no fingerprints. From all of the cigarette butts on the ground here, I deduced this was the unofficial smoking lounge, and the can was the regularly used doorstop.

Once inside, I looked around a half-lit cavern. We were in a vast open concrete space, maybe thirteen meters high, and it seemed to go on forever, held up by concrete columns evenly spaced throughout the structure. Here and there were storage containers, single, double, in small groups, stacked up to four high. If there was some order to it, I couldn't tell what it was.

Metal staircases rose up to the next level. They looked like the steps to forest ranger towers I had seen. Up, hit a landing, turn and go back the other way, hit a landing, and repeat. All told, there were seven landings before these steps disappeared above the next level. But we didn't use these steps. Instead, Adam led us to a back corner. He opened the door to a darkened stairway. There was no light on in this stairwell. Concrete walls enclosed the concrete steps. We climbed the steps as quietly as we could, certainly much quieter than the metal steps would have been. We encountered no one. We rested a minute when we got just above the next level. The door out of the stairs was obvious; there was a soft light above it, and the only light we had seen since entering the stairway. We went up two half flights from there and then rested. We wouldn't want to be surprised on that landing if the door suddenly opened. Noah and Adam put down their bags.

I offered wordlessly to help Noah with his bag. He shook it off. After a minute, we continued again to the next landing with a door. We stopped right there beside the door. Adam put up his hand to halt us, and he put down his bag. Noah did the same. Adam motioned for us to stay put while he took a look around.

He opened the door just enough to slide through and then closed it. I never heard a sound. Amy was looking at me. Thank God for my night vision goggles. I knew she couldn't see my face.

Adam opened the door and motioned us forward, and then he reached back for the bag he was carrying and fell in. He pointed to our left toward a row of containers. As we got closer, it became clear that there was a space, an aisle between the containers and the wall. A trap if anyone came to either end and a shelter and cover from the cavern beyond otherwise. This floor was much like the lowest level, large open, concrete columns in formation, containers stacked here and there. The ceiling was even higher, I estimated twenty meters, and everything seemed more cared for, more ordered.

We moved slowly. We rested twice, and then Adam led us out between two stacks of containers, and there was *Eternity*. We were across from the midsection of the stern deck of *Eternity*, slightly above it. We moved forward through the concrete cave and across it at the same time. We were watching in all directions but mainly toward *Eternity*. We slipped in and out of shadows and behind and between stacked containers.

When we were about fifty meters from the edge of the dock building, Adam tucked us all in behind a storage container. He went alone to scout the ship. Noah and Amy shared a bottle of water and offered me a drink. Insisted by motion is really what Amy did. When I took a sip, I realized how dry my mouth was, so I drank more deeply.

Adam was back and crouched down beside us. His lips moved in a whisper, and I heard clearly in my ear, "Okay, we're very close to where we want to be, parallel with the front deck, and I see the only passageway between the stacks on the front deck up there a bit. I see a beat-up yellow and red container about halfway between the deck's rail and the quarters. A light is on on the bridge and some lights on the ship, but I didn't see anyone. The deck is about five meters below us, so we'll use the rope ladder in the bag to climb down. Noah will go first and make sure everything is clear, making his way down to the other end of the passageway near the ship's quarters and make sure no one is coming. Then Noah will wave us on. When he does, we must move quickly. I'll go next, followed by Amy and Jack, you'll be last. Before you climb down, look around here to try to be sure we aren't surprised and cut off from behind. That could be disastrous. Ready?"

Amy and Noah had been unpacking the bags while Adam was talking. There was a rope ladder already laid out, three compact automatic rifles, flashlights, a tablet displaying a map of *Eternity*, a lock pick set and bolt cutters, a first aid kit, and burner cell phones, one for each of us. They all picked up the gear leaving me to get the first aid kit and my burner phone. Adam had already explained the first aid kit was mainly if Maddy or Li Wei needed it and the burner was to use if we got separated. We didn't want to leave evidence. I understood everything except exactly why we needed to rescue Li Wei as well. I wanted to find Maddy and get the hell out of here.

Noah and Adam were fastening the end of the rope ladder to the railing on the port building. Adam was right. It looked to be about five meters to the deck below. The floor here was about level with the top of the second layer of stacked cargo containers. I looked onto the ship. I immediately saw a yellow and red container. It was slightly rusty; the two doors were pulled together and locked with what looked like a padlock. The deck of the ship was also about two meters out from where we were standing.

Noah secured the ladder and climbed over the building's railing and, holding the railing with one hand and the ladder in the other tossed the ladder gently toward *Eternity*. Too gently, it fell short of the ship's deck rail and landed against the building. The ladder, made entirely of rope, made only a slight sound. Still, we waited and watched. Had anyone heard? Was anyone coming?

Nothing. Noah pulled the rope back up and threw it again. This time it landed softly on the deck of *Eternity*. Adam was now over the rail. He had a short pole with a lip on the end he used to hold the ladder away from the building so Noah could climb down without having his weight pull the ladder off of the ship's deck. Noah was quickly onboard and tied the ladder to the rail of the vessel. Adam put down the pole and watched as Noah walked down the passageway. The lighted bridge loomed overhead. Adam had one hand on his automatic rifle. I watched the bridge. Noah gave the all clear, and Adam was down the ladder in a couple of seconds. Amy was over the rail and on her way down. As I climbed over the railing, I remembered to look around behind us. All clear.

I was standing on the deck of *Eternity*, only a few meters from the container where Maddy was captive.

Noah held his position, just into the passage, now and then sticking his head out and looking up and down the ship. Amy was now watching the bridge. Adam and I moved right in front of the yellow and red container. Adam silently lifted the lock and examined it. He lowered it back down. He decided on the bolt cutters and held them up. Then he got the bolt cutters nearly in position and looked to Amy and Noah and finally to me. With one mighty stroke, he cut the lock. It fell into his hand. Adam opened the doors and shone his light inside; there were containers of white powder stacked floor to ceiling; some had leaked some of their contents.

"Cocaine?" I whispered.

Adam caught some and smelled it. "Milk." He smiled. "Wrong container."

We moved down the row, looking at each container. The boxes weren't identical but weren't as described either. We went around the corner toward the bow. We found no other passageways except the open path all around the quarters of the ship. We stopped against the crew area of *Eternity* directly below the bridge. We couldn't see the bridge, and the bridge couldn't see us, but we could sense variations in the light coming out from the bridge. Someone was up there. We discussed our choices.

Adam said, "Could Zhao have confused port and starboard?"

"Not likely," Amy said. "We checked. He's an old hand at being a Captain and was a sailor before that."

"Maybe he intentionally misled us?" Adam tried.

"Maybe, but I don't think so," Amy said.

Adam made a decision. "Okay, then we go back and check that first row one more time. If we don't find anything, we'll have to abort. We don't have the time or manpower to search the entire ship. Sorry, Jack."

Sticking close to the quarters' sidewalls, we made our way back to the row where we had first climbed aboard. Noah stood watch again, and Amy and Adam, and I crept down the row examining each container. When we were almost to the railing, I thought I heard something as I passed a green and yellow box. It looked like all the others, maybe a little newer.

"Adam," I whispered and motioned him over. I must have been a little too loud because there was immediately a knock and something said in Chinese and then "Hello?" It was definitely not Maddy's voice.

Adam cut this lock open and yanked open the door with his pistol at the ready and his flashlight in his other hand.

The light shone in the eyes of a man, a Chinese man who blinked into the intense beam. Adam flashed his light around the container. Maddy wasn't there.

Was this Li Wei? Was Maddy dead?

Adam said, "State your name."

The man stuttered and then said, "My name is Wang, I am a Chinese State Security Officer, and I wish to surrender."

I decided this Wang had calculated that he was far better off in a civilized prison than a Chinese one. Besides, he might yet get a chance to redeem himself. No reason to try to be a hero and no reason to alert those that had locked him up.

Adam had Wang's hands behind his back and was cuffing him before I knew what was going on. *Where is Maddy?* Amy moved up to join us.

"Where are the other prisoners?" she said. I was surprised how loud she sounded when she spoke to Wang in a standard command voice.

"Sickbay," he said, "they are locked in sickbay."

Adam consulted the map of the ship. He pointed out where sickbay was, inside the boat's quarters but just inside, maybe only a few meters and above the deck where the crew would generally be.

Adam turned back to Wang. "Are they guarded?"

Wang shrugged and said maybe as he looked toward the ladder, but made no move toward it. Adam changed his position to block his way.

"What do we do now?" Amy throat whispered.

"Lock him back up?" Noah said.

Amy said, "No and we can't let him go either. Someone will have to take him back while the rest of us continue."

Amy said, "Jack?"

Adam said, "No, this man is way too dangerous. I'll have to take him back via the SUV. You three complete your mission and return via the raft. Best I can think of."

Adam uncuffed one of Wang's hands, pulled his arms in front of him, and re-cuffed them. "You make one sound, Wang, and you're dead, and I'll be thrilled about it. Do you understand?"

Wang smiled when he whispered, "I understand."

Adam went to the ladder and climbed up while Amy stood behind Wang with her automatic rifle trained on him. When Adam got to the top, he and his rifle turned around, and Wang was sent up the ladder. He was gagged and had to climb with his hands cuffed together. Twice he stopped to get a better grip. I watched Amy and Adam both keep tight aim on him. Finally, he reached the top and climbed over the rail. He disappeared into the building, and Adam waved off.

Amy and I walked toward where Noah still stood watch, and toward where the door to sickbay was.

CHAPTER

37

Onboard Eternity
Port Vila Harbor
Port Vila, Vanuatu
March 19, 2033
1:01 a.m.

We weren't as sure of ourselves without Adam, and we were running out of time. But we were so close. I could feel it. Amy took charge. She and I moved to the end of the row. She signaled to move ahead to Noah, and he slid across and down until he was beside the door to the quarter's area of the ship. The door had no window and sealed tight; it was the shape of an elongated oval. It opened by way of a wheel that turned before the door could open. This was a perilous moment amid an absurdly dangerous operation. If someone were on the other side of the door, they would see the wheel turning and be waiting to ambush Noah.

And there was movement on the bridge again. Someone was moving around up there, changing the light spilling out of the windows on the bridge. From the feel of things, I guessed it was more than one person. And if they looked at the port side, Amy and I were easy to spot. Amy moved over with her back against the quarters' section of the ship and motioned for me to do the same. With our backs pressed tightly against the ship, we were directly below the port window to the bridge. Someone there wouldn't be able to see us. But now, we were vulnerable to anyone, such as a watchman, coming around the accommodations area's front or back. There was nothing to use for cover. Amy watched the stern, and I watched the bow.

Noah touched the wheel and then turned to be sure we were paying attention.

Noah turned the wheel until it stopped. He paused and slowly pulled the door open, taking cover behind it as he did. Nothing happened. Light spilled out onto the deck, and Amy and I hurried in behind Noah. He closed the door. We were in a narrow hallway, lit with low light. Amy and Noah kept their goggles down, and I followed their lead. We listened and heard nothing. Amy looked at the map of the ship on the tablet, turning it to get her bearings.

"There." She pointed to a door with paper taped over its top portion. It was only a few meters from where we stood. And beside the door was a small plaque, made of plastic that read *'Bing wan'* and a danger sign.

Amy tried the door, locked

Amy took the lockset and got to work. Noah closed the wheel on the door; a surprise could work in our favor, too.

Near the sickbay, there was a hallway running across the ship. I could see an identical entry on the starboard side. There was a stairway near each door, going down on each side and going up on the port side. I crouched in the center hallway and watched the starboard side knowing Noah would watch the port side. I looked again at Amy, willing her to get the door unlocked, willing Maddy to be safe inside.

She whispered, "In." She slowly opened the door to the sickbay with her rifle pointed in front of her. She looked into the sickbay a moment and then went in saying, "Come," to Noah and me. I could immediately see Maddy wasn't there. My heart fell. Noah pulled the door closed behind us.

There, standing against the back wall of this small medical room with two cots, was a frightened-looking Chinese man, who was staring into the mask covered faces of three people in black pointing weapons at him and who had just broken into the sickbay.

Amy said, "Li Wei?"

He breathed out, "Yes," he said, a little too loudly. Amy put her finger to her lips.

She whispered, "We're here to rescue you and Maddy Gamble. Do you know where she is?"

No one had ever had my more complete attention.

Li Wei shook his head. "She is on this ship, but I do not know exactly where, somewhere below this deck." He whispered, "Hu took her when we came to port. Said he would kill her if I tried to escape and vice versa."

Amy turned toward Noah and then me.

"Who are you?" Li Wei said.

"I'm Maddy's husband," I said, lifting my goggles so he could see my face.

And Amy said, "And we are friends."

"Jack," Li Wei whispered. "I am so sorry, all of this is my fault."

You bet your ass it is, buddy. I was about to light into him when Amy put out her hand.

"Stop. Not now, there's no time. Come, Li Wei. Come with us." Amy moved toward the door.

Li Wei said, "Will we go and search the ship and find Maddy?"

Amy said, "We can't. There aren't enough of us. We're out of time and need to get out of here while we still can. Now. Come on!"

I was determined to find Maddy even if I had to do so alone.

Li Wei crossed his arms over his chest and said, "I cannot. I thank you, but I cannot go with you."

Noah said, "Why the hell not?"

"If I am gone, they will kill Maddy."

Amy tried again.

Noah said, "Amy, we have to go," And pointed at his watch.

Amy nodded. She grabbed my arm. "Sorry, Jack, we have to go. We have to abort."

I pulled my arm out of her grasp and shook my head. I was going to find Maddy.

Noah backed out of the room, then Amy and then me. I saw the steps going down to the lower decks. Li Wei stood still against the back wall, arms folded across his chest. He looked lost.

A door opened on the deck above, and two men dressed in black started down the steps. The first man had a weapon on his hip. There was nowhere we could go. The steps were coming straight down toward us, and as soon as the first man got low enough to see below the deck above, he saw us, and his eyes grew wide, and he fumbled for his gun. That's when Noah shot him. His automatic rifle exploded into the small space and ricocheted off the metal stairs, and the man fell the rest of the way down the steps. The man behind him shouted out a warning and retreated to the deck above.

Noah went over and felt the neck of the man he had shot. He moved his hand across his throat, signaling that he was dead.

We heard running along the port side of the door and noise from the steps below us.

"Shit," Amy said, "let's go. This way." She pointed to the starboard door.

I was still looking at the steps to the lower decks but I moved along behind her. Noah was crouched and backing toward us with his gun trained on the port door.

"Hurry," he whispered, "someone's coming." He motioned down the steps.

Amy reached the starboard door, listened, and then turned the handle and pushed open the door. Just as Amy went through the door, the door on the port side opened, and gunfire erupted down the center hallway. I was out the door as Noah sprayed a burst back to the port.

Suddenly there was Maddy at the top of the steps from the lower decks. A man stood behind her with a gun to her head. Was he smiling? She looked so frightened.

Then she saw me. "Jack?" I couldn't tell what else she said. The man pulled her back down the steps and I crowded around Noah as Amy pulled me back. "It looks like a trap."

The port door opened again and the man there unleashed a spray of bullets toward us. I saw Noah fall near the starboard door.

Amy swung back toward the door and stood straddled over Noah. She leveled her automatic rifle and fired across the ship. "Grab him, Jack! He's hit. We have to go. Now!" she shouted.

I reached under her while she was still firing and pulled Noah past her and onto the deck. Noah was breathing hard, bleeding from his left thigh. Amy kept firing as she stepped back through the door and swung it closed. Shots pinged off the inside of the closed door.

"Take your body armor off now!" Amy said.

"What?" I was still planning to go back for Maddy. I looked at Amy, who was pulling the straps at the side of her body armor and pulling it over her head. She tossed it over the side. She looked at me to hurry. Reluctantly, I did the same. *Didn't we need this stuff? Especially right now.* I saw her struggling to get Noah's armor off. I helped from my side and together we pulled Noah to his feet, lifted him, and the three of us jumped off the starboard side of the deck.

CHAPTER

38

Port Vila Bay
Port Vila, Vanuatu
March 19, 2033
1:49 a.m.

I held on to Noah all the way to the water. The impact shook my grip loose. When I surfaced, Amy called, "Over here." She had Noah and was swimming along the side of the ship. "Stay as close as possible to the ship." I was startled to realize our communication gear was still working. Noah groaned softly. He probably didn't realize we could hear him.

We were touching the side of *Eternity as we moved,* Amy leading, then Noah, and then me. Noah was doing his best, but we had to try to keep his head above water. Being alongside the ship helped, but it still wasn't easy. *Maddy, Maddy,* my mind cried out as I spit out a mouthful of seawater.

From above, I heard excited voices and two powerful spotlights swept across the bay, close to the ship but not as close as we were. Several gunshots were fired into the water, making a 'sploosh' on impact. The shots were near where we had first jumped in but were not particularly near where we were now. *They can't see us,* I thought, relieved. To confirm that thought, I heard an order barked in Chinese from the deck of *Eternity*, and the shooting stopped.

The lights swung back and forth, and slowly, we made our way to the stern of the ship, trying not to create any telltale ripples or noise. Sirens were blaring; there was more light from somewhere; a halo of light seemed to radiate from the ship's deck. Good, I thought, let them be in the light trying to find us in the dark. Two police boats with flashers left their dock in town with spotlights fixed on the water ahead of them. One came straight at *Eternity* and straight at us, and the other swung around the other end of Iririki Island. No one was sure what was going on or what to do.

Amy pointed to the police boats. "We have to get out of the water, get Noah out of the water." Noah was conscious but weak. We didn't have much time; the police boat didn't have far to travel. It had slowed slightly and was now sweeping the light on the front of the boat back and forth. We swam quietly around the back of the ship toward the dock. The ship was now between the police boat and us. The lowest level of the building loomed twenty feet above us but still seemed dark. There was a wooden dock down here, just wide enough for a person to walk on and just above the surface of the water. We ducked under it just as the light from the police boats swept by the rear of *Eternity*. It swept along the dock building behind us, an empty concrete wall running down into the sea, with an opening here and there, dark but for the police light.

"Nothing here," I heard from the boat, and the police turned and continued back toward the front of *Eternity*.

"Now, hurry," Amy said as soon as it passed.

We moved to the end of the dock, and I climbed on top and then leaned over and pulled Noah up as Amy lifted him. We were not quiet. There was a lot of other noise. Amy found access into the dock building, and we hauled Noah in and laid him against the wall. Amy took her flashlight and looked at his wound. I could see that he had lost a lot of blood. Amy reached over to the side pocket of my pants. The first aid kit! I had forgotten I had it. She took out gauze and balled some up, and pressed it against Noah's wound. He groaned. Then she took another strip and tied it tightly around his leg. He groaned again but nodded. Then she gave him a pill of some sort. At first, he refused, but Amy pushed it toward him again, and he swallowed it dry. A pain pill, I guess.

We got Noah to his feet and hobbled in the dark toward the far door where we had first entered this building. There was a small light over the door. It looked like it was in a different time zone. It was still quiet, almost spooky. Our shuffling, dragging gait seemed to echo off the walls and the stray containers that were here and there.

Thank God we didn't run into anyone. We got to the door, and Amy peeked outside. "Looks clear; let me check," she said. She slipped out, making sure to put the pop can in the door opening to keep it from closing and locking. Noah was sitting against the wall; his breathing ragged.

Amy was back quickly. We got Noah to his feet. He wasn't able to do much for himself. His head hung forward, and he couldn't lift his injured leg. We pulled him out the door.

"Almost there, buddy, almost to the raft. Hang in there. You can then lie in the raft, and we'll get you to safety and get you some help. Come on, Noah." The words came out of my mouth as if someone else had put them there.

We started across the gravel area toward the mangroves and the bank and the raft. Noah fell. I guess he was unconscious. Amy bent down and tapped him lightly on the face, "Noah, Noah, come on, Noah? Can you hear me?"

And at that moment, a police SUV with its bright lights on came down the gravel slope from the dock building's land side. It skidded to a stop when its headlights picked us up, and it put on its searchlight and shone it on us. It was blinding.

"Don't move. Hold it right there," said a deep voice from behind the light. Amy and I slowly lowered Noah to the ground and put our hands up over our heads.

I heard two vehicle doors open and vaguely saw two shapes behind the light. "Is one of you, Jack Gamble?"

"Here," I said.

"And Amy Wirihana?"

"Right here," she said.

So, they knew our names. I couldn't see how that was good. Amy's commander, I guess.

The spotlight went out. "I'm Captain Renee Laurent, at your service. I'm a close friend of Sara Singh. Let's get you the hell out of here."

What? Wait? Renee who? Suddenly Sara's friend was here to help us? I could tell Amy was still unsure of our situation.

The Captain and a younger man came around where we could see them. The younger man bent down to look at Noah. "Not good, Captain; he needs a doctor."

"Come then, let's hurry." He and the other officer picked up Noah and took him to the back seat. Amy climbed in beside them. I rode shotgun with the Captain. He quickly turned around and sped up the gravel drive. When he got near Wharf Road, he put on his siren and his flashers.

He moved past all traffic, got waved through two roadblocks, and we were on our way out of Port Vila on Ring Road.

Captain Laurent said casually, "I guess there was some trouble at the docks tonight. Someone went onboard *Eternity*. I think they were trying to steal drugs from the ship's infirmary. But no friends of Sara's need to get mixed up in all of that." And he smiled.

Thank you, Sara. I looked back at Amy as Noah slumped against her. The other officer gave Noah an injection into his injured leg, but Noah did not react.

The Captain turned onto a small road and then into a dirt driveway lined with vegetation. The headlights fell on a darkened house ahead of us. Captain Laurent got out and went to the door and starting pounding vigorously, "Hello. Wake up. Get up, it is your good friend Renee, and I have work for you. Hello?"

A light came on in the house as we were getting Noah out of the back seat. A small man came to the door and greeted the Captain with kisses on both cheeks.

"Come," he said to us, holding the door, "bring him in here."

"This is my old friend. He is a doctor. It's better if you don't know his name." Renee turned to his doctor friend and said, "And these are my new friends; they are friends of Sara's."

At the mention of Sara, the doctor took a new interest in us. "Put him on the table."

CHAPTER

39

The Gamble House
Victoria Road
Nelson, New Zealand.
March 19, 2033
3:10 a.m.

"Sara, Adam here. Did I wake you?"

"Hell, yes, you did. It's three in the morning here. The kids and I don't get up for another three hours."

"It's only two here, and my work is just winding up. Wait until you hear what I have to tell you."

"Hang on a minute."

Sara got up and closed her bedroom door. She didn't want to wake JJ or Allison. She shook her head awake, put on her glasses, and turned on the lamp beside the bed and sat.

"Okay, what have you got, Adam?"

"I have Wang."

"Wang, you mean?"

"Wang, the same. We took him off *Eternity* tonight."

Wang! Sara had waited years for her shot at this bastard. He was the one who had planned and led the brutal murders of her family. And not just her family, hundreds of others had been tortured or killed by Wang. She tried to swallow the rage that was building in her throat. Wang.

"Where is he, Adam?"

"He's in an SIS safe house in Port Vila; you remember the one we used in the oil theft case?"

"Yes, when we worked with Renee?" Renee had been a savior to her in the months after Wang had killed her family. She knew he was married and to a wonderful woman. But she had needed someone, someone strong and good like Renee, someone to hold her and love her and tell her everything would be all right even if it wouldn't be, not ever again. But maybe now she could have a measure of justice. She smiled, thinking of Renee. "But I am French, Sara, of course, it's okay if I take a lover," he had said.

And he had. For the six months they worked the oil theft operation together, they had been lovers, against all the rules, in violation of all convention, and against her better judgment. But she had been wrong; Renee had helped heal her, helped her move on. And she would be forever grateful to him. When it was over, he had let her go. There were some things the French understood so well.

Renee had been instrumental at catching the Chinese operatives who were stealing millions of gallons of oil from Vanuatu but had made sure she got all the credit because her bosses had been trying to retire her after what had happened to her family. She would have died without her work; she knew that.

"The same, Sara. My men have him there. Want to join us?" Sara did not hesitate. The unwritten code was that Wang belonged to Sara. She could do whatever she wanted to him, with him, and she knew Adam and his men would back her all the way. Whatever Sara intended, this bastard had it coming. Wang probably thought he would make a deal, spend a little time in a cushy New Zealand prison where he was fed, allowed to sleep, and not tortured. You didn't have to be a genius to know Wang had given up so quickly because he was on his way to a Chinese prison or worse. Why? Who knows, but Sara would find out.

"You know I do, Adam. As soon as I hang up, I will book flights. I need to make arrangements for the Gamble children and take the time to explain to them. What about Maddy Gamble? And Li Wei? I would love to have some good news to tell these children."

"Not sure yet. We found Wang first, and I left with him while Amy and Noah, and Jack stayed on board to continue to search. They weren't where Zhao had said they were; that was where we found Wang."

"I hope they're all right," she said. "Let me know if you hear any more about them. I'm on my way, soon as I can."

"Great, my guys might soften him up a bit, but he's all yours."

CHAPTER

40

Main Deck, Eternity
Port Vila Port
Port Vila, Vanuatu
March 19, 2033
3:50 a.m.

The deck of *Eternity* was bathed in light. Bright lights shone down onto the deck from above it on the port building. All of the ship's lights were on. They were much softer than the glaring lights from above. In some of the crevices between cargo containers, the bright lights ruled; in some, only the softer lighting of the ship showed, and in some, the darkness remained. Patrol boats were sweeping the bay with searchlights that occasionally flashed by. On Wharf Road, flashing red and blue lights interrupted the night with their look at me attitude, splashed onto the white palette of the lighting on the deck.

Standing on the main deck of the ship were about forty people. Captain Hu and the first mate discussed the night's events with Captain Abbott from the Vanuatu Police Maritime Wing.

The rest of the crew, including all the security agents, stood at ease on the deck, all but one. Noah had killed one, and he lay wrapped in a plastic bag in one of the large freezers in the galley. Many of the men had on crew shirts and various pants and shoes. Some had just come back from town and were wearing casual clothes. Nothing fancy, no one had anything fancy on this ship. Some of these men were swaying on their feet, trying desperately to stay awake. The smell of alcohol was strong. The dark clothing usually worn by the security agents was nowhere in evidence.

There were a dozen or so police officers on the deck also. They were all straight-faced and watching the crew. They were all in uniform, including caps, and each of them had a sidearm holstered at his waist. No women were standing on the deck.

After the three, very well-equipped professional intruders had gone overboard, Hu had done some quick thinking. A professional assault on his ship would likely warrant an extensive investigation, and that could take days. Meanwhile, his vessel would be confined to port here and probably searched. And the longer they were here, the riskier it was. A crew member might talk, the ship might be searched, and while here, he had no good way to eliminate his prisoners and get rid of their bodies. Not that he wanted to, he preferred to take them to China as instructed, but at least if they could get back to sea, he would have the choice to kill them and dump their bodies overboard at night. He did not need a lengthy investigation; he wanted to get out of here as scheduled or as soon as possible. It had only taken the police twenty-five minutes to arrive at the ship, far faster than Hu was expecting. They had heard the gunshots across the water. Hu had kept the police at bay until one of his men had signaled that all was ready. Hu was sure that if he could pull this off, he would become a hero.

That's why he had hidden the dead crewman in the freezer. The security agents had cleaned all traces of blood, including some blood in the central hallway and on the starboard deck, that Hu was sure came from one of the intruders. Hu had found the sickbay door unlocked, and after tying and gagging Li Wei, he had relocked it and marked it "Contagious." Even he couldn't leave Maddy in the freezer with the dead man. Maddy and the other four prisoners were locked in a storeroom in the galley and armed guards were stationed inside and just outside the storeroom. He hoped it was not searched. He didn't have anywhere else to conceal them.

There were too many bullet casings in the central hallway and on the decks for this to have genuinely been a simple robbery attempt. Hu personally collected most but not all of the casings and threw them overboard. The few bullet dings on the ship shouldn't be enough to raise any suspicion.

Captain Abbott was looking around. "Why do you think this was a robbery, Captain?"

Hu said, "Look at what they did. They came onboard by a ladder from the port building. It is still there, as you can see. They brought bolt cutters, which they also left behind. They used those to open two cargo containers. One was empty." Hu had made sure it was empty now, and all evidence of its use as a prison was gone. "And the one container filled with milk they tested. I think they thought it was cocaine." He laughed. "And then they went straight to sickbay looking for drugs. They picked the lock. My men found this tool near the door, and the door to sickbay was unlocked." He handed a small pick to Captain Abbott. "There is a very sick man in there, very contagious. No one on this crew would have gone in there or left the door open. No drugs that thieves would find interesting are kept there. They are all locked up on the bridge." And they had been ever since Li Wei and Maddy had become confined in sickbay.

"I have spoken to the infected man there. He confirmed three people came in and searched the room but didn't find anything and didn't take anything."

"What happened next is also important. There were three intruders, and they confronted one of my men. He said they looked like locals. You can ask him for yourself." One of the security agents took a step forward and nodded. "And they ran right away. They fired a few wild shots, but they were panicked and running. And who in their right mind jumps off the side of a cargo ship?"

Captain Abbott smiled at that. "Are you sure it wasn't a professional attack? We have reason to believe some New Zealand agents are interested in this ship and that they recently arrived here."

Hu realized Abbott had not caught on. He wished he had a better team for support. "Whatever you think, Captain, we will cooperate. It seems that this was a failed robbery, and we hope to get underway as soon as possible without being involved in some extensive investigation. We found nothing missing. We would like to be cleared to leave soon if we can. My men have been at sea for a long time and are eager to see their families. I am sure you understand that."

Abbott said, "Are you certain? We were warned by a police commander from a friendly jurisdiction of a likely attack on your ship. We have been on high alert all night."

No one had warned Hu. That did explain the fast police response both by sea and in blocking the roads. But how did he make this functionary understand he didn't want him to 'do his job'. China didn't want him to 'do his job,' not his official one anyway.

Hu asked, "Don't you have security cameras on this island? What did they capture?"

"That was one of the first things I had checked, Captain. Unfortunately, the cameras aren't working right now, some technical issue."

Hu and Abbott shared a look, the cameras being off was too convenient to be a coincidence.

Hu tried again, "Of course, Captain Abbott, we would like to see these criminals apprehended and punished as much as you would, more even. But Captain-to-Captain, I know I can tell you, and you will understand. Sometimes there is a greater or a higher purpose that must be fulfilled at the cost of lesser goals. There was an attempted robbery, but nothing was taken, there is no serious damage to my ship, none of my crew was injured, and my highest goal is to get this ship to China. Do you understand now, Captain, when I put it that way?"

Hu could see that Abbott was beginning to understand correctly. Abbott said, "Yes, Captain Hu, I see your point. Let my men look around to see if we can find anything that might help us identify the robbers. Would you mind unlocking the sickbay for my men?"

"Not at all," said Hu retrieving his keys from his belt, "but I must warn you the man in there is very sick and is kept isolated for his own good and ours. Your men should know that before they go in. Do you have any protective medical gear?"

Abbott's men who had come forward stopped.

"What does this man have, Captain Hu?" Abbott asked.

Hu leaned in so he could keep his voice down. "Ebola, and not the kind vaccines work against," he said in a stage whisper.

Abbott's eyes widened, and he took a step back. "Are you certain nothing is missing?"

Captain Hu said, "Absolutely certain."

Abbott waved his officers away. "We did not bring any protective gear with us tonight. We will forego an inspection of the sickbay for now."

One of the other police officers asked about possible fingerprints. Abbott looked at Hu. Both men wished this helpful officer would just stay out of it.

Hu motioned for his crewman to stand forward. "Didn't you tell me that you saw that all of the intruders wore gloves?"

The man nodded again and stepped back into line.

Abbott said, "I don't think we need to waste time looking for fingerprints from gloved robbers, especially in a small contaminated room. Your safety is more important than looking under every rock to solve a simple robbery. We would like to check the rest of the ship, Captain Hu. To make sure there is no one still hiding here who could harm you or your crew."

This Abbott was starting to wear thin with Hu. But maybe a good show now would work to his benefit.

"It's your investigation, of course, but we know these intruders never made it off of this deck. Because we had crew members in town, two crew members were stationed on the deck below where both stairwells empty. They keep track of who has returned to the ship and who is still ashore. If a crew member doesn't come back, we become alarmed. When everyone has returned, one of these men can go to bed, but someone is on watch all night. No one came below the main deck at all. With no offense to your men intended, we would just as soon not have our personal belongings or personal spaces invaded and searched. Is it essential under the circumstances? And some of these men are drunk and need to go to bed." Hu laughed slightly and added, "They haven't been ashore for a long time, Captain."

"I guess we can let them get some sleep and forego a search of the lower decks. It is your ship, and I know I can take your word that no one intruded below this deck," Abbott said as one might speak to a superior.

Hu said, "Please feel free to have your men search this deck thoroughly; there are many places one could hide. But stay away from the sickbay, for your own good."

Abbott motioned for his men to search the main deck, and they spread out to explore the area that Hu had defined. Hu knew they wouldn't find anything. He asked Abbott, "Sir, my men are tired, can I let them go down to their quarters now and get some sleep? We hope to be underway later today. And if for any reason you wish to speak to any of them, I will make them available."

One crew member that Hu had identified as encountering the robbers was being interviewed by one of the police officers in the central hallway.

Abbott agreed the others could go below and get some sleep. The crew filed past. Chang was the last crewman to leave the deck. As he passed, he looked at Captain Abbott, who was standing right beside Hu. Abbott looked more Chinese than he did.

When Hu and Abbott were alone, Hu snarled at Abbott, "You imbecile an American heroine, Maddy Gamble and Li Wei, a Chinese dissident and others are prisoners onboard this ship. We need to get to China without your men or others discovering them. Do I make myself perfectly clear now? Get us out of here without further issue!" Hu turned and walked away before Abbott could respond.

***

Maddy heard the sound of many feet clamoring down the stairs; down all the stairwells it seemed to her. There were stairwells fore and aft of the storeroom they were in. Neither she nor any of the other prisoners had spoken since there were armed guards standing over them. Maddy recognized the four prisoners as former students in her class and she could tell by facial expressions they recognized her. Two of the men showed signs of torture and two looked like they hadn't been touched. Maddy wanted badly to talk to them, there was so much she wanted to find out and she wanted to enlist them in an escape plan. Together they might have a chance.

She turned when she heard the door being unlocked. It was Chang. She tamped down her relief at seeing him. Chang spoke to the armed guards in Chinese and they left. Chang then passed out small meal packets, rice and meat and water. The rice and meat were warm and the men ate hungrily. Maddy touched Chang's hand when he passed her a meal. He looked at her but didn't say anything.

Maddy heard a strange sound, music of some sort. Chang reached into his pocket and pulled out a cellphone. It was an Apple phone and looked like the same model phone she had. Chang silenced it and put it back in his pocket.

Maddy said, "Can you get phone service here?"

Chang looked at her and then answered, "Not down here, we are too deep in the ship, but on the deck it is no problem. We are in port so service is very close."

Maddy felt like she should have known that, but she simply nodded. Chang looked at her one last time as he closed and locked the door.

Maddy put her fingers to her lips and went to the door. As soon as she heard his footsteps moving away, she turned back to the four men. "Is it safe to talk in this room?"

They looked around at each other and then one of them said, "We think so. At least nothing we have said has been brought up during interrogations and we tested that early on. So, we think it is safe. What are you doing here, Maddy?"

Maddy decided not to play all of her cards at once. "Okay, English only. The Chinese took me. What are you doing here?"

"The Chinese took us, too, as we were preparing to leave New Zealand. Why did they take you? You have done nothing."

Maddy said, "I don't know, but you apparently know why they have taken you."

The men again looked around at each other and nodded. One of them said, "Yes, Maddy we are agents of the NSB, Taiwan's state security. That's why we were taken."

Maddy understood. She pretended not to and asked, "But in class you all said you were students."

The same man said, "We don't broadcast that we are intelligence agents." There was no false apology. That was just a fact. He added, "We all trained together along with Li Wei for several years. We were about to start our first missions. So, we know China has infiltrated NSB."

"Maddy, have you seen Li Wei? From questions and statements during interrogation we believe he is onboard but none of us have seen him."

Maddy relented, "Yes, he and I were taken at the same time and have been held together."

"Where were you taken?"

"At the Palazzo Motor Lodge."

The men were all silent. Finally, one of them asked, "Were you visiting him?"

"I was there, tutoring him when six men dressed like ninjas came in and took us."

"How is Li Wei or how was he the last time you saw him?"

"Not great. He was tortured by Wang with some electric stick, but has been healing the last several days while we were held together in sickbay. As far as I know he is still there."

She filled the men in about Wang and the rescue effort from what she had seen and what she had overheard when she was moved from the freezer. She said, "So, the way I see it, someone knows we're here and this is likely the last port before China, so if we're going to make an escape it looks like now or never." She didn't mention that she thought one of the rescuers was her husband, she wasn't sure and it seemed so unlikely.

CHAPTER

41

Outside Port Vila
Vanuatu
March 19, 2033
4:15 a.m.

Renee's French doctor friend made a small incision across the bullet wound, both across and up and down. Then he began to probe the wound. Noah moaned softly but did not move. A few minutes later, the doctor had asked for the tweezers and then wrestled them into the bullet hole. The other police officer acted as his assistant. The search with the tweezers seemed to be agonizingly long. Noah squirmed and moaned; Amy squirmed, too, in sympathy. Forehead sweating, the doctor finally pulled out the bullet. He leaned back and told all of us it didn't look good, that the bullet had struck bone. He packed the wound with clean gauze, covered that with a tight mesh sheet, and then wrapped it in sterile bandages. He sponged off the blood on Noah's leg below the wound. He cut off the rest of Noah's pants leg and dropped it on the floor. The bowl that had once held clear hot water was now blood red. We had been here for three hours. I was in a haze. I was tired, worn from the comedown from the night's adrenaline journey, I was sick about Maddy, about our failure and if that would cost her her life. And I was worried for Noah. Very worried. Amy seemed no better off, maybe worse. She held Noah's hand through much of the procedure and spoke to him. Noah never answered her, never opened his eyes.

The doctor looked at Noah, who was still not moving, and finally, he looked up at his friend Renee. He spoke only to Captain Laurent, "I do not know, Renee. I have done all I can do, but I do not know. He has lost so much blood. And the bullet struck bone, but here I am not able to tell how much damage the thighbone sustained. It does not seem broken, but," he shrugged his shoulders, "you must take him to the hospital. It is his only chance. He needs blood badly."

The Captain and the doctor embraced, and we loaded an unconscious Noah into the back seat and turned the SUV around. It was almost dawn. Captain Laurent looked at us. We were in black fatigues, and Amy had a sleeve missing. We wore high top shoes. We were dirty and looked drowned. We had remnants of our communication gear hanging from our necks. We were exhausted, physically, mentally, and emotionally even spiritually.

Captain Laurent knew to take charge.

"So, here is what we are going to do. I will drop the sergeant here off at the hospital with your wounded friend. The sergeant will say he found the injured man near the dock; he must have been involved in the ship's attempted robbery. Robbery is what the official report now says. I expected as much. The sergeant will say he was like this when he found him, unconscious, but someone had tried to tend his wounds. They had decided he was dead or could not help him and left him near the end of the dock building. I am talking about the exact spot where we picked you up. And if they have not done so already, sooner or later, they will find the raft, and who knows what else on or around the ship or in the port building, so we may as well be consistent.

And he will leave your friend to the hospital, a wounded captured criminal. If he survives, he will have to face the courts unless we can find another way, and if he doesn't..."

Renee let his voice trail off, and we knew what that meant. Amy and I looked at each other. Neither of us had a better plan, nor any plan at this point, so we were silent. *Poor Noah. Come on, Noah*, I thought to myself.

"You two need to get back to your penthouse on Iririki Island. I suspect the Maritime Wing of the police will be looking for you if they haven't been already. But you can't go back on the ferry looking like that. I'll help you find some more suitable clothes. And if the Maritime boys ask where you've been, say you spent the night in the park, say Freshwota Park. They won't believe you, but it may buy you some time. And I turned off the security cameras all across the island so they'll have no way to prove you're lying to them."

I looked at Amy and nodded. "How long will you be able to keep them turned off?"

Laurent smiled. "Long enough, my friend, long enough."

"Won't that alert them?"

Laurent smiled again, "It will definitely make them suspicious, but my office handles the cameras. They may suspect something, but boarding their ship has already alerted them." He shrugged.

Captain Laurent took us to his home and sat us in his kitchen. I could hear him talking to someone upstairs, a woman, I think. Then he came back downstairs with clean touristy clothes for each of us, including two pairs of flip flops. Both of us freshened up in his bathroom, just off the kitchen. When he dropped us off near the ferry back to the resort, he said, "Adieu, my friends; give Sara my best." And then he was gone.

We missed the first water shuttle to the Iririki Island Resort and Spa, just barely. It was about thirty meters out from the loading dock when we arrived. There were benches on the pier to sit and wait. So, we did. It was only about fifteen minutes round trip, including loading and unloading. Especially early in the morning, most resort guests weren't out and about, unless, like us, they had been out all night.

Amy leaned her head against my shoulder, and I put my arm around her. I hoped we looked like a loving couple instead of the grieving warriors we were. Noah was wounded and may not make it. And whatever happened there, I was sure Amy would pay dearly with her commander, maybe even with her job. I had seen that her career meant everything to her; it was who she was. She looked up at me and said, "You did good back there. Very good." She reached over and pulled my arm to get my hand out of my hair.

I just nodded. And I grieved for Maddy. We had failed her. *What now? What would become of my wife? Was there any hope? Any chance? What would happen to her?* Amy knew I loved Maddy very much. Very much. "We were so close Amy. Maddy was there within a few feet. I should have gone after her!"

"Maybe Jack," Amy said, "and maybe you would be dead if you had. We will find a way to try again." It didn't help. I still felt deflated, like I had let Maddy down.

I looked at Amy closely. She held my gaze.

When she came into my room last night, Amy had stopped and taken a long look at me. Then she had said, "If Maddy doesn't know what she has in you, I do." Time was I would have tried to turn a comment like that into something, not now. On the night before I planned to risk my life and the lives of others to save my wife, who I loved immensely. I couldn't take a comment like that seriously. I couldn't live without Maddy. I had to rescue her. For just a second, I considered whether what Amy said was a compliment or a come on. I quickly decided on compliment.

Still, I sensed I hurt Amy's feelings. Afterwards, she said she just wanted someone to love her as much as I loved Maddy, don't make too much out of it and that it would never happen again. It brought tears to my eyes to remember. But Amy wasn't watching. Maybe Amy was right that Maddy and Li Wei were having a fling. Maybe, but I trusted Maddy and wanted to hear her side of the story. And if she wanted to be with another man, it would destroy me, but I would let her go if that's what made her happy.

Amy sat still in the tan Bermuda shorts that were a little too big for her and the floral blouse she had tied in a knot above her firm stomach. She had on a big sun hat and sunglasses. That was good. I had seen her eyes, and they looked terrible. Mine must be, too. They felt terrible. My ball cap matched my t-shirt, both dark blue, and I had khaki shorts also and, of course, sunglasses.

The ferry completed its journey to the island and now was starting back. From just down the island, a boat started and came into view; a Vanuatu police boat. They pulled out and turned away from us, back toward the port and *Eternity*. I hadn't thought about that; the Vanuatu Police Maritime Wing was nearby: only a few buildings down the street or down the bank, depending on where you were. I wasn't ready to deal with them yet. And Amy wasn't either; she hadn't even noticed the boat.

The ferry pulled in, and the operator secured it to the dock. A young couple got off, talking excitedly about their day ahead of them. The operator grandly motioned for us to come aboard. Amy walked on without a word. I smiled or tried. The operator seemed to pay us no mind, and in a couple of minutes, we were on the island walking toward the penthouse.

When we got close, Adam came out to help us in. His eyes widened as he took in Amy. He looked behind us, I guess, for Noah, but he didn't say anything until we were in his room on the first level and all doors were closed.

"Where's Noah?" Adam asked.

"In a hospital, with a bad gunshot wound in his leg," I answered.

Adam looked down and away.

"He might not make it," Amy added. "And it's all my fault. He would never have done this on his own; he was only in this because I asked him to."

"What happened?" Adam said.

I explained the search of sickbay, finding Li Wei, and his refusal to leave. Amy took over. "And then they found us. Two of them were coming down from the bridge right on top of us. We had nowhere to hide or run. So, Noah shot the first guy, and the second guy retreated to the bridge. I could tell Noah wanted to go after him. That's our training. Then Maddy was pushed up the stairs by someone with a gun to her head, who immediately pulled her back down the steps. We were about to go after her when more guys came running down the side of the ship where the ladder was, so we had to break for the other side of the boat. Noah was our rearguard. It should've been me, but Noah did it. Just when we were almost out the door onto the starboard deck, he got hit. We pulled him out, and then the three of us went over the rail into the Coral Sea."

"Jesus! How did you get out of there?"

I explained about Laurent and all that had happened and leaving Noah at the hospital.

Adam nodded like he knew the place. "Laurent is the best. I've worked with him several times, and I know he and Sara have worked together, too." He looked at Amy and said, "You couldn't have left Noah in any better hands. And it's not your fault. Noah knew what could happen. Jack, kudos to you. Good job, man."

Amy looked at Adam but didn't say anything. I couldn't tell what she was thinking.

"Then I guess Laurent got you some different clothes and dropped you at the ferry?"

"Right," I said. "What happened to you after you and that Chinese guy left *Eternity?*"

"That Chinese guy named Wang is a mean son of a bitch by all accounts. He's the guy Sara believes killed her family."

"No shit?" I asked.

"No shit. Wang didn't give me any trouble getting to the SUV, but I didn't like my odds trying to manage him and drive without any help, so I knocked him out with the butt of my pistol, tied his feet, gagged him, and put him in the back of the SUV with a blanket over him. When I left, Laurent still had the roadblocks on Wharf Road, and he himself looked into my vehicle and let me pass. I told him you three were still on the ship. Anyway, I took Wang to a safe house used by the SIS from time to time and called in some friends. One of these guys recognized Wang and got Wang to confirm who he was. On *Eternity*, I thought he just made up a name. Wang is ubiquitous. When I found out, I called Sara. I bet she'll be on her way here. She's the best interrogator there ever was. The best. I had to get back here, so I left two guys with Wang, and one guy brought me across to the island in a little fishing boat. I thought you guys would be right behind me. I left my gear with my buddies, and also got rid of anything incriminating."

Amy said, "Thanks, good thinking."

Adam said, "But we better give it a second look. The Vanuatu Police, the Maritime Wing has already been here, and they were asking about the three of you. They'll be back, and they'll know about Noah soon."

"What did you tell them?" Amy asked.

"Nothing. Said I didn't know where any of you were."

"Good," Amy said, "best you could do."

Together we searched all three floors of the penthouse. We found some additional communication equipment and a Smith and Wesson revolver that was apparently Noah's. Adam destroyed the communications equipment with the heel of a shoe and put it in the dirty linens bag near his doorway. When he opened the bag, I could see his fatigues and some other gear already in there. Catching my look, Adam said, "Guy that will pick this up is in our employ sometimes."

Adam looked from Amy to me. "You may not like this, but the best thing is to get in the plane with Joe and get back to New Zealand, now this morning. You could be airborne in forty-five minutes. It would solve a lot of issues."

I could see *Eternity* from where I stood. "As long as Maddy is here on that ship, I'm not leaving."

Amy said, "And I'm not leaving Noah, not until we know."

Adam nodded his head. "Yeah, that's kind of what I thought, but I had to try. If you're both going to stay, get some sleep. You'll need to be sharp when the police get back, and it won't be long."

We nodded and I said, "Captain Laurent suggested what we should say."

"Go with it then," Adam said and then added, "And stay in the same room. Remember the police think you're a couple. Act like it."

CHAPTER

42

Headquarters, Vanuatu Police Maritime Wing
Port Vila, Vanuatu
March 19, 2033
2:45 p.m.

Captain Abbott pulled all of his ranking officers together for a meeting: everyone sergeant and above; three men in total, one lieutenant and two sergeants. They all reported to him, all of the Maritime Wing, and he reported only to the Commissioner who was over all Vanuatu police. Headquarters was in Port Vila in a lovely older building on Lini Highway. Because they were the maritime division, they also had a boat dock out back right on Port Vila Bay. Abbott's office looked out over the bay, including the port and Iririki Island. His land-based counterpart, Captain Laurent, called the maritime wing the resort police because much of their activity took place on the resort island. Captain Laurent was longer serving than he was, but they were of equal rank, which he often had to mention to Laurent. They both reported directly to the Commissioner. The differences lie in the locus of the crime or need for police activity. And also, in that Laurent had sixteen officers of the rank of sergeant or higher reporting to him. Abbott loved his view, but he would have gladly traded it for more direct reports. In 2028 Abbott had been instrumental in expanding the maritime wing's duties from enforcing fishing regulations and immigration issues to general criminal enforcement and authority over the port and the resort islands in the bay. That was the same year Australia gifted its second Guardians Class Patrol Boat to Vanuatu. Two patrol boats, five smaller boats, and four motor rafts comprised the flotilla under his command. At least one of the patrol boats and about half of the other boats were always at Port Vila; sometimes, both patrol boats were here like they were at the moment.

Just now, he was looking at the island. From his office, he could not see the penthouse where the New Zealanders were staying, but he knew where it was. The surveillance cameras still were not working. Abbott checked them several times each day.

After this meeting, he would confront the New Zealanders. He knew they were involved in this. Somehow. He just didn't know how or why. And he knew the incident on *Eternity* wasn't a failed robbery.

He started his meeting by asking his officers where they were investigating the attempted robbery on *Eternity*. "Lieutenant, why don't you lead off with what evidence we have?"

"Thank you, sir. From *Eternity*, we have the rope ladder, the bolt cutters, and the lock pick. We also found a suspicious-looking pole in the port building near where the ladder was secured. We're having all of those dusted for fingerprints along with the two cargo containers that were opened and the outside doorknob of the sickbay door." Abbott knew he would have to find a way to squelch the check of the doorknob. Hu made that clear.

He asked, "Have the container doors and doorknob on the ship already been dusted?"

"Yes, Captain, late this morning."

Abbott was relieved; He would not have to intervene since the dusting was already done. And he knew how to handle any complaints Hu might have. He knew it would take a week or more for the fingerprint results to come back, and by then, *Eternity* would be long gone. That is what Hu wanted, and Hu outranked him.

"What else have we got?"

"Bullet casings, nineteen in all. Look to be from all sorts of weapons. I'm not surprised; merchant sailors carry all manner of ordinance and robbers, too. I sent those to ballistics. Plus, we have some pictures and diagrams showing bullet marks inside the ship."

"Anything else?"

"I have a written statement from the crew member who encountered the robbers, and the Captain has promised to write his answers to written questions I submitted to him and to get answers to written questions for the guy quarantined in sickbay. I should have those late today."

"Excellent. You guys are on top of things."

"Well, sir," one of the sergeants said, "we still have no idea who tried to rob the ship."

The other sergeant said, "We might. You didn't hear this from me, but Laurent's boys have a wounded man in the private hospital. They picked him up last night just outside the port building forty-five minutes after the bungled robbery. And a black raft was parked under the mangroves near the same end of the building where this guy was supposedly found. Our guys spotted it half an hour ago. They're examining it now."

Abbott sat forward. "I want to know about the raft as soon as possible. Tell me what you know about this man in the hospital."

The second sergeant said, "Look, I wanted you to know, but a buddy of mine who works for landlubber Laurent told me in confidence, can we keep him out of it?"

"Of course," Abbott said, not knowing whether he could or couldn't.

"Okay, there's not much to tell. The guy is a John Doe. No ID, and last I knew, he was still unconscious. My guy said he might not make it. Laurent has two guys guarding his hospital room; he claims that the guy was found on dry land and belongs to him."

Abbott grunted.

"I know one of the nurses on that floor. She says he looks pretty bad. White guy, younger, fairly fit. He was dressed in black when he came in. Someone had doctored his leg wound before he got there, bullet removed, wound cleaned and dressed. Doesn't sound like work done by or for typical robbers, does it?" Abbott looked for more.

"That's all I know."

"What hospital?"

"The Private Hospital."

"They don't handle gunshot wounds."

The sergeant shrugged.

"Who the hell is paying for that?"

"Laurent, I guess."

***

Sara's estimated flight time was two and a half hours. Sara called Adam in Port Vila to let him know she was coming, the additional equipment she would need, and she asked him to pick her up. Then she settled in to plan her interrogation of Wang. He had been a Chinese operative many years and undoubtedly had much to share: the names of agents, the identities of counter agents, current operations, funding sources, cover companies, agent smuggling routes and methods in and out of New Zealand and other countries. But would he talk? And could she get him to talk quickly enough to help Maddy and Li Wei if they weren't already beyond help. She would like to have three weeks at a minimum and realized she might not even have three days. She had established contact with Wellington, so they knew what was going on and would be available to approve any deal. The idea of offering Wang anything made her sick to her stomach. Wellington said, "Sara, we have other agents. Maybe it would be better if someone else handled this. Someone who is not so personally involved."

"Screw that," Sara said, "I'm going." And no one had tried to stop her.

The children had been upset that she was leaving, but what else could she do.? Nickau and his father had taken over caring for them.

Wellington arranged for her to bypass security at the airport. She decided she liked it this way. It was way more comfortable than explaining to airport security what those devices were in her carry-on. Even with her government ID, it was sometimes tricky. She would need those tools plus what Adam would get to get the truth out of Wang. Thank goodness Port Vila had fixed its runway. Sara could remember when commercial flights stopped going there. She shook her head, an island nation with no commercial air service. That was all fixed, all good for now. The private charter from Nelson had been expensive enough without also needing a private plane from Auckland to Port Vila. Even if she wasn't paying, she kept an eye on costs.

Sara made notes, pages of them. She knew a great deal about Wang already. She had studied him since determining he was behind the deaths of her family. She was irritated that he had been in Nelson; it seemed taunting, disrespectful. She would make him regret that. And she would get him to confess to abducting Maddy. That could go a long way in stopping *Eternity* at sea or in negotiating Maddy's release from China.

The pilot of the New Zealand Air flight from Auckland announced that they had been cleared for landing in Port Vila. Sara was the first one off the plane and used her government ID to bypass customs. She made her way quickly through the airport and out the front door.

Adam was waiting for her in front of the airport in a small white sedan. She climbed in, and they started to pull away when police flashers came on behind them.

"Uh oh," Adam said.

Captain Abbott left the flashers on and came up to the driver's door. "You again? Who are you picking up this time? I got an alert that yet another New Zealand spook was paying us a visit on this flight. Is this her?" He bent and looked in the window at Sara.

"And just who the fuck are you?" Sara growled.

"Ma'am, I'm Captain Abbott of the Vanuatu Police, and I will thank you to mind your manners and your language."

"Abbott, you say. How does a full-blooded Chinese come to have the name, Abbott?" Sara said.

Adam tried to calm things down. "I'm sure what she meant to say was..."

Sara would have none of it.

"I meant exactly what I said. I want to know who the hell he is. He says he's Captain Abbott, but he doesn't look like any Abbott I ever knew. I want to make sure I know with whom I am dealing. That's all."

To Adam's surprise, Captain Abbott produced and showed his ID. As Sara was studying it, he said, "For what it's worth, I was adopted by my stepfather, Abbott was his name. My mother was Chinese; we both took his name. My real father is unknown."

Sara nodded and handed back his ID. "And you are, ma'am?" Abbott said.

"I'm a friend of Captain Laurent. That's all you need to know. I'm sure you'll hear from him about your stopping passengers at the airport and interrogating them. Your authority stops at the water's edge, as I recall. Good day, sir," Sara said. And then to Adam, "Come on, let's go."

Sara watched as Abbott stood red-faced. Adam pulled away. She had intentionally overplayed her hand. Now let's see what this Abbott did, see if it revealed whose side he was on.

Adam was laughing. "Same old Sara, I see. I could never pull something like that off."

"Nothing to it," Sara said. "What we need to be concerned about is who he's working for and how he knew I'd be on that plane."

"I have a theory," Adam said. "Amy's commander busted on her for coming here; ordered her not to. She told him to pound salt or something, and she and Noah Montgomery came anyway. This same guy, Abbott, was here when they landed to warn them against violating any local laws. Maybe the Nelson Commander said something about you, too."

"Maybe. What's the latest on the rescue effort?"

Adam's face grew serious. "Not good, I'm afraid. They couldn't find Maddy. They found Li Wei, but he wouldn't leave with them, said the state agents would kill Maddy if he did. Amy got a couple of pictures of him on the ship. And Noah's badly wounded. He's in the hospital, still out, under the watch of your friend, Captain Laurent. He's the only reason any of them got away. Now Renee says *Eternity* and the Maritime Division, that asshole you just met, are calling it a failed robbery."

"I was afraid of something like that," Sara said. "They're just trying to get out of here as quickly as possible. We need to move Wang somewhere that only you and I and maybe one other person knows about."

"Amy and Jack?"

"I guess they'll have to do."

CHAPTER

43

Iririki Island Resort and Spa
Port Vila, Vanuatu
March 19, 2033
9:30 p.m.

Sara and Wang were alone on the top floor of the penthouse. I now had the second floor, and Adam and Amy shared the first floor. Adam had several other operatives on standby, but he wouldn't tell them where we were. It was a terrible location. Everyone agreed. We were trapped or easily could be, and the headquarters of the Vanuatu Police Maritime Wing was just minutes away. There were cameras everywhere and I wasn't sure if they were part of island security and turned off or belonged to the resort. Who could see through them? Even with the adjoining units empty, it was a risky spot. It was what we had.

Sara called down and asked Adam to come up and spell her. In a few minutes, she came down, and Amy and Sara and I were together on the lowest level.

"How's it going up there?" I asked.

"Slow," Sara said. "I need to see if I can buy some more time and at least need to know how much time I do have." She called Captain Laurent.

"Renee?"

"*Ma cherie*, I would know that voice anywhere. Where are you, my darling?"

"In Port Vila, better if you don't know exactly where. I need to check in with you on some things."

"Anything, you know that."

"So, for starters, tell me about *Eternity*. Where is the investigation, how long will it take, how much time do I have while it will still be in port here."

"I'm afraid I have awful news there, Sara. The crime was committed on a ship, and so the Maritime Wing claims jurisdiction over the investigation. The crime is nowhere near being solved. It will never be solved because the whole idea of a robbery is a fabrication. It's not our fabrication: the Chinese are anxious to get out of here. And we know why. The US Naval ships out of Palau have continued their journey toward us and may block *Eternity*'s escape. No one knows what the Americans' plans are, but we're watching closely, and I must assume the Chinese are as well. Captain Abbott, the head of the Maritime Wing, declared the investigation sufficiently complete, and all aspects related to the ship itself sufficiently investigated. He ordered the ship released. The tugs will tow it out of the port tomorrow afternoon at five."

"Shit," Sara said. "That's not much time. I met that asshole, Abbott, at the airport. Whose team is he on anyway? He knew I was on the flight and pulled us over to intimidate us. I told him to go back to the water where he had jurisdiction."

"Oh, I am sure you did. And he may very well have mixed loyalties, if you know what I mean. I feel much more like we compete than cooperate."

"Is there anything you can do, Renee, to give us some more time? Anything?"

"I will try, my love. It may be difficult, but I will try."

"Let me change topics. With this officially being a robbery, are my friends here able to tell Abbott to go take a hike if he comes to question them?"

"Hmm. Not exactly, but you can try this. You can all say that Captain Laurent has already interviewed you and that I told you my division had jurisdiction over this matter and not to speak with anyone else. Abbott will be furious, and ultimately this is his case, but it may buy some time. So far, I've claimed jurisdiction over the wounded man. I do not wish to know his identity so keep that to yourself. My claim to jurisdiction comes from finding him on dry land. The Commissioner will not be happy with me, but Abbott and I have these little spats all the time."

"Any news on the wounded man? Some people here would like to know but can't go to or call the hospital for obvious reasons."

"Yes, *ma cherie*, finally I have some good news for all of you. The doctors say he will make it. His leg is broken and must be set and put in a cast at some point. They are waiting to see if the swelling will go down a bit first. The poor man is in terrible pain, so he regularly receives pain medication, which largely keeps him knocked out. It will be at least a couple of days before anyone can talk to him. Your friends will be gone by then, no?"

"I understand, Renee. Try to make it three days on all things if you can. Please. Any other news?"

"Only this. The Maritime Wing found a raft today hidden near the dock building, near the same end where I have reported finding the wounded man. Everyone presumes the wounded man is one of the robbers. The Police cannot tie the raft to any others, can they?"

"Let me look into that. How about the cameras, are they operable?"

"No, do not worry about the cameras. We have known for a while they were compromised so my staff has taken control of the technology that runs them, and right now they are down and will stay down until I say so. Abbott calls to check on them regularly. And every day we tell him of a new technical difficulty. But if we need the cameras, I can have them back in operation within fifteen minutes."

"Perfect, Renee. Thank you."

"And what will you do after you complete your work here, my sweet?"

"I'm afraid I can't stay, not this time, Renee. Perhaps another time."

"Perhaps."

After Sara completed her call, I asked, "What about Maddy? What will happen to her now? Have we only made things worse?"

Sara blew out her breath, "I wish I knew, Jack. I hope not, but they know we tried to rescue her. They will certainly be on high alert now, but will they..." She let her thought trail off, unsaid.

I pushed back the hair on the sides of my head.

***

Captain Abbott sat in his office and looked out at the water. It was a calm night; the water lapped gently at the boats moored offshore. He could hear music coming from the resort across the water. Should he gather some men and go to the penthouse to see if the couple had returned? To make sure they knew he knew they were involved even if he couldn't yet prove it? He was working on identifying the wounded man in the hospital. He had been there three times, and Laurent's men stopped him each time.

"You'll have to clear that up with him, sir." "We can't let you in. Captain Laurent claims this is his case." "Up to you, sir, if you want to involve the commissioner." And more excuses. The man's doctor claimed he was unconscious, but some of the nurses claimed to have seen him with his eyes open. Laurent couldn't keep this up forever. And in another day, it wouldn't matter. *Eternity* would be gone. For now, all he had to do was keep up the pressure, pretend to be pursuing things. He called at least once every day about the cameras. He knew Laurent had done something to disable them. He would keep up the pretense that he didn't know that and wondered when they would work. Tonight, he would not go to the penthouse. Perhaps tomorrow. Tonight, he would enjoy the cool soft breeze and another glass of wine.

***

Sara went back upstairs with Wang. Adam came downstairs. "I don't know," he said, "As good as Sara is, he is one tough customer."

"Has he said anything at all?" I asked.

"Nothing about *Eternity*. Wang denies having anything to do with the murder of Sara's family. He says he knew nothing about it. But he made a mistake; he knew how many children she had. I think the bastard killed them himself. Bastard. Let's hope Sara makes him talk before she goes off on him. We need to know about Maddy and *Eternity*. I can see Sara is barely able to control herself. This may be too much even for her. If we had more people, we would never leave her alone with him."

"Can we get more people?"

"Yes, but it will take a couple of days, maybe more. The CIA is actually sending some people. Sara thinks my group here has been compromised and won't work with them or let me keep them informed. And she may be right. The CIA may want to stay out of it. I'm not sure. They did ask, and I did describe what was going on. They seemed very interested in when *Eternity* would be back at sea. They asked if we could slow things down. And, of course, they would tell me nothing in return."

We all thought about our situation and our choices.

Amy said, "Adam, I have an idea. The Maritime Police know we're here, and it's only a question of time before they come back to question us. What do you think of moving Wang's interrogation to the property next door? You said your agency rented the adjoining villas."

"I think that's an excellent idea, Amy. Blindfold Wang and move him and then keep him in a darkened room. Still close, but if the maritime boys come back and we can't put them off, a search here will reveal nothing."

Thirty minutes later, Sara held the arm of a blindfolded Wang and led him out. As they passed by, I punched him in the stomach with more force than I have ever hit anyone. He doubled over. Sara shook her head, but no one moved to stop me. I kept all of my angry words inside my head and let Wang worry about who had just hit him and why. What had he done to Maddy?

Wang and Sara both disappeared inside the villa next door. From the outside, no light was visible. Amy and I tried to get some sleep while Sara and Adam took turns questioning Wang into the wee hours of the morning.

CHAPTER

44

Iririki Island Resort and Spa
Port Vila, Vanuatu
March 20, 2033
6:30 a.m.

Adam's phone rang and woke both of us. Amy was upstairs asleep, and Sara was next door with Wang. Adam answered, "Hello?"

"Yeah, boss, Police come now. Maritime."

Adam hung up. His unofficial early warning system might not meet Sara's strict secrecy guidelines, but it sure came in handy.

"Jack, that was a friend. The Police are on their way. Go up and wake Amy. Better yet, crawl in bed with her."

Adam sent a text message of three asterisks to Sara. As soon as he knew it had been received, he deleted it.

There was a loud banging on the door. "Police. Open the door."

Adam called out, "Coming." He ran his hand through his hair to make it look mussed and walked barefoot to the door. When he opened it, he stood in the door opening with one hand on the door jam and one hand on the edge of the door. "Yes," he said sleepily.

Captain Abbott was leading a contingent of six officers. Their uniforms identified them as Maritime Wing policemen. Abbott said, "We want to search your premises. Get out of the way."

I came down the steps with Amy to see what was going on. We sat on the steps to the upper levels and watched.

Adam said, "The police have already searched our premises and said we would not be bothered again."

"When?" Abbott said, stepping closer.

"Yesterday," Adam said. "Three officers under the command of Captain Laurent searched this place from top to bottom. And they said if anyone from the Police bothered us again to call Captain Laurent or have them call him to straighten it out. Said it was their case and not Maritime Wing's case." Adam made a point of looking over their uniforms, particularly the "maritime wing" patches.

He looked straight at Abbott. "That's who you are, Maritime Wing, right?" Abbott knew Adam knew they were. He made no move to leave.

"Do you want to call Captain Laurent, or shall I?" Adam said.

Abbott turned to Amy and me and said, "I see the newlyweds have returned. Where were you yesterday morning and the night before that?"

I said, "We slept under the stars in Freshwota Park; it was a great night for that." I brushed my hair back with my right hand and hoped it looked casual.

Abbott said, "No one sleeps under the stars there. It's only a tiny park."

Amy leaned into me and said, "It was so romantic. The palm trees were fluttering in the wind high above us."

Abbott looked to one of his men and said menacingly, "Check the camera footage from Freshwota Park for these two."

By the slow way his officer pulled out a pad to make a note, I thought Abbott was bluffing, trying to intimidate us. I decided not to push it any further and gave no indication that I thought the cameras weren't working.

Abbott looked up the steps. "And where is the other man, your cousin, I believe." His tone of voice made it obvious he didn't believe any of it. Adam said, "We haven't seen him for a couple of days. Maybe he met someone."

"Aren't you worried? Could he be hurt? Could he be in a hospital somewhere? Have you looked for him?"

Abbott suspected much more than he knew.

Amy said, "I got a text from him last night. Said he was doing fine and having fun. He'll show up."

"When he does, make sure you contact me," Abbott snarled. "And where is the woman you picked up at the airport yesterday?" he said to Adam.

"Whoa! Wait just a minute. You're here because of some robbery on a ship that occurred the day before this lady even arrived here, and you want to question me about her? We'll have to leave that for Captain Laurent to sort out as well."

Abbott looked hard at Adam, glanced around at the adjoining units, and then led his men back up the pathway toward the main lodge and the boat dock.

His lieutenant moved up beside him and said, "Is that what you were expecting, sir?" It was not at all what Abbott had expected; he enjoyed throwing his weight around. He did not take well to being challenged. Abbott answered, "Yes, pretty much. I know they're involved in this. I can smell it."

"What now, sir?"

"See if you can get me a photograph of the wounded man in the Private Hospital. Is he still supposedly unconscious?"

"As far as I know, he is. I will check with the nurse there, and while I'm at it, I will ask her to take a photograph for me."

When he was alone in his office, Captain Abbott called the Vanuatu Civil Aviation Authority at Bauerfield Airport.

"Yes, hello. This is Captain Abbott of the Vanuatu police in Port Vila. I need a copy of the landing permit for a small plane that landed there on March 17, at about six p.m.. Can you get that for me, please?"

"Sure, do you need the permit itself, or do you want any attachments like passenger or cargo lists?"

Abbott could hear keys clicking in the background.

"Everything, please," he said.

"Okay, got it. Want me to send it to your division like always to whatever her name is in Captain Laurent's office?"

"No, not this time. Send it to CAbbott@VPMW.gov."

"What did you say your name was?"

"Abbott, Captain Abbott."

"Hmm, I'm aware of Captain Laurent. I didn't know we had two Captains in Vanuatu. No matter, this is a public record. There, you should have it now."

"Yes, I see it. Thank you."

Abbott opened the attachment; there was the passenger list: Amy Wirihana, Jack Gamble, and Noah Montgomery. If those were their real names, he now had to figure out who wasn't on Iririki Island, Gamble, or Montgomery. The one not there was more than likely the wounded man in the hospital.

His search didn't take long. By typing Jack Gamble into his computer, he got many, many articles and images. Gamble was the American that years ago had liberated Ebola Island, Madagascar really, and been a hero worldwide. He remembered the story even if he had forgotten the name. From the multiple images, there could be no doubt that Jack Gamble was on Iririki Island, and that was probably Amy Wirihana with him. Who and where was Noah Montgomery?

***

Captain Laurent strode onto *Eternity*, accompanied by two of his officers. The crew of the ship was busy making preparations to depart. One of Laurent's men instructed a crew member to get the captain. Laurent stood with his hands behind his back, holding a clipboard. He seemed bored.

In a few minutes, Captain Hu appeared on deck. The two captains shook hands.

"You seem to be preparing to set sail, Captain Hu."

"Yes, later today. Captain Abbott has cleared us to go."

"Oh? Well, he has forgotten something."

"Forgotten what, Captain Laurent? I understood we were all clear."

"It's just a little paperwork, nothing much. It can all be completed and submitted on your computer, but for your convenience, I have taken the liberty of printing out a copy for your use."

Captain Laurent handed Hu a twenty-page form.

Hu said, "What is this?"

"Ship certification forms, Captain. Vanuatu law requires that anytime a ship is the scene of a crime or is in any way involved in a crime, its certification paperwork must be updated before it's permitted to set sail."

Hu's face tightened. "Captain Abbott never said anything about this, and the robbery is his case, is it not?"

"Apparently, he has forgotten this provision. You can look it up if you'd like. There is a reference somewhere in that form I just gave you. And yes, releasing your ship is normally a maritime wing function, but this certification is required. I'm just trying to help out."

Hu looked down at the forms, fingering through them. "This will take hours, maybe days to complete."

"Yes, I'm afraid it might. Do the best you can. There is a number for someone in my office you or your crew can call for help."

Hu's face tightened again, but he did not wish to get into an argument with this police officer. He simply nodded.

Captain Laurent turned to go. He stopped and said, "I've taken the liberty of canceling the pilot tugs scheduled to take you to sea later today. Let me know when you have completed that form." And then he and his officers strode off the deck of *Eternity*.

Hu went to the bridge. The first mate and Chang were busy making final preparations to set sail. Hu did not speak to them. His lips were tightly pursed which made his scar even more red and obvious. He threw the papers down on the desk and picked up his cell phone.

When Abbott answered, Hu exploded even though Chang and the first mate were still on the bridge. "Abbott, that Captain Laurent has been on my ship today saying we need to file certification documents before we can leave here. Is that true?"

There was a pause while Abbott responded and Hu continued, "Two things, a long form he says needs filling out and a citation that he says he must lift before we can set sail and which will only happen when the form is completed and approved. Can he do that?"

Abbott knew that he could. It was very rare to have an incident on a ship in their port. Typically, he would waive the certification for a minor matter. He had meant to do so here but had forgotten.

Hu shook his head as he listened.

"Do something, Abbott. Are you working on my behalf or not?"

Again, Hu listened. Then he threw his arms up.

"Now, how in the hell would I know that? This is not my real job, as you know. There is a hold order on my ship. I thought I could count on you to take care of things so this would not happen. You can be sure this will be in my report, Abbott," Hu shouted.

Hu hung up and threw down his phone. He looked up at the first mate and Chang as if aware of them for the first time. They both looked away. They had heard his end of the conversation with Abbott. He needed to be more careful.

"Belay that," he said to the two crewmen. "We will not be leaving today." Hu handed the certification form to the first mate. "We need to get this all completed as soon as possible. No sleep until it is done and submitted. Do you understand me?" Hu's lip was quivering.

The first mate nodded, and Hu stormed off the bridge. The first mate handed the form to Chang. "You do it."

Chang protested, "But I have never done this before."

The first mate smiled and said, "Neither have I, none of us have. Captain Zhao has always handled these official forms. Now we will learn, you will learn. That's an order, Chang."

CHAPTER

45

Headquarters, Vanuatu Police Maritime Wing
Port Vila, Vanuatu
March 21, 2033
4:15 p.m.

Abbott was looking at a picture on his phone of a Caucasian male about thirty-five years old, lying in a hospital bed with his eyes closed.

Abbott studied his face. He looked peaceful and stressed at the same time. So, now this injured man had a name and a picture. He knew the guy that had picked all of them up at Bauerfield Airport was a New Zealand agent. New Zealand and Vanuatu were friendly toward each other. But that didn't mean all the citizens of either nation agreed with that. And each country jealously guarded its sovereignty, especially tiny Vanuatu.

Abbott suspected this Noah Montgomery was from New Zealand. He started in Tauranga, where the flight to Port Vila had originated. Abbott found nothing on a Noah Montgomery from Tauranga. He tried Noah Montgomery, New Zealand, and got lots of hits but no images and nothing definitive. After three pages, the search results left New Zealand behind and showed Noah Montgomery from the United

States and Australia, and the United Kingdom. Of course, they were all possibilities, but he didn't have the time or people to run them all down. No, he needed to tailor a tighter search. Montgomery? Noah? Could that be short for something? Tauranga? Tauranga, where had he heard or read about that place recently?

Eternity! That was it. Tauranga had been *Eternity*'s last scheduled stop before Port Vila, but not its port of origin. Could it be a coincidence? Like all good policemen, Abbott didn't believe in coincidence.

He dug out *Eternity*'s earlier itinerary from the records he had on the ship. The records followed a vessel as it journeyed. *Eternity* had left from Nelson, New Zealand, on March ninth. He sat back and thought about what that might mean. He knew the small plane carrying Noah Montgomery and Amy Wirihana and Jack Gamble had something to do with things. He had gotten a discreet warning from his contact in China that New Zealand agents would be trying to compromise *Eternity* while she was in port and that it was imperative that they not succeed. There was no other information. Compartmentalization meant keeping sources and some specifics hidden. It was enough if you knew what to do; one did not need to know all the whys and wherefores. Maybe it was as simple as that. Wirihana and Montgomery were SIS agents, and these were not their real names. In that case, he would never find them. While he had the *Eternity's* records he noted Laurent's order preventing its departure. He had meant to waive any minor deficiencies by placing an order to that effect in the file, but he had forgotten and Laurent had acted first. He could see where someone, probably Laurent, had printed out the computer file just prior to the hold order. Backdating and filing an order now would not work. Laurent would not outsmart him again. And Hu didn't need to know any of this. Compartmentalization worked in many circumstances.

Abbott decided to recheck the landing permit of the small plane that had brought Montgomery to Vanuatu. He had found the passenger manifest right below the landing permit itself. Abbott pushed a little further and was pleased to discover that planes, like ships, traveled with their paperwork for a particular journey. He knew things hadn't always been this transparent, but right now, he was happy with the computerization of all travel records. The plane had originated in Nelson, New Zealand, on March 12 and had been chartered initially by Detective Noah Montgomery of the Nelson police. Got you! Abbott thought. *You have been following Eternity all along. He* searched the Nelson police, and there was a picture of Detective Noah Montgomery. The official police photograph looked a few years old, but it was the same man now lying in a hospital bed across town. Abbott scrolled down, and there was Detective Amy Wirihana, so those were their real names. Two Nelson police detectives had followed *Eternity* from Nelson to Port Vila, had failed to rescue Gamble's wife and the Chinese dissident Li Wei but may have been successful in capturing Wang.

None of this was shocking to Abbott, but he still liked to connect the dots. Captain Abbott unlocked the safe behind him. He removed another cell phone, turned it on, and entered a password. Then he held the phone in front of his right eye for iris identification and entered another password to unencrypt the phone's contents. Abbott scrolled through the contacts on this secret phone until he located Bo Peng, known to most people as Commander Li.

"Commander Li."

"Commander, this is Captain Abbott of the Vanuatu Police Maritime Wing."

The Commander knew who he was. "Captain."

"Yes, Commander, I'm sorry to call you." Sorry was an understatement. Both Abbott and Li knew they were never to contact each other directly. It could endanger their entire network and was an offense that others had paid for with their lives. No one was more important than the cause went the saying. That is why the Commander had sent his warning to Vanuatu via contacts in Beijing.

"What is it, Captain?" the Commander said, irritation apparent.

"I have a situation here involving two of your officers, a Noah Montgomery and an Amy Wirihana," Abbott said, reverting to an official script.

"I see, Captain. In Vanuatu?"

"Yes, sir. Montgomery is seriously wounded in a hospital here, and Wirihana, I believe, is pretending to be someone else and was involved in an operation conducted at night against a Chinese ship."

"Can you prove that, Captain?"

"Not quite yet, sir, but I know it to be true and feel confident I will be able to prove it when Montgomery comes to and is available for questioning."

"Yes, Commander, and I believe your officers together with New Zealand SIS agents may have taken a Chinese man off of *Eternity*, a man who goes by the name of Wang."

"Oh no, not Wang. What is it you would like me to do, Captain?"

"Sir, my priority is to find this Wang."

"Agreed."

"And secondly, I would like to get these New Zealanders out of my country. We will handle our own affairs."

"I understand, Captain; I warned my detectives not to go to Vanuatu for that very reason. They disobeyed my direct order and will face the consequences upon their return."

"The sooner you can get them back there, the better for all of us, especially Montgomery."

"I'll see what I can do, Captain. Anything else?"

"Yes, do you know who Sara Singh is?"

"Sara Singh is the false name of Mina Kaur, the most decorated woman in the history of the SIS, a woman whose family Wang slaughtered."

Both men paused at the enormity of Li's statement. Had he really said that out loud.?

"I'll see what I can do to get my detectives home, Captain, soon. You don't need to call me again." *Ever*! He thought as he prepared to hang up.

"Wait a minute, Captain. Can I call you back on another line? I have to take an important call."

Abbott gave him a number, they both knew it was a private number, and Li would not be calling back on a police line.

Abbott's phone rang within just a few seconds.

"Abbott. You are not to use my official number, ever, do you understand?"

"Yes. I thought it was important."

"Proper channels are important; the security of the network is important. You should have communicated via China. You have put us both at unnecessary risk."

"I didn't have a choice. Communication via Beijing can take days, Li, and we don't have days. I need to find Wang and rescue him or eliminate him."

"I agree he is a danger to all of us in enemy hands, especially with Singh as his interrogator. Where is he being held?"

"Not sure. Can you reach your female detective and see if she will tell you?"

"I can try. What has become of the Gamble woman and the dissident?"

"They are still hidden onboard *Eternity* now under Hu's command."

Commander Li laughed. "Hu? Smart-mouth in command of a ship? He knows about as much about ships as I do. He must be furious at the delays. When will they leave?"

"Not sure. They're hung up on paperwork right now; I'm trying to help them through it."

Abbott saw no reason to explain everything.

"That must be secondary to finding Wang, and I suggest eliminating him. He is a much greater risk to all of us, to China, than a two-bit dissident or the American woman. Wang is a fool to have even taken her. He should have eliminated her before his first port. Li Wei would never command so much interest from New Zealand on his own. Has there been any communication from Taiwan about Li Wei?"

"None, they seem to be denying him."

Li grunted. "They trained him for four years, set up a job and an identity for him and now they abandon him? China will do the same in regards to Wang."

Abbott asked, "See if your detective will at least tell you where this Sara Singh is. If we find her, we find Wang."

"Yes, I will try. I have an idea. Should you disclose that a New Zealand detective was shot while intruding on a cargo ship owned by another nation? He may be a detective here, but he is no friend of mine."

"Maybe Commander, I am still thinking that over. Right now, I hope to hold that back until I can get *Eternity* out of here and then make an international issue out of it."

"You are there. I am not. Remember, eliminate Wang first, then deal with *Eternity*. If it continues to be problematic, eliminate the two prisoners and Hu and dispose of the bodies. You can do that, can't you?"

"Yes, I can do that."

"Good, and then leave the ship to its fate."

CHAPTER

46

Onboard Eternity
Port Vila, Vanuatu
March 22, 2033
5:30 a.m.

Chang unlocked the storeroom door in the galley. Maddy lay huddled against the back wall. He held Li Wei's arm as he escorted him into the storeroom. The four others were squatting or standing and talking quietly. They were pleased to see Chang, who had hot food for breakfast, a rare treat and they were overjoyed to see Li Wei alive. Even with Chang present they shot out questions and greetings to Li Wei. For his part Li Wei said little, he just eased down onto the floor near Maddy.

***

All night long, Chang had worked on the certification of ship paperwork. Alone on the bridge, he had at last found some of the paperwork previously submitted by Captain Zhao. He missed him.

Hu knew nothing about the ship and cared even less, and without Zhao, the first mate had slid back into his nightly drinking.

Manning. How many persons are on the ship? Chang knew not to count the prisoners, so he had counted the crew and the security agents and gotten twenty-five. He had filled that in on the paper.

In charge of the ship: Captain Hu.

Officers certified in navigation: the first mate and one other.

Identity of all crew members. Chang had copied this from a prior report by Captain Zhao. The crew was the same, and he didn't know the security agents' identities; they were supposed to be secret.

Ineffective or inoperable refrigeration equipment. One refrigeration unit is not working, two others work.

Hygiene issues. Cockroaches in the kitchen and elsewhere. Toilet in kitchen area leaks dirty water.

Crew quarters. Crew residing in the infirmary? Yes. Chang remembered what Hu had told Abbott about the infirmary.

Hours on the ship's engines since repair: Chang had used an earlier report and made some calculations.

Fuel supply. A simple check of the gauges answered that one.

Cargo. He had attached a copy of the manifest.

Calibration of navigation equipment. Chang attached the most recent report.

Last port. Chang was unsure of this one, whether to put Nelson or Tauranga. At about three in the morning, he decided on Nelson.

He copied tonnage and all the other ship capacity questions directly from prior reports. They were half of the form.

Owner. China COSCO shipping.

Flag: Belize. He checked three prior forms on that.

At five a.m., he finished. It was the best he could do. He noted that a complete ship inspection was part of the process to release the ship. The first mate and the Captain could make any changes they wanted to. He was sure they would have to make some.

At ten after five, Chang was in the galley. He fried rice, he boiled water for eggs, and he got in the freezer for steamed buns that could just be warmed up. Twenty minutes later, he unlocked the door to the storeroom. Air hissed into the unit. When the door was closed, it was pitch black. Maddy blinked into the light. "Chang!" she said, truly glad to see him.

*****

"Fried rice for breakfast," Chang said, holding up four bowls, each one with fried rice and a steamed bun and a boiled egg on top. Chang handed Maddy and Li Wei and two of the others a bowl. As he passed out the bowls, his phone buzzed. He pulled it out of his pocket, looked at it, pushed something to silence it and laid it on an empty shelf near Maddy. "Be right back," he said and left, leaving the door propped open. Li Wei and Maddy took in the light and the air. Maddy breathed deeply. She motioned to Li Wei to stand lookout at the open doorway and she picked up Chang's phone. All the letters were in Chinese, which she had knew; the icons looked just like her phone.

There was a message in Notes. It was in Chinese of course, so she motioned for Li Wei. One of the others took over watching the door. She didn't read Chinese as well as she spoke and understood it. She handed Li Wei the phone.

Chang was taking his time in the galley, pouring Coca-Cola for all of them and gathering up three more bowls. It took him three more trips to bring everything back in. Li Wei had replaced the phone before Chang returned the first time and Maddy and Li Wei were back in the exact spots they had been in when he left. Chang returned with four glasses, "Coca-Cola?" he said. Maddy looked to Li Wei, who explained some Chinese typically had Coca-Cola at breakfast. Maddy laughed and reached for a glass.

Maddy's laugh was like magic. Chang's admiration for her was apparent and Maddy played up to it.

They ate breakfast together and talked. Sometimes Li Wei had to interpret. They spoke of many things but never the present, never what was going on on the ship or what might happen to them.

Only when Maddy said, "Chang, you look tired. Is everything all right?" did Chang respond with anything about the ship. All he said, "I was up all night working on some paperwork needed to get the ship free to sail. And lucky for all of you, after that, I remained awake to give the papers to the first mate. Since he is not yet awake, I decided to make a hot breakfast. I hope you liked it. Like my mother used to make."

"Excellent. Thank you. Thank you very much," Maddy said.

"Reminds me of home," Li Wei said. The others all said their thank you's. All bowls and glasses were emptied.

Maddy looked at the open door. The guards weren't paying them any attention. She asked, "Chang, do you know Captain Hu's real name?"

Li Wei stared at Maddy. For a moment Chang did not speak. Maddy assumed he would deny Hu had any other name. Chang said, "I do not know for certain. His nickname is smart-mouth, but you cannot call him that. He is very high up in security. That much you already knew."

Maddy and the other prisoners nodded as if they did already know all of that.

Chang let them each use the restroom, one at a time, so it took a little while. He stood in the kitchen but left the storeroom door open and did not guard the restroom door.

Chang said, "I am sorry, but I must go now."

The six prisoners returned to the storeroom. There were two armed men also in the galley. Chang bowed, took all the bowls and glasses, and then he picked up his phone from the shelf, looking at Maddy as he did so. Slowly he closed the door.

***

Chang cleaned up the kitchen and then went up to the bridge to wait for the first mate. No one was there, so he sat down and tried to sleep a little. At seven-fifteen, the first mate stumbled onto the deck, still smelling of last night's alcohol. Chang offered him the certification form he had worked on all night. The first mate took it and glanced at the first three pages. "Give this to the Captain, Chang. He'll be here soon. I need some coffee." And the first mate left.

Hu did not know much about sailing, but he was punctual. Precisely at seven-thirty, he appeared on the bridge. He said nothing to Chang as Chang sprung from the chair when the Captain arrived. Chang said, "Good morning, Captain. I have finished that report you wanted." Chang extended his arm holding the report to the Captain and said, "After you have approved it, it needs to be entered into our ship's computer and submitted. That is the fastest way."

"Put it there, sailor," Hu said. Chang did not know if the Captain knew his name. Chang put down the report, bowed, and went down to his quarters to get some sleep.

When the first mate returned to the bridge at eight a.m., the Captain handed him the report and told him to have it keyed into the computer. "And remember you are responsible for this report." The first mate sat down to go through the report carefully. He got through two pages before he fell asleep in his chair. It was ten a.m. when he woke; the report had spilled onto the floor. The Captain was gone, and no one else was on the bridge. He took the information to the communications officer. He was very good with computers, and the first mate told him to input the information and submit it according to the instructions on the first page of the form.

***

"Why did you take the woman?" Sara asked Wang for the one-thousandth time, "She was no threat to you."

Wang answered, "She was there, with her little boyfriend in the hotel." He smirked at her.

That was the most answer Sara had gotten from him yet and at least it was an admission that he had taken Maddy. His bragging would be his undoing.

Her phone rang. She looked down at the screen and walked away to answer, "Jack?"

"Yes, Sara. Sorry to call, but the Nelson police commander just called me and asked me to get a message to you as soon as possible. He said two cars were creeping around our house. He was worried about the children. Said he thought you would want to know."

"Did he say how he knew that?"

"Yes, he said Sergeant Taylor had called him."

Sara checked her phone; Charlie Taylor had not called her. "What did you tell him, as far as getting a message to me?"

I said, "Sure, right away."

"And did the Commander seem to know where you were?"

"Must have; he called on the resort phone."

"Put Adam on, please."

"Adam, here."

"We have to go, Adam. Right now!"

Wang had overheard. He said, "Trouble in paradise, darling?" Sara struck him fiercely with the back of her hand.

Darling. That was it. "Hello, Renee. I was hoping you could get me out of here right away. All of us."

"But, of course. I am on my way. Abbott?" he said.

"Yes, I think so. Are those damn cameras still off?"

"But of course, *ma cherie.*"

***

Abbott hung up from the short call from Commander Li and began mobilizing his forces. Not the Maritime Wing forces, although a couple of those men also worked for him in other ways. No, he was marshaling his clandestine mercenaries. He would need at least six. But he was already too late. Renee left his office and walked to the dock where his division kept their boats. He took six trusted officers with him. Fifteen minutes after he had hung up from Sara, they were speeding across the bay on the far side of Iririki Island from and therefore not seen by the Maritime Wing headquarters.

While he waited for his forces to assemble, Abbott checked his computer. Still no camera footage. He pulled up *Eternity*. The hold was still prominently displayed, but the hold now noted "Ship Certi-fication Filed 11:30 a.m.. 03/22/2033. Review and approval pending." He and his men would see to the ship's inspection right away so that Laurent's men wouldn't.

CHAPTER

47

Onboard Eternity
March 22, 2033
8:15 am

Maddy asked·Li Wei what the note on Chang's phone said. Li Wei replied, "It was like a note to self. Something about remember to use the front steps as they are used much less often and you can reach the deck without being seen by the bridge. I guess he prefers to avoid the Captain and company."

"Hmm, curious, don't you think?"

"Maddy, I apologize for changing subjects, but I need to tell you something important."

"Yes?"

"The other night when there were gunshots on the ship?"

"Yes, I remember."

"Well, it was an attempt to rescue you. And one of the rescuers was your husband."

"Jack?! How do you know?"

"He lowered his mask and he told me and he looked just like the picture in your office at the school, the one behind your desk."

"What did he say?"

"He asked where you were and I said I didn't know and then they tried to get me to go with them."

"And?"

"I refused. I told them Hu would kill you if I escaped. Eventually when they left without me was when all the gunfire broke out."

"Was Jack shot? Is he okay?"

"I do not know, Maddy, I was l still in sickbay. And the door was closed."

Maddy took several audible breaths. *So Jack had come to save her. And he had some help anyway. Jack!* She said, quietly, "You should have gone with them Li Wei; you could be safe now."

Li Wei shook his head.

After a few minutes Maddy looked hard at Li Wei and said, "Do you think he meant for us to find that?"

"Who meant for us to find what?"

"Chang, the note about the front steps."

All the men were paying close attention now. "Hmm, maybe so. Maybe so," said Li Wei as one of the others helped him to his feet. Li Wei shuffled over to the storeroom door, turned the knob and pushed gently on it. It opened! He put his finger to his lips and pushed it a little further open and then peeked around it toward the galley. He motioned for Maddy and she also peeked around the door. There was only one guard visible in the galley and he was sleeping, his head was slumped to one side and his breathing was rhythmic.

She leaned back into the storeroom, nodded her head and stepped out into the hall and started toward the front steps. One of the others helped Li Wei next and the other three followed, the last man shutting the door after he came out. As quietly as they could they moused their way down the hall. The stairway was to their left around a corner. Maddy sent the others ahead and looked back toward the galley as they began to climb the steps. The guard was still asleep.

The stairwell was challenging. It was metal and Li Wei was unable to move gracefully or stealthily. Two others determined to carry him up the steps without ever uttering a word. As quietly as possible they made their way up to the main deck. The noises of the ship at anchor helped cover their escape.

Oh please Lord, let me, and let us get off of this ship. Let me see my children again. And Jack? Please Lord, please.

At the top of the steps was a door with a wheel in the middle. One of the men slowly began turning the wheel. When the wheel was opened, he turned and looked from face to face, pausing on Maddy. Maddy nodded and moved forward to go first. This man put out his arm and shook his head and pointed to himself. Maddy settled in second in line, the two men carrying Li Wei would bring up the rear. The lead man turned again to Maddy and motioned for her to stay with him. Again, she nodded.

He pushed the door open a few inches and pressed his face against it to peer down alongside the ship. His eyes grew wide and he quietly pulled the door close and stood back on the landing with his finger to his lips. He motioned that there were two men with guns out there. No one so much as breathed listening to the two men walk by the door. After thirty more seconds the man again opened the door a few inches and peered alongside the ship. This time he opened it further, far enough that he could stick his head out and around the door to see the other way.

He motioned to come on and stepped onto the deck with Maddy and the others right behind him. The deck was deserted except for the rows of storage containers. The bridge was directly above them. Maddy looked for cameras and didn't see any. To their left and ahead of them was an opening between rows of containers; it looked like the access to the container where she and Li Wei had been held. She pointed and pushed forward into this aisle way. She just hoped no one from the bridge was looking and that there was no one in the aisle. The lead man was right behind her. The access row was empty. The lead man put his hand on Maddy's wrist and leaned around the corner and looked up and down the ship and up at the bridge and then motioned the others to come. They had to bring Li Wei. Then he pulled

Maddy's arm and they moved quickly to the rail of the ship, which adjoined the port building. About eight feet down and three feet away was the concrete floor of one level of the port building. Normally Maddy would never attempt a jump like that but this was not normally. The Taiwanese climbed over the ships rail, braced himself, bent down and then jumped out from the ship with his arms extended out in front of him. He landed on the concrete, and fell forward catching himself with his hands.

He turned and looked and Maddy was already outside the ship's rail, ready to jump. Before she did, she looked back over her shoulder to see the others safely in the aisle, carrying Li Wei toward the jumping off point. *How would Li Wei ever make this jump? Would they throw him? Could they?*

No time for that she thought. She looked at the lead man; he was ready for her. She took one deep breath, squatted and then pushed off as hard as she could. She landed hard even with the agent there to sort of catch her. She blew out her breath. She took one last look at the ship as the agent led her into the cavernous port building. Li Wei and the others were peering down from the ship's railing.

CHAPTER

48

Outside Port Vila, Vanuatu
March 22, 2033
9:00 a.m.

It looked different in the daylight. I recognized the remote home of Renee's doctor friend who had saved Noah. In the light, it didn't seem as run down as I had thought. And there were three other buildings I hadn't noticed before, a garage and a large storage building behind the house and a vacant chicken house. I didn't see or hear any chickens.

Renee had called ahead, and when the three trucks carrying us pulled in, the doctor was on the porch waiting for us. A police sergeant was in the second vehicle driving Amy and Adam, and me. All of the vehicles were unmarked black SUVs. Behind us were five police officers and a bound, gagged, and blindfolded Wang, and in front, an SUV with two more officers plus Renee and Sara.

I watched Sara jump out of the lead vehicle before it had even stopped.

"Honoré!" she shouted and rushed onto the porch to embrace him.

Honoré? I thought. In all of our hours here before, I don't think I ever heard his name. Then I remembered Renee had intentionally kept us in the dark, So much for that.

Sara and Honoré embraced, kissed each cheek, and excitedly held on to one another, both talking at once. Renee got out of the lead vehicle as we got out of ours. He said, "As you can see, they are acquainted."

Sara was pulling up her shirt and showing Honoré a scar. He made a show of looking carefully at it and then smiling and shaking his head.

Renee told us, "Honoré saved her life one time. She and I were running an operation, and she got shot. It was my fault. I felt terrible and stayed here by her side for three days until Honoré made me sleep. A few hours later, when I awoke, she was sitting up eating soup and talking with Honoré. Look how they carry on."

Renee was smiling. Then he looked behind us and saw his men pulling Wang out of the rear vehicle. "Take him to the large building in the back. We will be right there." All emotion had left his face. I looked up, and Sara had stopped talking and was staring at Wang. He was handcuffed and blindfolded still. One of Laurent's men retied his gag. Sara watched him coldly until they had passed out of sight along the side of the house. Honoré was looking intently at Sara. "Is he the one?" he asked.

Sara just nodded. After an uncomfortable silence, Honoré said, "Come in and let me see if I can find you some food. Come in, all of you." He nodded to Amy and me to let us know he recognized us.

We walked past the table where Honoré had treated Noah. It was clean and looked only like a small dining table.

"Sit here, please," Honoré said. "I have good news about your friend. His doctor set his leg during surgery this morning. The surgeon said everything went fine, and he should recover normally. He should be out of the cast in six to eight weeks."

Renee and Sara, and Adam were in the back in the kitchen arguing about something. I couldn't make out what they were saying, but I could sense the tone of disagreement. The backdoor slammed, and Renee and Adam came to join us for some food. I went out and followed Sara.

Sara opened the door to the large building in the back of the property. Wang was sitting in a chair in the middle of the room. She tied his legs to the chair and checked the binding on his wrists. Then she removed his blindfold and his gag.

Wang smirked. "Aren't you afraid I will yell for help?"

"Yell, all you want. No one can hear you. No one will hear your screams. No one but us." Sara opened her arms to include the others on the property.

She turned to the two police officers, who were in the large space with her and Wang. "Please wait outside," she said.

When we were alone, Sara lifted her bag up onto the counter atop the base cabinets across the room. The bag Adam had brought for her was already there. She looked inside that bag first. She looked all around the room. I could tell she had been here before.

She pulled out a water board and a towel. Wang remained quiet with a bemused look on his face. Next, Sara found an electric shock stick in the bag from Adam, and she lit it up. It made a startling buzzing sound. In an outside pocket of her duffel, she found a pair of pliers and placed them down on one of the cabinets.

In another area of her bag, she found leather gloves and tried them on, and she examined a hammer and a long nail. Sara opened a drawer and looked into it. Then she turned and looked at Wang. She lifted a locking iron mask out of her bag. It had holes to breathe through, but no eye or mouth holes. She held it up and gazed across it at Wang, making sure he could see it. Then she put it back into the bag.

For her last piece of equipment, she selected a garrote, wire with wooden handles. She snapped it tight and placed it on the cabinet beside the other tools.

"That should be all I will need, Wang. You can think about which one you would like me to use first. You never know I might be feeling generous and go with your choice."

She stepped toward Wang until she stood just inches from his chair. I could see the hatred in her eyes; and I could see Wang feeding on that hatred. He would try to use that against her. She composed herself.

"Now I'm going to get something to eat, but I will be back." The menacing hatred had returned. "I don't want you to be bored while I'm gone, so I have something for you to listen to," she said. "Can you guess what it is?"

Sara put a small speaker on the cabinet; it had its own digital memory. "Actually, Wang, this is something you sent me years ago. It's the soundtrack of you murdering my family one by one, of them crying and pleading for mercy and you giving them none. Listen as you laugh as they died and called my name. I want to make sure you remember it. And you can think about how your family's cries and pleas for mercy will be different."

Wang smirked again. "You Western democracies don't have the guts for the tough actions that are sometimes required."

Sara leaned down, so they were face to face, about three inches apart. "Take a good look, do I look like a Western democracy to you? This is personal. Tit for tat. You have been given to me, Wang. You're mine." Sara looked up at me. "And you will tell me where Maddy Gamble is being held on that ship. And anything else I want to know." She turned on the speaker and we left the room.

She said to the two officers outside the building, "Stay out here for three hours and let the speaker play. Then go in and give him a little food and a little water. Do not untie him for any reason. If he has to go to the bathroom, he will have to do so in his pants. Then leave again within five minutes and turn the speaker back on and leave it on all night. Tomorrow at five a.m., turn it off and leave without a word."

The officers nodded their understanding of their orders, and we hurried away. Even outside the building, she could hear the cries of her family. Renee and Adam had warned her against hearing this re-cording. They thought this was too tough on her, and one of them should do it. She insisted the impact was much more significant if she did it herself. She had finally agreed to Adam calling in two more agents to help her with this interrogation; they would be here some time tomorrow. She walked quickly to the back of Honoré's house and collapsed into Renee's arms.

I wanted to go back and question Wang myself and torture him to tell me where Maddy was. Instead, I gathered my strength and went into the house with Sara. My hands never left my sides., my fists clenched tightly.

CHAPTER

49

Port Vila Port Building
March 22, 2033
10:15 a.m.

Renee hurried toward the sound of gunfire, his weapon drawn and in front of him. With him were a dozen more officers; guns at the ready and their guns were better than his. There had been a report of a gunfight between men from the ship and watchmen in the port building. It sounded like it was ongoing.

His men spread out and cautiously looked into the open area where the shots were coming from. They remained partially shielded by the stacks of containers in the building. One of Laurent's men shouted out, "Police, put down your weapons." He ducked back behind the storage container just in time to avoid the fusillade of bullets fired at him in response.

Laurent ordered his men, "Full engagement!" and they all began firing into the open area. Cries of surrender came almost immediately. Laurent and his troops moved carefully into the open area. Six bodies lie motionless on the ground; three men stood with their hands above their heads. In the near distance Renee saw two men carrying something heavy as they slipped back onto *Eternity*. That would have to wait.

Laurent was certain the two of the men he had now taken into custody were Chinese State security because of their smug attitudes and the weapons they had had. His men were taking note of the bodies when one of them moved out from under another body. "Don't shoot! My name is Li Wei, I am an agent of the Taiwanese government and I have just escaped from imprisonment on *Eternity*. Some of these others were with me." All weapons remained trained on Li Wei. He said nervously, looking at the guns, "Some of these others escaped with me. Or tried to." Laurent moved closer and asked, "Where is the woman?" Li Wei looked frantically around and then turned his eyes back toward the ship. "Oh Maddy, where are you? Did they recapture you?" Then to Laurent he said, "The woman's name is Maddy Gamble and I do not know what has come of her, she escaped with us. The last time I saw her was a couple hours ago when she jumped from the ship to the port building." Laurent's eyes widened. "Lower your weapons, men. He knows the name of the American woman. I believe he is who he says he is." After the guns were no longer pointed at him Li Wei helped the Vanuatu police make sense of the dead bodies and the men with their hands still up. One of these men was a Taiwanese compatriot of Li Wei's. He was allowed to lower his hands. Three of the bodies were Chinese State Security. They were dressed the same as the two new prisoners so that made sense. Two of the other bodies were of friends of Li Wei. They were also Taiwanese agents. State security agents had returned to the ship with at least one and maybe two other people, maybe with Maddy. Laurent ordered his men to search the port building from top to bottom. He took Li Wei with him in his vehicle and left his officers in charge of the scene and the search.

CHAPTER

50

Outside Port Vila, Vanuatu
March 22, 2033
10:40 a.m.

Sara walked into the large storage building carrying a cup of coffee. The room was silent. Wang was awake but looked exhausted. Good. Two policemen stood outside the building. The speaker was off.

Sara put on the gloves. She picked up the pliers and approached Wang. She went back to the cabinet and turned and said, "Are you ready to talk to me now?"

Wang sneered but said nothing. Sara found the gag she had removed from Wang last night. She spit into it and then tied it tightly into his mouth. "Let me know when you do want to talk." Sara walked around behind Wang, where his tied hands were. She lifted his right hand and extended his right index finger. Sara placed the pliers over the middle knuckle of Wang's right index finger. She pressed until she knew it must hurt, until the finger bone resisted against the pliers. Wang's eyes smiled. Sara could tell he thought she was bluffing; and would not torture him. And then she slowly applied pressure and crushed his knuckle while he screamed in pain into his gag. Without a word, she moved down to the knuckle where his right index finger sprang from his right hand. Sara took one look at Wang and crushed that knuckle with a strong pull on the pliers. She said nothing as she moved to the top knuckle of his right index finger. Again, she pressed until she could feel the resistance of bone paused and crushed it.

Then she said, "That finger will never pull another trigger." And she moved the pliers to his left index finger. Wang was sweating despite the chilly morning. Sara crushed all the knuckles in his left index finger. Then she went back to the right hand, to Wang's right middle finger. Slowly she worked through every one of the knuckles on both of his middle fingers, taking time between each knuckle to make sure he could feel the pain, realize which knuckle had just been crushed and anticipate what was next. Like a robot, she moved to his right ring finger and wordlessly crushed those knuckles. Then she stopped. Never once did she ask him if he was ready to talk. She came around to look at his face. He was sweating, and she wasn't positive, but he may have been crying. She saw that he had wet his pants. Good.

She tasted her coffee, where Wang could see her. It was cold. She threw the rest in his face. "You are mine, Wang."

Wang motioned for her to remove the gag. When she did, he sneered at her and said, "Why don't you go ahead and finish the job on my hands. Crush all the joints, or are you too weak?"

Sara stepped directly in front of Wang's chair and snarled, "You fool. I have intentionally stopped partway. If the Chinese can trade for you or otherwise secure your freedom, they will see that I stopped and will assume you told me everything that I wanted to know at that point, and you will not be able to persuade them otherwise. They may kill you for that, Wang. You know how they are. It always ends in death or imprisonment for people like you. Where is Xi Jinping now? No one stays on top forever, and then the ending is always bad. Why can't you people figure that out?" Wang looked up at her but said nothing.

Sara said, "And I now get to move on to something else." She stepped back and called in the two officers who were right outside.

"I need more coffee. Clean him up, not his pants; he should know better. Leave him gagged and take off his shoes. Tie his ankles more tightly to the legs of the chair and tilt the chair back. And put the speaker back on for the son of a bitch. I'll be back."

***

Abbott's cell phone rang just after ten in the morning. He was still settling in at his desk.

"Abbott, we have to get out of here. Now. Some of the prisoners escaped."

"What? When? How did they escape?"

"I don't know exactly, yet. But they did. All of them. And my men went after them into the port building where they first got into a gun battle with the security there and then were attacked by your police in force."

"Not my police, you mean Laurent's."

"Whatever. Three of my men are dead as are some of the prisoners. Two of my men returned with one prisoner. He will be disposed of. And two of my men were captured."

Abbott blew out a whistle. "Shit. Will your men talk?"

"Sooner or later, that's why we have to get out of here. Now."

"I agree but there is no way your ship will be released if your men were in a gunfight with Vanuatu officers."

"I am aware of that, Confucius. We are leaving with or without permission or assistance."

Abbott paused. "This is quite a disaster, Captain. I will report it to Beijing shortly. Meanwhile, I will try to arrange the tugboats to assist you. My other forces will be standing by, but we must now be even more careful. What about the American woman, Captain? Where is she?"

"My people do not know. See what you can find out. And let me know."

***

Honoré made the best pastries I have ever had. Butter, butter, and more butter. That's what he said his secret was. I had already had two and was looking hard at another. The coffee was good, too, if a little intense. Amy was barefoot with her feet, propped up on an empty chair. Honoré was entertaining us with stories from the old days. Apparently, he could remember when there were real pirates in Vanuatu. Sometimes Honoré rolled his eyes to make sure we kept our healthy skepticism. Sara and Adam came back and forth, taking turns interrogating Wang. Neither one of them would say much. Only that he hadn't talked yet. Late in the afternoon, two men arrived, and they began to help with the interrogation. I saw Adam introduce them to Sara through the back window of Honoré's house. I could not hear what was said, but Sara looked to be in charge.

Sara came back into the house. "I need more time. He will crack, they all do, but I need more time. Even with the help from Adam's men so we can interrogate him nonstop, I need more time."

Renee came driving up to the house, kicking up dust and slammed to a stop in front of Honoré's home. He got out of the vehicle quickly without bothering to close the door behind himself. Then he went to the front passenger side and helped a frail looking Chinese man out of the other side. We all rushed to the front door to help and see what was going on. Renee filled us in as quickly as possible with details from the Chinese man who we learned was Li Wei.

I couldn't hold back. "Where is Maddy? When was the last time you saw her? Is she okay?"

Patiently, Li Wei repeated that he didn't know, the last time he saw her she was jumping off the ship, that she made that jump safely and he didn't see her after that. Something new came out, I could tell by Renee's intent interest.

Li Wei said, "When I jumped into the port building, I hurt my leg, hurt it even worse I should say and was having trouble walking. The lead man, the one who had gone ahead with Maddy came back to help the others with me. Maddy was not with him and he did not say any-thing about her. We were all hurrying to get away. Then the Chinese security came after us with guns ablaze. Clearly their orders were to kill us, not to capture us. But fortunately, port security was nearby and came to our rescue. Some of them were shot I think and then while a cat and mouse gun battle was ongoing, Captain Laurent and his men showed up and the Chinese surrendered. Before they did two Chinese security agents and at least one person, one of us I presume and maybe Maddy returned to the ship."

"Did you see her? Did they have Maddy?" I moved closer. Li Wei did not shrink away. "I am very sorry, I do not know. I just could not see. I was under the body of one of my countrymen who died protect-ing me."

"Holy shit." Sara said. "How much time do we have Renee? We should have enough to board and search the ship? Surely."

Renee said, "Agreed. I am working on it. We are trying to find the magistrate. But we don't have much time. It may already be too late."

"When?" Sara said.

"Hmm, there is no real way to tell exactly, *ma cherie*. A warrant is required. I will send my men there shortly with instructions to look in every part of the ship. I am pushing as hard as I can. Perhaps, they can find Mrs. Gamble and rescue her."

I sat forward, listening.

Sara put her hands on her hips, "Perhaps, Renee. I will only feel better when it happens. There is no other ship in port. How busy can they be?"

I agreed with Sara on both points. "When will this search of the ship take place, Renee? Can I go along?"

"Later today. As soon as possible. And I don't think it is a good idea for you to go onboard. My men can handle it. You and I can stand by somewhere close."

I nodded. A cool calmness had come over me, similar to the feel-ing I used to get when I was about to start a big trial.

Renee returned his attention to Sara. "Two ships are scheduled to come into port over the next twenty-four hours. They will need to be loaded and unloaded but should not affect *Eternity* in any way. Perhaps it would be better if the port were even busier."

Renee added, "I guess there are ways the Chinese could leave port under their own power."

Sara said, almost to herself, "Under this timetable, only brutality has any chance to make Wang talk."

"Do not do it, *ma cherie*. Do not become like them to fight them. It is easy for the hatred to overtake you until you are like the one you hated. Fight it, my love."

"What if it's already too late, Renee?" Sara asked.

"Don't be like them, Sara. No matter what," I said.

CHAPTER

51

Headquarters, Vanuatu Police Maritime Wing
Port Vila, Vanuatu
March 22, 2033
11:00 a.m.

"What is taking so long?" Abbott asked.

"Almost done, sir. I had some other things come up," the clerk said.

Yeah, like her boyfriend, Abbott thought. For a moment he was concerned.

Abbott tried to guide her, "There are eight deficiencies noted, and I filed an amended certification form to address them."

"Yes, sir. I see that. Can you hold a minute while I look at them? Okay, I see now, the manning issue and crew identification issues are approved. There is a new owner and new flag for this ship. That's unusual but looks fine. And we were provided a copy of Captain Hu's successful navigation certification from Beijing two months ago, so that is current, but..."

"But what? You can see that he is navigationally certified, can't you?"

"Yes, it's just that I have never had to review and accept a test itself; it has always been filed and certified somewhere else wherever all ship data is collected."

"I understand, and I assure you this method is perfectly acceptable." He let her think for a minute. "Are we okay on that?"

"Okay, sir, if it's good enough for you, it's good enough for me. But you will need to sign off on it. What about the refrigeration and hygiene issues and the inspection of the ship?"

"Yes, as I told you, mark the refrigeration and hygiene issues waived per Captain Abbott. I will sign off on those as well. They can deal with those issues when they get back to China. And my men have conducted a thorough investigation of the ship which disclosed no additional issues. The inspection report has also been filed."

"Fine by me; waived. That will complete the application. Anything else, sir?"

"Yes, before you go home, and by the way, thank you for staying to take care of this for me. But before you go, can you schedule the pilot tugs to pull *Eternity* out to sea?"

"Yes, sir, I think so. Hang on a minute." Abbott listened through clicks and then, "Okay, sir, all set. Anything else?"

"Just this. I appreciate your help on this and I know you have had a long week, being the only clerk in port this week, so why don't you take the rest of the day off? It's the least I can do."

"Really, sir? But what if there is port business and no one here to handle it?"

"I looked, and this is the only outstanding paperwork on all ships in port. So, just do like you do on the weekends and put the messages on the phone and computer saying that you are closed and directing anyone to call my office if they have issues that won't wait. We will take care of them like we always do and you can enjoy a well-earned long weekend."

"Thank you, Captain Abbott, thank you very much."

"Now can you schedule the tugs to get *Eternity* out of here immediately?"

"Yes, Captain Abbott. Taken care of."

***

"Do you think she will be okay, Renee? You know her best," Adam asked.

I had been wondering the same thing but hadn't wanted to ask. This interrogation of Wang was getting to Sara. And why not? The bastard had murdered her family. According to Renee, 'slaughtered in a purposefully painful way.' The interrogation was bringing all of that up again. Now she had a chance to get revenge. And I needed her to focus on Maddy and where she was.

"After what he did to her, she may kill him," Adam said. "I would."

"She may," Renee said, "and if she does, we will just have to deal with it."

I couldn't help thinking of Maddy. What had Wang done to her? I didn't want Sara to kill Wang, but brutality was fine with me as long as she got all the information we needed from him. But did he even know where she was or what had become of her. We needed that warrant now. I kept my thoughts to myself. Everyone was well aware of the urgency. I held my head in my hands and blew out my breath.

"Sara is stronger than you think, Adam," Renee said. "She is the best, the strongest, the smartest, the toughest I have ever worked with, and always she keeps her moral compass. Always."

Adam said, "She's taking on too much of this, putting too much pressure on herself. I brought in two interrogators from the CIA, but she has hardly used them."

Renee said, "She doesn't know them, Adam, not yet anyway. Sara is one of those people whose trust you have to win. If you do, then she will stand by you through anything, but first, you must earn her trust."

Renee and I went to the building out back to check on Sara. The police guards stood aside as we entered. Just then, Sara stood in front of Wang, snapping the garrote. Wang couldn't see her, she had locked him into an iron mask, but he could hear her. Snap. Snap. Snap. "You know that sound, don't you, Wang? You remember you used a garrote on my husband. You remember, don't you?" Under the mask, Wang made a muffled sound. The mask looked horrible to me, difficult to breathe in and surely claustrophobia inducing. Sara walked around behind him and slowly, gently even, let the garrote fall across the front of his neck. "We're running out of time, Wang."

I watched, spellbound.

Renee's phone buzzed an alert. He had told me he had registered for notifications about *Eternity*. He called Sara and me out of the interrogation room. He showed us his phone. 'Departure Approved' was noted at eleven-fifteen this morning. Just five minutes ago. *Eternity* was leaving right now. Renee called right away and was sent straight to the message. He played it over the speaker so we all could hear. "The port office is now closed and will reopen at seven a.m. on Monday, March twenty eighth. If you have urgent business that will not wait, please call Captain Abbot's office at the Vanuatu Police Maritime Wing." Laurent hung up and scrolled farther down on the information about *Eternity*. "She is scheduled to leave port today! Right now. Damn. Damn Abbott, he set this up so there would be nothing I could do."

Damn. Damn. Damn.

Renee called everyone into the kitchen. "I have horrible news, and it is my fault. Abbott outmaneuvered me, and *Eternity* is now cleared to leave Port Vila, and the port office is closed until Monday morning, so there is no way I can file something to stop it." He looked at Sara and then at me, "I'm so very sorry."

"What about that warrant?" I asked.

"It is no good if the ship has left the port."

"There must be something." Adam said.

Renee said, "Nothing really. As the officer who requested the certification, I can appear and sign off on the departure, but my authority is limited to confirming an existing approval. These last-minute approvals are not done anymore because the computer already notes the approval. If not, the tugs would not be there. It's a nothing."

"What about inspecting the items noted about the ship or the crew identity or making Hu prove he knows how to navigate?" I asked.

"I am sorry, Jack. Abbott has approved or waived those items, and his men have already completed the inspection. The crew identity paperwork will be in order; the Chinese are not stupid. And as much as I would love to, I cannot insist Hu demonstrates his navigational skills." Renee touched my shoulder. "*Eternity* is leaving and I can't do anything more. Unless there are new and powerful developments, I cannot legally stop that ship once it has disembarked."

"But Maddy may be on that ship." I protested.

Renee put his hand lightly on my shoulder.

"Can we disable the ship?" I asked.

Laurent just shrugged. "With the Maritime Division standing guard on deck and in small boats? That is what you must expect from Abbott."

"Well, can we try?"

Laurent shrugged again.

Sara sighed heavily, still carrying the weight of the world. "Jack, I am so sorry. I can't think of anything either. I guess I better get back to work. Adam, can you spell me in two hours?"

"How about one of my guys?" Adam said.

"No, I prefer you, Adam. Please," Sara said.

Adam threw up his arms and nodded his head.

"Sara, wait a minute," I said. "We can all see how this is affecting you. None of us can speak to what Wang did to your family. That's for you alone to work through. But I can tell you this. I don't want you doing anything to Wang that you will later regret to try to help me, to try to help my family. I thought about it, and I know Maddy would not want that, ever. Even if it costs her her life. And besides, Sara, you're not really getting anywhere and we're out of time. Please let someone else try. And you come with us."

"Where are we going, Jack?"

"You and I and Laurent and whoever else he wants to bring are going to the port. There may still be something we can do. We have to try."

Tears ran down Sara's cheeks, but she held her head high. I blinked through my own tears to hold her gaze. Sara came and hugged me, and I hugged her back, and I cried. *Maddy, I have lost you.*

Laurent led us to his vehicle with his eyes downcast. Three of his officers followed us in another vehicle. With sirens blaring and lights flashing we moved rapidly through Port Vila to the port building and pulled directly into the building.

CHAPTER

52

Port Vila Port Building
March 22, 2033
1:02 p.m.

As soon as I got out of Renee's vehicle, I could see *Eternity* in the bay. Well away from the port building already. As I watched the tugs were being untethered and *Eternity* was ready to proceed under her own power. I fell back against the police vehicle. I might have fallen to the ground but Sara was there to catch me. I buried my face in Sara's shoulder. I had just lost the most wonderful woman in the world. *Maddy. I have failed you. I am so sorry. How will I ever live without you?* My tears were unstoppable. Unstoppable, just like *Eternity* I thought. I knew Sara of all people could understand.

I heard Renee and his men wander off. I guess they were just giving me some room.

I turned and looked again at *Eternity*. A small white wake appeared behind her as the ship's engines propelled her out of the port and out to sea and on to China. *How could this be happening? How would I raise two children by myself?*

Sara still had one arm around me. "I have some sense of how you must feel, Jack. I am so very sorry. I failed to break Wang in time to do your Maddy any good."

I shook my head. I couldn't speak, but it wasn't her fault. "If it comes down to it, Jack, I will help you with the children. I am quite fond of them."

I tried to smile, to find strength to go on.

Renee called out from somewhere behind us, "Jack, Sara, over here, quickly."

Sara and I looked at each other and then ran to find Renee. We could just see his back around the corner of a storage container. "What is it, Renee?" Sara asked.

When Renee turned toward us, he had a huge smile and he pulled Maddy from around the container. My Maddy! And she was alive! Standing there, looking at me. My jaw dropped as I ran to her and picked her up in my arms. "Maddy, I thought I had lost you. Oh my God, Thank you, Lord, Thank you, thank you, thank you."

Maddy was crying and wouldn't let go of my neck. I held her for the longest time. Finally, she looked up at Sara. I introduced them. "Sara this is my wife Maddy and Maddy this is Sara, she has been watching the children so I could come find you."

It was all I needed to say. The two women embraced. "And I have already met Captain Laurent and some of his men." Maddy said.

"Where were you? How?" I stammered and looked helplessly around. "We thought you were on that ship, *Eternity*."

"Yes. If you are able, can you fill us in, please?" added Renee.

"I'll try. A man named Chang, the only name of his we knew, helped us escape. I think so anyway. He left the door unlocked to the room we were all kept in and he allowed us to see a note suggesting we use the forward stairwell. Yesterday, after an early breakfast we snuck out past a sleeping guard and jumped from the ship to this building. I went first with one of the other men who had been a prisoner. Li Wei and the others are all Taiwanese state agents, I think. Anyway, we were fine and were moving away from the ship but when

Li Wei and the others jumped down, Li Wei injured his leg. It was bad before due to the Chinese torturing him. A man named Wang who we haven't seen for a couple days."

Wang! We all looked at Sara. She looked back but remained composed.

"Anyway, the man I was with went back to help with Li Wei and told me to stay out of sight and that if anything happened, I should hide somewhere. That he would find me when it was safe. At just about the same moment, he reached Li Wei and the others men jumped from the ship and opened fire with guns. Then gunshots rang out from behind me and I saw one of these new men from the ship fall. Someone was shooting at them too. And then I hid. I found this storage container with the door partially open." She put her hand on the storage container to show us which one. "I closed the door and listened. The gunfight went back and forth for several minutes and then I heard voices shouting and the sounds of much more intense gunfire and then it stopped. I couldn't tell who was who. I heard men searching and even calling out, but I wasn't sure who they were so I remained quiet."

Renee said, "The more intense gunfire is when I showed up with my men. And the searchers were my men after we found Li Wei among the bodies and took two Chinese security agents' prisoner. Li Wei is injured but will be okay. All but one of the others were killed or recaptured."

"You mean the other Taiwanese?" Maddy's lip quivered. "Oh no."

"Yes, well one may have been taken back aboard *Eternity* we don't know for sure. We thought it was you who had been recaptured." Renee gestured toward *Eternity*. "We may know more soon. Two of the Taiwanese were killed for sure."

"Thank God you weren't recaptured Maddy. That's what I thought. I thought I had lost you." I held her hand. I wanted to never let it go. I squeezed Maddy to me.

Maddy continued, "Just now I heard you just outside this container and I was hoping it was one of the Taiwan agents looking for me. I couldn't stand it in that container any longer, not after being locked in one on that awful ship." I would have to get these details later.

Renee said, "Yes, we heard you but we couldn't make out what you said. My apology for opening the door with drawn weapons." Maddy waved that off, "I understand. Thank you for rescuing me.

Renee smiled and shook his head and pointed to the bay, which he was facing. "Well, will you look at that?"

Pulling back into port in reverse was *Eternity*. In front of her was a small US Navy warship with guns bristling and aimed at *Eternity*.

As I turned, I said, "Mitch," under my breath and then added more loudly to Maddy, "You remember Mitch Drummond from law school?" Maddy nodded, "Yes, sure. Last I heard he was working at the Whitehouse."

"Right," I said, "I will fill you in later. Come on. Let's get out of here and you can check in with Li Wei as well."

CHAPTER

53

Honoré's House
Outside Port Vila, Vanuatu
March 24, 2033
11:33 a.m.

Renee popped the champagne. "To Mr. and Mrs. Gamble," he said.

"And to Li Wei," Maddy added.

We all raised our glasses and took a sip: Renee, Amy, Maddy and Li Wei, Honoré, me, and several officers.

Amy said, "You did it, Renee. You pulled off an impossible rescue. Congratulations! And Jack, you were a damned good husband. Nice work." She smiled. "Now just stop touching your hair."

Maddy and Amy both laughed at that. The comment went over Renee's head. He said, "Oh, my dear, we did it; all of us together. Only a team can accomplish something like this. Have I told you how beautiful you look when you are happy?" Renee was beaming.

"Don't you start on me, Captain," Amy said in mock indignation. She did look beautiful when she was happy.

"Beautiful women surround me," Renee said, taking Maddy's hand.

As if on cue, Sara came in the back door. She was a striking woman in her own right. She looked worn out at the moment. I knew she had been up all night, interrogating Wang. Even though I could tell she was tired, there was a certain lightness to her as well.

Sara went straight to Maddy. "Sorry to miss the celebration. I'm so happy." She nodded to Li Wei. Sara pointed out the back door. "I just had to finish something up, something that started a long time ago."

"Well, *ma cherie*? Aren't you going to tell us? How did it go with Wang?" Renee asked.

"It went well," Sara said, collecting herself. "Very well."

"Adam and his men are finishing this session up because I wanted to get in here and meet Mrs. Gamble. You are lovely, dear. Now I see why your children are so gorgeous, Jack." She shot me a sideways glance and a smile.

"Maddy, Sara Singh; our babysitter also happens to be the most decorated intelligence agent in the history of New Zealand."

Maddy's eyes widened.

Renee chimed in, "Yes, she is the best. The absolute best."

Amy handed Sara a glass of champagne. "What have you learned from Wang?"

"Oh, that's a big, big question, but I can tell you some things. Wang has identified over forty-eight Chinese agents in government positions in nations around this area, here in the Pacific. Forty-eight, there may be more. Among these agents are Captain Abbott and two of his men here in Port Vila."

Renee broke in, "Those three have been taken into custody and are being questioned now. I am told it is going well. And that is before Wang's revelations."

"What else can you tell us, Sara?" Amy asked.

Sara had a little twinkle in her eye and said, "I think you'll be pleased to know that Commander Li of the Nelson Police was a Chinese agent and SIS arrested him."

"Commander Li? No. Son of a bitch." Amy said.

"Yes, he is," Sara said, which brought laughter from everyone. "I really shouldn't identify any of the others until after our intelligence agencies have captured them. And Captain Hu is not really Captain Hu. I fear the real captain has come to a bad end so a very high-ranking member of Chinese state security could assume his identity. I'm sorry I cannot give you his name but the man masquerading as Hu is the highest-ranking Chinese state security agent we have ever captured. There is no telling what he may know. I can tell you his nickname, smart-mouth. The information we will get from him will set Chinese intelligence back a decade. They must be very perturbed about now." She smiled.

"Smart-mouth?" Maddy said. "I heard that on *Eternity*."

Sara chuckled. "The story is when he was a boy he said something smart-alecky to his father who smashed his fist into his young mouth telling him not to be a smart mouth and then every day for two weeks his father hit him again to be sure he would learn his lesson, leaving him with a permanent scar and a nickname. Some of my sources say he now has learned to like the nickname because Beijing often asks for smart-mouth's thoughts." She shook her head.

I shook mine, too. Who were these people?

Renee took Sara's hand and said to Maddy, "I told you she was the best. What else have you learned from this rat?"

"Oh, very much, Renee. The Chinese used fake sea captains to smuggle spies in and out of countries, their communication system, the control hierarchy in this region, certain code words, bank accounts' locations and how they use security cameras in Western nations for their own purposes. The United States is collecting those accounts as we speak and we are working on how to shut down Chinese access to security cameras but that will take a little longer. Wang has promised to tell us which Western intelligence agents China has identified, and the identities of three agents who have infiltrated the CIA and MI6. They should be working on that now."

"Wow, Sara, that's quite a haul of information," I said.

"Yes, Jack, but let me tell you the most important thing I learned from Wang, which was with your help."

We were all intently listening. "I learned not to be like Wang. I learned that he represented nothing, no loyalty, no love, no kindness; I didn't want to be like him, and if I was, I had lost, I had not defended the values that make me a Kiwi, that made me want to serve my country. I listened to you and my dear sweet Renee." She blew him a kiss. "Last night, when I went back into the storage room, I put away all the implements of torture I had gotten out to both scare and use on Wang. I'm not proud to say I had already used some of them, but no more. I told Wang; I will not be like you. I had Honoré attend to him, got him food and water, and had others take him to the restroom and clean him up.

When he came back, I sat down across from him and said, the truth will come out, Wang. It always does, and it will here, and when it does, I will be here waiting. And Wang asked me, "What about your family?" with an evil smirk on his face. I realized he was playing on my anger, so I let it go, right then and right there. I told him it was a tragedy, and I would forever remember, but it would not define me; I was better than that, that I was part of something bigger and better than that. And I told him I was here with him because of Maddy. And then I just sat there and looked at him. He was expecting me to continue to torture him, to break bones in his feet and maybe more, and he was ready for that, but not for my change of heart.

"Not long after that, Adam came in with an audio recording of a call between Abbott and Commander Li. Don't ask how we got it." She put her finger to her lips. "In that call Abbott and Li, two agents in Wang's network talked of the importance of eliminating Wang. And, of course, Hu had already dishonored and imprisoned him. That's what did it. He has worked thirty-some years for Chinese intelligence, done all manner of work for them, including some truly horrific things, and they're ready to cash him in right away, to protect the mission, to protect China. Adam helped, and we convinced him there was nothing there, nothing of substance, only a continuously rotating cast of petty tyrants. He had built nothing in all of his years, was worth nothing to his superiors or underlings. And he realized I think that by not breaking all of his fingers, the Chinese would assume I had stopped because he had talked. I had marked him if you will. And he knew the Chinese would eventually kill him if they got him back.

"And then Wang started talking and still is. So, thank you, Jack and Renee, for helping me step back from the edge. I can't tell you how much better I feel. I'm working on recovering my humanity and letting go of the hatred."

I went to her, misty-eyed, and hugged her. "Oh, Sara, thank you. Thank you for everything. You are wonderful, a wonderful human being."

"And thank you, Jack. You saved me." Sara stood back and wiped her eyes. Then she added, "And I can't say much, but your contacts in Washington helped get the recording to us. Whew, it's been a long night. I need to get some sleep."

"Would you like some company, *ma cherie*?" Renee asked.

Sara held out her hand, and the two of them walked down the hall together.

Amy went out back to discuss something with the two police officers, and Honoré insisted Li Wei let him look more closely at his leg wounds. They went to the dining/operating table at the front of the house.

Maddy was holding my hand. "Can you believe it's only been two weeks? Two weeks since my life went from normal to this."

I decided to come out with it. "Has it only been two weeks, Maddy? Or were things changing before that?"

"What do you mean? What are you talking about?"

"I'm talking about Li Wei and you. You'd been secretly meeting him in that hotel room for a couple of weeks, parking down the street to be discreet. You were hugging him, added him to the toast to us;

you can hardly pay attention to me now for trying to listen in on his care by Honoré. Is there something you need to tell me?"

Li Wei was standing in the doorway to the kitchen. Honoré had wandered off to find something, and Li Wei had escaped the exam table.

He said, "I heard your question, Jack, and I can answer it. Maddy loves you. She and I are friends; we have now been through a lot together. We will always be friends. And that makes me very happy. We began our friendship as teacher and student, and then I asked for special help. And she helped me, and Jack, I would have let there be more if I thought it was right. Maddy is magnificent. But it was always clear to me that she loved you, and her life with you and the children. She is a very good woman; surely, you must know that."

I looked over to Maddy; she was looking at Li Wei, crying. *Did she look grateful? Was this the truth?* "Jack, why did you even come after me if that's what you thought?"

"Because I love you, Maddy. More than anything. And I wanted to hear your side of the story. Because I want to believe in you."

I had not heard her come back in, but Amy was standing at the back door. "Let me add something, Maddy. You are one lucky woman; that's all I can say. This guy here, and he's no slouch when it comes to good looks, came all the way across the ocean to rescue you despite having doubts about how you felt about him? I wish someone would love me that way. And the reason was that he loves you. I hope you get that. I feel a little guilty for raising the idea in the first place that maybe you and Li Wei had just run off together. That's usually the way it turns out." Li Wei and Maddy looked at each other.

Having held our marital discussion for us, Amy and Li Wei retreated. I reached out my hands to Maddy; she took them. For a moment, I just looked at her and her at me. Then I came around the table and got down on my knees beside her and hugged her, really held her, and she held me back, and she sobbed.

A few minutes later, Renee came into the kitchen in his underwear for more champagne. When he saw us, he said, "Good. Good, hugging is good. Events like this can be so stressful; let nothing interfere with your love. You two are obviously in love."

Honoré came back loaded down with clean bandages. He smiled at his old friend Renee. "Why don't you let that poor girl rest?"

When Honoré turned back to the front room, calling out, "Li Wei? Li Wei, where are you?" He was nowhere to be seen. Maddy and I stole down the hallway to another bedroom.

After a one-hour nap, we walked hand in hand back into the kitchen.

Sara and Renee, and Adam were in the kitchen when we got there. Everyone was tense.

Sara asked Adam, "How could you let this happen, Adam? Wang had so much more to tell us."

Adam said, "Please, Sara. I had no idea. I had only turned my back for a second when I heard the gunshot. That was the first warning I had that anything was wrong and by then it was all over."

"Damnit, he had so much more to tell."

Honoré was looking at Adam's arm. He wrapped it in gauze and said, "The bullet only grazed you, and you will be fine. I can give you something for the pain if you like."

Sara looked at Adam's arm. "And who shot you exactly?" Her tone was not altogether friendly.

Adam said, "One of Li Wei's men, the other prisoner we rescued from the ship."

"And where did he get a gun, Adam?" Amy and I looked at each other but didn't say anything.

Sara growled, "Damnit, Adam, I told you to be especially careful."

"I know, and I should have listened," Adam said. "But I had no way of knowing Li Wei was a Taiwanese spy."

Maddy leaned forward. "What happened?"

Adam looked to Sara for permission to tell the story. Sara nodded.

Adam said, "I took a break from interrogating Wang. I left one of my men in charge and two officers at the door. They said one of the former prisoners distracted them and Li Wei apparently snuck into the interrogation room. Wang screamed and the officers went running into the room to find Li Wei shoving a lit electric stick down Wang's throat."

"Oh no, Li Wei," Maddy said and her hand went to her mouth.

"When Li Wei wouldn't obey their order to stop, they shot him point blank. I heard the shot and came running but by then it was too late for Wang. One of Li Wei's accomplices shot at me to stop me and wounded me. And then one of the officers killed him, too. It all happened so fast."

More softly, Sara said, "It always does, Adam, it always happens fast. I'm glad at least that you'll be okay. Where is Wang's body?"

"I don't know," Adam said. "I honestly don't. Other SIS men removed it from the work building immediately. After a conversation with someone they said the CIA was insisting on getting the body and since they supplied the audio of the phone call we used to get Wang to talk, which they reminded Wellington of several times. Wellington made this decision to give the body to them. I assume they have it by now."

He was almost pleading.

Renee said, "*Ma cherie*, you and I can go travel around the clandestine world and search for his body. Oui? Do you simply wish to see him dead?"

Sara smiled and shook her head. "No, Renee, but thank you. No one grounds me as you do. No one. This damn business, yesterday I wanted to kill Wang with my bare hands, and today I'm sorry he's dead before he could give us more information. And if the Taiwanese would kill him here with the CIA standing by, there must be more going on than we know. What we already have will devastate the Chinese. Wang told me Li Wei and the others were Taiwanese agents. I just hadn't had the chance to warn everyone. But I don't know why the Taiwanese would want Wang dead."

Maddy said, "Maybe it wasn't the Taiwanese although Li Wei wasn't honest with me about who he was. But maybe Li Wei just wanted to get revenge personally for all the torture Wang inflicted on him while we were on the ship. After all he used the same kind of electric stick he was tortured with to kill Wang. Maybe it was as simple as revenge."

"Maybe," Sara said. "We're questioning the other Taiwanese to try to find out. We know they all trained together over several years, those are the years when we lost track of Li Wei. And since these men were picked up by the Chinese on the way to their first mission, we know Taiwan has a Chinese spy in its security services." She turned to Adam and said, "And Adam, it's okay. Shit like this happens in our world. I'm glad it didn't cost you your life."

"Yeah, me, too. Thanks, Sara," Adam said, relieved.

Adam let a few minutes go by and then said, "Okay, here's the plan. Tomorrow at nine a.m., I will take Amy, Jack, and Maddy to the airport. Joe and his plane will be waiting there."

I asked, "Are you okay to drive, Adam?"

"What? This? No problem, Jack. Under my shirt sleeve, you will never be able to tell anything at all."

"And my men will be monitoring the airport entrance so that you will have no problems," Renee said.

Adam added, "And Sara, you can go, too, if you want. It is really up to you."

Sara didn't hesitate. "Yes, I'll go back. I promised those children I wouldn't be gone long."

Maddy took my hand and smiled at that, at Sara's dedication to our children.

Renee, incorrigible as ever, said, "At least we have tonight, *ma cherie*."

Honoré shook his head, smiling, the rest of us laughed out loud.

CHAPTER

54

Bauerfield Airport
Port Vila, Vanuatu
March 26, 2033
1:30 p.m.

Noah Montgomery had been waiting with Joe at the airport. He was cleaned up and in a fresh white shirt and khaki shorts. On one side of the shorts, the leg was cut open at the outside to make room for Noah's full leg length cast. He was on crutches. On his foot on the other leg was a bright red Olukai slip-on. He saw Amy notice it and said, "Look what they gave me at the hospital. I have the other one in my bag." Amy hugged him tightly. Joe had to help keep him from stumbling or falling.

Amy stood back and wiped her cheeks. "And how about that other thing they gave you at the hospital?" She looked at his cast.

Noah said, "Oh, this old thing?" He knocked on it like it was a door. "I saved a place for you to sign it if you'd like." That I could see, there wasn't a single signature on it.

Joe loaded our bags, and we piled into his plane. Joe and Adam helped Noah into the front passenger seat, the only seat with enough legroom for his cast. Maddy and I cuddled into the back back seat, and Sara and Amy sat across from us, facing us. Just before we took off, my cellphone rang. The caller ID said, Drummond. He was calling me on his personal cell.

"Mitch! I don't know how I can ever thank you properly."

Mitch asked, "So, is Maddy okay?"

I looked over at her and took her hand. "Yes, Mitch. I need to put a little weight back on her, but she'll be fine. Thank you for helping us."

"Glad to do it, Jack. Besides, you're just no good without her."

I laughed. "Guilty."

"I'm going to have to go here in a second, Jack. Is there anything else I can do for you? I mean, that we can do for you? As you can tell, the President took this very personally."

"It might not be proper on this phone, but can you tell me what will happen to Hu and Abbott and the others?"

"Don't worry about this phone, Jack. It may be my old cell number, but it's encrypted, shielded, monitored, and I don't know what else. I don't know what will happen exactly, and I don't want to. We don't want to. In addition to Hu and Abbott, Chinese spies are being apprehended all over the South Pacific and elsewhere. Eventually, I would expect most of them to arrive at the same place. It makes questioning them so much more coordinated. I doubt it will be in the United States. And we may never know. I really have to go. You can't believe what's happening. China is marching across Siberia, essentially unchecked. In two weeks, they will be at the eastern foothills of the Ural Mountains. They bypassed the cities, and those cities are now stranded, surrounded. The Russians are preoccupied with their current conflict with USEU and yet the Russians battle on successfully at sea. Vladivostok remains in Russian hands, and China has lost nearly half of its naval fleet. So far, no one has used nukes. China sank a Japanese ship, and the Japanese are talking about declaring war on China, which would bring us into it. The Chinese naval authorities say it was a rogue captain who sank the Japanese ship, and Beijing says the Japanese started it. And, well, that's all on my plate right now."

"Wow, Mitch, I don't want to hold you up. Wow. I guess I haven't been paying attention. I remember when Russia and China were acting in concert against us in threatening Taiwan and Ukraine at the same time. I guess things change. Thank you for finding the time to help us with everything. If you ever need anything, ask."

"Glad I could help a couple of old friends, Jack. And as far as things changing, China never lets up on its desire to rule, other countries even Russia are just convenient pawns along the way"

"Thanks, Mitch, and I'll remember that," I said, and Maddy called out, "Yes, thanks, Mitch. Thank you, thank you, thank you."

I hung up, and immediately the plane started forward. As we took off, we were all talking at once; it seemed. Then we slowed down to take turns. Noah filled us in on his experiences, He said Laurent's guards had never left his side, and he had never been questioned. Amy told the story of rescuing Li Wei and then finding Maddy.

"Where is Li Wei?" Noah asked.

Maddy said, "He's dead. He was killed after he killed Wang. It turns out Li Wei worked for Taiwan's National Security Bureau."

"No shit," Noah said, "a spy?"

Sara looked at Maddy. "Yes, he was a very well-trained spy. He took us all in, but Wang knew who he was and he knew who Wang was. He nursed his injuries and found his chance to get at Wang when we were at the doctor's property."

Maddy looked over at me.

"The doctor with the farmhouse?" Noah asked.

"The same," answered Amy. "I'm surprised you remember any of that."

"You mean, like you holding my hand and speaking softly to me?" Noah said.

Amy acted like she was going to punch him and then laughed.

I filled everyone in on Mitch Drummond and especially the conversation they had just overheard.

When I looked out the window, I saw Kaluas, the giant banyan tree below. I was telling Maddy all about it when I caught Joe's eyes twinkling in the mirror. I was telling her everything Joe had said to me as if I knew all about it. I winked at Joe, and he laughed out loud.

For a while, we were all quiet. The north coast of the north island of New Zealand came into view. The sight of home started the conversation again.

Amy asked Sara, "Can you tell me where Commander Li was taken? What will happen to him?"

"Li is a spy, so SIS took him. He's being held somewhere discreet, and being questioned. Depending on how cooperative he is, he will later be taken to Wellington and charged with espionage, and who knows what else at this point. From there, he'll likely go to prison and could be the subject of a prisoner exchange. And you heard what Mitch Drummond had to say. It's all too hard to predict."

"Do you know who the acting commander is?"

"Yes, Deputy Commander Barron has taken over on an interim basis. He's a good man."

Amy agreed. Sara was seated directly across from me, and she had that little twinkle in her eye again. "And Amy, my friends in Wellington have let the acting Commander know that you and Noah were acting undercover on a mission at their request and that the reason Li wasn't informed was that they had already started to suspect him. It makes you all look good."

"So, no discipline? Do you hear that, Noah?"

"Loud and clear," Noah said.

Sara said, "No discipline; in fact, I bet you get a medal."

"She deserves one; both of them do," I said.

Sara continued, "And what about you, Mr. Jack. First, you saved the world from itself at Ebola Island, and now you and Maddy outsmarted Chinese state security and set them back a decade; what will you do for your next adventure?"

While everyone else erupted in laughter, I thought, a decade? That's not nearly long enough; JJ will only be sixteen, and Allison only fifteen. Three decades would be better. I only said, "Maddy did it." And I squeezed her hand.

***

Amy drove us all from the Nelson airport to our house in her police vehicle. Noah's car was still there, too, but he wouldn't be driving for a while. We pulled into the driveway, and JJ and Allison came running out with Nikau and Charlie behind them on the porch.

"Mom!"

"Dad!"

"Are you okay?"

"Did you get the guys who did this?"

"Did you shoot them, Dad?"

"Mom, you look skinny. Are you sure you're alright?"

"Will you tell us all about it?"

"I got an 'A' on my science test."

"Mom, this is my friend, Nikau, and his dad, Charlie. Can they live with us?"

Allison still had her arms around her mother. Maddy and I were basking in their love and trying to answer some of their questions. I looked at my family, all together, all at home and I breathed out loudly. The children didn't notice, but Maddy hugged me tightly and exhaled only a little quieter than I had. She felt skinny in my arms. Lovely, magnificent, perfect, but skinny.

"Aunt Sara!" both children shouted at once. "Thanks for bringing our mom back."

Aunt Sara? Maddy and I looked at each other and smiled. We all had a new friend.

"Aunt Sara. Aunt Sara, can we make chocolate balls?"

ACKNOWLEDGMENTS

Any novel is the culmination of many efforts. This, my second novel, wouldn't exist without the support and encouragement I have been given about my first novel *Ebola Island*. Many have asked when my second novel would be coming out. I am sorry it took so long. The fault is entirely mine.

Family and friends supported this novel, offering suggestions and support along the way. My editors, Carolyn and Amy made this a better story. So did my volunteer first readers. My author friend Mike made a great classic suggestion that gets the story off to a faster start.

My wife offered suggestions and encouragement all along the way and took care of all the technical details of formatting and self-publishing. And I continue to love Mary Beth's work on the cover. Over the years I have enjoyed so many chocolate balls made by my friend Sara that I just had to work her into the story.

I apologize if I have overlooked anyone. My sincere thanks to all of you!

Gregor

BOOK REVIEW QUESTIONS

1. How does politics play out in this novel; the politics of the United States, China, New Zealand and Vanuatu? And how do they mix together?

2. Have you ever faced a seemingly overwhelming challenge like the one in this book? What did you do? What would you do if this happened to one of your loved ones? Who would you turn to for help?

3. Who is your favorite character in the book and why?

4. Which scenes seem most realistic? The book takes place halfway around the world from the United States; which, if any, descriptions were well done and made you feel like you knew or understood the place?

5. What would you like to see Jack and Maddy do next?

6. Much like in *Ebola Island*, Jack gets essential help from very capable locals. Why is this important? What does it say about humanity?

7. Is Maddy a strong character in Dragon's Eye? Why or why not?

8. Sara is introduced as a figure of some historical importance in New Zealand. Do you like her? Why or why not? Can you understand her motivations?

9. There is a love scene near the beginning of the book. Is it helpful to the story? Why or why not?

10. When I finished *Ebola Island*, I set up the second novel to take place in New Zealand because I always have wanted to go there. That didn't work out for me. Have you been there? What did you observe about the people there, the countryside, the country?

11. What parts of the world do you find interesting to read about? Why?

12. What were your thoughts about the portrayal of Chinese State Security? Realistic or not? Why?

ABOUT THE AUTHOR

Gregor Pratt a retired trial lawyer grew up in Middletown, Ohio and now splits his time between Sarasota, Florida and Cincinnati, Ohio. Gregor's first novel, *Ebola Island*, was eerily prescient being released just weeks before the 2020 coronavirus pandemic. It was very well received with an overall 4.5 star rating, receiving many 5 star reviews.

Dragon's Eye is the second thriller in the series of Jack and Maddy Gamble novels.

Feel free to reach out to Gregor via his website
www.gregorpratt.com or by email prattgregor@gmail.com

www.ingramcontent.com/pod-product-compliance
Lightning Source LLC
Chambersburg PA
CBHW031119160726
47991CB00004B/1460